Love in Key West

SUSAN BLACKMON

With the exception of historical figures, all characters in this novel are fictitious. Any resemblance to living persons, present or past, is coincidental.

Dream Publishing

Dream Publishing
Lawrenceville, GA

ISBN: 10: 0-9886648-9-5
ISBN-13: 978-0-9886648-9-0

www.susanblackmonauthor.com

Cover illustration: John (Jack) H. Morse III

Printed in the United States of America

DEDICATION

This book is for those who love stories and for those special people that have blessed my writing journey. It is dedicated to the ones who kept asking for more, who motivated me, who helped me get past writer's block, and inspired a better story. They are fellow authors, readers, fans, co-workers, friends, family, email buddies, Facebook connections, and so many others I've met along the way. You are an author's gift, and I want to give you something to say

Thank You.

AUTHOR'S NOTE

This story parallels *Salvaged Love* so you will notice overlapping passages, but it is told from Jason and Victoria's perspective. I hope you enjoy their romance as much as I enjoyed writing it.

Chapter 1

August, 1828, Midanbury, England, a small hamlet outside Southampton

Lord Jason Albert Duncan Malwbry, future fifth Duke of Rothebury, walked through the large foyer of his family's ancestral estate smoothing his dark hair after a brisk morning ride on his favourite chestnut stallion, Shelton. The mid-summer morning proved too beautiful to resist, worthy of inspiring poems and paintings, not that he was of a prosaic or artistic nature. Jason immensely enjoyed the fresh air and exercise.

Upon hearing the raised voices of his parents coming from the study off to his left, he resigned himself to leaving the beauty of the day outside. Within these walls were heartache and strife. His mother, the overbearing Duchess of Rothebury, was again lecturing his father, the beleaguered Duke of Rothebury, about his gambling at the dog tracks. Jason started up the stairs, hoping to avoid them, but alas his mother must have sensed his return for she stepped into the foyer and called for him to join them. With a fatalist sense of the inevitable, he turned from the stairs and walked towards her. He paused at the entry awaiting his mother to precede him, and then he shut the heavy oak door behind him. He saw no sense in subjecting the servants to more than they had already heard.

The Duchess launched into her questioning without delay. "How are you progressing with Miss Bennington?"

Jason tersely answered, "Fine."

"Then why was she seen riding alone with Marcus Danvers in the park yesterday?"

His mother didn't wait for him to answer, which was just as well since he didn't have one. He couldn't pretend to understand any female, much less one as unconventional as Abigail Bennington.

"Do you know how much trouble I went through to arrange for her and her father to be invited to Lady Waverly's dinner party so you two could be introduced? If not for his money and a favour Lady Waverly owed to me, she would never have agreed to invite someone from the working class to one of her dinners. You assured me you had Miss Bennington in hand. I merely assumed the matter was settled when you visited her father. Nevertheless, I informed her of how a future duchess is expected to behave."

Jason's jaw dropped, "Say again?"

"I saw Miss Bennington at the modiste's yesterday. I made her aware of her improper behaviour, and told her to expect to see you today."

Jason was at first dismayed, then angry, and if truth be told, embarrassed by his mother's audacity. He sent a note to Abigail this morning before he went riding. His intention was to gauge her feelings for Marc, since he already knew his friend's affections lay elsewhere. Now he worried that Abigail would believe the note was his mother's doing, and he was nothing more than a puppet. He allowed his anger to rule the tone of his response. His jaw clenched. "Mother, you are not helping. I will see Miss Bennington today as you wish, but if you dare to interfere again, I will walk away from this whole marriage idea. Do you understand? Once more, and I am done!"

His mother's eyes narrowed to slits as she spoke through her teeth, "No, you are not done. You do not have the luxury of being done. She is one of only a few ladies with a dowry sizeable enough to cover your father's gambling debts. You do not want to see him go to debtors' prison, do you?"

Jason lost his temper and answered back without thought, "Stop exaggerating, Mother. You are simply not ready to give up your pricy luxuries or worse, for your friends to find out you cannot control your husband."

"Why you ungrateful...." His mother was so angry she couldn't even finish her expletive.

With Jason's last comment striking hard at his pride, his portly father finally spoke, "Now see here son that will be quite enough!"

Jason replied in a deceptively quiet voice, "You are right, Father. I have had enough." He turned on his heel and quit the room, as both his parents sputtered their displeasure at his retreating back.

He strode quickly to the stables and stopped the groomsman from leading Shelton to his stall. Jason, too impatient to wait on the stable hand, returned the saddle to the horse's back and cinched it. He then grabbed the reins and leapt unaided onto Shelton's back. Turning him sharply towards the exit, he kicked him into a full gallop out of the stable and down the drive, shocking all who witnessed his uncharacteristic behaviour.

With the house out of sight, Jason was able to regain control of his emotions. He slowed Shelton to a trot trying to decide where to go. His thoughts were too dark and heavy to stand the beauty of the day, so he headed for the nearest pub. He was sure not to be disturbed, as it was too early for most to be there.

The dank and dingy room complimented his mood. He chose a table in the far interior corner away from the light and waved off the barkeep as he approached.

He was used to his parents arguing, but he was not used to being dragged into the vortex of anger with them. He was not proud of his reaction this morning. The best he could attribute it to was a built up resentment resulting from courting a woman of his mother's choosing.

What was he getting himself into? Would he end up in a marriage like theirs? No. The bloodline would end with him before he accepted such a fate. He sat there considering his next course of action until three o'clock when he was scheduled to meet Miss Bennington.

* * *

Jason's arrival in the drawing room of the Bennington town home was announced as the clock struck three. His determined stride faltered when the butler stepped aside revealing the presence of the lovely petite blond, Lady Elizabeth Kendall. He muttered his dismay under his breath. He had hoped to speak with Abigail alone, but he should have known not to expect it.

Abigail greeted Jason with a small curtsey and gestured to the chair across from the settee. "Good afternoon, Lord Malwbry. Please join us." She resumed her seat next to her good friend, Elizabeth, as she introduced her, "You, of course, remember Lady Kendall."

Jason bowed to Elizabeth before taking his seat. "Yes, of course. How are you Lady Kendall?"

"I am well, Lord Malwbry, thank you for asking."

"And your husband? Is he well? I have not seen him at the club."

Elizabeth nodded, "Yes, quite well, though his business dealings keep him occupied of late."

Jason acknowledged her reply with a nod. "I am here to take Miss Bennington riding. Would you care to join us?"

Abigail intervened, "Milord, would you mind postponing our ride? I wish to discuss something with you."

Jason's gaze returned to Abigail's striking visage framed with red-gold tendrils. Her luminescent grey eyes held his in steady regard. He was surprised by her directness but not displeased.

Riding in the park was an excuse. He was more than amenable to skipping it.

"As do I but..." He cast a glance toward Lady Kendall. He was not at all comfortable discussing their affairs in front of her friend, even though he was fully aware Abigail likely had already shared all the details with her ladyship. Apparently, Lady Kendall was very astute, for she rose without a word and moved to the far side of the spacious room.

The sharpness in Abigail's words brought his gaze back to her.

"May I ask why you are directing your attentions towards me?"

He had never met such a forthright female and found it convenient to respond in kind. He ignored her question to get straight to the point of this meeting. "What is your relationship with Marcus Danvers?"

Abigail frowned. "We have been friends since childhood. You did not think it was more, did you? He is engaged."

"I am aware of that fact. I was not sure you were, since you risked both of your reputations."

"Why are you interested in me? Your mother does not seem to approve."

"On the contrary, you are at the top of her very short list."

Abigail's jaw dropped. "Why?"

Jason believed in honesty, but telling Abigail her dowry was the reason would be counterproductive, so he prevaricated. "She may believe she can mold you into the daughter-in-law she desires."

"Obviously she does not know much about me or I would be at the bottom of her list. She should set her sights on one of those flighty young debutantes without a thought of their own."

Jason studied her for a moment trying to determine how much truth to reveal. "I think she was looking for someone like herself and maybe, unconsciously, I was too, but I do not want the same angry and bitter relationship as my parents."

"What, or should I say, whom, do you want?"

Jason was momentarily taken aback. She was the first to ask him what he wanted. "I really have not given it much consideration until this morning. I have avoided the marriage mart for the better part of a decade. At this point, I am afraid I hardly know any of the girls or their families. Other than my mother's list of choices, I do not have much to guide me."

"I could help. If you like?"

"How?"

"You could attend the next assembly room dance. I will save the first dance for you. I can point out some of the more favourable candidates, and with Marc's help, we could introduce you to the ones you might find appealing."

"Why a public dance? Surely the next private ball will do."

Abigail laughed lightly, "'Tis the end of the season, and I do not hold an invitation to any of the remaining private balls."

He could get them invitations to one but that would involve his mother. "Then I suppose a public one will have to suffice." He impulsively reached for her hand and kissed the back of it.

Relief to have a way of finally taking back control of his life made him speak more openly than he normally would have, "I appreciate and sincerely thank you for your generous offer *mademoiselle*. I look forward to the next dance." He rose from his seat to take his leave. Abigail followed suit. "Ladies," he bowed to Lady Kendall and Abigail in turn, "I bid you *adieu*. Enjoy your afternoon."

Jason paused on the stoop as the butler shut the door behind him. He felt the warm sunshine on his cheek and breathed deeply the scent of roses growing profusely on either side of the entry. The day still held its beauty, and once again it was reflected in his mood—thanks to Abigail and her offer of assistance. He stepped lightly down the stairs and accepted Shelton's reins from the groomsman. He lithely mounted the stallion and kicked him into a trot headed for the ready entertainments of his gentlemen's club.

* * *

Nearly a week later, Jason paused in the doorway of the assembly hall to scan the crowd in search of Abigail. A hush fell across the room as soon as his presence was noticed, and it was followed by a wave of whispered conversations ripe with gossip. He pretended not to notice as he scanned the chamber.

The building's structure was sparse but spacious, or at least it would have been spacious if not filled with what seemed to be hundreds of colorfully dressed and heavily perfumed attendees. Three large multi-tiered wooden chandeliers hung in a row down the center of the ceiling holding hundreds of glowing tallow candles. A gallery ran the perimeter with stairs leading to it from either side of the landing he currently stood upon. On the far end of the upper level, the orchestra was tuning their instruments. In the colonnade beneath stood a long table heavily burdened with cups and two large silver punch bowls. Small tables and chairs lined the side walls occupied by the elders of the gathering. The young gathered in clusters about the dance floor. The crowd was so thick the pattern of the parquet flooring could not be discerned.

Every eye in the room seemed to be focused on him. He supposed he couldn't blame them. They all were fully aware, since he had never attended a public dance before, the only reason he, a future duke, would be there was to seek a future duchess. The few balls he had attended previously to seek out Abigail were private ones arranged by his mother. He begrudgingly had to thank her for sparing him this feeling of a fox suddenly discovered by the hunting party. Every unwed female and her mother was now speculatively eyeing him and moving forward en masse like a wave to the sand. He took a deep breath to dispel the unwelcome feeling of being cornered.

He discovered Abigail standing with Lord and Lady Kendall off to his right. With controlled motions, he descended the steps into the room and headed in their direction while carefully avoiding eye contact with any and all in his path. From the corner of his eye, he noticed Marcus Danvers making his way from further in the room. They met up with the group at the same time. Greetings were shared all around before the gentlemen broke off to their own conversation while waiting for the dancing to start.

Marc clapped him on the shoulder. "Never would I believe you to set foot in one of these dances without seeing it with my own eyes."

Lord Kendall said, "Neither would I."

Jason grimaced. "Desperate times call for desperate measures. I assure you." To Marc he said, "Are you here alone? Where is your charming fiancée?"

"She is currently visiting relatives on the coast."

Jason said, "Then why ever would you bother being here?"

Marc smiled. "I am escorting my youngest sister since my parents were not able to attend."

Jason saw Marc frown at something over his shoulders. Just as he started to turn, Marc gave warning, "Don't. You will only encourage them."

'Who?"

"The hungry mamas desperate to gain an introduction for their daughters."

Lord Kendall said, "But isn't that the reason he is here, to meet them?"

Jason frowned. "To meet only a select few, I assure you."

It was Lord Kendall's turn to frown. "How do you plan to select them?"

Jason cast his glance in Abigail's direction to see her and Lady Kendall with their heads close together rapidly whispering behind their fans.

Lord Kendall's gaze followed. "Oh! So you are to blame for my wife's insistence on attending this lowly gathering instead of enjoying a quiet evening with a cigar and brandy."

Jason's look turned sheepish. "My apologies, sir."

The first dance was announced. Jason turned to Abigail. He bowed and held out his hand to her. "I believe you have promised this dance to me."

She curtsied and placed her gloved hand in his. They joined the other couples lining up in two rows with the gentlemen facing the ladies. As the movements of the country dance brought Jason and Abigail together, she would point out the various ladies deemed suitable. Jason nodded after each one sometimes not even looking in the direction she indicated. His attention was focused on his feet. He had not practiced these dances in many years, and feared he might tread on her toes.

When he chanced to look up, she nodded to the side. He risked a glance where she indicated to see his friend, Robert, and his current love interest, Bridgette, standing by the refreshments.

"At least they are behaving this evening."

He couldn't help the brief smile her comment evoked recalling a very uncomfortable carriage ride they all shared a few weeks earlier. The lovers had openly displayed their affection for each other, causing Abigail's cheeks to bloom brightly.

As the dance ended, they moved to the side of the room. Jason noticed Abigail's dismay. Wanting to see her smile restored, he whispered a confession, "I am sorry I was so distracted. I am quite out of practice. It was all I could do not to make a fool of myself. Tell me again the name of the tall blond by the balcony doors." In truth, it was the only face he could recall. Trying to keep up with the dance steps he missed seeing most of the ladies she mentioned.

Abigail's mood brightened considerably. "That would be Lady

Jane Torrington. Her father has an estate south of here. Good connections and she has a pleasant demeanor. Would you like for me to introduce you?"

Jason offered his arm in response and led them to Lord Torrington and his daughter. Lady Jane Torrington was a conventional beauty with blond hair and kind blue eyes. Abigail made the introductions, and the conversation flowed smoothly to the weather and fashion with a brief mention of politics. After an appropriate amount of time, Abigail excused herself on the pretext of greeting another acquaintance.

Jason offered his hand to Lady Jane. "I would be honored if you would share this dance with me." Jane accepted with a very becoming blush. They joined the couples lining up for a cotillion. He noticed Abigail and Marc were partnered further down the line. He felt a twinge of jealousy and frowned. Unfortunately, Lady Jane noticed. He gave her a smile meant to encourage them both and complimented her dress for good measure. Her smile returned, and the music began.

The steps of this dance were more familiar to him giving him time to contemplate Abigail's choice for his wife. Sweet is how he would describe Lady Jane. Sweet and plain. She seemed like the perfect prospect to meet his mother's wishes, which made him wonder why Lady Jane was not on his mother's list. She was certainly pleasant enough, but he kept finding himself distracted whenever Abigail would dance by on Marc's arm looking so radiantly happy. Jason acknowledged to himself he was a little jealous of Marc's ability to be at ease with Abigail.

He and Lady Jane said little to each other as they danced, and when it ended, he held out his arm. Lady Jane slipped her hand in the crook of his elbow, and he led them to the nearby refreshment table. He picked up two prefilled cups, and as he turned to hand one to Lady Jane, they were joined by Marc and Abigail.

Marc handed Abigail a glass of punch. "I hear you are planning to quit our fair country for distant shores."

Jason's eyes flew wide leaving Lady Jane's face to seek confirmation from Marc and then Abigail. "What is this you say?"

Abigail's face lit with enthusiasm. "My father and I will set sail on the first for the Caribbean and then onto my uncle's plantation in the States for the holidays."

Jason's jaw dropped. He was quite shocked; she had neglected to mention it to him before now. That she had so little regard for him was yet another reason he should focus on other prospective ladies. Lady Jane moved imperceptibly reminding him of her presence. He sobered his expression aiming for indifference.

Marc teased Abigail, "You have no remorse for the spot you have put me in. Mary returns next month. She will hear the gossip of our carriage ride and that you have suddenly left the country, and she will think the worst."

"I have no doubt your sweet charm will persuade your fiancée of your innocence. In fact, I believe you can even take on the repercussions of a second dance with me." Abigail deposited her cup on the table behind her. "Please excuse us Lord Jason, Lady Jane." She grabbed Marc's hand and pulled him towards the couples lining up for the next Quadrille. "Come Marc, I leave in less than a week, and you are the best dance partner a lady could ask for."

Marc threw an apologetic smile towards Lord Jason and Lady Jane as he was forced to follow the hand in Abigail's grasp.

As Abigail was swept away from him, again with Marc, and he was faced with Lady Jane, Jason couldn't help but feel his enthusiasm for the evening vanish. He exchanged an uncomfortable smile with Lady Jane and asked, "Would you care for another dance?"

"I don't believe so. Besides, we have just met. It would be unseemly to dance twice in a row."

"Of course, I seem to have forgotten my manners." The rules of courtship forbade dancing two dances back-to-back with someone of new acquaintance.

Silence followed for a few moments in which they both sipped their punch and watched the dancing.

Lady Jane took a deep breath and said, "Surely you wish to ask another to dance."

He turned to her and shook his head. "I am not so keen on dancing."

"I see. Then perhaps you wouldn't mind escorting me to my father."

"Of course." He took her cup and placed both of theirs on the table, and then gave her his arm. They leisurely strolled the colonnade to where her father was seated.

Lord Torrington greeted Jason warmly before turning to his daughter. "My dear Janie, I am tiring. I hope you don't mind if we leave now."

Lady Jane gave him a doting smile. "Of course father. We shall leave at once." She turned to Jason to dismiss him.

Jason was more than ready to leave. He did not want to seek out Abigail to find another lady on her list and without Abigail's aide there was no point in remaining at the assembly. Lady Jane presented him with a good excuse to leave. "I would be pleased to assist in seeing your carriage brought round."

Lady Jane's smile was warming. "Thank you, Lord Malwbry."

Lord Torrington gave a nod. "Yes, thank you, good sir."

Jason excused himself and made his way directly to the front exit where he requested the Torrington carriage. Rather than wait for the groomsman to bring his mount, he made his way to the stable to retrieve Shelton himself.

* * *

It was one month to the day since the assembly ball when Jason last saw Abigail Bennington. He was slumped in a leather chair at his gentlemen's club smoking a hand-rolled Cuban cigar; a half empty decanter of brandy and an empty crystal tumbler on the table beside him. His surroundings, while not as ornate and lavish as the well-known London clubs, was comfortable enough for a gentleman of his station. Rich leather sofas and chairs were scattered about the room with highly polished dark rose wood furniture. The walls were covered in dark damask paper above walnut wainscoting. Large floor to ceiling windows allowed for enough light during the day and a vast array of oil lamps and candle sconces lit the dim recesses at night. The establishment was clean with enough of the amenities to make one comfortable, and, most important, it offered a quiet place for a man to take stock of his life. Jason was doing just that, contemplating the events of the last few months leading to his current situation.

The whole marriage hunt started with his mother's push to replenish the family coffers. When she arranged for him to meet Miss Bennington, he decided to go along not having any strong feelings either way. His life had become dull with so many of his friends having recently wed that he was willing to take a small step into the marriage mart.

He enjoyed the first evening with Abigail. She had a quick wit and an impertinent attitude to match his mood that evening. The venue he chose for their next meeting turned out to be a disaster. He was so embarrassed by his friend Robert's brash and inappropriate behaviour with Bridgette during the carriage ride he couldn't face Abigail. He kept his gaze focused outside the carriage for fear of blushing himself. Next, he found himself attending balls at his mother's insistence. He only stayed long enough at each one to accomplish his mission of dancing with Abigail before making his escape from all the matchmaking mothers and debutantes vying for his attention.

He still was not sure how it happened, but his mother convinced him that since *The Ton* was already speculating on their upcoming marriage, he should speak with her father, which he had done. Mr. Bennington agreed to his courtship, but Jason had the impression he was not as thrilled with the prospect as one would expect. Jason had never dealt with anyone not in awe of his family titles and who didn't treat him like royalty but instead judged him for himself and dared to consider him inferior. He wondered what it was Mr. Bennington found lacking in his character. It was bothering Jason more than he cared to admit.

Then, he heard the tales at the club of Abigail being seen alone with Marc Danvers. He sent a message to meet her but before that was the angry episode with his parents. The meeting with Abigail led to the ball and Lady Torrington. He considered the assembly ball to have been a failure along with all the others he had allowed Marc to talk him into since then.

As if materializing from his thoughts, Jason noted Marc's entrance in the arched wood paneled foyer of the club. Marc scanned the room as he removed his leather riding gloves, saw him, and headed his way. Jason rose to greet his friend before slumping back in his chair and signaling the barkeep for more libations.

Receiving their drinks, Marc raised his glass in a silent salute and downed a large swallow before commenting on Jason's demeanor. "What's wrong old chum? I have never seen you look so serious, as if your future depended on this very moment's decision."

Jason returned a wry grimace. "As a matter of fact, that is exactly what I am contemplating—my future and my future bride."

"Your bride? I had no idea you had made a decision. Pray tell, who is to be the next Duchess of Rothebury?"

"And there is the rub. I do not know. But it is time to figure it out. Time to produce the heir and all that."

Marc nodded in understanding. "Which one of our fine lasses are you considering? I have introduced you to several these last few weeks."

"Lady Jane Torrington would be top choice of those here in England, but there is one not on this soil who still holds my attention."

Contemplating but a moment, Marc's eyes widened as he realized to whom Jason was referring. "No! You are not seriously still considering Abby are you?"

"Why? Is there some reason I should not?"

"Besides the fact she risked all sorts of scandal to remove herself from your presence, no."

Jason grimaced. "I came across that poorly, eh?"

"I would say so. You used to be so charming with the ladies during our school years. Did you know we dubbed you 'Prince Charming'? Combine charm with your title and the rest of us did not stand a chance. Have to say, I was a little surprised Abby was not enamored with you. I thought maybe she was running scared."

Reflecting back, Jason realized his mistake. "Charm was the one thing I did not show her. I was letting my mother control my actions. Abigail was her choice. I was only going through the motions rather than committing to the idea. I did not put any effort into courting her, and now I realize I am left with simpering spoiled debutantes when what I want is Abigail's spirit. She probably was running, scared off by my boorish behaviour. And now it is too late."

"Why would it be? If you are really serious about her why not follow her? What lady could resist the idea she is unforgettable? Show her how charming you can be."

Jason brightened at the idea. It could work, and it had more appeal than his other choices. "Do you know where she is headed?"

Marc grinned at the hope lighting Jason's expression. "I do. Her uncle, James Bennington, has a plantation near Montgomery, Alabama. Abby and her father plan to visit with them until spring."

Having a new goal and being one of his own choosing, Jason was now in a hurry to put it in motion. He stood up and moved next to Marc's chair to lay a hand on his friend's shoulder. "Hope you do not mind if I take my leave. I believe I will head to the docks and see when the next ship is leaving for America." Jason didn't wait for a reply but hastily headed towards the door; a new fervor lengthening his stride.

Marc wondered if he had done the right thing in telling Jason to pursue Abby. He felt Jason's change of heart was sincere and there really was no reason he would not be a good husband to Abby. He couldn't say the same about Abby being a good wife for Jason. He couldn't picture her as a duchess, but then again, stranger things have happened. He wondered how Abby would handle Jason showing up on her doorstep after all her maneuvering to get away from him. If he didn't have his own wedding to attend, he probably would have volunteered to go with Jason so he could witness their reunion. It was sure to be entertaining.

* * *

Jason rode Shelton at a leisurely trot through the seaport town of Southampton. After leaving Marc at the club, he returned home to gather funds and have his valet pack an overnight bag. On his way out the door, he told the butler, "Inform my parents I am out for the evening and likely won't return until late tomorrow."

"Yes sir. And where shall I say you have gone, sir?"

He wanted to say it was of no concern of theirs, but he feared his mother would harangue the poor butler for not having an answer. "Southampton." He turned and strode from the house, anxious to avoid being discovered by either parent. After securing his bag, he untied Shelton from the hitching post at the foot of the wide stone steps fronting his ancestral house, and lithely mounted. He turned Shelton's head and nudged him into a gallop down the long drive for the three-mile ride to the city in search of a ship bound for America, preferably Mobile.

By good fortune, he happened upon Mr. Bennington's shipping offices. He reasoned the surest way to follow was in a ship likely bound for the same ports of trade. He fortuitously discovered one was leaving in a week's time with a passenger cabin available. He booked it without hesitation. If only telling his mother of his plans could be as easy. Next, he visited his solicitor to withdraw extra allowances from his Malwbry estate to cover travel expenses.

With ticket in hand to sail one week hence on the *Merchant's Pride*, Jason made his way back home the following afternoon thinking of all he needed to do to prepare for his voyage. This trip was the most exciting thing to ever happen to him, and he was looking forward to the journey and all that he might see and discover along the way, but even more stimulating was the smiling face he hoped to find at his journey's end.

Jason heard the stilted tones of his parent's latest disagreement as soon as he set foot in the foyer. He shared a tight look with the butler as he pulled off his leather riding gloves and laid them on the waiting white gloved palm. His jaw firmed as he removed his hat and coat. He may as well get past the inevitable confrontation now, rather than wait, despite their already raised ire. In all honesty, if he waited for a peaceful moment to deliver his news, he might as well wait for eternity. He approached the parlour with a stiff spine refusing to acknowledge the trepidation he really felt.

The Duke and Duchess abruptly ended their terse argument upon sensing his presence and turned of an accord to stare at him. He almost smiled thinking it was the first time they had done anything in sync in many years. His father was sitting in a chair almost facing the door, while his mother stood a few feet closer. He saw her lips purse, and without even the courtesy of a greeting, she opened the subject weighing on his mind.

"And where have you been?"

"In Southampton."

"Harrumph! I am aware of that. For what purpose did you find the sudden need to go to town?"

"To book passage on a ship."

Both pair of eyes widened in surprise, but his father remained silent. His mother's eyes narrowed as she said, "Where do you think you are going?"

Jason lifted his chin a notch, unconsciously mimicking his mother when challenged, and boldly said, "To America."

His father's eyes widened again, while his mother's narrowed in a deep frown. "The colonies? Whatever for?"

"I have my reasons." He steadily held her gaze refusing to say more.

She turned to his father with a sputter of disbelief and then abruptly turned back to him. "We will not fund a gallivanting crusade. You have the serious business of searching for a wife to attend to here at home."

Jason couldn't help the slight lifting of the corner of his mouth. "You are not funding my voyage. I am."

"You are? With what funds?"

"If you must know, from my estate."

She took a step closer to face him directly. "I forbid it."

He refused to give ground. No longer was he the boy she could control at will. "You cannot forbid it. I have reached my majority, and you no longer have a say."

His father rose from his chair, "I think a voyage is an excellent idea. The boy needs to broaden his horizons."

Jason looked to his father, surprised by his sudden support, while his mother spun around to confront him. "You will not condone his folly."

Jason refused to tell her under direct confrontation but now to diffuse the escalating tension he spoke, "The purpose of my voyage is in fact to bring home a wife."

His mother turned back to him, surprise and speculation quickly passing over her features, before she whispered, almost to herself, "An American heiress."

He opened his mouth to contradict her but then thought better of it. Let her think what she would.

His father said, "Where do you plan to find a lady of means?"

"Alabama."

His father frowned. "A southern state? Why not search the New England states? That is where the rich industrial families reside."

He was surprised how quickly the excuse came to mind. "Those are city girls who would be quite dissatisfied living in the country as we do, and I imagine are spoiled as well. I am aiming for the cotton plantations. Their daughters are used to the country and trained to manage a large household."

Both his parents were silent, and if he wasn't mistaken, a little proud of his forethought. His father smiled. His mother's face relaxed and after a moment she said, "When are you leaving?"

* * *

Jason was smiling as he took the stairs to his room. His spirits were light now that he had confronted his parents and garnered their approval. He reached his room to find his valet, Reginald, hanging his freshly brushed coat and hat. For his overnight stay in Southampton he was perfectly capable of taking care of himself, but this voyage would be weeks, if not months. He would need his valet, but he only purchased one ticket. One very expensive ticket. Plus he would need money for food, travel, and other expenditures, which would be doubled if Reginald accompanied him. But he hadn't a clue how to care for his clothes without him. Reginald was hired to be his valet, replacing his nursemaid, when he moved out of the nursery. He couldn't imagine leaving him behind, and he must admit, travelling alone was daunting. It would help to have company, even that of a servant. *Why hadn't he thought of this yesterday?* He would return to Southampton tomorrow to purchase a second passage and withdraw the extra funds.

"Reginald, let us have a talk."

Concern tightened the man's features. "Certainly, milord."

"We will need to pack for a voyage to the States."

"Of course, milord. When do you sail?"

"We leave in a week."

"We, sir?"

Jason gave him a puzzled look. "You and I, of course."

Reginald was dismayed. "Respectfully, sir, I cannot go with you. My family needs me. I could not leave them for so long a journey."

Now what was he to do? It wasn't right for a lord to press his own clothes, and how did one go about brushing out a coat or polishing shoes? At least Reginald could pack his valises.

Jason was so concerned with what he was going to do without his valet that he failed to notice the distress in Reginald's eyes.

"Perhaps, sir, I can assist in finding you a replacement before you leave."

Jason shook his head having come to a decision. "No. I daresay I can find a way to manage on my own. I mean to travel light, perhaps a carpet bag or two. I see no need for a trunk."

Reginald gave him a speculative look. "Ships and hotels typically have laundry service, and I can show you a few tips for the in between times."

"That would be most helpful." With his most urgent problem resolved, Jason finally realized the full hardship he was putting on his valet—it was likely he would have to take a lesser position, given his age. Reginald said he had a family and Jason was, in effect, leaving him unexpectedly unemployed. "Is there something I can do for you to reward your years of faithful service?"

"A letter of recommendation would be appreciated, milord."

"Of course you will have a letter, but I was thinking more of a bonus."

"Whatever you deem appropriate would be appreciated more than you can know, milord."

Jason laid a hand on the shoulder of the man whose importance he was only beginning to appreciate. "I will miss you, Reginald."

The faithful servant's jaw tightened as he controlled his emotions, and all he could do was nod in response.

Chapter 2

Jason's building excitement during the course of the long voyage from England to America reached a fevered pitch in his breast as the *Merchant's Pride* finally made port in Mobile Bay. He left Southampton eight weeks ago on this ship sailing due south. They made a stop to resupply in Cape Verde before turning west to cross the Atlantic and into the Caribbean Sea. A trade stop in Jamaica lasting more than a week gave him time to explore the mountainous island before they sailed into the Gulf of Mexico. An hour ago they passed between Alabama's barrier islands with Fort Gaines on the left and Fort Morgan under construction on the right to protect Mobile Bay. He now stood at the railing facing the city of Mobile waiting for his turn to descend into the long boat taking him to shore.

He still had to travel overland to reach Montgomery, but he was getting close to his goal. Close to reuniting with Abigail. He had no idea what lay ahead in his journey, but he was happy to be starting the final part of it. He preferred the solidity and vegetation of land to the barren fickle waves of the sea.

He was surprised to discover Mobile was only slightly larger than Midanbury, but very much a growing settlement. He had no trouble finding the only posting inn, and was informed he could reach Montgomery via steamboat or stagecoach. The latter was still faster, and having just gotten off the water, Jason was in no hurry to return to it. He secured passage on the next stagecoach due to depart three days hence, and he was fortunately able to secure the last room at the inn for his wait. He spent his time exploring the coastal town. He discovered three churches, a multitude of taverns, a thriving government, and, for the most part, genteel people. The countryside beyond was much like home—covered in trees holding on to the last vestiges of their fall color but intermingled with a prolific number of pine trees.

On the morning of his departure from Mobile, he boarded the well-maintained red and gold stagecoach with six other passengers. A lad of ten climbed to the top to ride with the luggage behind the driver, which left the rest of them filling the interior to capacity and forcing him to hold his limbs tightly to his body. The ride was smooth enough out of the city, but once they entered the countryside, the road turned into a narrow pitted path enclosed by trees on either side. The jarring ride added further discomfort. Fortunately, the carriage was a newer model with the body supported by straps rather than springs, so the passengers were swayed rather than bounced over the ragged road. He resigned himself to enduring this latest hardship for the three days it would take to reach Montgomery. The end was near, and he smiled softly as he thought of reuniting with Abigail.

What was supposed to be three days turned into six. A sudden afternoon downpour on the second day lasting several hours turned the roads into a quagmire. They were fortunate to make it to the next overnight stop before they became mired in the mud, so at least they had a reasonably comfortable place to sleep and eat. Two days later, the ground was determined to be firm enough again to proceed onward.

When they finally entered the outskirts of Montgomery, Jason found great relief to see something other than trees from the window and to hear noises other than the coach and its chatty occupants. He was first out of the door ready to stretch his limbs and turned to assist the other ladies before retrieving his luggage. He then looked for the closest livery stable in hopes of finding a horse for hire so he could be on his way.

Montgomery was considerably larger than Mobile and full of bustle. The first stable did not have any horses available nor did the next three. He walked to the fifth recommendation with little hope. It was a combination livery stable and blacksmith shop. He stepped into the three sided lean-to smelling of hay, horses, fire and heated iron. He waited for the owner to hammer the finishing touches on a horseshoe and dunk it in a bucket of water to sizzle and steam before coming to greet him.

The middle-aged muscular man removed his heavy work glove from his right hand and wiped it on his dirty leather coveralls before holding it out to Jason. "Name's Johnson. What can I do for you?"

Jason shook his hand. "Malwbry." He made the mistake in Mobile of introducing himself as Lord Malwbry. He was used to his title bringing instant attention and respect, but in this country it opened up a lot of questioning at best and ridicule at worst. He quickly found it expedient, albeit humbling, to drop it. "Do you have a horse for hire?"

"I have one mare left, but..."

Jason was so relieved there was a horse, he didn't care if it wasn't a stallion, and whatever Mr. Johnson was about to say didn't matter. "I'll take it. What's your price?"

Johnson cocked his head, "Depends on how far and for how long. Where are you headed?"

Jason frowned. He didn't know yet in which direction he was headed, let alone how far it would be. He only knew Abigail's uncle had a plantation near Montgomery. "I don't suppose you know the whereabouts of James Bennington's plantation?"

The man's brow puckered. "Bennington, you say." Jason nodded. "I don't reckon I do. Cotton?"

"Yes, I believe so."

"Most of the cotton plantations are west of here, but there's one or two on the road to Tuscaloosa. Best thing to do is go ask at the cotton exchange or the courthouse."

Jason gave the man a coin. "Please hold the horse for me. I'll be back soon." He made his way to the large, newly built, courthouse at the foot of Market Street. He had to weave his way through strings of coloured people chained together in various states of health and dress waiting for their turn at auction in Court Square. In the distance he could hear the shouts of the auctioneer and bidders trading money for lives. The degradation angered him. Men were needed to work the land, but surely tenant farming was a better system than slavery.

He climbed the steps of the courthouse, putting the disturbing thought aside. It was a large building with many offices, but he finally found the one he needed. He was dismayed to learn from the clerk that his destination was nearly thirty miles outside of town. It was more than a man could travel in a day by horseback, at least not without tiring an unconditioned man and beast past the point of exhaustion. He made his way back to the livery thinking there was no help for it; he was going to be spending the night alone in the wilderness unless he happened upon someplace he could impose upon the famous southern hospitality.

He would need food for the journey, so on the way back to the stable, he entered a dry goods store to pick up whatever ready to eat, portable food he could find. He thought about asking for help, but as he looked around the store, embarrassment kept him silent. Even the children of the patrons seemed perfectly capable of making a fire to heat a can of beans, if necessary. He filled a small burlap bag from the barrel of mixed nuts, and then picked up some apples, soda crackers, jerky, and a canteen. He passed a display of flint and matches and picked up both so he at least had the tools he would need, if not the skills. He silently paid for his purchases and returned to the stable.

Mr. Johnson greeted him with a friendly wave. "And what did you learn?"

"He owns Mulberry House, twenty-seven miles due west."

They negotiated a weekly price since Jason was unsure how long his stay would be. Considering the lateness of the afternoon, he decided to wait till morning to head out to avoid spending two nights in the wilderness. He found a room and a hot meal at a nearby inn and went to bed early. He hadn't had much rest since leaving the ship. The three previous nights he shared a room at the various posting inns along their journey and tonight was no different. Besides the uncomfortably tight quarters, one of his fellow roommates snored so loudly it was impossible for him to sleep.

At dawn, he sat down at the boardinghouse table with the other inhabitants to share a meal of eggs, bacon, biscuits and gravy before making his way to the livery.

Mr. Johnson gave him a friendly greeting. "I'll bring the mare around."

Jason was pleased with the appearance of a reddish-brown palfrey with black stockings, mane and tail. When the first stable was empty he resigned himself to riding less than a stallion. When the next ones also proved to be empty except for this one horse his expectations dropped even lower. Based on Mr. Johnson's reluctance of yesterday, he presumed to be saddled with an old nag. It lifted his spirits to be handed the reins of a vigorous young mare. He handed over enough coin to cover a fortnight per their agreement. He would settle any difference upon his return.

Mr. Johnson shook his hand and said, "You take care of my girls and bring them back safe."

Jason silently frowned. *Girls?*

Mr. Johnson gave a nod indicating he should look behind the mare.

Jason took a step sideways and discovered a matching bay filly with a bit of white on her forehead. "Oh no! No sir. The foal must stay."

Mr. Johnson grinned. "I'm afraid, Mr. Malwbry, you don't have a choice. Where the mare goes, the foal goes. No foal, no mare. It's as simple as that."

Jason's brow furrowed. He had no idea how to care for a foal. His stable hands handled them, and he hadn't ridden a mare since he was in shortpants further limiting his experience. He was loath to expose his ignorance by admitting what to this man would be a shortcoming but neither did he want to inadvertently harm the filly with his lack of knowledge. It was yet another lesson in humility. "I don't know anything about caring for foals."

"You don't need to worry. Her momma will tend to her. She's about four months old so she shouldn't slow you down too much. You just need to keep her safe from the wild animals."

Jason's mind froze. Wild animals. That hadn't crossed his mind. His eyes widened as another thought occurred. *What about the natives?* "Sir, do I need to worry about Indians?"

"Well, I suppose there could be a few hanging about, but General Jackson pretty much cleared them out of this area a few years back. If there are any left, they tend to stay clear of us whites. No sir, it's the mountain lions, black bears, bobcats, wolves, coyotes, and foxes you need to be worried about." He gave Jason a speculative look, "You do carry a gun?"

Jason nodded, "It's in my bag." Foxes did not overly concern him. Having participated in fox hunts since boyhood, he didn't consider them a huge threat, even without his hounds or his rifle. On the other hand, although bears and wolves roamed the woods of England, he had never hunted nor encountered them, but the stories of other men who had were terrifying. Worse, he had never heard of mountain lions, bobcats or coyotes. *What had he gotten himself into?* Now having fire took on a whole new importance. He fingered the flint and matches in his pocket. They kept the fear at bay but failed to give him any confidence of being able to start a fire.

Mr. Johnson was beginning to wonder if he would be wise to change his mind. This young dandy was not instilling confidence in his ability to protect his horses. "You best keep it on your person. Trouble comes calling, you won't have time to retrieve it much less load it."

Jason saw the sense in his advice. He passed the reins back to Mr. Johnson and removed his revolver from his satchel. He slipped it in his coat pocket and put the powder and balls in his other pocket. It uncomfortably weighed down his coat, but there wasn't anything to be done about it. He had no other means of carrying it.

"Here let me secure your bag." Mr. Johnson traded the reins for Jason's bag and tied it behind the saddle.

"What are their names?"

Mr. Johnson looked up from his task. "These aren't pets. I don't name them. When I have to I refer to this one as Red." He patted the mare's neck as he stepped to her flank.

Jason's mouth thinned at his gaffe. He led the mare away from the lean to and swung into the saddle with a confidence born of his title. It was certainly far from what he was feeling. Pride kept him from admitting his shortcomings to Mr. Johnson. With his back straight, he tipped his hat to the livery man and set the mare to a trot with the morning sun climbing the sky behind him. The mare whinnied and tossed her head. He turned to see the foal nimbly run up to her side and a little ahead, kicking out her back legs and tossing her mane in carefree abandon before settling into a walk.

This lasted until they were a good distance away from the city dwellings and the dirt road, now strewn with leaves and pine needles, was enclosed by gray tree trunks crowned with faded fall color intermingled with the plethora of dark green pines. Dried leaves were piled thick on the sides of the road adding an earthiness to the crisp air. Occasionally, they were stirred by the breeze to dance across his path. Silence reigned except for the call of birds and the steady staccato of the mare's pace with the faster undertone of the foal.

He pulled his collar tighter around his neck to ward off the morning chill. The smattering of sunlight that filtered between the trees teased him with its promised warmth later in the day. Jason and the mare kept a steady gait while the foal pranced ahead a bit before turning to circle behind and leap ahead again. Jason found the exuberant antics amusing so long as they didn't delay his forward progress.

The sun climbed higher adding warmth to the fall morning, and the solitary ride through middle Alabama gave him time to think. It was the first time since leaving his home he was truly alone and the solitary miles gave him plenty of time to consider what lie ahead.

Ideally, Abigail and her family would welcome his arrival and invite him to stay giving him time to woo her. In his mind, he saw idyllic days of stimulating conversation, horseback riding, and evenings spent playing chess in front of a fire after which he would propose and she would accept and they would return to England as husband and wife.

He frowned as his mind warned him of all the pitfalls in his musings, the first being his reception. How would Abigail greet him? Would she be happy or dismayed? In all likelihood it would be her uncle or her father he would face first. Would they turn him away out of hand or allow him to stay? Having traveled so far he could perhaps count on common courtesy to allow him to at least stay the night. Then he could charm Abigail into pleading for his extended visit. Considering how quickly she pawned him off at the dance and avoided him after he had to admit he was nervous about her reception. She very likely would be the one to turn him away out of hand without...

The horse suddenly stopped beneath him while momentum threw him toward her neck. "What the devil?" He righted himself and nudged her sides, but she didn't budge. She was standing still in the middle of the road for no discernable reason. He used the same clucking sound from this morning, but still she didn't move. Then he noticed the foal was not in sight. He turned in the saddle looking to the right and then the left and behind. The flicking of the foal's tail brought his gaze downward to discover she was suckling. *Now?* He pulled out his pocket watch to check the time. He had been riding for barely an hour and judging by their pace he guessed they had barely covered two miles.

His brow furrowed. The foal could eat later. He was not going to stay alone in this wilderness any longer than absolutely necessary. He tried again kneeing the mare's sides more emphatically. The mare only tossed her head and snorted in annoyance. He moved his foot in an attempt to shoo the foal. The mare turned her head and nipped at his knee. He was considering getting down, dislodging the foal, and pulling the mare forward when he remembered a long forgotten conversation with one of his groomsmen lamenting the vagaries of working with nursing mares. Jason's will meant nothing to this mare. He was over-ruled by a little bit of a horse.

It was a hard fact for him to accept. All his life people had done his bidding. Few ever dared to defy him knowing his father would terminate their employ upon a simple word of displeasure from Jason. His personal horse and dogs obeyed his command. Others had seen to their excellent training before he had possession of the animals. And of course, he had no experience with mares. It wouldn't do for a duke's son to ride anything less than a stallion, even as a boy.

Unexpectedly the mare took two steps to the side of the road to reach the grass. Clearly he was not the one in charge of this situation. Anger flashed through him and he tried one more time to turn the mare's head and get them moving, but she refused to budge. Jason took a deep breath and reluctantly accepted the fact he was going to have to find patience. He slipped from the saddle careful not to kick the nursing foal. As long as he was stuck here, he might as well make use of the time to stretch his legs and eat the leftover biscuit stuffed with bacon he had wrapped up in his pocket.

Jason sighed. It was going to be a long day.

About ten minutes later the foal was satisfied and prancing about again. Jason mounted up and urged the mare into a trot anxious to make up for lost time. One night spent alone in the forest was bad enough. He had no intentions of it turning into two nights because of a little bit of a horse.

Another two hours later he came to Catoma Creek, the first of three significant water crossings according to the crudely drawn map the clerk made for him from the larger map on display in the courthouse. The creeks range forty to fifty feet wide and he was assured all were shallow enough to easily cross on horseback. *But what about the foal?*

The mare eagerly stepped to the edge of the sandy shore to drink and the foal followed suit. Jason assessed the depth of the murky green water. A few feet from shore it was impossible to see the bottom. He watched a leaf lazily drift past and took some comfort in the slow current until he remembered it usually also indicated deeper water.

Large birds circled overhead drawing his eye upward to the partly cloudy sky. Here in the open, the sun warmed his back. Soon the day would be warm enough to remove his coat. The mare lifted her head from the water, and Jason urged her forward at a careful walk. A few steps in, she stopped and whinnied. His first thought was she sensed trouble, but then he realized the foal was still on the bank pacing back and forth. The mare turned her head to look back while her offspring continued to dance at the water's edge. It seemed like minutes passed by before the foal grew brave enough to step into the river. She jumped back at the new sensation of swirling water on her legs with a distressed cry to her mother. The mare's whinnying assurances eventually coerced the foal to try again and she came running and splashing forward as if the water would hurt her. The foal stayed close to the mare's flank until they were safely on the far shore. Jason was relieved the water's deepest point was just above the mare's knees making it an easy crossing. He hoped the other two would prove to be the same.

They had not gone far on the other side when the mare suddenly stopped again. He looked around for the foal, first to be nursing and then along the road, but he didn't see her. *Where could that little bit of a horse be?* He was sure it was not ahead so he turned the mare around and was mildly surprised when she capitulated. He still did not see the foal, and it was beginning to worry him. He gave the mare her head, and she stepped to the right side of the road and began to feed on the grass. Jason's body relaxed when he finally noticed the foal laid out sleeping behind a stand of tall grass; her long legs stretched out full length, the front ones crossed. Even in sleep this little bit of horseflesh looked feisty. While he was relieved no harm had come to her, he was frustrated by yet another delay in the day's travel, and it wasn't even noon yet. He contemplated waking her, but a sleep deprived foal would not help his cause. Besides horses usually took short naps during the day; he could only hope foals did so as well.

He dismounted and removed his overcoat laying it across the saddle. The sun was getting high, pleasantly warming the air, and if he wasn't chafing over trying to cover another twenty-something miles, he would be enjoying it. As it was, the idleness was rousing his ire. He paced as far as the mare's lead would allow and back shaking his head. The breeze ruffled his hair, but unfortunately could not cool his growing frustration.

As a man used to dictating his desires to those around him and having them carried out without question, he was having trouble accepting that a four-month-old filly was now dictating to him. Jason kicked the dirt, stewing in his vexation. He cast a discomfited glance at the filly sleeping peacefully in a sunny patch of grass. Part of him acknowledged the tranquility of the scene, and the enticement the tired foal must have felt upon discovering the sweet warm grass. With the softening thoughts came the voice of his nursemaid when he was about ten years old admonishing him for his lack of patience. The corners of his mouth lifted. It was a virtue he never mastered, and apparently a little bit of a filly was going to teach it to him or send him into a madcap rage. A self-deprecating chuckle escaped his lips sounding overly loud in the surrounding quiet. The mare momentarily lifted her head from grazing in response to the out of place sound.

With nothing to do but think, Jason looked down the shadowed road highlighted with bands of sunlight. He still had a long way to go, and the sun would soon reach its zenith. It would set a mere five hours later. The coming night ahead gave him some trepidation—actually, more than a little. He was a fair shot with his rifle and pistol, but learning to camp out was not encouraged training for a future duke. How to direct another to do so was more in keeping with his education. He saw the deficiency now and was beginning to understand Mr. Bennington's reservations with his character. What skills did he really possess? What was he worth without his servants? In this situation, the answers were dismal. Tonight, he who had never started a fire in his life, would be on his own, in a strange land, responsible for the safety of these horses, which were a livery man's livelihood. Jason grimaced. He was about to get a long overdue lesson in self-reliance.

The filly lifted her head and rose to her feet full of energy. A glance at his pocket watch told Jason twenty minutes had passed. He eagerly mounted ready to cover some ground. He turned the mare to the road and glanced behind him calling to the filly, "Come on Little Bit. Show us how fast you can go." He nudged the mare into a light gallop as they climbed the gently rising slope in the road. He turned to watch the foal and grinned as her legs went in all directions as she eagerly tried to keep pace with her mama.

The rest of the day included two more feedings and an afternoon nap. In between these delays, they made slow progress except for one point when they came across the terrible stench of something dead in the brush. Bile rose in the back of Jason's throat. He kicked the mare into a gallop attempting to escape the foul odor. In the afternoon, they approached an opening in the trees not caused by water. It was a curious swath of felled trees, their trunks splintered. It was not as if they were cleared by man, but more the haphazard work of nature, for the trees lay where they fell twisted and torn from their trunks. In front of him lay a large pine across the road with a section cut away by axe some time ago large enough to allow passage for a carriage. He continued on wondering what could have caused such destruction.

The sun was dropping in front of him. He could continue about another hour before he would have to find a place to camp for the night, preferably near a creek or stream with grass for the horses. They should have crossed the second river by now, but the best he could figure they had only traveled perhaps a dozen miles today, putting them well short of reaching it. He sighed again in frustration knowing it was not to be helped. He turned his mind to what needed to be done to prepare for the night ahead. First thing he would need to do is gather wood for the fire. If he could get a fire going, the rest he hoped would be easy.

The mare nickered and tossed her head pulling him from his thoughts. He realized Little Bit was not in sight. He turned to find the filly sniffing something on the side of the road. She tossed her head in the air, and come bounding towards them. It wasn't a gallop or a trot but an exuberant run with legs sometimes going akimbo, sometimes to the side and sometimes kicking back and head bouncing. Jason couldn't help smiling. If nothing else, Little Bit was good amusement.

The acrid scent of burning wood reached him. Hope flared; he would find a residence nearby. He walked the horses forward and soon found a path leading off the road and an opening in the trees revealing a cultivated field with the withered remains of summer crops. Beyond the field was a small white-washed farm house and a good sized barn of weathered grey wood. Jason pulled on the reins bringing the mare to a halt. He briefly debated making more progress in the remaining daylight or taking advantage of this opportunity to avoid spending the night alone. The sight of a lad on the front porch waving to him settled his mind. He turned the mare to canter down the lane leading to the house.

Reaching the porch, Jason dismounted as the lad ran forward to take the mare's lead.

"Hello mister. My name's Daniel Hudson, but folks call me Danny."

Jason smiled at the lad he guessed to be about eight or nine. He removed his riding glove and held out his hand. "I am Jason Malwbry."

The boy shook his hand, pleased by the adult gesture. He turned to the porch as his mother stepped from the house. "This here's Jason Malwbry."

Jason nodded to the woman, who appeared to be in her mid-twenties with honey colored hair smoothed into a bun and a well-worn brown dress covered with a stained white apron. She faced him with confidence and surety. She didn't smile, but her demeanor wasn't unfriendly.

"I'm Mrs. Hudson. My husband's in the barn. What can we do for you Mr. Malwbry?"

Jason took a step toward the porch to address her directly. He removed his hat and bowed to her. "Pleased to meet you, ma'am."

"Judging by your accent, you're a long ways from home."

Jason nodded. "I am, and I am faced with spending my first night alone in an unfamiliar wilderness. I was hoping I could impose upon you for shelter for the night, in exchange for coin, of course."

She nodded toward the barn. "Go ask Mr. Hudson. It will be his say."

"Of course ma'am. Thank you." Jason turned and took the reins from the boy to lead the mare toward the barn. By now Danny had spotted the foal and eagerly relinquished the mare's reins to dash over to the filly to rub her forehead. She nickered and nudged him. Jason smiled to see the instant rapport between the two youngsters.

Danny turned to him with bright eyes. "What's her name?"

Jason's mouth quirked remembering Mr. Johnson's reply to his same question. "I've been calling her Little Bit."

Danny started walking toward the barn. "Come on Little Bit. Let's get you something to eat and drink."

Jason and the mare followed. At the barn door he could hear a man speaking softly to one of his animals and the sounds of hay being moved.

"Papa, we have a visitor."

The man straightened and set aside his pitch fork. He stepped forward with his hand extended. "Rafe Hudson."

"Jason Malwbry." Jason shook the calloused hand of the burly sandy-blond man with dark blue eyes.

"Where you headed?"

"Mulberry House."

"James Bennington's place. Big spread. Friend of his from England?"

Jason grimaced. He didn't expect the personal question. "Not exactly, but I am acquainted with his brother and his niece."

"Oh. Can't say that I've met them." Mr. Hudson gave him an appraising look. "You looking for a place to bed down for the night?"

Replying in the manner he heard other locals use, Jason said, "I would be much obliged."

"I can let you bed down in the barn for the night with your horses. You can have feed for them and share a plate from our supper table. It's not much, but my wife's a good cook."

"On the contrary, sir, you are most generous, and I am more than willing to pay you."

Mr. Hudson shook his head. "The money isn't necessary. Just being neighborly. You can put up your horse in that stall there after I throw some clean hay in it, and I'll bring you some bedding you can use in the loft."

"Thank you sir."

"Danny, why don't you lead the horses down to the creek for a drink?" The boy was quick to do his father's bidding. "Mr. Malwbry, I'm sure you would like to wash off a bit of travel dirt before supper. Help yourself to the rain barrel out back."

"Thank you, sir."

"No trouble a'tall."

Supper was a quiet affair. After the blessing, the Hudson family's attention was focused solely on enjoying the hearty soup of smoked ham, beans, and potatoes with freshly baked sourdough bread. Afterwards, the family settled by the fire. Mrs. Hudson crocheted a blanket, Mr. Hudson sharpened his knives, and Danny worked on his reader, occasionally asking his mother for help. For the first time in his life, Jason was uncomfortable with his idle hands.

After speaking about the weather, Mr. Hudson ventured into personal questions again, but Jason's reluctance to answer soon quieted him, and the room was silent except for the noises of their various industries. Jason was trying to find something to say to fill the silence when Mr. Hudson began speaking to Mrs. Hudson about local affairs, leaving Jason content to quietly listen and draw comparisons between his life and theirs. The hardships they mentioned had never crossed his mind, and he realized they were probably very similar to those faced by his father's tenant farmers. His brow furrowed. For the first time in his life he considered how he came to have the coins in his pocket. He had always accepted they were his birthright, but now he appreciated they were earned by the sweat and labor of others.

Jason looked at the sun-browned face of his host. "Sir, are you a tenant farmer?"

Mr. Hudson turned to his guest and broadly smiled. "No sir, I own this land. About eighty acres." The pride behind his words was unmistakable.

"You are not beholden to others?"

"No." He frowned, now, unsure what Mr. Malwbry was implying.

Jason could feel his host's displeasure, and so he dropped the subject with a nod.

A few moments later, Mr. Hudson told Danny it was time for bed.

Jason decided it was a good time to excuse himself too. Mrs. Hudson bid him to wait as she stood. A few moments later, she returned from the bedroom with two heavy wool blankets. "To ward off the night's chill."

"Thank you, ma'am." Jason nodded to both of them and left the farm house.

He was thankful for the blankets as he stepped into the crisp night air. Mr. Hudson thought they might have their first frost of the season by morning. It made Jason thankful for the barn as well when he thought of waking on the cold hard ground covered in frozen dew.

He climbed the ladder to the barn loft with his saddle bag and the blankets and inhaled the sweet smell of hay emanating from the heaps of fresh cut straw surrounding him. The last time he was in a hay loft he had been eight and hiding from his governess. He arranged five of the bails lengthwise in a row to form a bed and spread the blankets upon it. He pulled out his own much thinner blanket from his saddle bag to use for a pillow. The result was not to be compared with his bed at Rothebury Hall, but it was a far cry better than the hard ground he previously anticipated for tonight. A mule's snort reminded him of the barn's other occupants. Jason grinned. He was getting another lesson in humility: a duke's son sleeping with the animals. How Marc Danvers would laugh if he could see him now.

A beam of moonlight breached the space between the loft doors. Intrigued, Jason made his way to the doors and unhooked the latch. The full sized doors used for loading the hay into the loft slipped open. The incoming breeze made him shiver in his coat, but the view kept him from immediately pulling the doors closed. Light from a nearly full moon bathed the surrounding hills and treetops, turning it from black to a muted palette of blue-grey. To his right was a recently harvested field of hay; otherwise, as far as he could see, the land appeared undisturbed by man.

He pulled the doors closed and latched them again. Due to the cold, he remained dressed for added warmth, including his boots. He laid down on his makeshift bed and pulled the second wool blanket up to his chin. Slumber quickly overtook him. Sometime during the night, he woke up feeling the cold on his cheeks and ears. He shook out his 'pillow,' folded it in half, draped it over his head, and wrapped the ends around his neck. The next thing he knew, the rooster was crowing and Mr. Hudson was entering the barn to begin his morning chores. Jason rose from his bed with the blankets still wrapped around him, loathe to leave their warmth, and approached the loft's edge.

Mr. Hudson looked up. "Good morning, sir. Mrs. Hudson is fixing porridge if you would care to have some."

"I would appreciate a warm meal. Can I help you with your chores?"

"Thank you for the offer, but no. I am milking the cow now and will return after my meal to take care of the rest. I am sure you will want to be promptly on your way. I reckon you still have fifteen miles to go, and that filly will make it difficult to reach your destination by nightfall."

Jason nodded in agreement. He turned and packed up his few belongings and folded Mrs. Hudson's blankets after shaking off the hay clinging to them. He carried it all down the stairs just as Danny came rushing in to summon them to eat. Jason laid his belongs next to his saddle by the barn door. Mr. Hudson carried the now full milk pail back to the house followed by Jason with the blankets, and Danny, eagerly telling him all about the puppy he would soon receive from the neighbor's litter.

The meal was again silently consumed, and at its end, Jason thanked his host and hostess and offered them compensation, which was politely refused. Danny followed him out to the barn to help saddle the mare and pet the foal one last time. He ran after them for a short distance before effusively waving them off. Jason returned his wave with a smile.

Shortly after leaving the Hudson farm, Jason crossed the Pintlala Creek without any trouble. It roughly signified the half-way point in his journey. The day went much like the previous one. At first, he kept the mare to a faster pace hoping to cover more ground, but it tired Little Bit that much sooner, so by midday, he resumed a steady pace and hoped for the best.

He wondered what Abigail was doing today. Perhaps she was sitting in a sunny corner of the parlour reading a book or wandering the grounds of the plantation with her father. How was she going to react to seeing him? She would certainly be surprised, but would it be a good surprise or a bad one? Did he come all this way for naught? Jason frowned. He wouldn't accept that. The gesture alone of traveling so far just to see her should certainly endear him to her. His spirits lifted. He was the future Duke of Rothebury. What woman could resist becoming a duchess? He frowned even more. Abigail resisted. In fact, she left the country to avoid him. How was he going to change her mind? He brightened once again. He was here to show her the man he could be, not the lord she dismissed. He was here to woo and sweet talk her. Once he showed her how much he enjoyed her company, indeed, how much she had come to mean to him, how could she resist?

The mare halted for Little Bit to suckle. Jason dismounted to stretch his legs, and his mind wandered conjuring up scenes of him and Abigail engaged in pleasant conversation with undercurrents of affection, strolling in the sunlight with her arm tucked in his, and dancing at a country ball. In all these scenes, her grey eyes gazed adoringly into his.

Little Bit's moist muzzle nudging his hand broke into his reverie. He turned around and rubbed the forehead and ears that barely reached his chest before the energetic foal scampered away. Jason smiled. His pleasant musings and the amusing foal put him in a good humor for the afternoon.

Shadows were growing long, and too soon the colors of sunset would fill the sky. Jason stared down the road trying to decide what to do. He estimated it was another four or five miles to the plantation, and it would be dark in another hour. Little Bit was going to suckle again soon. If he tried to keep going, it would be well after dark before he arrived. While his impatience to reach Abigail drove him onward, his late arrival may not be well received by her uncle and father. Also, it would be difficult to find his way in the dark, even with the moonlight. And then there were the horses to consider. He wasn't at all sure the mare would keep going with the filly after dark. Even if she did, Little Bit could suddenly decide it was time to sleep, and then he would be stuck without a campsite. And he couldn't forget about the wild animals. A fire was necessary to ward them off, and he had little confidence in building one in the daylight. In darkness... He shuddered even considering it. No. All of the facts pointed to finding a place to camp for the night.

A dart of wind brought the smell of decaying death, and he reflexively squeezed his knees urging the mare to quickly pass the area.

Jason heard the faint sounds of gurgling water, and a small creek soon appeared. A slightly elevated sandy bank was on the opposite side with a small clearing. It would make a good place to spend the night. He urged the horses to take the couple of steps necessary to cross the tributary. Jason dismounted and walked with the horses to the water's edge. Paw prints on the bank, evidence of the mountain lions or bobcats mentioned by Mr. Johnson, sent a shiver down his spine. He scanned his surroundings, listening intently. All seemed peaceful. A gentle breeze rustled the remaining leaves in the trees. Here and there birds chirped. The mare was content nibbling on a patch of grass with Little Bit at her side. Nothing around him seemed threatening... except for those impressions in the sand.

Jason secured the mare next to the creek and began gathering wood. Little Bit followed him until he was out of site of the mare. Her whinny called the foal back to her side. Jason's mouth twitched at the way the filly seemed to jump and turn at the same time. Her legs kicked out behind as she made a quick return to her mother.

He gathered a pile of twigs and branches, but knew he would have to feed the fire all night unless he could find something larger. There was a log nearby, but he had nothing with him to chop it up. His further search revealed a rotting, fallen tree broke into two and three foot sections. He picked up the smallest, hoping there would be enough solid wood for his fire. The top half separated from the bottom, and as he stepped back, he caught sight of a snake slithering away. Apparently, he had disturbed its nest. Jason thanked his good fortune it was not an aggressive or poisonous snake. That one careless act could have led to his death, alone, in the Alabama wilderness. There was no one expecting his arrival to be concerned enough to come looking for him. And what would happen to the horses? He shuddered. Those two lives were depending on his survival. He would have to be more careful.

He looked down at the crumbling half log he now carried. The wood wasn't much, but it would do. He hauled it back to his makeshift camp and then carefully retrieved two more pieces.

The sun was close to dropping behind the trees. Jason knelt in the center of his campsite, which he cleared of debris. He began piling the wood up in the manner he had seen the servants do so many times when lighting fires in the fireplaces of Rothebury Hall. Small pieces on the bottom. Big piece on top. The stack looked good. Jason reached into his pocket and pulled out the box of matches. He pulled one out and put the rest of the box back in his coat pocket. He looked around for something to strike it against. Not finding anything within reach, he got up to retrieve a rock he saw closer to the creek. Sitting down again, he struck the match and touched it to a small stick at the bottom of the pile. The match burned out before the flame caught on the wood.

Undeterred, Jason retrieved another match and tried again. Although this time a flame started, it didn't hold. A third attempt proved no better. He sat back to figure out if he was missing something. Always before, there were servants to do his bidding. This entire trip he had been around others taking care of the necessities; providing food, fire, and shelter. Tonight was the first time ever he had to rely solely on himself, and he was failing.

What in the world had he gotten himself into? Here he was out on his own in a foreign wilderness all because of a woman. A woman who probably wouldn't welcome him when he did finally reach her. The whole idea seemed preposterous in hind-sight. He crossed his arms over his chest, frowning at his own folly. He was a fool.

A noise in the brush behind him made the hairs on the back of his neck stand up. The mare lifted her head and listened too. Jason pulled the gun out of his coat pocket. He tried not to notice his hand was trembling. In the fading light, a rabbit appeared from the underbrush. Jason released his breath in an audible whoosh while the mare calmly resumed her grazing.

Jason turned back to his unrealized fire with a confidence further shaken by the burst of fear. He placed the gun on the ground beside him within easy reach just in case next time, it was something less benign. What was he going to do if he couldn't get the fire lit? It would be a long, cold, sleepless night if he didn't. Likely it would be anyway, but at least the fire would give him a small measure of comfort and security.

He tried another match and failed again. He was definitely missing something. Jason tried to recall the details of the servant's actions. Instead, for a moment, he visualized the comfort of his room in Midanbury with a crackling fire, and his bed with the smooth cotton sheets turned down under warm blankets on a soft down mattress, and him settling in to slumber without a care in the world. If he had known this night was in his future, he never would have left Midanbury. He would have settled for marriage to Lady Jane Torrington, and perhaps now, he would be sleeping comfortable in his bed after performing his husbandly duty. He smiled at the thought, until he realized the face he envisioned was not that of Lady Jane, but

Abigail's.

Abigail.

Just five more miles and he could be reunited with her, but first he had to make it through this night. He focused his attention on recalling the one time he watched a servant build the first fall fire in the cold summer hearth. He piled the wood. He struck the match. He lit the tender.

That was it!

He was missing tender. Jason looked around for something to use as tinder. All he could find were dried leaves. He gathered the larger ones, layered them together in a pile, and stuffed them in an opening under the twigs. They would burn fast but hopefully just long enough. With a deep breath of hope and a bit of concern for the dwindling supply, he struck the fifth match and touched it to the leaves. They lit easily, but as he feared, they burned too fast. He needed something that burned slow and easy. He stood in his clearing, turning in a slow circle, looking for anything that might work.

He pulled his coat tighter against the evening's chill, noticing how deep the shadows had grown. There was not much daylight left. He picked up his gun and slipped it into his pocket. He squared his shoulders and stepped towards the trees. He would have to find something quickly. Dried leaves and pine needles were strewn everywhere. His heightened nervousness made him jump when a twig napped under his foot. He frowned at the offending branch, and then he noticed the large pinecone resting near his foot. It was dry, thicker than the leaves, but thinner than the twigs. Perhaps this would solve his problem. Actually, he recalled seeing a basket of them beside the fireplace in some tenant's cottage as a youngster. Excitement made him rush back eager to try the pinecone, sure now that it was the answer.

He again knelt beside his wood pile and choose what he hoped was the best place for the pine cone. He lit the match with fingers trembling in excitement and breathed a sigh of relief as the strobile caught and held the flame which steadily grew. When the twigs finally caught, he jumped to his feet with a huge silly grin. He did it. He made a fire. The strong sense of accomplishment was more than he had ever felt before. Sure, he felt accomplished when he learned to shoot and finally hit the target, when he learned to stay in the saddle, and a hundred other little things a young lord learns as they grow, but this time it was something meaningful and significant. There was no one to help him figure it out, so this accomplishment meant more to him.

His smile faded as he saw how fast the twigs were burning. The pile of extra wood he thought to be sufficient earlier now seemed paltry. In the last of the daylight, he gathered all he could find around the perimeter of the clearing. He hoped it would be enough.

Now fully dark, Jason settled by the crackling fire sitting cross legged on his blanket spread upon the ground to help insulate him. Other than his coat, it was the only protection he had against the cold of night. He hoped there would not be frost by morning. Reaching for his bag, he pulled out an apple and the bag of nuts. It wasn't much of a supper, but it would do. By the second crisp bite of apple, Little Bit wandered close to investigate. Her nostrils flared as she picked up the sweet scent. Jason smiled and reached for his knife. He cut the apple in half and fed one part to the foal before getting up to give the other half to the mare. Seated once again, he pulled out a second apple. This time when Little Bit came over Jason ignored her until she nudged his shoulder so hard it pushed him sideways.

"Go." His stern command seemed overly loud as it broke into the silence. Perhaps more so being the first words he had spoken all day, other than a few commands for the mare. He was not a stranger to being alone. He often sought the comfort of solitude from his parents' constant bickering, but never before had he gone a complete day without contact with another person. It was a novel experience but not one he would choose to repeat without strong reason.

Finally being still after the day's journey allowed the weariness to settle over him. With heavy eyes, Jason threw more sticks on the fire and laid down on the blanket with his head cradled in his upward facing palms. The sky was clear and the moon was rising. He couldn't see it yet, but the brightness in its path told him it was there. He turned his thoughts to Abigail, but Morpheus stole her vision from him as he slipped into a dreamless sleep.

Chapter 3

Jason awoke with a shiver. The world was dark except for the meager light of the setting moon. He turned his head and saw that the fire was almost out. Quickly he rose and dropped more twigs on the embers. When they sufficiently caught he added another log. A yawn overtook him. He shook his head to clear it but sleep was not to be waved off. He laid back down and fell into a deep slumber.

The next time he awoke, it was much the same; still dark, and the fire was once again smoldering embers. Just as he was about to get up, he heard a horrifying cry of an animal in pain and movement in the underbrush. Jason reached for the gun lying by his head and rolled to face the trees behind him. His grip reflexively tightening on the hilt, he stared into the darkness, ready to shoot whatever may appear.

The specter of a bird flew overhead momentarily breaking his concentration. After a few moments of silence, he rose stealthily and began rebuilding the fire trying to make as little sound as possible. He inwardly laughed at himself for being quiet when noise was more likely to help ward off whatever creatures were hunting in the dark.

It was still a few hours until daylight. He tried to stay awake, but boredom, and the warmth of the flames carried him back into slumber, even sitting up. When he jerked awake for the third time, he gave in and laid back down.

Sometime later, he awoke to discover the eastern sky was a lighter navy behind the dark silhouette of trees. Sunrise was approaching. He sat up and stretched the muscles along his back and neck. He stood and stretched a moment longer before relieving himself in a nearby bush. He coaxed the fire a little brighter but not too much knowing he would have to put it out soon. The horses were feeding on grass, so he finished off the rest of the food in his bag and squatted by the water's edge to wash his face. Feeling the stubble on his chin, he retrieved his shave kit and did the best he could to improve his appearance in the less than ideal situation.

His stomach grumbled, reminding him, he hadn't eaten a full meal since yesterday's breakfast with the Hudson's. If he hurried on his way, perhaps, he could be at the plantation in time for breakfast leftovers. As the early morning grey began to fade from the sky, he kicked dirt on what was left of the fire, loaded the mare, and walked her through the creek to the road with Little Bit at his

Jason mounted and started the mare forward down
was getting easier to see with each passing minute. Two ho
foal feeding later, he finally reached his destination. Tall
pillars marked either side of a drive cut through the trees. An eng
and painted wood sign hung on one pillar announcing Mulb
House. He turned the mare to the right passing between them an
started down the lane. The dense trees and undergrowth kept visual to
a minimum. Horse and rider clipped along the narrow road in the
space between the wagon wheel ruts. A deer darted across his path,
tail up, startling them both.

Several minutes passed and he was still unable to see the house.
Just as he was wondering how much further it could be, the trees
opened up to a clearing with a gentle downward slope to a large—at
least compared to others he had seen since arriving in America—two
story house of white washed wood siding. Four white columns
spanned across the entire front of the house supporting the hipped
roof high above the second story with Ionic capitals. The wide,
centered steps spanned a third of the house's length leading up to the
portico and elaborate front door. Two double windows flanked either
side of the front door with matching windows on the second floor
above. Another shuttered door, with side lights and transom to match
the main door below, opened onto a balcony with wrought iron railing
painted black to match the front door and shutters. The front of the
house faced west and was in shadows with the morning sun sitting
picturesquely above the roof framed by tendrils of smoke drifting up
from chimneys bracketing either end of the house. The perfect
symmetry of it all was pleasing to the eye, and though not as large as
Rothebury Hall, it made quite a statement in its own setting.

Spanning out behind the house were small cabins and out
buildings and beyond them were acres upon acres of dormant cotton
fields. Past the fields, he could see a river from his vantage point on
higher ground. Small groups of people were everywhere across the
property working at various tasks like clearing the fields, burning
debris, digging up root vegetables, and sharpening tools. Even though
it was past the summer harvest, there was obviously still much to do
around the plantation. Jason suspected his tenant farmers were doing
much the same thing.

He looked back to the main house. All he had to do was ride
down this hill, and he would finally be reunited with Abigail. After

el culminating in a cold night spent alone
und, he would finally have the chance to court
ke his future wife.

the front steps and dismounted. A small
ke the reins.

: of yore horses. Don't you worry about 'em
rses."

reins and a coin for his trouble.

ad with wide eyes. "I can't take that." He
around in distress. "You's trying to get me in trouble?"

Jason frowned. "Why would you get in trouble?"

The dark chin went up and his mouth thinned. "Law says slaves can't have money. This is a good place. Don't want no trouble."

Jason slipped the coin in his pocket. He momentarily forgot he was on a plantation operated with slave labor. While untying his two bags, he cast a glance at the two men raking leaves in the front yard confirming their dark skin. There was not another white person in sight until a young man suddenly came galloping around the corner of the house on a spirited white stallion. The men paused in their raking to return his wave as he rode past. It was a friendly gesture and appeared to be freely given. So far, Jason did not see any evidence here of the horrors he had heard of slave owners. He was glad that was the case since Abigail's family owned this estate.

The young man came to a sudden halt a few yards in front of Jason. The little boy smiled wide despite the cloud of dust kicked up by the horse's hooves.

The man dismounted and tossed the reins in the direction of the lad, "Take care of Prince for me."

"Yes sir, Master Robert."

The boy walked off leading both horses and followed by the foal. The young man with reddish-brown hair and grey-green eyes similar to Abigail's approached Jason with his hand held out. "Hello. I'm Robert Bennington."

Jason shook his hand. "Lord Jason Malwbry of Midanbury." For some reason, this man's self-assured confidence made Jason feel like he needed his title to give himself equal footing, socially speaking. Belatedly, he realized the man likely didn't know where Midanbury was located so he added, "England."

Robert's welcoming smile broadened into a mocking grin. "I've heard of it. My uncle lives there. And a lord, you say? What brings you, a titled Englishman, to the middle of Alabama?"

How should he state his intentions of speaking with Abigail? He should ask for her father first. "I would like to speak with Mr. Richard Bennington, please."

Robert gave a burst of laughter. "I'm afraid my uncle is not here at present."

Jason inwardly smiled in relief to not have to work his way past Abigail's father. "Then Miss Abigail Bennington. She and I are acquainted." He hoped Robert would not refuse his request.

Robert squinted in assessment. "What is your interest in my cousin?"

Jason was not going to let this man prevent him from seeing Abigail, so he prevaricated a bit. "I am her *fiancé*. I hoped to surprise her for Christmas." It was only a partial lie. He had her father's permission to marry, just not the lady's consent.

The corner of Robert's lip quirked. *"Fiancé?"*

Before Jason could respond his attention was drawn to an older gentleman emerging from the front door. The similarity was striking enough, Jason knew who he was without need of introduction. He walked forward as the man descended the porch steps and extended his hand. "Mr. James Bennington, I presume."

Robert stood just behind his shoulder, interrupting Jason. "This is his lordship, Jason Malwbry of Midanbury. He is here to see my uncle and cousin. He claims he is to wed Abigail."

Mr. Bennington gave Jason a benevolent smile. After shaking hands he gestured towards the front door. "Come in out of the cold. You've had a long journey. I'm sure you could use a drink."

A maid with dark coffee skin, her hair wrapped in stark white fabric, hovered inside the front door. Mr. Bennington sent her for refreshments. He led Jason through the grand foyer into what appeared to be his study. He gestured to a pair of comfortable looking deep leather chairs facing an impressive cherry desk. "Have a seat."

Jason waited until Robert and his father were ready to sit before he did as requested.

Mr. Bennington cleared his throat. "I am afraid my brother and niece have been detained on their journey. I received a letter a few weeks ago that they were abiding in Key West due to a shipwreck."

Jason's disappointment was bitter. In all the scenarios he imagined, he never once considered she wouldn't be here to greet him. He swallowed hard. "Key West?"

"Yes, it's a small island off the Florida peninsula between the Gulf of Mexico and the Atlantic Ocean."

"Did Captain Bennington say for how long?"

"I am afraid not. As far as I am aware, he is still there awaiting repairs to the ship."

Jason stood and nodded to Mr. Bennington. "Then I am intruding and will be on my way."

Mr. Bennington and Robert both rose as well. The elder said, "Nonsense. You must at least stay the night. Rest yourself and your horses. You can be on your way again in the morning, refreshed."

Jason shook his head. "I wouldn't want to put you to any trouble."

"I assure you it is no trouble a 'tall. Actually, I would recommend you wait here for their arrival. There is all probable chance you will cross paths in your journey and miss them altogether."

Jason saw the wisdom in his advice, but he had no desire to infringe on Mr. Bennington's hospitality for weeks on end. No. He would rather head toward Abigail and if he missed her, turn around and head back this way, or maybe consider it fate and return home. "I thank you for your kindness and I will gladly accept it—for tonight only."

"I will have the maid show you to your room so you can freshen up. Have you ever visited a cotton plantation before?"

"No sir."

"Then I will give you a grand tour today. Of course, it was much more exciting a few weeks ago when it was harvest time, but there is still much to be seen."

Mr. Bennington ushered Jason out the door and instructed the waiting maid which room to settle him in. To Jason he said, "Return here when you are ready."

The men nodded their heads to each other, and Jason followed the white turbaned dark skinned maid to a small but luxurious second floor bedroom. It was lavishly decorated in navy and maroon. He emerged a quarter hour later having washed his face and changed his clothes. The maid promised to have his travel clothes cleaned and pressed by morning, and a warm bath would be drawn for him after the evening meal. The pleasure of a bath was at least some measure of consolation for the disappointment of not finding Abigail in residence. He hadn't had a proper bath since he left home.

Jason cast a longing look at the bed wishing he could indulge in a nap rather than tour the plantation. He was exhausted and uninterested in agriculture, but it wouldn't do to insult his host so he returned to the study.

Mr. Bennington led him outside. "Lord Malwbry, I assume with your title you have property and perhaps tenants."

"Yes sir. Though my father's holdings are considerably larger."

"How many tenants do you have?"

"I am unsure of the current number." The truth was he had never taken an interest in the details of the estates.

"What method of irrigation and fertilizer do you employ?"

"I'm afraid I do not know, sir."

"I have always been curious. How is the income divided?"

Jason simply shook his head this time.

"What crops do your tenants raise?"

"I'm afraid I do not know. My holdings are in the care of a steward who reports to my father."

"I see. Do you intend to take control of your inheritance at some point?"

"Yes. At some point, I do, sir."

"You and my son seem to have the same lack of initiative in common."

Robert cast his father an aggrieved look. Jason had the feeling it was a subject of much contention between them. Unfortunately, Jason's father also lacked any concern for properly overseeing his holdings. He also seemed to have as little interest in passing on the estate as Jason had in taking it over. Jason assumed they were both satisfied with the current state of control. It did not occur to him to feel the deficiency in his character until this man pointed it out. Perhaps that was part of what Abigail's father had noticed as well. Until now, Jason never considered all that he took for granted; things that men like Richard and James Bennington had to work hard to attain.

They were now outside where a groomsman held three horses in waiting for them. He recognized the white stallion as belonging to Robert. Mr. Bennington was handed the reins of a light brown bay stallion, and he was given a black one. They mounted and Mr. Bennington led the way to the closest field from the house.

Jason decided if he had to tour the plantation, he might as well make the most of it and perhaps learn something useful. "Mr. Bennington, how many acres is your estate?"

"Eleven hundred and thirty six all together with three hundred currently cultivated."

"All of it cotton?"

"Yes, except for what is raised for our food supply and a few acres of indigo. Every year we cut and plant new fields of cotton, and as the old fields lose their yield, they will be converted to another crop."

A man Jason assumed to be the overseer approached them on horseback. Mr. Bennington moved forward to meet him so they could speak in private. He then motioned for Robert to join him.

As Robert urged his horse forward, he said for Jason's ears only, "Off to do the dirty work."

Mr. Bennington sent Robert with the overseer. He called out after the retreating figures, "Be sure to handle it fairly, I'll check in on the situation later." He kneed his horse and returned to Jason. In answer to his questioning look, Mr. Bennington said, "There is a dispute between the workers and the overseer."

Jason had many questions he would like to ask, but refrained instinctively knowing his host would not want to share the dirty details of plantation life. Instead, he listened politely as Mr. Bennington pointed out the various outbuildings and their uses. The slaves' quarters behind the outbuildings were quickly mention before turning their horses in the opposite direction. It left Jason with the impression Mr. Bennington was ashamed of owning slaves.

They cantered down the dirt road, cleared of autumn's debris by frequent use, and past several fields before turning towards the river. Mr. Bennington silently led Jason to the edge of the ten foot sloping bank overlooking the one hundred and fifty foot expanse of turbid waters. At first he thought the river to be slow moving, but soon he noticed the telltale lines of the swift current disturbing the waters' surface in the center. The banks were lined with a dense mixture of evergreen and bare deciduous trees. The slight breeze carried with it the earthiness of harvested hay and manure and the sound of the workers singing. Overhead, a large bird swirled in the updrafts.

Mr. Bennington spoke after a moment, "The river traffic was heavy a few weeks ago with the flats and barges hauling cotton down to Mobile. It's quiet now. Just the occasional steamboat. Amazing creations those are. My brother said one day they'll replace sails, even for long ocean voyages. He has been talking about getting into coal production somewhere on the coast." He chuckled. "Richard is always looking for a way to capitalize on progress." He turned his horse around and Jason followed suit. Mr. Bennington gazed across his holdings. "There was nothing here but the overseer's house and a few cultivated acres when I bought the land. It may not be of my sweat and blood, but all of this exists because of me. I built this plantation from nothing to one of the largest cotton producers in the area."

Jason heard the pride in his voice, saw it in the firmness of his jaw, and in the blaze of passion in his eye. He looked again at his surroundings through Mr. Bennington's eyes. It was a great accomplishment. The man wasn't handed a ready-made inheritance. He built it. Jason could only imagine the effort it must have cost and the profound sense of accomplishment he must feel.

Mr. Bennington turned to Jason. "My only regret is having to use slave labor. The laws of this land and the economics of the trade limit other alternatives. Even if I found another way, the people I do business with will allow for nothing else."

"Do you believe tenant farming to be better?"

"Even with the flaws in that system, it is better than slavery. At least the people can make their own choices, earn their own coin, and move at will. These people can do none of that. I believe happy people are more productive, so I am as fair as I can be, but even so they cannot earn money, nor can they leave this plantation without my permission, and even that must be given for a particular purpose. For example, allowing one of my slaves to go to a neighboring plantation simply to visit a family member is frowned upon. I would do better to send them on an errand to borrow sugar. It's nonsense!" HIs frown deepened. "My neighbors think these people can't survive without us. They don't seem to realize the slaves take care of us. They do all the manual labor, cook, and clean. It is because of them the plantations are profitable. We are the ones who wouldn't survive without them. At least not this way of life. At best, we are interdependent on each other—a symbiotic relationship—but at its worst, it's abuse of unimaginative proportions."

"Slavery is abolished in England. Why can it not be here?"

"My dear boy, slavery may be abolished in England, but I assure you it is alive and well in her colonies, especially the ones in need of cheap labor such as the sugar plantations in Jamaica. Remember this when you take your place in parliament. Maybe your generation can find a way to rid of us of this institution once and for all."

Jason had never given much thought before to what it meant to serve in parliament. He felt uncomfortable now with this future burden Mr. Bennington was placing upon his shoulders. Not wishing to discuss it further, at least not at this time when the idea was so new, he sought to change the subject. "Perhaps we will." He nodded towards the fields in front of them. "How much cotton can be produce on an acre?"

Mr. Bennington obliged his desire to change the subject. "Each acre has about five thousand plants and currently yields on average a bushel an acre. I am working on ideas of how to increase it to two bushels."

They rode their horses at a gentle pace between the expanses of cultivated acres bordered in the distance by the ever dark pine trees. Mr. Bennington continued speaking of yields, harvests, profits and loss, his dealings with the ginners, and the cotton market. It occurred to Jason, as he listened to James Bennington passionately speaking of his land, that he had never once heard his father refer to his holdings as anything other than a burden. Perhaps it explained why, until this day, he himself was uninterested in the workings of the estate he would one day inherit. His interest was piqued now.

After the tour, Mr. Bennington bid him to rest until supper, but Jason found he was too restless with the thoughts running through his mind. He paced in front of the large window in his room overlooking the fields towards the river. From the second floor, he could see the wide ribbon of water cutting through the terrain and a small boat sailing past the landing. It was as if this day had stripped the blinders of youth from him, and now he saw the world truly from the eyes of a man. He wanted the answers to Mr. Bennington's questions. He wanted to know if his and his father's estates were truly profitable. Was it solely his father's spending that caused the need for funds or was the problem deeper? He wanted to know how well their tenants were doing and if their methods could be improved to produce more yield.

Despite the distractions of his own thoughts, he learned much from Mr. Bennington today. When he returned home, he planned to start learning the management of his inheritance; a cluster of small tenant farms a few miles from his home. Once he had that in hand, he could take over managing the Rothebury estate. He didn't expect his father to object so long as the income remained fluid.

The excitement of this new venture made Jason anxious to find Abigail, convince her to wed him, and return home to put his plans in motion. He no longer wanted to marry for money to fill the family coffers. He wanted to earn it and in so doing have the same satisfaction of accomplishment that Mr. Bennington enjoyed and to feel the same pride of ownership Mr. Hudson exuded. But, he did still want to marry Abigail. He would need an heir, and she was still the finest catch of all the maidens he had met.

He would leave first thing in the morning, and if fortune was on his side, reach her in Key West before she and her father resumed their journey to this place. The possible delay of crossing paths and having to backtrack dismayed him, but he knew he could not stand to wait here for their arrival. He had all the impatient energy of an untrained colt running through his veins. He was anxious to be on his way.

The sound of a bell being rung drew his attention to a dark girl-child pulling the string of a black iron bell on a pole a few yards in front of the house. Movement drew his eyes back to the surrounding area to see the people all leaving their tasks to return to their quarters. He was somewhat startled to realize the sun had set and dark was approaching. The bell must signify the end of the day or mealtime. The aroma of roasted meat tantalized him. His stomach rumbled. Jason brushed the dust from his jacket and trousers. He washed his face and hands and dressed as best he could for supper. He wandered downstairs following the sound of voices coming from the parlour.

Upon his entrance, Robert gave a silent nod in greeting while his father stepped forward to welcome him into the room. He was introduced to Mrs. Bennington. In spite of her years, she was a lovely woman. Jason could easily understand why James Bennington still doted on his bride. She was also a lovely woman on the inside who genuinely welcomed Jason to her home. As a good hostess, she made sure his glass was always filled and his meal was to his liking. In turn, Jason raved over the roast beef and vegetables covered in rich brown gravy, served with plenty of warm bread and creamy butter, followed by plum pudding for dessert. He could truthfully say it was the best meal he had eaten since leaving England.

After supper, Jason joined Mr. Bennington and Robert in the study for a drink but soon excused himself to retire for the evening. The excitement of the day and the continued lack of sleep were finally catching up to him. His eyes were heavy and his legs ached around his knees. He was asleep as soon as his head hit the pillow.

The sky was just beginning to lighten when Jason awoke. He quickly took care of his morning toilette and gathered all his belongings. When he arrived downstairs, Mr. Bennington instructed him to leave his belongings by the door and have breakfast with the family while a stable hand prepared the mare and foal for travel.

Mr. Bennington blessed the meal. Mrs. Bennington opened the conversation with, "Lord Malwbry, are you sure you won't stay a bit longer? Surely you must still be weary from your journey here."

"Thank you, ma'am, but I am anxious to be on my way. Every day I delay increases the chance of unknowingly crossing paths with Miss Bennington."

Mrs. Bennington frowned. "It seems more sensible to remain here in the comfort of our hospitality and avoid the likelihood of such an occurrence all together."

Mr. Bennington nodded in agreement. "I said as much yesterday. We would be happy to have you."

Robert's frown clearly indicated he did not feel the same, but it mattered not to Jason. His mind was set. "Thank you for your generous offer but I must decline. I am afraid I do not have the patience to wait."

Mr. Bennington smiled. "I understand." He cast a lover's glance to his wife as they both recalled the memory of a time when he felt the same impatience to reach her.

After the meal, Mr. Bennington followed Jason outside to see him off. "I suppose the next time we see you it will be in the company of my brother and niece."

"Yes, sir. I sincerely hope so."

"Until then, may you have a pleasant journey."

Jason shook hands with James Bennington. "Thank you, sir, for your kind words and hospitality. It has been a pleasure meeting you and your family. I look forward to seeing you again soon." He mounted the mare, gave a wave to his host, and then turned her towards the drive leading back to the main road. He glanced back to be sure Little Bit was following, then set a steady pace to cover as much distance as possible before a feeding or nap forced his return journey to a halt. He tried to rein in his impatience knowing he was still weeks away from reaching Abigail.

* * *

Nine days later, James Bennington welcomed his elder brother,

Richard, as he exited the carriage. Both were exuberant in their reunion having been many years since they had last seen each other. As they stepped apart, James looked over his brother's shoulder expecting to help his niece from the carriage. He looked to Richard for an explanation for the empty doorway.

"She is in Key West."

"Why would you leave her behind? She is not too ill to travel, I hope."

"No, no, nothing like that." Richard paused, seeking the words to explain.

"Well, it is an interesting turn of events. You crossed paths with her fiancé just as I said you would, but I suppose he was also right in that he will find Abigail in Key West."

Richard frowned in confusion. "I don't understand. Max was here? When? Why?" The furrows in his brow deepened as he shook his head. Max couldn't have had enough time to visit his brother. It didn't make sense.

"Who is Max? I am speaking of Lord Malwbry. He was here looking for you and Abigail. He left last week. He said he intends to wed her."

Richard chuckled and then the chuckle turned into a full laugh.

James shook his head. "What is so funny, brother?"

It took a moment before Richard cleared his throat to say, "Jason Malwbry is going to be very disappointed when he discovers Abby is wed to another which is why she is not with me now." Richard's humor faded. "I did not think the boy's intensions were serious enough to follow us. I hope I did not do Abby a disservice marrying her to Max Eatonton. If Jason's affections are true, she could have been a duchess."

* * *

A fortnight had passed since Jason left the plantation. Two days were spent travelling back to Montgomery. Little Bit still slowed him down but not as much as before. He was able to spend the first night at Mr. Hudson's farm in the warm comfort of the barn, and he made it back to Montgomery just before dark the following day. He hated to leave Little Bit behind having become quite attached to the little horse. Another four days spent on the stagecoach to Mobile, where he spent too many days waiting for a ship headed east. Due to the Christmas and New Year's holidays, such ships were in short supply and to date none of them had room for passengers.

It was the ninth morning since his arrival in Mobile and the second day of the New Year. He hoped today would bring news of passage. Every day's delay made him increasingly aware that James Bennington's prediction of his unknowingly crossing paths with Abigail would likely occur. And so it was with great relief, he noticed the encouraging smile of the ticket agent who was well acquainted with his request.

"Good morning, Lord Malwbry. I was hoping you would be here early today. A merchant ship, the *Southern Belle*, arrived this morning and plans to sail again in an hour or so. The captain is willing to make a stop in Key West for an extra fee."

Jason could hardly contain his excitement. He booked his passage and left to retrieve his belongings. He planned to wait on the dock by the ship until such time as he could board. He wasn't taking any chances of missing its departure.

* * *

Friday morning, January 9th, after a week's sail, Jason disembarked from the *Southern Belle* and stood at the foot of the wharf taking in the view of the small island town. Finally, he reached his destination. Now, if only he wasn't too late, and Abigail was still here. The thought of retracing his journey back to Mulberry House was disheartening.

He scanned the waterfront buildings from left to right wondering which way to go in search of a boardinghouse. He thought his eyes deceived him. He blinked expecting to discover what he saw was only a trick of his imagination, but no, it truly was Abigail walking down the next pier only a score of yards away from him.

Waving his arm to gain her attention, Jason called out to her with jubilance, "Miss Bennington!"

Chapter 4

Jason dropped his arm as he watched Abigail continue to walk away from him. He sprinted down the wharf closing the distance and called out to her again, "Miss Bennington!"

Thankfully she heard him. He froze as she turned and made eye contact. He saw his name form on her lips and her eyes widen. Seeing her surprise turn into a smile of welcome was worth the weeks of travel he endured. He resumed walking towards her unable to believe he found her so quickly after so many weeks spent trying to reach her.

"Abigail Bennington, is it really you?" He dropped his travel bags and clasped her hand as she offered him a curtsey.

She smiled, "Lord Malwbry, as I live and breathe! What brings you to this island?"

He was so overjoyed to see her his mind could not prevaricate. "You, actually." He held his breath waiting for her response. Her cheeks bloomed and her eyes flew to those around her. She turned slightly away. He was not sure if it was to hide her response from him or from those around them. Now he felt an urgent need to explain himself. He moved to face her side blocking her from the view of others.

"I have chased you across two oceans and over land and am quite shocked to find you within five minutes of debarking, not that I expected to have any trouble finding you on such a small island. It is just... I was sure you would no longer be here."

She turned her head to look at him directly, eyebrows raised. "You really just arrived?"

"Stepped off the gangway of the *Southern Belle* only moments ago, recently departed from Mobile." Jason gestured to the ship behind him. It was still being unloaded adding credence to his declaration.

"Mobile? You really were following me. How did you know to look for me here?"

"At the direction or your relations."

"You met my Aunt Virginia and Uncle James? I would love to hear more about them, but I am in a dreadful hurry this morning. Would you like to come for dinner tonight? I am hosting a small party and there is plenty of room for one more."

"I would be delighted to attend."

"You must be staying at the boardinghouse."

"Right you are. I am told it is the only accommodations so you

51

must be staying there as well."

"Not anymore. We have a house on the other end of town. I will walk you to the boardinghouse and introduce you to Mrs. Mallory. I can point out our house too so you will know where you are going later this evening."

"Excellent." Jason offered her his arm, and they strolled down Front Street to Fitzpatrick Street. As they walked, Abigail asked him about her family. "Are my aunt and uncle well? Did you meet my cousin?"

"Yes. They seem to be enjoying good health. Of course, they were very disappointed by the delay in meeting you. You know they asked me all about you."

"You were kind, I hope."

"You have no reason to fear otherwise. I will have you know they generously welcomed me into their home." He neglected to mention posing as her fiancé. He hoped it would be truth before she learned of his falsehood. "Although, I only put them out for one night choosing to leave promptly the following morning to return to the coast after they explained what happened to you."

Reaching the boardinghouse, Abigail continued walking past it and pointed to the rental house she occupied on the other side of the pond. In jest Jason asked, "Must I traverse the pond in order to get there?"

Abigail laughed. "Good Heavens no! You will walk back the way we came, and then follow Front Street to the end and turn left on Simonton."

"Walk?"

"I know, I thought it strange at first too but I have only seen one buggy on this island, and as you can see, the distance is not great."

Mrs. Mallory had gone out, and so Abigail left Jason in the capable hands of one of her helpers. Jason watched Abigail leave before turning to check in. She seemed happy to see him. He felt hope take wing in his chest.

* * *

Mrs. Mallory saw her latest guest, a debonair Englishman, in the foyer ready to step out for the evening. She hurried to greet him. "You must be Lord Malwbry. I am Mrs. Mallory, the proprietress of this establishment. If there be anything I can do to make yer stay more enjoyable, please let us know. Have you had yer supper, milord? We have a lovely turtle soup tonight."

Jason bowed his head to the Irish matron. "Thank you, madam. I am pleased to make your acquaintance. I am afraid I will have to forego your turtle soup. I was just on my way to dinner with the Bennington's."

Mrs. Mallory frowned. "Pardon?"

Jason assumed she must not be well acquainted with her former guest. "Miss Abigail Bennington. She invited me this afternoon."

"Oh. Perhaps you're not aware having just arrived. She be Mrs. Eatonton now. She and her *husband*," Mrs. Mallory emphasized, "live on the other side of town."

Jason kept his face from showing his surprise at the astonishing news Abigail had a husband. Her aunt and uncle had not mentioned it. He, apparently, wrongly assumed during their earlier conversation that 'we' and 'our' referred to Abigail and her father. A husband never crossed his mind. It had only been a few months since she left England. Mrs. Mallory didn't mentioned her father. Jason wondered where he was. Had something happened to him forcing Abigail to marry? It was not a question he wanted to ask Mrs. Mallory, although she could probably answer his query. He had the feeling Mrs. Mallory was very protective of Abigail and may not let him pass if she continued to question his intentions. "Yes madam, I momentarily forgot. You see I am a friend of the family from England. Mrs. Eatonton pointed her residence out to me this afternoon."

Forced to accept that nothing untoward was going on, Mrs. Mallory replied, "Well then enjoy your evening, Lord Malwbry."

Jason stepped from the porch relieved to have survived the interview but feeling keenly disappointed, after finally finding Abigail, to learn his quest was for naught. She was effectively out of his reach... Unless she was in need of rescuing. He would see for himself if she was in a good marriage before returning home.

* * *

Jason approached the house of average size for the island - albeit less than a cottage by his family's standards. Lanterns lit the front porch revealing a cozy domestic scene of curtains blowing in the open windows and rocking chairs suggesting a happy couple spending evenings together in pleasant conversations. The image created an aching empty place in his soul for what could have been his if he had not been so stubborn. Pushing the unpleasant thought aside, Jason raised his hand to knock on the door. He was arrested by the sound of laughter from the occupants inside. Jason felt a strange feeling of insecurity begin to build. Reigning in that emotion as well, he knocked on the door.

An elderly gentleman opened it. Rightly assuming him to be a butler, Jason gave him his calling card upon which the butler welcomed him inside. Jason stepped into the house and turned to face the group of strangers in the parlour. He glanced past the others before locking gazes with Abigail as if she were a lifeline and he was about to drown.

Abigail stepped forward to greet him wearing a lovely gown of sea-green. "Lord Malwbry, how good of you to come."

"Thank you for the invitation. It is good to see an old friend after my long journey."

"I look forward to hearing about your travels. May I introduce your host, Captain Max Eatonton?"

Jason bowed his head in the English custom and then extended his hand to the man he had no trouble identifying as her husband. The captain made clear his claim on Abigail without uttering a word. "Pleased to make your acquaintance, Captain Eatonton." Jason noted the loose white shirt and buff breeches of his host's attire and frowned. Was he so poor, he could not afford a decent coat and vest to wear to supper, especially when entertaining guests?

Max tersely replied, "Likewise, Lord Malwbry. Everyone calls me Captain Max."

Anger simmered below the surface of Captain Max's demeanor, but Jason couldn't tell if it was directed at him or Abigail. He couldn't care less if Abigail's husband found offense with him, but if he in any way indicated harm to Abigail, Jason was prepared to call him out. Tonight he would closely observe their interaction.

Abigail turned to the side and held her arm out to the others in the room. "Allow me to introduce you to our guests."

Jason's gaze was caught by the dark-haired beauty standing behind the others. She was fascinating in her aloofness, for she refused to look his way. With effort, he pulled his attention to the lady Abigail was introducing first.

"This is Mrs. Betsy Wheeler. She is the island seamstress and quite talented."

Jason bowed his head to the petite brunette wearing a stylish lavender gown and the light scent of rose water, the same as Abigail. She was also dark-haired and fair-skinned but her wide eyes were blue instead of the sultry brown he had glimpsed of the lady standing behind her. "A pleasure to meet you Mrs. Wheeler."

Betsy bowed her head in return, "Nice to meet you too, Lord Malwbry."

Abigail turned to the other gentleman Jason guessed to be Mrs. Wheeler's husband but soon learned different. "This is Mr. Jonathon Keats. He is first mate of the *Mystic*, Captain Max's ship."

Jason shook hands with the sailor dressed in the same manner as his host. He sensed Mr. Keats was clearly ready at the slightest provocation to stand with the captain against him. They exchanged greetings, and finally, Abigail lifted her arm towards her last guest to be introduced. Mrs. Wheeler and Mr. Keats stepped aside to allow the intriguing lady wearing a strikingly fashionable light blue dress to step towards him with her bewitching smile. "And this is Miss Victoria Lambert."

The beguiling lady stepped forth bringing with her a heady sweet scent as lovely and intoxicating as the wearer. It was unknown to him and was as captivating as it was mysterious. Jason could not help himself. He took Miss Lambert's gloved hand and gave her a deep bow. "A pleasure to meet you, Miss Lambert." The lovely creature captured his attention like no other, especially when she withdrew her hand mid-bow with a feigned indifference. The others were openly curious about him, but he could tell Miss Lambert was more than curious even though she tried to hide it with disinterest.

Though she feigned indifference, Victoria was drawn to the handsome lord as soon as he entered the room. Jason cut a fine figure in his snowy white cravat, black waistcoat with threads of red, green, and blue, with a dark blue jacket, and trousers fastened under his highly polished square-toed shoes. It was quite a contrast to Max and Jonathon's casual attire. She smiled inwardly when she realized from his repeated glances that he was attracted to her as well. Instinct told her it would not do to let him know her feelings too soon, so when he presumptuously took her hand in greeting she intentionally pulled it away in rebuff.

Abigail said, "Lord Malwbry, please have a seat." There was a sofa and two chairs in the room. Victoria and Betsy sat together on the sofa set under the window. Max indicated Jason should take one of the chairs as he seated Abigail in the other one taking up a position behind her. Jonathon moved to stand in the opening to the dining room allowing him to face the group at large.

Realizing the room had settled into an uncomfortable hush, Abby sought to end it with general conversation. "Lord Malwbry, how was your voyage? No storms, I hope. My father and I were caught in the tail end of a hurricane during our trip across the Atlantic. Being tossed about one's cabin is quite uncomfortable."

"Only a few mild ones."

"And how were your parents when you left?"

"They are much the same as when last you saw them. Thank you for asking. I notice your father is absent. Nothing untoward has happened to him, I hope?"

"Oh no, he is well. As a matter of fact you crossed paths with him. He left just over a month ago to continue on to my uncle's estate. Your ship carried a letter from him telling me of his safe arrival in Mobile."

"Indeed. Our coaches likely travelled right past each other without notice."

Searching for something to redirect the conversation, Max's eyes came to rest on the pianoforte across the room. He asked his wife, "Do you play?"

Puzzled, Abby peered up at her husband. "To what do you refer, sir?"

He gestured towards the instrument behind her. Abby grimaced and then gave him an apologetic smile. "No. That is not a talent I was able to acquire much less master."

Victoria was going to say she played very well, but hesitated long enough, she missed her opportunity. She wanted to turn Jason's attention towards her but did not want to be obvious in doing so.

Jason nodded, "I would have to agree. You are much better suited for dancing to music than making music."

Clearly surprised, Abby turned to Jason. "When did you hear me play?"

"A long time ago. I believe it was at your friend, Lady Kendall's, debutante ball. You and Marc Danvers and a few others were gathered around her grand piano entertaining each other with much hilarity as I recall."

Blushing, Abby remembered the evening and couldn't help the fond smile. "I do not recollect your presence."

"No, you would not. I remained in the doorway not wanting to intrude on your *coterie*."

Victoria had never been jealous of another person in her life—until now. She truly envied the history her friend shared with the intriguing young lord and was afraid it might show on her face. Victoria cast a surreptitious glance to the others in the room. All were focused on Lord Malwbry with open curiosity except for Max. From her vantage point, she could see what the others could not; his fists were tightly balled at his sides.

Mr. Baxley approached the doorway and announced supper was ready to be served. Mr. Keats stepped forward to assist Mrs. Wheeler. Jason eagerly approached Miss Lambert and offered his hand to assist her to her feet. Covertly, he glanced over to see Captain Eatonton tend to Abigail. He looked for any signs that all was not well between them, until he was distracted by the provocative scent trailing in the air around Miss Lambert. It was more exotic than rose water. It teased his senses adding to the pleasure of following her.

Captain Max led Abigail to the right seating her at the foot of the table while Mr. Keats placed Mrs. Wheeler on the closest side next to Abigail. Jason did the honours for Victoria on the far side against the wall, placing her next to the captain, so he could take the seat next to Abigail. Max took his place at the head of the table, and the gentlemen all sat down. The first course of turtle soup and warm yeast rolls was served with wine and ale.

With a hinted gesture from Abigail, Captain Max raised his mug in a toast. "To friendship, old and new."

Jonathan raised his mug and the others lifted their wine goblets all echoing his toast. "To friendship."

The conversation began with Jason and Abby speaking of people they knew in common in England as well as her aunt and uncle. Victoria discovered, while it was fine and dandy to ignore him during their introduction, she did not like it one bit when he ignored her. Waiting for an opening in their conversation was trying her patience but hold her tongue she would. She thought it best to keep at least a figurative distance from the man to her left. It seemed the prudent thing to do since she did not fully understand Abby's relationship with him, much less how he felt about Abby. It would be horrible to let him see how much he affected her if his feelings were still hopelessly tied to Abby. During the first course, she observed them and found only a casual interaction allowing her to unconsciously loosen the hold on her own feelings.

When the conversation opened to topics of interest to others at the table, Victoria unconsciously began flirting with the gentleman. She took full advantage of bringing his attention to her. "Lord Malwbry." She waited for him to make eye contact. She wanted him to see the message in her expressions meant only for him while her words were spoken for all to hear. "I am afraid I am not very familiar with English rankings. What is the highest title?"

Jason thought it was a silly question, until he noticed her eyes. They conveyed a deeper interest leaving him to believe the words were merely subterfuge. Her dark honey irises said she found him as attractive as he found her, so he answered her earnestly. "Why king and queen, of course."

"Well, yes, of course, but I was wondering what title comes next?" She tilted her head and intently looked up at him through her long lashes. Her gaze traced the pleasing line of his regal nose to his deep-set almond shaped eyes. His forehead rose above the delightful arches of his full eyebrows and his hair, though slightly long and tousled from the salty breeze, framed the whole of his face splendidly. She batted her eyelashes and allowed a hint of a smile to hover on her lips.

Jason swallowed against a surge of desire. "Duke and duchess."

Victoria wished she had a fan to aid in her coquetry. The attraction between them was instantaneous, mutual, and undeniably strong. She couldn't keep her eyes off him. If it were in any way proper, she would be touching him as well. She had never felt anything she couldn't control before. It dismayed and excited her. She affected her reply with as much innocence as she could inflect in her voice, lest the others notice. "And your father is a duke which makes you a future duke."

"Only if the title is hereditary."

She moistened her bottom lip holding back a satisfied smirk when his eyes intently followed her action. "And is it?"

Jason frowned. As delighted as he was with her, his interest would wane if his title was the reason for her sudden flirtation. "Does it matter to you?"

She gave him a coy smile. "Not at all, but I imagine it matters a great deal to you." She really could care less about his title, but she liked keeping him off-balance.

He could play her game as well. "It does have a way of dictating one's lot in life."

Victoria tilted her head up to acknowledge his non-answer. "A title gives one an assured position in life, of one's place in society, a certain security. The lack of a title leaves a person to have to earn those niceties."

He raised his eyebrows. "And which do you think applies to me?"

She was spared from answering by the arrival of the second course. A plate of perfectly seared red snapper and roasted root vegetables was placed in front of each of them. Victoria cast a quick glance around the table. Her eyes met Betsy's who dropped her gaze to hide her mirth. Victoria decided, perhaps it would be best, to remain silent for a while if she was being so obvious.

Jason was enjoying the conversation with Victoria, but at the same time, he was aware Max's gaze rarely strayed from Abigail except to cast a contemptuous glance in his direction.

After savoring a bit of tender flaky fish, Jason looked sideways at Victoria. "And what is your answer?" He was curious as to how she perceived him.

Victoria raised her napkin to delicately wipe a corner of her mouth. It seemed Lord Malwbry was not ready for a change in the conversation. Very well, she would play his game. "You, sir, are entitled. You have all the assurance of a man who knows his place in society, and expects, nay demands, to receive the respect as such a position requires."

He fought to hold his grin. "A respect, I suspect, you would deny to bestow if given the choice."

The side of her mouth lifted as if she too fought to hold a grin. "Perhaps."

Jason feigned wiping his mouth with his napkin to hide his smile.

Mrs. Wheeler asked, "Lord Malwbry, what do you think of our island?"

Jason sobered his expression to seriously reply, "It is lovely."

Victoria saw an opening to learn Jason's intentions. "Would you not rather spend a winter on this warm and sunny island than in your dreary old England?"

Jason smiled. "Your winter is nice but nothing beats spring in Midanbury, wouldn't you agree Abigail?"

Jason turned to the lady on his right as he finished the sentence but she didn't answer. Her gaze was focused on her husband. Jason turned to Max and saw that he was frowning in Abigail's direction. It reminded him of the reason he agreed to attend this party. All was clearly not well between these two. He returned his gaze to Abigail determined to gain her attention. "Abigail?"

Belatedly Abby realized Jason had spoken directly to her. She turned her questioning gaze to him. "Pardon?"

Jason asked, "Is there something between you two I should be concerned about?"

Varying levels of shock emanated from those around the table. Jason knew he was overstepping his bounds to ask such a personal question, but he was determined to know Abigail's true situation and a more private opportunity to do so was not likely.

Abby quietly answered, "No." She returned her gaze to Max.

The table remained quiet. Realizing Jason was still waiting, she looked him in the eye and firmly added, "No, of course not. What would make you ask such a thing?"

Jason looked from his host back to Abigail. Despite the simmering anger flowing between them, he noticed it was different than his parents who looked at each other with hate. Whatever was afoot between Max and Abigail, beneath it they truly cared for each other. He shrugged. "I felt it my duty in your father's absence to assure your well-being."

Captain Max responded with jaw clenched, "My *wife*, sir, is no concern of yours."

Jason responded in kind. "And you, sir, do not deserve her." He didn't really mean the words. He was jealous and hurt because he noticed the light in Abigail's eyes whenever she looked at her husband. He had never seen that look in her eyes before, and it bothered him knowing Max was the reason it was there.

Abby intervened telling her husband, "I am sure Lord Malwbry meant you no disrespect, sir." Turning to Jason, she laid a hand on his arm. "Lord Malwbry, thank you for your solicitude but I am well, and you have no reason to be concerned. My husband is a very honorable gentleman."

Jason accepted the truth in her eyes. Whatever was going on between them, it was not abusive. Abigail was not afraid of her husband. "Very well." He turned to Captain Max and gave a nod, "My apologies sir." Jason momentarily returned his attention to his plate.

Victoria's gaze dropped to her plate as well, suddenly aware of her folly in letting her feelings get carried away for the man sitting next to her. Jason still seemed to hold a *tendré* for Abby. She felt physically injured by jealousy and disappointment. Gathering herself together, Victoria tried to return to the aloofness she had begun the evening with only to have it disintegrate when next her eyes met his warm gaze.

Jason's concerns for Abigail vanished. He was now free to fully turn his attention towards Victoria. His gaze settled on her with heated warmth.

Victoria felt the change in him. If she looked, she knew she would see a lightening of his shoulders as if a burden were lifted. Maybe she was wrong about his feelings for Abby. Risking a glance, she cut her eyes sideways and blushed when she caught the intensity of his gaze towards her. He enveloped her, not with words or touch, but with his energy. She felt it focus on her, and her blush deepened.

For moments the only sound heard was the occasional clink of silverware against ceramic plate as the other guests made a pretense of continuing to eat in the ensuing silence.

Max made an effort to pay attention to their guests. "Mrs. Wheeler, have you heard from your mother recently?" He caught the look of gratitude his wife sent his way.

Understanding Max's intent, Betsy played along. "Yes, I received a letter in this month's mail. She is doing well and says they may come for a visit in the spring."

Max smiled for the first time all evening. "I look forward to meeting them."

When everyone was done eating, Abby stood to bring an end to meal. The gentlemen rose to their feet in respect. Abby softly smiled at the group. "We should adjourn to the parlour for drinks."

Max circled the table to pull away Abby's chair and escort her to the front room followed by the others.

Jonathon had had enough polite society for one evening. He looked to Betsy and seeing the same sentiments reflected in her eyes announced to the room in general, "Mrs. Eatonton, thank you for dinner. It's getting late and if you don't mind, Mrs. Wheeler and I are going to call it an evening."

Abby understood their real reasons for leaving and couldn't blame them for not wanting to risk subjecting themselves to more discomfort.

Jonathon turned to Victoria. "Miss Lambert, may I offer you an escort home?"

Max said, "An excellent idea."

Victoria had other plans for getting home. She demurred. "Thank you kindly Mr. Keats but I must decline. I have a private matter I wish to discuss with Abby. I'm sure Lord Malwbry will see me home."

Both Max and Jonathon offered protest, after all, this man was a stranger to them, and both counted Victoria as a friend.

Abby intervened. "She will be fine. Lord Malwbry is an honorable gentleman and she has her maid for chaperone."

With a nod to Victoria, Jonathon said, "As you wish. Good evening Miss Lambert, Lord Malwbry. Thank you for your hospitality Captain and Mrs. Eatonton." Jonathon bowed as he moved to the front door in an obvious hurry to escape their company.

Betsy bid them good evening as she passed through the door Jonathon held open for her.

Max caught the louvered door as it swung shut to keep it from banging against the door frame before facing the remaining company in his front room.

Victoria wanted to prolong her contact with Lord Malwbry. She was well aware his pursuit of Abby had brought him to Key West. With Abby married, he may leave as suddenly as he arrived not having any other reason to stay on the island. She wanted to guarantee herself one more day in his company, so she asked the others in what she hoped was her most appealing voice, "Why don't the four of us go on an outing tomorrow?"

Max's face tightened. "I'm afraid I can't. I was thinking of keel hauling the *Mystic* tomorrow."

Abby frowned at him. "Must you do it tomorrow? You just came home."

Max looked to his wife. "It is long overdue."

Victoria had known Max a long time, long enough to know when he was prevaricating. "You're just making an excuse to avoid something that might turn out to be fun, and what is Abby to think—that you don't want to spend time with her? I am sure you could put it off a while longer."

Jason recognized Victoria's manipulation and tried to deflect it from Max as an amends for his earlier rude behavior. "If Captain Eatonton has work to do I'm sure I can escort you ladies to some kind of entertainment."

Max's face tightened. "Very well then. I'll postpone the keel haul. What did you have in mind Miss Lambert?"

Victoria couldn't help the smile that spread across her face. "Well,

I'm not sure." Turning to Lord Malwbry she suggested, "Having just arrived today, we could show you the town."

Max smirked. "And what do you propose to do after those five minutes? Besides he's already seen most of the town just walking from the boardinghouse to here."

Jason had to agree with Max. There wasn't much he hadn't seen of the town. "Do any of you ride?"

Max grimaced. "Sorry mate, we don't have the horses or the pasture for that pastime."

Victoria said, "We could go for a sail."

Jason grimaced. "After sailing for the better part of three months, I have no desire to step foot on a boat so soon."

Max said, "Well there are really only two other points of interest on the island; the lighthouse or the salt ponds."

Jason's curiosity was piqued. "The salt ponds sound interesting."

Not having been there yet, Abby was of course interested. Max didn't even have to ask to know she would be in agreement.

Victoria could only wince at the idea of trudging through the hammocks in the heat to look at a brackish pond but she would go along to be with Jason. "Salt ponds it is then."

Max turned to Jason. "Malwbry, I don't suppose you have clothes for clearing underbrush with you?"

"I am afraid I do not."

"I'll loan you some of mine. Be back in a minute."

Abby asked, "Max, do you not think the heat will be too much for Lord Malwbry to be doing hard physical labor before he is acclimated?"

"Nonsense. It's not as warm as it was when you arrived."

Max left the room to retrieve the clothes. Abby excused herself to take care of a quick task leaving Jason and Victoria momentarily alone.

Jason turned to Victoria and lifted her gloved hand to his lips. "Alone at last," he whispered and kissed the back of her knuckles. His lips lingered.

Victoria's eyes were captured in the warmth of his darkened gaze. A shiver raced down her spine, her mid-section tightened, and her palms grew moist. *Was he flirting with her simply because she was available?* She hoped not. Much to her chagrin, her attraction for him had grown past simple flirtation. She considered herself skilled in the art, but under his gaze, she was unable to think clearly. There were many questions on her mind during supper she would have asked, if they had been alone. Now that the opportunity presented itself her mind was blank. She was focused on the warmth of his fingers still holding her hand. He stared into her eyes, and she could read their message now. He wanted to kiss her. Her breath shallowed and her lips grew dry. She unconsciously moistened them. He broke eye contact, dropping his gaze to her lips. She dropped her eyes to his slightly parted lips and wondered what they would feel like pressed to hers.

They leaned towards each other, drawn by attraction that over-ruled propriety.

A step was needed to bring them closer together.

She waited, breathless.

Just as he lifted his foot to do so, they heard the creak of the stairs. Jason stepped away from her. He let go of her hand with a gentle squeeze of her fingers. Victoria's cheeks burned in embarrassment. She turned her back to the room pretending interest in the oil painting. *How had she fallen so quickly?*

She turned back to the men. "I'll be back in a moment." She left them to retrieve her maid from the outdoor kitchen.

Max handed the clothes to Jason. "Shall we meet here in the morning? Say eight o'clock? Don't want it to get too warm in the day while we clear brush."

Jason refused to allow Max to think him a dandy. "Unless you would like to meet earlier?"

Victoria, returning to the room, shook her head. "Eight o'clock is early enough by my standards."

Jason shared a conspiratorial glance with Max and shook his hand. "Captain Max, it was a pleasure to meet you. I look forward to tomorrow. Thank you for the meal and for the loan of clothes."

Max gave an obliged nod. "Likewise, Lord Malwbry."

"Please, call me Jason."

Max gave a silent nod of acquiesce.

Jason walked to the front door to wait for Victoria just as Abigail reappeared from the side room. She handed him a piece of paper. "What's this?"

"A request for Mrs. Mallory to prepare a picnic lunch for tomorrow's outing." Next she handed Jason a lantern. "We do not have the luxury of street lights. It is awfully dark out there."

Jason accepted her offering as Max and Victoria approached. "Thank you. I will see you in the morning Mrs. Eatonton."

Victoria kissed Abby's cheek. She passed through the door, and then held out her hand for Jason to assist her down the front steps as Max shut the door behind them. At the bottom, Jason offered her his arm. Victoria tucked her hand around his elbow. He held the lantern out with his other arm lighting her path so she wouldn't trip. Her maid, Lydia, walked a few steps behind them carrying her own small lantern.

They walked several yards in silence. When they both started to speak at once, they laughed, finally breaking the remaining tension leftover from the Eatonton's.

"He does love her, you know." For some reason, Victoria felt the need to defend Max. She could barely discern Jason's nod in the pale light.

"I must admit, I started the evening concerned for Abigail, but by the end, I could see that they care for one another."

She smiled. "Eventually, they will realize they love one another despite their beginning." Victoria's next step landed on the side of rock twisting her ankle. "Ow!" She momentarily lost her balance.

Jason's arm tightened around her hand in the crook of his elbow. "Are you alright?"

Victoria gingerly tested her ankle. "Yes." Even when she regained her footing, he kept her hand close to his side. Taking advantage, Victoria walked a bit closer to him.

Jason spoke into the deepening twilight, "Abigail said your family was from Charleston. How long have you lived on the island?"

Victoria was glad he didn't want to continue discussing Max and Abby. "This winter marks our fourth year."

"What was it Abigail called you?"

"Tria. It's her pet name for me."

"Do you like it?"

She recalled the night of a ball when she first met her bosom friend and received the nickname. There was a smile in her voice when she replied, "Yes." Her voice softened. "You may call me Tria if you like."

"No."

Victoria frowned. His terse response was unexpected and for the briefest of moments she felt rejected until she saw his lips lift at the corners. When he turned to look at her, his eyes were softened with affection.

"I prefer Victoria. It is a beautiful name and should not be shortened, in any way."

Victoria's smile returned in full. She couldn't help it. She liked the firmness of his declaration, and she definitely liked the sound of her name coming from his lips, flavored with his English accent.

With a slight tug on his arm, Victoria indicated they should turn right on Front Street. She stopped in front of the corner house; a large square two-story with a low roof line nearly obscuring the second story windows giving it the deceptive appearance of a smaller home. Jason walked her to the front steps where Lydia slipped past them and up the stairs. Victoria turned and offered him her hand. "Good night, Lord Jason."

Dutifully he kissed her raised knuckles. "Good night, Miss Victoria."

He watched her enter the house before turning to make his way to the boardinghouse at the other end of Front Street.

Chapter 5

The following morning, promptly at quarter till eight, Jason raised his hand to the Lambert's brass front door knocker. He mentally prepared himself to meet her parents fully expecting one or both of them to greet him this morning. Instead, he was welcomed by a radiantly smiling vision wearing a yellow day dress that did more than simply flatter her figure. Her sweet scent floated to him on the morning breeze arousing his senses.

Victoria, on the other hand, was dismayed to find a very different Lord Malwbry. The elegant Englishman of yesterday now looked like every other sailor on the island dressed as he was in a loose fitting white shirt and tan breeches borrowed from Max. Victoria didn't like the outfit, but the man who bore them was still immensely appealing. Sleep had not cured her of her infatuation. Jason didn't seem to be fond of the clothes either. He looked very uncomfortable, as if he felt undressed in public. She smiled in sympathy. "Good morning, Lord Malwbry."

"Please, call me Jason. How are you this morning Miss Lambert?"

She answered with a smile in her voice. "And you are to call me Victoria, remember?" She was, of course, referring to their conversation of last evening. "I am very well, thank you. Is that a picnic lunch from Mrs. Mallory?" Victoria gestured to the basket hanging from his arm.

"Yes it is. Abigail thought of it last night, clever girl. Are you ready to go?"

Victoria leaned inside the door to retrieve her parasol and call her maid to join them before saying, "I am now. You, of course, remember Lydia."

Jason gave a nod to the quiet, middle-aged woman wearing a well-worn plain brown dress who would serve as their chaperone for the day. "Good morning, miss."

"Good morning, milord."

He smiled at hearing her faded British accent strengthen as she said the last word. He supposed since the term was not used in America, it was not subjected to the modified dialect.

Victoria smiled at Jason as they walked side by side towards the Eatonton's, followed by Lydia. His compliment of Abby stung her vanity a little, but as it was deserved, Victoria brushed aside her pettiness. "Have you traveled much, Lord Jason?"

"A little around England. This is by far the furthest I have been from home."

"And how does our island compare to your side of the world?"

Looking at her expectant face, he said the first word that came to mind, "Lovely."

Victoria blushed. The look in his eyes told her he wasn't describing the area around them. Normally, easy flirtatious banter came naturally to her, but with this man, she found herself for the first time in her life at a loss for words. She ducked her head to hide the bloom in her cheeks and tried to think of something clever to say.

They walked away from the wharves in silence for a moment before Jason asked her, "How long have you known Captain Max?"

Recalling Jason's bold questioning of Abby last evening, Victoria guessed his reason for asking her about Max. She was disappointed and perhaps a little jealous, again. Jason was still thinking of Abby. Seeking to put his mind at ease, she said, "Long enough to know you have no cause for worry. Max is a good man; one of the best on this island. Any woman would be lucky to have him."

She paused for a moment giving Jason concerns that Victoria may have had feelings for the captain.

"They were attracted to each other from the first. Max typically went out of his way to avoid romantic involvements. Until he met Abby. I believe they love each other. They just haven't discovered it for themselves yet. Abby's father may have pushed them to marry, but given time, I am sure they would have married anyway."

Jason felt the sting of wounded pride. Mr. Bennington may not have denied him to court his daughter, but he certainly had not been overly encouraging. He led Jason to believe whom she married would be Abby's choice. So why then had he forced his daughter to marry the captain? Did Mr. Bennington consider Max a fine catch? More likely, despite Victoria's ringing praises, Max must have taken advantage of Abby. "Why did Mr. Bennington insist on such speedy nuptials?"

The tone in Jason's voice and the continued concern for Abby were giving Victoria doubts that she had correctly interpreted his earlier meaning. Maybe he really had been referring to the island as 'lovely'. With their destination only a few hundred feet ahead, she carefully answered his question in an effort to protect her friends and for her own selfish reason. If she told him of the walk along the beach that precipitated Max and Abby's wedding, it would certainly lead to a strained relationship between Max and Jason, and probably ruin what could be her only chance to spend a day in Jason's company, so, while still being truthful, she gave the safer response. "Her father took ill while he was here. It was serious enough he wanted to ensure Abby's future. He also saw what everyone else could see; they were smitten with each other. Maybe even knowing his daughter better than anyone, he knew she loved Max. I do know he questioned many of the islander's as to Max's character before allowing her to marry him."

"And how was Mr. Bennington's health when he left? Was it the reason for his departure?"

"I don't believe so. He seemed well enough. Abby has not mentioned any concerns to me. I assumed he left to visit his brother as that was his original destination."

They had reached the Eatonton's front porch. Max stepped out to greet them and held out his hand to take the lunch hamper. "Here Malwbry, let me take that from you. I'm afraid we'll be leaving this behind for later." Max held the door for Jason and Victoria to precede him into the house. They turned to him expectantly in the parlour. Max crossed the room and set the basket on the dining room table. He then turned back to his guests. "Please, have a seat."

Lydia took a chair in the corner. Jason and Victoria both sat on the sofa keeping a respectable distance between them. They could feel the tension in the room. For a moment silence reigned. Finally Victoria asked, "Where is Abby?" at the same time Abby reentered the house from the backyard.

"Good morning." Abby held three canteens filled with water. She looked to Max. "Are we ready?"

"I believe so." Leading the way out to the front porch, Max leaned down to pick up the gloves and machetes he left earlier on one of the rockers. He handed a set to Jason before walking down the steps. Max led the way around the house to the Simonton Road footbridge that crossed the water's flow into the tidal pond and then across the cleared expanse of land beyond. They walked in pairs with Max and Abby leading the way followed by Jason and Victoria. Lydia was grateful to be left behind with Abby's maid, Maria.

Victoria looked up at the man walking beside her with the patrician nose and wavy dark brown hair. Only for the chance to be with him, to learn more about him, would she agree to such a preposterous outing as this one. It wasn't that she didn't like nature, she just preferred it to be more contained, such as manicured gardens and potted plants. Traipsing through the tangled wild growth that consumed the undeveloped parts of the island was not her idea of enjoyable entertainment, but she was willing to suffer a soggy, snagged hem if it meant spending more time with Jason. At least it was a pretty day with a bright blue sky and a gentle ocean breeze. "Jason tell me, what is Midanbury like? That is where you are from, same as Abby?"

Jason met the beguiling dark amber eyes turned his way and smiled. "Yes, it is. Midanbury is a tiny hamlet nestled in the hills. It is separated from Southampton by River Itchen. It is dense with hard woods and sparsely populated. It is beautiful. Especially in spring when so much is in bloom."

"And if you were there now, what would you be doing?"

Jason gave her a boyishly lopsided grin. "I would be riding Shelton."

She heard the wistful tone in his voice and felt its echo in her heart. "I love to ride too. In Charleston, I had my own horse. A gentle bay named Prince. He was sold when we moved here."

Jason heard the sorrow in her voice and understood. "Sometimes a horse is like a best friend—always there for you."

Victoria smiled wistfully. "Yes, they are. My parents offered to let me have a cat or a dog, but I turned them down. It just wasn't the same."

"No, definitely not the same."

Victoria could get lost in the depths of his blue-grey eyes under slanted lids. Pulling her gaze away, she looked to the couple in front of them, and realized, Max and Abby had barely spoken since leaving the house. She was worried about them, but she had faith they would eventually find their way to happiness. She sent a fervent prayer heavenward that it would be soon.

Jason asked the group in general, "Is it not warm for this time of year?"

Max replied, "No, it's about right—seventy degrees or so."

Jason's eyebrows rose. "Only seventy? I would have thought it was closer to ninety."

Victoria said, "It is the tropical moisture making it feel warmer. It takes some time to acclimate to it."

Now that they were outside of town, small trees and bushes became more prevalent. Ahead of them lay a canopy forest Max called a hammock. He led them to an old path grown over from disuse. He turned and called to Jason, "Malwbry, want to give me a hand with this?" Max gestured towards the undergrowth on the pathway.

Abby gave Max a stern look as she said under her breath, "Lord Malwbry."

Max gave her a direct look in return. "We're not in England—titles don't mean much here."

Jason overheard their terse conversation but chose to ignore it. Weeks ago, it would have offended him, but after his sojourn in Alabama, it didn't bother him if Max refused to use his title. He had a different kind of pride to worry about. If he read the undercurrents correctly, Max was challenging him to keep up in manual labor.

Abby handed each of them a canteen keeping one for herself and Victoria to share. She fell back to Victoria's side while the men worked together to clear the path. It didn't take long for the ladies to realize there was a silent contest going on between the men. Knowing it was useless to diffuse the situation, they let them work out their aggressions on the innocent vegetation.

Abby linked her arm with her friend and leaned a little closer. "You and Jason seem to be getting along very well."

Victoria gave a wry smile. "I suppose."

Abby turned her head in surprise. "You are not getting along?"

"We are. It's just..." Victoria wasn't sure she should say more but seeing Abby's concern she admitted, "He has been concerned for you."

Abby smiled. "That is touching."

"Yes it is except..."

"Except it makes you wonder how much he cares for me."

Victoria nodded. "He followed you here from England."

"Maybe so, but he never looked at me the way he looks at you. If he had, I would be Lady Malwbry right now."

Jason almost enjoyed the annoyance on Max's face when he realized Jason was keeping pace with him despite frequently wiping the sweat from his brow. Just as his energy was waning, the trees and brush suddenly opened to an expanse of barren ground with large puddles of water as the tide was currently out. A white heron, disturbed by the noise, took flight. Jason expected to find a pond of water rimmed in large salt crystals. The muddy limestone was a disappointment.

When Jason and Max turned around, the ladies were a hundred yards or so behind them. While waiting, they stood catching their breath and drinking the cool water from the canteens as they viewed their handiwork and the ladies. Jason noted that while Victoria did not move as gracefully as Abigail, she did have good carriage and spirit. And a willful nature. He smiled. He liked the inviting challenge she presented him of taming her. Just as his wayward thoughts were getting away from him, they were abruptly interrupted by the troubling tone of Max's voice.

"Malwbry, you'll want to step this way." He cupped his hands and called out. "Abigail, Victoria, stay to this side of the path and hurry."

Picking up their skirts the ladies moved to Max's side of the path and quickened their pace. Coming up to the men, Abby looked to Max with concern. "What is it?"

"Poisonwood." Max nodded to the waist high trees with spotted leaves. "Several of them on his side." Max looked intently towards Abby. "Do you know a treatment? Did Mrs. Mallory teach you anything that would help if Malwbry has come in contact with it?"

The intensity of Max's demeanor concerned Jason. *How serious was poisonwood?* Certainly the name was ominous. He looked at the plants and tried to recall if he had actually touched them, and then he looked at his exposed arms below the rolled up sleeves searching for any sign of trouble. Nothing looked or felt amiss.

Abigail's eyes closed in concentration, then flew open with the triumph of recalled knowledge. "Gumbo limbo. We need to rub the oily bark over his exposed skin and then cover it to protect it from the sun.'"

Jason thought gumbo limbo was a silly name for a tree.

Max glanced at the surrounding vegetation. "There should be one nearby."

Abby nodded in agreement. Max went to look for the bark while Abby moved towards Jason. "Let me see your arms."

Jason held them out for her inspection. "I do not feel anything. Mayhap you are worried for naught."

"You may not feel anything even if you did come in contact with the plant. Mrs. Mallory said the rash could show days later. Turn your arms over."

Jason did as she directed while Victoria wiped his brow with her handkerchief. When she was done, he gave her a half smile and a wink over Abigail's bent head. He enjoyed the responding bloom in Victoria's cheeks. Abby finished her inspection. He sobered his expression lest she noticed.

"I do not see any sap, but I think we should assume the worst and treat your exposed skin." Abby leaned down to lift the hem of her skirt and began tearing off a strip of her chemise to use as a bandage. Victoria did likewise so there would be enough to cover both of his arms. While they waited for Max to return, Abby moved around Jason to get a glimpse of the pond. "This is what we came to see?"

Jason grinned at her. "It would seem so. A bit disappointing, is it not?"

Abby continued past the brush to step out onto the dried pond bed for a better view.

Jason gave Victoria a bemused look. "Not exactly what you had in mind when you suggested this outing, is it?"

She gave him a rueful smile. "No."

Abby approached them as Max returned carrying bark. He stopped Abby from taking it from him. "No sense all of us getting sticky. Just tell me what to do with these."

"Rub the oily side over his skin." Max did as she directed.

Hating the feel of the sticky substance, Jason turned a skeptical eye toward Abigail. "Are you sure this is necessary?"

"Trust me. You do not want to risk getting the rash."

Max finished his task and discarded the bark. He then went to the pond to try scouring the residue from his hands while Victoria and Abby wrapped Jason's arms with the torn fabric.

Jason gave them a deprecating smile. "Is this the Key West version of 'tar and feather'?"

Both ladies laughed lightening the somber mood.

When Abby stepped away, Jason whispered to Victoria, "Do you think they did this on purpose to make sure I keep my distance from you?"

For a moment, Victoria thought he was being serious until she caught the wicked glint in his eye. "It was actually my idea."

Curious, Jason played along. "Yours?"

"I wanted to make sure you didn't leave too soon."

"And why is that?"

"So you would miss me when you return to England."

"I can think of better ways to ensure such an outcome."

"But none of them would be as memorable."

He lowered his voice to a bare whisper. "But they would be infinitely more enjoyable for both of us."

Heat instantly bloomed in her cheeks just as Max and Abby were returning. She ducked her head, pretending to improve tying off Jason's makeshift bandage.

Max bent to retrieve the machetes and gloves. "It's time we head back. A storm is approaching."

Jason looked up to see the sky was still the brilliant blue he knew it to be. He cast a puzzled glance at the others.

Victoria intercepted his look. "Captain Max has a feel for these things since he makes his living salvaging ships grounded during storms." She glanced at Abby surprised to see her calm. If it were her husband about to sail off into a storm, she would be anything but calm.

They started the return trip to the house at a much quicker pace. Not just because the way was already cleared, but because Max was in a hurry to return to his ship. Not even halfway through the hammock, Max turned for the third time to see how far behind they were trailing.

Abby called out loudly, "Max wait."

He halted for them to get closer and called out, "Is something wrong?"

Reaching him, Abby put her hand on his forearm. "Yes. Tria and I cannot keep up with your pace."

Max released a frustrated sigh. "All right, I'll slow down."

She smiled indulgently at him. "Thank you for the offer, but I was going to suggest you go on without us. You are obviously impatient to get to your ship. We will be fine. It is not like some wild animal is going to attack us, and we cannot get lost following the path."

Max looked at his wife, Victoria, and then Jason standing there in his ridiculous arm bandages. "Lord Malwbry." He waited until Jason took his eyes off Victoria and looked him in the eye. "Take care my wife gets home safely."

Jason was sure he had not heard him correctly. After all the animosity between them, Max was going to leave Abigail behind, entrusted to his care. He didn't understand the reason for Max's hurry, but he did understand the significance of the trust Max was placing in him. Even though it was unlikely Abigail needed his protection, Jason knew Max's request was not to be taken lightly. He answered just as seriously. "You have my word."

Max nodded to Jason. He kissed Abby on the cheek and took off running while they trailed behind.

The trio returned much quicker than the walk out thanks to the cleared path. Upon entering the house Abby asked, "Would you care to climb up to the Captain's Walk with me?"

Victoria immediately agreed. "I would love to."

Jason said, "Certainly." He followed the ladies up the stairs to the second story and then up a steeper set of stairs to the attic where they climbed a ladder to the hatch which opened to the roof. Jason went up first so he could assist the ladies in exiting the hatch.

Standing at the railing, Victoria commented, "It is too bad you can't see the wharf."

Abby nodded. "I know, but when Max came home the dock was full. The *Mystic* is anchored in the harbour. You can barely see her just over that building." Abby stretched to look where the *Mystic* had been this morning only to find she was already gone. Scanning the ships under sail, she found her headed east. "There she is." Abby pointed towards the distant sails. "I am sure the men were ready to leave as soon as Max returned." In the far distance, there seemed to be a bank of clouds on the eastern horizon. Putting a smile on her face, Abby turned to her guests and asked, "Shall we have our lunch now?"

Jason gestured with his outstretched arms. "How long must I be like this?"

"I think we can clean you up now, but you should stay indoors the rest of the day. If we missed any, the sunlight will make it worse." Abby left them to retrieve a basin, lye soap, a pitcher of water, and some towels.

Jason's eyes met Victoria's as soon as Abby turned her back. The warmth of his gaze made her cheek's flush again. "Where were we earlier? Ah yes, enjoyable things you could do to convince me to stay."

"I never said I wanted you to stay."

Jason caught the teasing note underlying her seriousness and responded in kind. "Then what were we discussing?"

Victoria knew this conversation was much to bold to continue, but she couldn't help herself. She knew him less than a day, and yet, she was immensely enjoying flirting with the edge of propriety. "How to make you miss me." Well, maybe a bit over the edge.

"Ah." Her answer pleased him. She was agreeing with him without being agreeable and with an underlying challenge to make her agreeable. He was fairly certain, she felt the same intense attraction that held him spellbound to her. It was as if their hearts intertwined at the moment of their meeting, and now, their minds were exploring and testing the strength of their affection.

Abby returned to the dining room table and deposited the supplies.

Victoria stayed her hands. "Let me do this."

Abby happily relinquished the task. She instead unpacked the picnic basket and started setting out their lunch.

The ladies worked in silence while Jason cast surreptitious smoldering glances at Victoria feeling victorious as each one deepened the stain on her cheeks. Her blush also heated her skin, delightfully increasing the musky sweet scent of her perfume. He wanted to know what flower's essence matched her so perfectly, but it was too indelicate a question for him to ask just yet.

Victoria desperately wanted to tell him to behave when her meaningful looks went unheeded but couldn't do so least it cause Abby to notice.

Once Jason was relatively free of the sticky tree sap, they ate their lunch.

Abby remained silent for most of the meal while Jason and Victoria spoke of casual topics sure to meet approval with even the most strict of proprieties. Or, at least, their words were proper. The looks Jason cast her way were anything but proper. Victoria fervently hoped Abby didn't notice.

When the meal was over, Victoria started clearing the table.

"Please leave it."

Victoria started at the crisp note in Abby's voice.

Abby gave her a soft smile and modified her tone. "Mrs. Baxley will help me clear this. You two should go enjoy the day. I think I will take a nap. It was an early morning." She rose from the table.

Victoria gave her a keen look. "You're sure you don't mind? If you need company, we'll stay."

Abby kissed her cheek. "No, I will be fine. I promise."

Victoria decided Abby simply needed time alone. She leaned out the back door to call Lydia in from the kitchen.

Abby ushered the three of them to the front door. "Enjoy your day."

As they stepped outside the house, Jason settled his hat and looked to Victoria. "Should we be concerned for Abigail?"

"No. I'm sure she just wants some time alone."

Jason held out his arm. "Well, Miss Lambert, what shall we do with ourselves?"

Victoria curled her hand around his bicep. "I have no idea."

"What was the other outing Captain Max mentioned?"

"The lighthouse."

"Yes. Could we not go there?"

"Abby said you should avoid sunlight."

"True but my arms are covered by my sleeves, and I am willing to risk the discomfort."

Victoria dubiously eyed the thin white sleeves of his borrowed shirt. "Well, I suppose we could but shall we walk along the beach? I believe we both have seen enough of the hammocks today."

"I whole heartedly concur." He held his free arm out towards the road. "Lead the way."

They descended the steps followed by Lydia. As they approached the beach, Victoria happened to look southeast out over the Atlantic Ocean. The edge of dark clouds, once distant, now threateningly enveloped the horizon. "Perhaps we should postpone this till another day."

Jason followed her gaze and then looked toward the lighthouse judging the distance. He was sure they could reach their destination, but the chances of making it back before the storm didn't seem likely. Reluctantly he agreed. "Another day." They turned around and by unspoken consent headed towards Victoria's house. When they reached her door, Victoria turned to bid him good day.

Jason wasn't ready to part company. "May I come in?"

The question surprised Victoria. "Of course."

She stepped to the side allowing him to open the door for her. As Victoria waited in the foyer for Jason to follow Lydia inside, her mother appeared in the doorway of her drawing room.

"Hello, Victoria. You have returned none the worse for wear, I see. How was your morning excursion?"

Victoria smiled. When she told her parents of her plans last night, her mother commiserated with her dismay as they both shared a dislike for the early hour and the wilderness. "Yes, I have. It was not as vexing as anticipated. There is someone I would like you to meet." Both ladies turned toward Jason as he shut the door behind him. "This is Lord Jason Malwbry, he is a family friend of Abigail Eatonton." Victoria felt compelled to add the last to head off any concerns her mother might have for propriety.

Jason gave a modest bow. He felt awkward meeting Victoria's well-dressed mother in his borrowed clothes. "I am pleased to make your acquaintance Mrs. Lambert."

Mrs. Lambert was charmed by his courtly manner and gave a slight curtsey in return. "A pleasure to meet you, Lord Malwbry."

Jason made note of his surroundings. The house was relatively large for the island suggesting her family was well off. The interior decor confirmed their affluence. Outside, it was a deceptively small looking two-story. He later learned it was referred to as a Bahamian eyebrow design. The front roof extended low, all but obscuring the second story windows, giving the two-story the outward appearance of a single story. The inside was spacious and elaborately furnished with high quality European imports. "You have a beautiful home, Mrs. Lambert."

"Thank you, sir. I have done my best to make this odd house feel like our Charleston town home."

Victoria jumped in before her mother could begin lamenting for her old home and the burdens of living in Key West. "Lord Jason, would you care to play a game of chess?"

"Indeed, I would enjoy a game."

"Perhaps you would like to play out on the piazza, so we may enjoy the afternoon breeze?"

He extended his arm. "Lead the way, my lady."

Her mouth quirked at his teasing address until she caught sight of her mother's frown. Quickly, Victoria led Jason out of her sight and into the parlour. She directed him to pick up the wooden box containing the chess set and follow her to the front porch. He had an awkward moment of holding the game and opening the door for her but managed to accomplish both. She led him to a small wicker table on the right side with two matching chairs. He set the box down and held the chair for her then took his seat. The box was inlaid with wood squares of natural and stained maple creating the playing board. The rest of the box was made of dark walnut with a carved vine pattern around the edge of the board. Victoria opened the drawer on the side revealing richly detailed ebony and ivory pieces.

Victoria looked to Jason but before she could ask her question he said, "Lady's choice." She gave him a coy grin before picking up the white queen and placing it on her side of the board. Lydia brought them lemonade, but otherwise, they were undisturbed. Silently, they set up the pieces and then began to play. For both of them concentration outweighed conversation and few words were spoken. The same could not be said for their eye contact which was often and intense.

A dozen or so moves later, Jason said with approval, "You are quite good."

Victoria gave him a serious look in return. "You are too."

"We seem to be well matched."

Victoria thought he was referring to more than just their chess skills, but it could be her wishful thinking getting the better of her. While she was distracted, he captured her rook, but after considerable effort, she managed to capture his queen. In the end, Jason claimed checkmate.

Victoria rose to congratulate him. Jason stood with her. She held out her hand to shake his. "You are a worthy opponent. I look forward to our next encounter."

Jason's eyebrows rose. "Our next encounter?"

Realizing her assumption, she took advantage of the conversation gambit. "Unless you have plans to leave soon, I would like a rematch."

"I have not made any plans as of yet. I suppose I will visit the docks Monday morning in search of passage to England. I expect at minimum, I will be residing on your island for at least a few more days. Otherwise, I have no plans."

She gave him a winsome smile. "Good. Then will you honor me with another game tomorrow?"

"It would be ungentlemanly of me to refuse such a request. What time shall I present myself?"

Victoria pretended to give it some thought. "I plan to take lunch with Abby. It is a trial for her while Max is away. We could play afterwards," she paused for effect, "unless you would care to join us for another meal?"

He knew she was cajoling him, and he had not the will to refute her. "I would be delighted to accompany you."

"Shall we say eleven o'clock?"

"Eleven o'clock it is."

They began putting the pieces away. The first brush of their hands may have been unintentional, but the multitude of touches that followed were contrived, enjoyed, and soon lingered over. The sound of footsteps on the limestone walk abruptly ended their play. They both looked to the source and discovered her father approaching. Victoria was surprised by the lateness of the hour. The afternoon slipped away while they played.

Victoria rushed forward to greet her sire. "Father, this is Lord Jason Malwbry, a family friend of Abby and Mr. Bennington. He is on holiday from England."

Jason closely eyed Mr. Lambert and noticed the way her father sized him up in a glance. It made him nervous considering how Mr. Bennington found him lacking. Once again, he felt uncomfortable in his borrowed clothes. *How would this man see his character?* Wanting to make a good impression, he stepped forward with his hand extended. "Good evening, Mr. Lambert. It is a pleasure to meet you. Your wife and daughter have graciously entertained me this afternoon with refreshments and a challenging game of chess."

Mr. Lambert shook the proffered hand. "Greetings, Lord Malwbry. Any friend of the Bennington's is welcome in my home. How long do you plan to stay in Key West?"

"I am unsure at the moment. It will depend on when I can find passage home."

"Was this not a planned visit?"

"No. I expected to meet the Bennington's in Montgomery, but upon my arrival, I discovered they had been delayed."

"And you chose to come here versus waiting for them there?"

"It was a risk, but traveling was more appealing than sitting idle."

"On that we can agree. Will you be staying for supper?"

"If I am invited then certainly I will."

Mr. Lambert turned to his daughter. "Have I been presumptuous?"

Victoria shook her head. "Of course not, father, but I planned on taking supper to Abby and hoped Lord Malwbry would join us."

They both looked to Jason.

"Of course, I would be delighted." He wasn't entirely certain to which supper he was agreeing to join.

Mr. Lambert glanced at the game and then at the two of them. "And who was the victor?"

Victoria answered, "Lord Ja… hmm, Malwbry." She saw her father's eyes tighten at her slip and knew she had betrayed her feelings along with the social blunder.

Her father returned his gaze to Lord Jason with a bit more scrutiny. "Come to the parlour when you have finished putting away the game, and we can share a drink."

Jason gave him a nod. "With pleasure, sir."

Wanting to spare Jason from what was sure to be an inquisition, Victoria prevaricated. "Father, I'm afraid we haven't the time. We should leave for Abby's immediately."

Mr. Lambert gave a knowing nod. "Next time, then."

When the door closed behind his host, Jason released a sigh of nervous tension.

Victoria absently resumed putting the chessmen back in the box as she considered what her father must be thinking and what all he might have learned from the short encounter. She was sure it was more than she would like for him to know.

Finished with the task, she said to Jason, "Wait here while I go get a hamper of food."

Victoria returned about ten minutes later flying through the front door in a fluster of skirts. Jason rose to take the hamper from her and silently wondered why Lydia was not trailing behind. He followed Victoria down the steps.

Abigail was surprised to see them but welcoming. Jason placed the basket of food on the sideboard in the dining room. Abigail set the table while he and Victoria removed the contents. There was a jar of applesauce, fried chicken, biscuits, and a bowl of green beans cooked with ham. The short distance from one house to the other ensured the meal was still hot. It was enjoyed with relish.

Victoria asked, "Have you heard any news of Captain Max?"

Abby shook her head. "No, but then, I didn't expect to so soon. I was told the storm hit hard in the upper keys so I hope he found work."

Victoria tilted her head. "You hope he found work for the income it will bring, and yet, you hope not, so he remains safe."

Abby nodded solemnly. "Such are the worries of a wrecker's wife." She turned the conversation to less troublesome topics.

After their meal, they companionably cleaned the dishes. Jason gave his assistance much to the surprise of the ladies. After he tossed out the dirty dish water, Abby said, "Shall we watch the sunset from the Captain's Walk?"

Victoria quickly agreed. "That would be lovely." She turned a dazzling smile on Jason that would have had him agreeing even if he objected, which he did not.

They stepped out onto the open decking facing the waters of the Gulf of Mexico. Mesmerized, they stood under a cloudless sky of light blue fading to the palest shade of pink before turning to rose as it touched the horizon. The luminous white-gold orb hung just above the water surrounded by bursting rays of the brightest yellow. Jason gaze strayed to the vision standing beside him. He didn't think

Victoria could look any lovelier than in this moment with the soft light of evening kissing her skin. He longed to touch her cheek, pull her close, and kiss her dewy lips. Abigail's movement on the other side of Victoria snapped him back from his treacherous thoughts. He dutifully turned his attention back to the western sky in time to see the picturesque view of a ship sailing across the sun, now turned red and just touching the horizon. They talked quietly as they watched the sun's downward progression. The blue dome overhead darkened and the pink horizon turned to a golden rose. Of an accord, they all fell silent as the last of the glowing sphere disappeared and the colors deepened with each passing moment.

Abigail bid them good evening when they returned to the lower floor. The two stepped into the evening's twilight for the short stroll to Victoria's house. Jason kissed her hand at the bottom of her steps having no desire to face any more of her father's questioning, but he found it hard to let go of even that small contact.

Victoria looked into his eyes feeling the same reluctance. "Thank you for today."

Jason smiled. "My pleasure."

"Don't forget tomorrow. Perhaps we will have better success cheering Abby up after a night's rest."

"Of course, eleven o'clock. Until then sweet lady."

Victoria's smile grew. "Until then, my lord."

He waited for her to go in the house before he turned away. He walked to the boardinghouse calling himself all kinds of a fool for agreeing to yet another outing.

Chapter 6

Sunday morning was bright and clear as if the azure dome had been washed clean by the fierce storm passing to the east of the island yesterday.

Jason stepped from the boardinghouse at half past eight feeling debonair to be dressed once again in his regular clothes instead of the borrowed work wear from Max. He flipped his top hat before placing it on his head and then jauntily walked with the other boarders to the custom house for worship services. It was a far cry from the Midanbury Chapel of aged brick, bright stained glass windows, and domed bell tower. The island did not even have a permanent clergy. The elders of the community took turns reading from the Bible except on the rare days when there was a visiting minister. Jason was only able to catch a glimpse of Victoria after service as she and her family left the custom house. He spoke with Abigail briefly before she excused herself, declining his offer to walk her home, forcing him to wander the wharves, biding his time.

A while later, Jason checked his pocket watch. He smiled as he clicked the cover closed. Time to meet Victoria.

Victoria could hardly contain her impatience as she waited for Jason to arrive. She surreptitiously lifted the edge of the curtain on the front window to look for his approach without giving herself away. She had done so at least a dozen times in the last ten minutes even though it wasn't quite eleven. Her restlessness was getting the better of her. She spun away from the window in a rustle of pale pink taffeta to storm a path from one end of the room to the other and back to the window again, much to Lydia's amusement. The scene was repeated twice more before a squeal of delight pierced the room. Victoria went rushing for the stairs to wait in her room to be called. She must not appear too eager to see him.

Lydia hid a laugh behind her hand at her lady's antics. The young and in love were always so dramatic. A moment later there was a knock at the door. She stepped forward to draw it open and moved aside for Lord Malwbry to enter.

"Good morning, milord. Miss Lambert will be down in a moment." Lydia turned to call for Victoria and was not surprised to see she was already making a gracious descent of the stairs.

Victoria smiled sweetly. "A pleasure to see you again, Lord

Malwbry. Lydia, be a dear and run to the kitchen and see if the hamper is ready."

Lydia did as she was asked even knowing Victoria made the request so she might have a few private moments with her suitor. Her parents being out of the house, lunching with friends.

Jason stepped to the foot of the staircase and held his hand out to Victoria. She slid her ungloved hand into his causing friction to further heighten his already well attuned senses. Her intriguing floral scent enveloped him. *What was a man to do when enticed by such a beautiful creature?*

As they delved into each other's eyes, the rest of the world ceased to exist. Breath became ragged, pulses flurried, hands moistened. Victoria licked her lips. Jason's head dropped a notch, pulled by his need to sample their sweetness. Her chin lifted ever so slightly. He leaned just a bit closer. Their breath mingled.

Lydia approached from the hall with basket in hand.

The couple quickly stepped apart. Both were disappointed by the interruption and embarrassed to have not been able to control their feelings. Jason took the heavy food basket from Lydia and opened the door for Victoria to exit the house.

Lydia stayed behind. Earlier, Victoria declared to her mother that she would not need a chaperone for the short walk in which they would never be out of sight of the house, and, of course, Abby would be with them otherwise. Her mother reluctantly agreed.

Jason offered his arm to the charming lady by his side wearing a dainty pink dress that perfectly matched the tint of her cheeks. He felt his heart skip a beat when she lifted her honey-brown eyes to his, with a joyous smile, as if he had given her the rarest of gems. Indeed, her smile was the rarest of beauties in his mind. He wondered how to coax it from her again.

Surreptitious glances were cast between them as they walked to the Eatonton's.

Victoria was feeling quite cheerful today, and confident she would get her way with this man in the end. Lord Jason Malwbry had no idea how tenacious she could be at getting what she wanted, and she had her heart set on sailing to England as his bride. She gave him another dazzling smile. "Lord Jason, I have heard English names are confusing. What is your full name?"

He smiled. "Lord Jason Albert Duncan Malwbry"

"Your name is simple enough."

"Aye, it tis, but perhaps what is confusing is that a nobleman's name can change over his lifetime."

"And yours will change?"

"Yes. When my father passes away, I will become the Duke of Rothebury and will be known to all as Rothebury instead of Malwbry. Although, I will still hold title to the Malwbry estate."

"Do you have any brothers or sisters?"

"No."

She nodded sagely, understanding the nuances in the tone of his reply. "Neither have I."

"I believe I was aware there were no other siblings around but had not really given thought to both of us being only children. Did your parents wish for more?"

Victoria frowned trying to recall any conversations she might have overheard on the matter. "I have no idea. It was never mentioned in my presence. And you?"

Jason gave a wry grin. "Oh, my father lamented on it often enough, but my mother insisted she had done her duty providing a viable heir, and there was no other reason strong enough for her to endure the process a second time—not the beginning nor the ending."

Victoria's jaw dropped. "And this was said within your hearing?"

Jason silently nodded.

"Does she love you?" The words were out of Victoria's mouth before she considered how they might sound. Upon hearing them, she instantly regretted having said them. "Oh, Jason. I'm sorry. I didn't mean that. Of course she loves you. You're her son. Her flesh and blood. She carried you under her heart."

Jason patted her hand on his arm. "My mother is quite curmudgeonly, and I daresay you are not the first to wonder at the true nature of her feelings, but I have always felt she loved me in her own way. However, I cannot say the same for how she feels about my father."

"How sad."

"Indeed, and quite the reason I will marry happily or not at all."

Victoria gave him a coyly radiant smile. His declaration gave her hope.

Jason shook his head. "Let us not ruin a perfectly beautiful day with talk of my unhappy parents."

"I agree."

Abigail opened the door at Jason's knock. He saw the distress in her eyes and started to ask if they should return another day, but Victoria breezed past them.

"Cheers, Abby. What a beautiful day it is, don't you think? Jason would you be a dear and set the basket on the buffet in the dining room?"

Abigail followed her into the room leaving Jason to trail behind.

"Tria, please lower your voice. Max is home. He is sleeping upstairs."

"No, he's not."

Three heads swiveled to the staircase where Max was descending.

They waited, a frozen tableau, for Max to enter the room.

Jason nodded to him. "Good to see you again, Captain."

Max returned his nod. "Malwbry." To Victoria he said, "Did I hear you mention food?"

She gave him an uncertain smile. "You did."

Victoria and Abigail went to work setting the table and unpacking the hamper.

Jason saw the tightness in Max's expression and felt it wise to keep silent. During the meal, he tried to keep the conversation light in the hopes of dissipating the tension in the room. He knew he failed when he saw Abigail send Victoria a pleading look with a nod towards the door.

Victoria's eyes flashed in understanding. She turned to him and whispered, "We need to go."

Both ladies stood bringing the men to their feet. Abigail silently led them to the door. Jason overheard Victoria whisper to her as she passed, "*Bonne chance, mon amie.*"

As they stepped down from the porch, Victoria said, "I wonder what happened."

Jason could only frown in puzzlement. "Why did you tell her good luck?"

"She'll need it to deal with Max and his suppressed feelings. Something happened out on the reef. Something bad. And I know just who to ask." She turned her gaze on him. "Will you walk with me to the wharf?"

The sincere need he saw in her eyes made his agreement a certainty.

At the corner of Simonton and Front Street, they turned left away from her house. A few blocks later, they cut down an alleyway on the right to reach the docks. They noticed a cluster of men talking.

Among them, Victoria found the person she was seeking; Max's first mate, Jonathon Keats. When he saw their approach, he broke away from the group to meet them. "I suppose you have heard the news."

Victoria shook her head. "No we haven't. I could tell something was wrong, but Captain Max wouldn't say anything."

Mr. Keats nodded. "I'm not surprised he is taking it hard. There was an accident. Billy fell from the rigging into the waves crashing over the reef."

Victoria inhaled a sharp breath and her hand flew to her chest. "Oh my! Is he alright?"

Sadly, Mr. Keats bowed his head. "He didn't make it." He lifted his gaze to theirs. "Captain's blaming himself." He looked off in the distance as if trying to separate his feelings from his words. "Some women are preparing the body now." He took a deep breath. "Funeral's to commence in an hour at the cemetery."

Victoria nodded. "Thank you for telling us."

She turned with Jason to walk back to her house. Quietly, she said, "Billy was the youngest of Max's crew." Her watery eyes lifted to Jason's. "Max has to be devastated. Though he will never admit it, his crew is like family to him. They're like a band of brothers out to conquer Mother Nature. He'll blame himself for Billy's death, no matter the circumstances."

Jason didn't know what to say. In sympathy, he squeezed her gloved hand still tucked in the crook of his elbow.

* * *

The cemetery was located on the beach south of the settlement. The gentle lapping of water several yards away made it a tranquil final resting place. Jason escorted Victoria to Abigail's side. Her husband was on her other side; his spine stiff and his face grim. The graveside service was simple with many sailors in attendance. Billy had been well liked by all who knew him. Max stepped forward to officiate since there was no clergy available.

At the conclusion of the service, Max rounded up his crew and sent them to the ship. He returned to face Abigail, but he addressed Jason. "Malwbry, will you see my wife home, again?"

Abigail protested, "Max, what is going on? Why are you not staying?"

Max's reply was cold, "There is still more work to be done at the wreck."

Abigail pleaded, "Then take me with you. I will not be a burden."

Max tensed. "No."

She started to protest but he cut her off, "No, absolutely not. Go home, Abigail."

And with that, he turned and left her standing on the beach, embarrassed, forlorn, and heartbroken.

Victoria put her arm around her friend's shoulders offering what little comfort she could as the three of them turned to walk back to Abigail's home. Jason kept silent having no idea what he could say to help. At her door, Abigail turned. "I am afraid I would make rather poor company today."

Victoria gave her a sympathetic smile. "Say no more. I understand. We'll leave you."

Abigail solemnly nodded.

The ladies hugged each other, and then Jason and Victoria retreated to her house. Earlier in the day, Victoria had plans of challenging Jason to another game of chess, but now, it seemed wrong given the events of the day. "Perhaps, we should have our rematch tomorrow?"

"I agree. I have business to attend to in the morning. Shall I come by in the afternoon?"

She was going to hate waiting so long to see him again, but she would find the patience. "Of course. Until then, my lord."

He smirked, for when she said 'my lord,' it seemed to have an entirely different meaning than the phrase intended.

Chapter 7

Monday morning was overcast and gloomy. The water in the harbour reflected the somber grey sky further darkening Jason's mood as he futilely searched for passage home.

It took all morning and into the afternoon for him to visit every shipping office. He found the clerks and proprietors very talkative, but to his frustration, he could not find passage to England. Apparently, it was the wrong time of year for sailing northeast across the Atlantic. He was warned the ships were few and far between. He frowned, realizing he was getting an additional lesson in patience. There was no help for it. He may be stuck on this island for the time being, but he would make the best of it. He nearly whistled as he jauntily wove his way through town to keep his appointment with the lovely Miss Lambert.

Lydia opened the door at his knock and informed him the ladies were awaiting him in the parlour. He was ushered into the formal room elegantly adorned in pine green and plum. Victoria and her mother stood up from the round table in the corner covered in dark green damask.

"Welcome, Lord Malwbry." Mrs. Lambert gestured to the chair closest to him. "Would you care for some tea?"

"Thank you madam. A spot of refreshment would be most welcome."

Jason approached the table and bowed to the ladies before helping, first her mother, and then Victoria to be seated again. Jason took his seat and watched as Mrs. Lambert gracefully poured him a cup of fragrant tea. In the center of the table was a glass bowl filled with what he assumed were tropical fruits as they were unfamiliar to him. Their bright colors were a stark contrast to the darkness of the cloth. A servant arrived with a plate of fresh scones. Mrs. Lambert graciously served him first, and then Victoria, and finally herself. As she stirred the cream in her tea, she asked Jason, "Lord Malwbry, how have your travels brought you to this island?"

Victoria's eyes flew to Jason's anxious to know how he would respond. Certainly not with the truth.

Jason was caught off guard by the unexpected question but felt compelled to be honest—to a point. "My mother has finally convinced me it is time I marry, but I felt the need to do a bit of travel abroad before making such a commitment."

Mrs. Lambert held his gaze. "I imagine it was a wise decision. And do you have a special lady in mind to take as your wife?"

"There was one but she has since married."

"I believe Victoria mentioned you are a future duke. What kind of lady are you seeking as your future duchess?"

Victoria's eyes widened, surprised by the directness of her mother's questions. Certainly, she would never ask such a thing, but she was deeply interested in his answer. It almost seemed as if her mother were interviewing Lord Jason on her behalf.

Again, the question was unexpected. Jason pondered if Mrs. Lambert was making conversation, or if she recognized the depth of his interest in her daughter. He considered giving her the description his mother had given him of an appropriate bride, but it would be untrue. His desires did not coincide with his mother's. "She would be spirited, willing to be a bit unconventional, devoted, of sound mind and body, able to hold her own in high society, but also prudent enough not to cause embarrassment or disgrace."

He couldn't tell how Mrs. Lambert felt about his answer, for she kept her expression neutral. However, it was clear Victoria approved by her satisfied smile.

Mrs. Lambert delicately returned her cup to the saucer before replying. "It is well you have put some thought into your choice of a bride, but I wonder if your ideals are not a bit high. It will take a special woman to be both avant-garde and conventional; to meet both society's expectations of a duchess and your desires while avoiding censure."

Jason frowned. His wants were based on his attractions to Abigail and Victoria. Both ladies were spirited and a bit progressive. He hadn't considered how such a wife would struggle to fill her position in society. For his sake, he was willing to flaunt his obligations to have what he wanted, but was it fair to subject a lady to possible ridicule for her lack of conformity? And if that wasn't going to be difficult enough, his bride would also have to contend with his mother's displeasure. He looked at Victoria and tried to imagine her fitting into Southampton and even Midanbury society as his duchess. Sadly, he could not. His mother's disapproval of Victoria would only increase the turmoil in the house, and he could well imagine the stress and strife bearing down on Victoria. It made his heart wrench. It was a physical pain as well as emotional.

With a steady gaze for Mrs. Lambert he said, "Thank you. I had not considered the burden's my prospective bride would face if not inclined to the strictures of society. It would be selfish of me to burden such a free spirit, or worse, to be the cause of her downfall."

Mrs. Lambert nodded in agreement, but then he saw the barest twitch of her bottom lip as if she were happy to have turned his attention from Victoria. Her point was valid but was it sincere? Was she simply trying to redirect him? He was relieved when her next questions were common and easy to answer.

A quarter of an hour later, Victoria returned her empty teacup to its saucer and rose with more grace than was her norm. "Shall we adjourn to the porch for our chess game?"

Jason rose with Victoria. "As you wish." He turned to Mrs. Lambert, "Will you excuse us?"

She gave him a small thoughtful smile. "Of course."

A curtain of light rain fell turning the porch into an intimate setting as Jason and Victoria tested their wits against each other. They may have tested more than their wits if her mother hadn't sent Lydia to the porch to do her darning. Having a chaperone curtailed Victoria from anything more provocative than glances. Jason noticed and returned them. He may be having second thoughts on how far to carry their relationship, but the attraction between them was still intense enough to make him amenable to her flirtations.

And so it was that Mr. Lambert returned from the office to find a similar scene as he encountered two days prior. "And who was the victor of this match?"

Victoria looked up sheepishly from putting away the game pieces.

"Ah, my cunning daughter prevails today. Will you be joining us for supper, Lord Malwbry?"

A glance at Victoria saw her gathering a refusal but not wanting to give the appearance of avoidance Jason spoke first, "I would be honored to, sir."

Victoria was startled by Jason's confident acceptance. While she rejoiced to spend a little more time with Lord Jason, she knew with certainty the forthcoming conversation would really be an interrogation. Her father was, after all, a skilled lawyer. He saw things most people wouldn't notice. She was certain he had already discerned her attraction to the young aristocrat.

Mr. Lambert grinned. "Join me for a drink when you are done here."

A few moments later, Jason followed Victoria into the parlour. Her father rose to greet them and then with a gesture toward the decanters on the sideboard, he asked, "Lord Malwbry, what is your pleasure?"

"Brandy, please."

Jason waited for Victoria to settle next to her mother on the sofa before he took a seat in an opposing chair. Her father handed him a snifter of rich amber liquid and then turned to hand his daughter a small wineglass of sherry. He took a seat adjacent to the sofa, next to his wife. Jason surmised he did so the better to see him.

"Lord Malwbry, what are your family's interests in England?"

Jason kept his smile in check. He was not surprised to be interrogated again. At least her father's approach appeared more subtle than her mother's earlier questioning over tea. He considered how to answer the question. Because of his visit to Mulberry House, it would certainly be a different answer than he gave to James Bennington.

"My father has an estate in Midanbury, and I have one on the outskirts of Southampton. The lands are worked by tenant farmers."

"I see. And are they profitable?"

"They do well enough, but I am anxious to apply some of the methods I learned while visiting the Bennington plantation. I am hopeful it might increase our yields."

Mr. Lambert nodded. "You sound excited. It is good to have a goal and ambition."

Jason was surprised to realize, he really was excited. What he said weren't just words to impress Victoria's father. They were aspirations, and the beginnings of a plan, he hadn't realized he was harbouring. Before this moment, it was a thought, but now he realized it was an idea that had taken root in his soul. Instead of dreading his return home, he was beginning to look forward to it. He looked to Victoria wanting to share his excitement with her, but her eyes were downcast and her features solemn.

A servant entered the room calling them to supper. Mr. Lambert gave his hand to Mrs. Lambert and led her to the dining room. Jason approached Victoria and offered his hand. She looked up at him and smiled, but it lacked the luster of earlier. He lowered his voice to ask, "Is something the matter, Victoria?"

Her smile brightened. "Not at all."

He didn't believe her, but etiquette would not allow him to question a lady.

She delicately sniffed the air. "Mmm, do you smell the mint? I believe we are having my favorite dish tonight, rack of lamb."

A large cased opening brought them into the navy and gold dining room. The long table was polished to a glossy shine and could easily seat eight, though only four chairs were currently in place; the side chairs being centered along the length. Two large silver candelabras were fully lit even though their light was not yet necessary. Victoria indicated Jason should seat her on her father's right. He then circled the table to sit across from her. Mr. Lambert said a simple grace, and the servants began filling their plates.

Mr. Lambert turned to Jason. "I believe Victoria mentioned your father is a duke. I am not well acquainted with English titles. Is it hereditary?"

Jason heard a note of concern in his voice and wondered what Mr. Lambert was thinking. "Yes. The Rothebury title and all the lands tied to it will pass to me upon his death."

"And is your father in good health?"

"He is. I expect to remain a lord for quite some time."

"And do you serve in parliament?"

"No sir. That honor will also be inherited."

Victoria came to his rescue. "Father please. Enough questions for one night."

Mr. Lambert nodded. "My daughter is right. I suppose it is my nature to be inquisitive."

Jason said, "May I ask you a question, sir?"

Mr. Lambert smiled. "Certainly. I would enjoy a bit of cross-examination."

"What brought you to Key West?"

"Opportunity. Salvage cases are very lucrative and human lives are not on the line, so the courtroom battle is more enjoyable as well."

"Is wealth new to you?"

"Heavens no. My father was not poor and my wife comes from Old Charleston money." He paused for a moment assessing Jason. "Is that your way of asking if Victoria has a dowry?"

Jason eyes flew wide. "No, sir. Certainly not. A dowry of any kind did not cross my mind. Heavens, sir, we just met yesterday, and I am to return to England soon. Courting is not my intentions." He was wrong about Mr. Lambert being subtle. He was more direct than his wife.

"So you are not one of those noble Englishmen we hear of

travelling about searching for an American heiress to save their sinking estate?"

Jason blanched as that was exactly his original intent in pursuing Abigail, but the journey led him to a different path, and now, he could answer with complete honesty. "No, I am not. I can see how you might think so and understand your wish to protect your daughter. I enjoy Miss Lambert's company, but there is nothing more between us."

Victoria suddenly stood, her chair making a harsh scraping sound against the hardwood floor, her face flushed with anger.

Jason and Mr. Lambert both rose as gentlemen should when a lady stands.

Her voice seethed, "Is that all I am to you; an afternoon's entertainment?" She lowered her tone but firmly said, "You lie! You have feelings for me. I have seen it in your eyes."

Jason was uncomfortably aware of Mr. and Mrs. Lambert's regard as he addressed Victoria. "You are without a doubt the loveliest lady I have ever beheld and your spirit draws my soul against my will, but you heard your mother this afternoon. When and if I take a wife, she will one day be a duchess so I must choose with care, but beyond that, I am not ready to settle down." His eyes pleaded with hers. "Miss Lambert, I do enjoy your company. You have made what could be a tedious visit most enjoyable, but I can see it is too much of a burden for you. I will excuse myself and leave this instant."

Panic bloomed in Victoria's chest. He mustn't leave. She wanted a declaration from him but realized now was too soon. She needed more time. "No, please stay." She offered an apologetic smile to all of them. "I am afraid my biggest folly is being too bold. I didn't mean to discomfort you with what must be a silly school girl crush. Please, as a gentleman, forgive and forget these last few moments. Let us continue on as friends."

Jason, wishing to put an end to the awkward moment, solemnly nodded. "As you wish."

Victoria smiled weakly. Her father held the chair for her to resume her seat, and then he and Jason resumed theirs. A strained silence accompanied the rest of the meal occasionally broken by stilted mundane conversation. Mr. and Mrs. Lambert exchanged many glances, but Jason kept his eyes stoically away from Victoria.

When the meal ended, Victoria excused herself on the pretense of a headache. She then snuck out the back of the house and circled around to secretly wait for Jason. She hoped her father would not follow him out on the porch, and she fervently hoped the neighbors would not take notice, for she knew the tongue lashing she would receive if this was mentioned to her mother. A mirthless laugh slipped out. She was already going to receive one of those lectures for her behaviour at supper. Her mother was sure to chastise her for failing to act like a proper lady, pursuing a man, and presuming too much. And yet, she was willing to risk further censure just to speak with Jason.

A few moments later Victoria heard the deep voices of her father and Jason and the closing of the door. Thankfully there was only one set of footsteps descending the stairs. She straightened from her crouch in front of an oleander bush as he came into sight.

"Victoria! What are you doing out here?"

"Shh, keep you voice down or you'll bring my father out." She inhaled a deep breath before continuing, "I am sorry for the scene I caused. Please, accept my apology. I am afraid I read more into your demeanor than you intended. It won't happen again. Please can we not continue on as friends?"

Jason's heart melted at her sincere pleading. He longed to assure her she had not imagined his feelings, but he could not. It would be cruel to give her hope. She was not suitable for his bride no matter how much he wished it were otherwise. But here she was giving him a way to still enjoy the bittersweet pleasure of her company, and God help him, he was not able to resist. "We can be friends. We will not speak of this again."

Victoria gave him a nod and turned away lest he see the smile she couldn't hold back. She quickly made her way to the back of the house leaving him standing there in bewilderment.

Jason watched her retreat, and for a moment, he wished his life were his own so he could follow her, declare his intentions, marry her, and live anywhere they wished.

He slowly walked to the boardinghouse with the sun setting behind him. Tomorrow morning, he would again seek passage home and with any luck at all, sail away from this island, before he truly lost his heart to a winsome girl with captivating eyes. Yes, it would be best to leave here soon.

Victoria tried to quickly move past the parlour where her parents had adjourned, but she was caught. Her mother rose from her seat followed by her father. They entered the foyer to stop her assent up the stairs. Her mother's words were angry. "Young lady, I have never been so appalled. I thought I taught you better."

Victoria was momentarily meek. "You did, and I am sorry I embarrassed all of us." But then her stubbornness returned. "I am afraid my heart got the better of my head, but it doesn't matter. I will marry him."

Both of her parents were aghast. Once past his shock her father said, "He will never ask, especially not after your behaviour tonight. You proved without a doubt you have not the skills to be a duchess."

Victoria's spine stiffened. "He will ask for my hand, and father, when he does, you will give your blessing."

"Victoria, I don't see how I could..."

She said it firmly leaving no room for her parents to doubt her sincerity. "Because I love him."

"Love!" Her father turned to her mother. "What does she know of love? She is too young."

Her mother laid a hand on his arm. "I was younger than her when we married."

Her father looked at Victoria again as if truly seeing her for the first time in years.

* * *

It rained off and on all day Tuesday keeping Victoria house bound. She had hoped to casually run across Jason while out walking. She hoped to challenge him to another game of chess. The weather prevented such manipulations. She fidgeted all day with her frustrations. By late afternoon, she was at her wits end and could hardly bear to sit still while having tea with her mother.

Mrs. Lambert looked intently at her daughter. "What is vexing you so?"

Victoria returned her look while silently debating how to answer.

Her mother's chin lifted as the answer dawned on her. "Lord Malwbry."

"Yes, Lord Malwbry."

Mrs. Lambert gave her daughter a thoughtful look. "Whatever you are scheming, put it from your mind. A lady never pursues the man. It will only bring you heartbreak."

"But, mother, what if he doesn't know his own mind? He could leave any day."

Her mother nodded sagely. "If it's meant to be it will happen and if not..."

Victoria huffed in frustration. According to her mother, she was supposed to content herself with fate determining the outcome of her happiness. It just wasn't in her to idly accept what will be, will be. She wanted to control her destiny. She wanted to do all she could to get the outcome she desired. She impatiently walked to the window to stare out at the rain. It was not in her nature to patiently wait and accept whatever outcome fate presented her. No matter what her mother said, tomorrow she would find a way to meet with Jason.

Jason spent Tuesday reading a borrowed book from the boardinghouse library rather than venture out in the rain, but Wednesday morning found him out bright and early looking for any vessel headed east only to be disappointed once again. Of course, the clerks all promised to send word to the boardinghouse if something became available, but it gave him something to do to call at their offices in person. Next, he decided to visit the barber for a trim and a shave. He left there in better spirits that rose even higher as he spied across the street the very person he was trying so hard not to think about walking with her maid.

Before good reason could prevail, he found himself crossing the street to intercept their path as if pulled to her. He tipped his hat, "Miss Victoria, what a pleasure to see you again. Good morning, Lydia."

Victoria's smile was full and genuine. It was not lost on her that he had gone out of his way to speak to her, and her spirits soared as a result. Her response was soaked in more than her usual amount of Southern charm. "Why Lord Malwbry, you sure are looking dapper this morning."

"May I escort you to your destination?"

Joy took wing in her breast. "If you would like."

Jason turned around and offered her his arm which was eagerly accepted. "Where are you headed?"

She couldn't very well say she was out in search of him, so she said the first excuse that came to mind. "To the mercantile for some embroidery thread. I am in desperate need of more red for a rose garden."

"Ruby red roses are my favorite."

She smiled. "The traditional flower of love. Perhaps, you are a romantic at heart. My favorite is a gardenia."

"Gardenia? I am not familiar with that flower."

"Do you not have them in England?"

"I am afraid my knowledge of horticulture is extremely lacking. I couldn't say one way or the other. Perhaps you could show me a specimen?"

"I haven't seen any here. I know it from Charleston. It was imported many years before I was born. The flower is named after Alexander Garden, a Scottish botanist living in Charleston."

"What does it look like?"

"The leaves are dark green, thick and glossy like a smaller version of a magnolia leaf."

Jason shook his head.

Victoria laughed realizing he wasn't familiar with the magnolia tree either. "The flower looks similar to a rose. The petals are of the purest white, velvety soft, and highly fragrant." She leaned in close and whispered, "Its meaning is a secret love."

Jason watched her pull away with an enchanted smile hovering on her lips. Her heady perfume further enticed him. Together it was becoming deucedly difficult to keep his feelings aloof.

"And what of its fragrance?"

"I adore it. It is my favorite perfume. An old family friend in Charleston has perfected the formula to capture the essence of the flower in a bottle. Since turning sixteen, my father procures one every year for my birthday." She stopped in front of the mercantile door and held her wrist up for him to smell. "What do you think?"

Jason inhaled the scent he would forever associate with Victoria. "Lovely."

Victoria's smile bloomed, fully satisfied with his answer as the inflection on the word told her far more than he realized.

Moments later, while perusing the various shades of floss, Victoria asked, as casually as she could, "Perhaps I could meet you tomorrow at the boarding house for another game of chess? To break our tie, of course." She paused before adding, "Chess and dinner?"

He grinned. "Or perhaps, dinner and chess."

She returned his grin. "Yes, dinner and chess."

She made her purchase and Jason walked them home. He declined her invitation to come in wanting to keep his attraction in check. He feared it was a losing battle.

Chapter 8

Thursday morning, Victoria coerced Lydia into walking the length of town, needing a way to work off her nervous energy. Glimpses of the wharf were visible between the buildings lining Front Street. They noticed Max's ship was tied to Mr. Greene's dock. Victoria smiled thinking Abby must be happy to have him back on shore again. At the end of Front Street, they encountered Betsy on an errand to get more thread.

The three greeted each other enthusiastically under the bright morning sun before Betsy's expression turned somber. "Have you seen Abby this morning?"

Victoria shook her head. "No."

Betsy's lips pursed. "I was wondering if she and Max reconciled."

"Reconciled? Betsy, I beg of you, tell me to what are you referring?"

"They had a very heated argument in front of the mercantile yesterday and then parted ways."

"And what was the argument pertaining?"

Betsy shook her head. "I am not sure. I didn't witness it. My customers were all too eager to share the gossip. They called it a 'lover's quarrel'. I really like Abby and Captain Max is a good man. I sure hope they can work out their differences and find happiness with each other."

Victoria could well imagine her friends were arguing, but in the middle of the street was unseemly for either Max or Abby. Victoria turned, linking her arm with Betsy, and started walking. "I couldn't agree with you more. Thank you for sharing. I think I'll invite Abby to tea this afternoon to learn her side of it."

Betsy smiled. Knowing Victoria, she would have the full story within five minutes of speaking with Abby, and then spend the rest of the afternoon devising a scheme to help her. Betsy parted company from Victoria in front of the mercantile.

Passing by Mr. Greene's wharf, Victoria paused to look at the *Mystic*. Max was on deck directing his men. It sounded like they were loading supplies. Guessing Abby might need a sympathetic shoulder to lean on, Victoria and Lydia extended their walk to visit her. Arriving at Abby's home, Mrs. Baxley directed Victoria to the Captain's Walk while Lydia waited downstairs. Maria was out on an errand so she and Mrs. Baxley chatted in the parlour.

Abby appeared at the hatch opening. She held out her hand to assist Victoria over the edge - always a tricky maneuver with long skirts. Victoria couldn't help but notice the sadness in Abby's eyes. For someone who was normally cheerful, it was a marked difference. Looking closer she saw telltale signs of crying. "Abby, what is the matter?"

Abby tried to dismiss her concern.

Victoria gave her a stern look. "You know I won't give up asking until you tell me."

Abby's smile turned watery as the tears started to well again. She visibly worked to control her emotions before plaintively saying, "I love Max."

Victoria waited but Abby didn't say more. "Well, of course you do, but why are you crying?"

Abby gave her a puzzled look. "He does not love me."

Victoria couldn't help her grin. "Of course he does. What would make you think he doesn't?" Just then a frequent visitor to Abby's observatory swooped over Victoria's head. "Oh!" She instinctively ducked down and twisted sideways to keep her eye on the huge bird. Up close and personal, pelicans were quite intimidating. "What is wrong with your pet?"

Abby gave her a wry smile. "You are standing where he likes to perch."

"Well by all means, let me get out of his way." Victoria moved to the other side of Abby and warily watched, Percy, the pelican circle several times.

"He said he did not."

Victoria was momentarily lost in the conversation due to the distracting bird. She cast a puzzled glance to her friend for clarification.

"Max said he does not love me. In the middle of the street, no less, and he has been avoiding me."

Percy finally settled on the railing instantly making Victoria feel more at ease. She turned her full attention to Abby and frowned. Something didn't make sense. She had never known Max to lie and she was positive he loved Abby. "What exactly did he say?"

Abby thought back to his response. "I never said I loved you, Abby."

Victoria was relieved but kept her voice level. "He hasn't said 'I love you', has he?"

Abby shook her head in despair, "No"

Victoria looked her in the eye, "But he also hasn't said 'I don't love you.'"

Abby looked at her with guarded hope.

"He can't say it because he does love you. He just hasn't admitted it to himself yet. Apparently, you have just realized how you feel." Abby nodded. "Sometimes, it takes men longer. Especially when they have no intention of falling in love in the first place. They fight against it. You just have to show him, it's not a bad thing."

"I tried to tell him…"

Victoria shook her head. "Uh-huh. I said show him. Reasoning isn't going to work. But first you have another problem."

"I do?"

"Part of Max's problem is he didn't get to complete the courting ritual."

Abby frowned, "What do you mean?"

"First there's interest—you both felt it—then there is the chase and then the prize of winning your hand in marriage."

"I do not understand. He won my hand. We are married."

Victoria shook her head. "No. He didn't win your hand. You were handed to him with a 'take her or she'll go to someone else' threat."

"Worse. He had to accept me or lose his ship."

Victoria didn't believe that was the case, but she didn't want to get off point debating it. "Regardless, he may have chosen to marry you, but he didn't chase you. And he didn't chase you, because he didn't make the decision to choose you and therefore to chase you."

Abby shook her head in confusion. "Tria, you are going in circles!"

"You have to make him want to be married to you by getting him to chase you."

"How am I supposed to get him to chase me?"

Victoria smiled mischievously. "By playing hard to get."

Abby gave her a skeptical look. "How do I play hard to get when we are already married?"

"By ignoring him. Make him work for your attention. Withhold your affections. Desire is a very strong motivator."

"And how can I do any of this when he is away from home or avoiding me?"

Victoria's brow furrowed. "Um, that is a problem."

They were interrupted by Maria's call from the bottom of the stairs. "Mrs. Abby, will you come down from there? I have something I need to tell you."

Victoria asked, "Why doesn't she come up here?"

"I tried to get her to when we first moved in, but she is afraid of heights." Abby maneuvered onto the stairs. "Coming Maria." At the bottom she turned to her distraught maid. "What is it? Has something happened?"

Maria was so upset she spoke rapidly—her Jamaican accent thickened—making it difficult for Abby to understand her. "No, nothing bad. At least not yet. I heard men talking in town. They are going to do something bad. Somehow the Captain is involved. I heard them say his name."

Victoria stepped off the ladder behind Abby. "Who were the men?"

"I didn't know one of them, but the other was the man from the shipwreck."

Victoria looked to Abby for enlightenment.

Abby asked Maria, "Our shipwreck?"

"Yes. The other captain. The one who took your chest."

Abby's hand flew to her throat in alarm. "Captain Talmage?" Maria nodded. "Did he see you?"

Maria nervously answered, "Maybe. I'm not sure. He looked behind him just before I turned the corner, but I am just a maid. He probably didn't pay me any attention."

Abby was pensive. "We cannot trust that he did not notice you. Maria, right now, while it is fresh in your mind, we should write down everything you can remember hearing."

Victoria and Maria followed Abby to the office downstairs where she sat down at the desk, took out a fresh piece of paper, and dipped the pen in ink, poised to write.

Abby looked to her maid. "Now Maria, start at the beginning. What was the first thing you heard?"

"I don't know which one but one of them said, 'Will Captain Eatonton be a problem again?' Then the stranger wanted to know how to find Alligator reef. The captain wanted to know why they had to wreck the ship, why not just meet. The stranger said they had to damage the ship in case someone passes by 'cause the reefs are always..." Maria paused to think, "I don't remember the word he used."

Abby said, "You are doing fine, Maria. What else?"

"Captain Talmage told him not to wreck the ship 'til he was there. Then he asked him the name of the ship. The stranger said it was the *Anna Rose*."

Abby's gaze flew to Maria in alarm. "You are sure he said, '*Anna Rose*'?" Maria nodded her head yes. Abby asked, "Did he say anything else?"

"The stranger said, 'they would stop here first,' and 'Monday next,' and he asked Captain Talmage if he was worried about clear weather, but I didn't hear his answer. That's all I heard ma'am."

Victoria asked, "Maria, what did the stranger look like?"

"Dark hair, lanky, taller than the Captain. Oh and he was missing part of his thumb," Maria held up her right hand, "on this hand."

Victoria nodded her approval. "Excellent observation, Maria."

Abby read over what she had written, then looked to Victoria. "We should take this to the marshal, right away."

Victoria shook her head. "He won't believe us. It will be our word against Captain Talmage. I hate to say this, but we are only women. Our word does not count for much. He won't be able to do anything about it, anyway. The crime hasn't happened, and he doesn't have jurisdiction over the reefs."

Abby saw her point. "It is too bad Max has left. He would want to know about this."

Victoria was surprised Abby was unaware of her husband's proximity. "He hasn't left yet. I saw his ship tied at the dock a little while ago."

Abby frowned.

Victoria was sure if Jason were here, he would suggest they do something reasonable, like going to the marshal anyway, but Victoria had another agenda in mind. Her smile spread. The more she thought about it, the more she liked her idea. "This is the answer to your problem, Abby."

Abby looked at her questioningly.

"You need Max to stop ignoring you. Max needs to know what Talmage is planning. You should go to him."

Abby gasped, "I could not."

"Go to him," encouraged Victoria. "Get yourself on his ship, preferably for a few days, and then hold yourself aloof. You are simply there to share information, not yourself. Show no emotional interest on your part. Then, and you will know when, give him a look, but make it quick so he wonders if he saw it at all."

Abby shook her head. "I do not think I could do that. I wear my heart on my sleeve. Besides, he got really angry the last time I was determined to go after him."

Sagely, Victoria said, "This time you have a practical reason, not an emotional one. Men really don't like emotions. They're complicated and they get in the way."

Abby was silent a few moments but then her chin firmed. "All right. Maria and I will go to his ship and tell Max, but I still think we need to tell the marshal too." Abby stood up from the desk, holding the paper. "Let me retrieve my hat and gloves, and we will leave directly."

They promptly left the house, Lydia included, and walked two by two down Simonton Street; the ladies in front and the maids behind. As they approached Front Street, Victoria felt Abby stiffen. Following her gaze, she saw Captain Talmage standing on the corner, as if waiting for them. A shiver of ominous foreboding ran down her spine.

Talmage bowed to them. "Good morning ladies. Lovely day for a walk isn't it?"

Outwardly he projected a gentlemanly demeanor, but Victoria sensed an underlying malevolence. Well, she would show him they were not withering females he could easily frighten. Exaggerating her southern accent, Victoria cheerfully replied, "Why it certainly is, Captain Talmage. Don't we have such lovely tropical weather in the middle of winter? Why back in Charleston, I would be shivering in front of the fireplace this time of year instead of enjoying the sunshine, and I do so love a warm afternoon stroll. You have a nice day now, Captain Talmage."

Victoria nudged Abby who finally found her voice to echo, "Good day, Captain."

They tried to act like they were having a normal conversation with each other as they continued walking towards the wharf.

Maria nervously whispered, "I think he is following us."

Victoria stopped them in front of the next store window and pretended to point out something of interest to Abby while they were really watching Talmage's reflection in the glass. He was on the other side of the street, and had stopped also, ostensibly to speak with a sailor.

Victoria said, "If Talmage is suspicious, maybe it's best if we wait until he's gone for you to go to Max. Let's go into the mercantile and see what he does."

They walked past the next few buildings bringing them past the last warehouse on the other side of the street and finally allowing a view of the dock. Abby discretely looked over, and to her dismay, discovered the *Mystic* was pulling away from the dock. "Oh no!" She whispered to Victoria, "We have a problem. Max is leaving. We will have to come up with another plan."

They entered the general store and gathered around a front table holding sewing notions where they had a clear view of the street, but to an onlooker, they appeared to be shopping. The *Mystic* had cleared the dock now. Talmage was casually strolling past the last warehouse, and the marshal could be seen coming out of one of the warehouses behind him. The two men stopped to speak to each other.

Victoria said, "Now what do we do?"

Abby said, "You are sure the marshal would not believe us?"

Victoria didn't even hesitate. "I'm sure. Even if he did, he is not going to do anything on hearsay."

Abby suddenly grabbed Victoria's arm and pulled her from the store. "I have a plan."

The ladies left the store *en masse* headed away from Talmage and the marshal. Abby called a passing errand boy to her. Puzzled, Victoria could only watch as Abby gave the boy a whispered message and a coin, and then a second coin in exchange for his cap. As the boy ran off, and they resumed walking, Abby said, "We need to see Betsy."

Victoria said, "What was that about?"

"I'll explain everything when we are safely off the street."

Betsy greeted them in her front parlour. "What a nice surprise to see you ladies. Welcome."

Abby quickly returned her greeting, and then asked, "Do you have any ready-made clothes appropriate for a cabin-boy of my size?"

Betsy looked at her questioningly. "I might. I'll go look." A moment later she came back with a shirt, trousers, and socks. "Will this do?"

"Yes." Abby took the clothes from her and rushed to the changing screen set up in the corner of the room used for fittings.

Victoria had no idea what Abby had in mind, but if she was dressing as a boy, it was bound to be interesting.

Guessing Abby would be wearing long ones, Betsy held up a pair of short pantaloons. "Will you be needing these as well?"

Abby looked up then reached for the underwear. "Yes, thank

you."

As she changed, Abby hurriedly told them her plan. "Captain Graham owns a fishing smack down by the beach. I sent the boy to give him a message to not leave until I speak to him of an urgent matter. I stitched up his hand a while back, and I am hoping he will still feel grateful enough to take me out to Max's ship. To get past Talmage, I am going to dress as a cabin boy and sneak out the back way to meet Captain Graham. Meanwhile, Betsy, will you help us by leaving with the others so Talmage sees four women leave here?" Betsy nodded in agreement. "That should keep me safe. Maria, I do not think it wise for both of us to try and get to the ship. However, I fear Talmage may suspect you overheard him, so I want you to stay with Tria until I return."

Victoria couldn't find any fault with the plan. In fact, she whole-heartedly approved, as it would most likely mean, Max and Abby would be stuck with each other's company for a few days. "Sounds good to me. Just be careful getting to the ship. What will you do if Captain Graham won't help?"

Abby emerged from the screen. "I guess I will have to make my way to your house. What do you think? It will not pass a close inspection since I did not bind my chest, and I will have to wear my own shoes, but will it work from a distance?"

Victoria looked her over critically as Abby turned. The shirt was a tunic with a string closure at the neck. The short pants revealed her shapely calf muscles. "Your profile gives you away, but otherwise, from a distance, you should be fine."

Betsy excused herself and left the room while Abby sat down to put on the socks and her boots.

Maria asked, "What about your hair?"

Abby's hair was in a bun at the base of her neck. She pulled it free and then secured it in a knot on top of her head before putting on the wide-brimmed sailor's hat she borrowed from the errand boy. "Well?"

Victoria said, "It will have to do."

Betsy returned with a drawstring sack. "To put your dress and undergarments in. I added some other items you may need." She handed it to Abby, then picked up her discarded dress and carefully folded it. Abby passed the bag to Maria who held it open for Betsy to place the clothes inside. Abby took Maria's account from her reticule, tucked it into her corset, and then added the reticule to the sack.

Maria returned the sack to Abby. "Take care, Mrs. Abby. Tell

Thomas I'll be safe."

"I will." She turned to Victoria. "I hope you are right." Both knew Abby was referring to Victoria's earlier advice concerning Max.

"I am. Trust me. Now hurry! A smack is going to have a hard time catching Max's clipper."

Abby hugged each of her friends before leaving out the back door. Betsy covered her dark hair in the simplest bonnet she could find and walked out the front door with Victoria, Lydia, and a very worried Maria.

Victoria said in a hushed whisper, "Don't look back. We mustn't give Talmage any reason to suspect something is amiss. Betsy keep your face turned toward mine, so he can't see you clearly. Natural ladies. We must act natural."

Maria said, "I hope all goes well for Mrs. Abby. How will we know if she makes it to Captain Max?"

Victoria said, "We'll know she made it if she doesn't return."

Maria said, "But what if Captain Talmage catches her?"

Betsy said, "We must trust in Providence to keep her safe."

Victoria had one other concern to dispense with. She flagged down an errand boy and sent him to the boardinghouse with a message for Lord Jason that she regrettably was not going to be able to meet him as planned.

Fortunately, they made it to Victoria's house without running into Captain Talmage. While that was good for them, Victoria secretly worried it may bode ill for Abby. "Maria is staying here at Abby's request. Might I suggest, Betsy, that you do the same for tonight?"

"Nonsense, I have a business to attend to. I must get back to my shop. If you will recall, I left my shingle 'open' to further the illusion."

"Then at least wait long enough to have a cup of tea, and for Talmage to grow impatient, if he is, perchance, watching the house."

Lydia said, "I'll go fetch the tea." Maria followed her.

Mrs. Lambert came into the parlour as they left. "Hello, Mrs. Wheeler. How nice to have you join us for tea. It has been a long time."

"Yes ma'am. I am afraid my business does not allow much time for social calls."

Mrs. Lambert nodded, "I can imagine so. Well, I'm glad you are making time today. Please have a seat."

The three of them sat down, but the suspense was worrying Victoria. "Excuse me for a moment." She hurried from the parlour, up the stairs, to the unoccupied bedroom across from hers with a southern window. She couldn't see much of Front Street, but at least what she could see, revealed nothing untoward. She crossed the house to her bedroom window. Again, there was no one in sight. Back down the stairs she went, to the front window to the left of the front door, and peered out in the same manner as when she was watching for Jason. No one was in sight. At least Betsy should be safe to return home.

Chapter 9

Victoria woke up Friday morning still feeling a lingering thrill from yesterday's excitement. She couldn't wait to tell Jason, so even though they didn't have plans, she decided to take a chance of catching him at the boardinghouse. First, she had to impatiently wait for a decent hour to call. She intended to leave around eleven, but by ten, she could wait no longer. She called for Lydia, grabbed her parasol, and set out on a brisk pace down Front Street. When she realized Lydia was having trouble keeping up, she made a valiant attempt to slow down.

It was only three blocks to the boardinghouse, but it felt like ten to Victoria. Her nerves were overwrought, as they finally approached the front steps. A sailor exiting the building mumbled a greeting to them as he passed. It gave her a half second of reservation about the impropriety of her mission. Victoria opened the door with a confident smile on her face. She entered the large foyer and hesitated. It opened to a parlour on one side, and a dining room on the other, both of which had lingering gentlemen guests. Jason was not among them. What was she to do now? She hadn't thought this through.

Even if she knew which room was his, it would be highly improper for her to knock on his door. An unattached lady simply didn't call on a gentleman. It would be scandalous. Seeing Mrs. Mallory's approach from the rear of the house made her panic. What could she say to the matron that wouldn't get her in trouble with her parents? Ideas were whirling and discarded through her mind with dizzying rapidity.

Mrs. Mallory stopped in front of her and smiled. "Good morning to ye, Miss Lambert."

"Good morning, Mrs. Mallory."

Cheerfully she asked, "What brings ye here this fine morn?"

Victoria couldn't think of anything to offer but the truth. "I am here to see Lord Malwbry." Any hope of not being questioned was immediately dashed.

The matron didn't frown but her smile disappeared into concern. "Tis he expecting you?"

Oh dear, what to say? Yes, and Jason could reveal her deceit, or he may not be in at all, and she would appear to have been stood up. No, and she risked the appearance of a trollop. Aware of the other men nearby, she made her decision. "Yes." She reasoned that it was not entirely a falsehood. He was expecting her—yesterday.

"Pardon me while I inform him of your arrival." Mrs. Mallory lifted her skirts to ascend the stairs.

Victoria's heart fell, when a few moments later, Mrs. Mallory reappeared alone at the top of the stairs. As she waited for Mrs. Mallory's descent, she happened to see Jason's approach from the far side of the dining room. She turned to him with a radiant smile on her face, and a silent plea in her eyes to not betray her.

Jason was on his way back to his room when he was surprised to discover Victoria in the foyer. He met her widened eyes and saw the plea for help. It took him but a moment to assess the situation and realize it would bode ill for Victoria's reputation if he did not collaborate with her.

He approached Victoria with a smile. "My apologies, Miss Lambert, if I kept you waiting."

Relief flooded Victoria. "Not at all, sir."

The planned game of chess from yesterday under the watchful eye of Mrs. Mallory did not appeal to Jason. He could only think of one other acceptable activity. "Would you care for a stroll?"

It was as if he read her mind. "A stroll would be lovely."

Jason stepped to the door and held it open for Victoria and Lydia to precede him. The disapproving look on Mrs. Mallory's face clung to his mind, reinforcing his belief that Victoria would make a poor duchess. Once they were a few paces from the boardinghouse, he broke the silence between them. "What were you thinking? A lady shouldn't call on a gentleman. It isn't proper."

Victoria was hurt by his tone and lashed back at him. "How is today any different from our plans of yesterday?"

Jason gave her a sideways look trying to determine if she was really that naive or playing some kind of game with him. "Yesterday you were invited. Do you know how it would have looked if I hadn't been there? It would have damaged your reputation."

"Oh fiddlesticks! My reputation has been bruised before. It would have passed."

His frown deepened. *How could she have such little regard for her reputation?* Morally, he was concerned by her lack of propriety but as a man, her boldness intrigued him. He had never met a woman like Victoria. Abigail's behaviour may have been rash but her actions were still tempered with reserve. Abigail pushed the limits of society's boundaries but Victoria broke them. Life with her would never be boring. But then again, for all intents and purposes, they were having a disagreement. It brought to mind his parents and the life he didn't want.

Victoria kept speaking in the hopes her story might distract him from whatever was causing the awful frown on his face. "You wouldn't believe what happened yesterday. I just had to tell you. I was visiting Abby when her maid returned to the house in distress. She overheard two men threatening Max. We couldn't go to the sheriff, so Betsy helped us divert Captain Talmage's attention while Abby, dressed as a boy, snuck past him, and with the help of a friendly captain, hopefully made her way to Max's ship to warn him. Trying to keep Captain Talmage from suspecting anything, Betsy returned to my house for tea, and so I missed our appointment."

Jason wasn't paying attention to her first few words, but what he did hear disturbed him greatly. He didn't know where to begin unravelling all the frightening concerns he was experiencing. He stopped walking and shook his head. "You did what?" His voice was sharper than he intended, but he wasn't surprised. As if the scene in the boardinghouse wasn't enough of a shock, now this fantastic story. No. She would never make a suitable duchess, but he had more pressing concerns now. He needed to sort out this tale, and ensure all the ladies involved were safe. "Let's go to your house and you can tell me the story from the beginning."

Horror flashed across Victoria's face before she could contain it. Her mother mustn't hear this tale. She gave Jason a cajoling smile. "I have a better idea. Let's go to Betsy's shop. It's nearby."

Jason recalled she had mentioned Betsy, so the seamstress would be one of the ladies of concern. It would suit his purposes as well to head to her place, but Victoria didn't fool him. He could well imagine her mother had no idea what her daughter was involved in. Betsy's shop was only a few houses away around the corner on Whitehead Street. Her shingle was turned to open so they entered after knocking.

Victoria took a few hurried steps into the front room calling out, "Betsy! Betsy! Are you here?"

The petite brunette with bright blue eyes appeared from the back room. "Victoria! I am here and all is well. You can lower your voice."

"Thank goodness. Did you have any trouble getting home?"

"None at all. I didn't see anyone."

Jason looked from one lady to the other. The high color of their cheeks suggested they rather enjoyed their *risqué* clandestine activities. He supposed one couldn't blame them when most days were dreadfully routine. "Now that we have a modicum of privacy, I would ask, Miss Lambert, for you to tell me the whole story, in detail, if you please."

Victoria found it endearing the way Jason acted all lordly when he was really trying to hide his true feelings of concern.

Betsy raised the counter opening separating her front room dress shop from the rest of her house so her guests could enter the parlour. "Please make yourselves comfortable."

Jason nodded as he passed. "Thank you, Mrs. Wheeler."

"Would you care for some refreshments?"

Victoria's, "Yes, please," overlapped Jason's, "No, thank you."

Betsy waited for their consensus.

Jason resigned himself to waiting a few moments longer. "Refreshments would be nice."

Without a word, Lydia followed Betsy to the outdoor kitchen to assist leaving Jason and Victoria momentarily alone. Victoria wished the mood between them was different. Oh, how she longed to pick up where they left off two days ago with that almost kiss in her foyer. Unfortunately, the tension emanating from Jason was anything but amorous. She wondered why he was so upset. He was carefully avoiding eye contact with her, so she settled on the sofa without speaking to await Betsy and Lydia's return.

Once the tea and biscuits were served, Jason looked to Victoria expectantly. She took another sip of tea and began with her visit to Abby. Although the conversation with her friend was pivotal in the motivation to get Abby aboard the *Mystic*, Victoria had no intention of relaying it to Jason. "Abby and I were chatting when Maria returned from her errand quite upset. It seems she overheard a disturbing conversation between Captain Talmage, a former adversary of the Eatonton's, and another stranger, threatening Captain Max. As you can imagine, Abby was anxious to get word of this to her husband, but there was a frightening concern of what would happen if Captain Talmage caught her, so she disguised herself as a boy in order to sneak aboard his ship before it left the harbor. The rest of us left the dress shop, Betsy included, to keep Captain Talmage from suspecting anything."

Jason's gaze pierced hers with a sharp intensity strongly conveying his disapproval. His words were acute, "Putting aside why you ladies considered such an undertaking to be your only course of action, are you certain Abigail made it safely aboard the *Mystic*?"

Victoria's brow furrowed in dismay. Perhaps his feelings for Abby were unchanged, and she was merely a distraction for him. "I have no reason to believe she didn't."

"But you didn't see her."

He said it as a statement, not a question, but she softly answered anyway, "No."

Jason mumbled, "Someone must know." He looked up at the other ladies, "How did Abigail reach his ship?"

Betsy said, "A fishing captain took her. Someone she knew. Victoria, do you recall his name?"

"Grant... Gardiner..." she shook her head, "something that starts with a G."

Betsy's smile bloomed. "Graham. Captain Graham. She said he has a fishing smack."

Jason nodded, "And her maid, Maria, is she safe?"

Victoria nodded, "Yes."

Jason rose and bowed to Betsy. "Thank you for your hospitality. I will walk Victoria home, and then see if I can find this captain, and ascertain that Abigail indeed made it to her husband." He held out his hand to assist Victoria.

She wasn't ready to leave, but his set face warned her not to protest. It also cut a wound in her heart. He obviously still cared a great deal for Abby. She gave Betsy a weak smile. "Thank you."

Seeing the emotional distress in her friend's darkened irises, Betsy gave her a quick kiss on the cheek. "I'm sure Abby is fine." The momentary flash of puzzlement in Victoria's eyes told Betsy she made the wrong assumption. Victoria was upset about something other than Abby. Unfortunately, there was no time to ask. She gave a nod to Jason as he silently followed Victoria out the door.

Jason's brisk pace as he escorted her home heightened Victoria's distress. He was showing little regard for her, and it rankled; more than she wanted to admit. Her feelings for him were in danger of being trampled, and she was helpless to prevent it. His feelings may have diminished, but she couldn't control her desire for him any more than she could stop breathing, which was becoming difficult with his riotous pace. As usual, her hand was curved around his bicep. She pulled slightly against him feeling the muscle tense beneath her fingers. He gave her a sharp glance, but immediately understood her silent request and slowed his pace.

Within minutes they traversed the short distance of Front Street from Whitehead back to Simonton. Jason walked her up the steps to the front door, but when she turned to invite him in, he said good day to her, pivoted on his heel, and quickly left. For the first time her confidence in the outcome of their relationship faltered.

Jason knowingly left Victoria, standing in her doorway, confused and dismayed. His concern for Abigail was only part of the reason. Day by day his attraction to Victoria, and in reciprocal her attraction to him, deepened. It would be cruel to both of them to encourage feelings between them when the outcome was certain disappointment, or worse, devastation on her part. He cared too much to subject her to such cruelty. The pain she might feel from this day's parting was better for both of them.

He came to this conclusion yesterday, as he listened to the errand boy deliver Victoria's message. He was unexpectedly and deeply disappointed. He didn't realize how much he was looking forward to another challenging game of chess in the company of her vibrant allure. She garnered his affections like no other, despite his best efforts to put her aside.

He shook his head in wonder at the suddenness of it all.

One week, that was all it took for Victoria to become the center of his thoughts. Her warm brown eyes drew him in and her plump lips enticed him to all manner of impropriety. The girl herself showed no hesitation in following him. In any other, it would have seemed wantonly, but Victoria was not wanton. He was sure she was feeling the same strong, unbreakable attraction that he felt. It was explosive and heady whenever they were together.

And addictive.

His certainty that she was not to be his wife hadn't changed. To protect them both, he had to put distance between them.

And so, he came to realize, her note was also a relief. Instead of having to extricate himself from further plans she was sure to suggest after their game of chess, he could easily withdraw from her society by simply avoiding her, and thereby avoid any uncomfortable and awkward explanations. Unfortunately, she thwarted his plan with her unexpected arrival at the boardinghouse this morning and her fantastic tale of yesterday.

He set out with her to ensure the safety of those involved, starting with the seamstress. Nothing more and nothing less. Having done so, he planned to find Captain Graham to ensure Abigail was safely aboard the *Mystic*. Doing so did not require Victoria's assistance which gave him the opportunity to cut his ties with her for both their sakes.

He didn't take into account how the hurt look in her honey-brown gaze would affect him. He nearly changed his mind. Even though he was resolved, he still had to clench his fist to keep from reaching out to touch her one last time. Turning from her was the hardest thing he had ever done.

* * *

How could finding one man on a tiny island be so difficult?

After leaving Victoria, Jason walked down to the beach where the fishing boats occupied the shallow side of the harbor. He found it practically deserted. Realizing it was mid-morning, of course, all the fishing smacks were gone; the captains were out fishing. Forced to wait till their return in the late afternoon, he returned to the boardinghouse.

Boredom soon overtook him. He wished he could relieve it with a visit to Victoria. Time always flew when he was with her. But of course, seeing her was not an option. Instead, he engaged a fellow boarder to a game of chess which he lost since his mind was elsewhere.

When Jason checked his watch to find it was finally a little after four, he gladly left the boardinghouse. With a flick of his wrist, and a lift of his arm, he dropped the top hat on his head. He stepped off the porch dressed in his usual shirt, vest, and trousers. He did forego the jacket in deference to the heat.

As he approached the beach, this time he could hear the shouts of sailors before he rounded the last building to see boats being unloaded on shore and at the nearby wharf. The men were hard at work in various tasks: unloading, hauling buckets, repairing sail and nets, sharpening knives, and other things he couldn't identify.

He walked up to the closest group of ragged fishermen and used the greeting he had often heard on his sail from England, "Ahoy!" The word felt strange on his tongue and sounded even stranger to his ear.

A second of silence was followed by raucous guffaws.

Jason's mouth dropped. He had never been laughed at before. It was unsettling and perturbing to say the least. He cleared his throat in a manner that would have had his Midanbury servants snapping to attention but phased naught these plunderers of the sea. Deciding it was best to ignore their merriment, he spoke with authority, "Where can I find Captain Graham?"

The eldest of them narrowed his eyes with a hint of suspicion. "We don't know no Captain Graham."

The glances tossed between them gave lie to his words.

The youngest said with a grin. "Weren't he the bloke, what sailed for Cuba yesterday?"

Another looking a bit friendlier said, "What do you want with the captain?"

Jason was relieved at least one of them knew how to be civil. "He knows the whereabouts of Miss Bennington."

All of them turned their attention to him, but three chimed in together, "We don't know a Miss Bennington." One of them continued with avid interest, "What's she look like?"

Jason sighed. Of course these men would be more interested in a woman; there were so few of them around. And so few would mean they would recognize this one. "She has reddish hair and grey eyes. A real lady. She's been here a few months."

"Sounds like Mrs. Eatonton."

The eldest of the group said, "Son, you aught naught to be chasing married womens."

"Didn't I see you steppin' out with Miz Lambert the other day?"

The young one said with admiration, "Tristin' with two womens at the same time."

Several more chimed in with ribald comments.

They wouldn't listen any further. Jason's frustration grew with their belligerence. He was getting nowhere with these men. He tried a few other smaller groups on the beach, but they were too involved with their work, and treated him like an intruder and an unwelcome interruption.

He decided it would be best to wait till later when their work was done, and they had a little brew in them to mellow their feelings. An hour later, he followed one group of fishermen into a bar. They were young sailors and entirely too rowdy to pay him any attention despite several attempts. Fortunately, the bartender quietly suggested he try the tavern two doors down preferred by the older sea men. He gave the man a tip and followed his advice. There he found a row of seamen, with varying heads of thinning grey hair, sidled up to the bar, quietly talking, and seriously drinking tankards of ale. They ignored him too until he offered to buy a round of drinks.

One captain looking friendlier than the others said, "Tweren't you down t' the beach lookin' for some-un?"

Seven pairs of eyes swiveled in his direction. Jason gave a nod, "Aye."

The friendly captain's face brightened. "Ah yes, the lovely Mrs. Eatonton." His aged brow furrowed low over his sharp eyes. "Captain Max is a friend o' mine. Don't take kindly to you messin' with what's his."

Every one of his comrades was ready to stand with the friendly captain in defense of Mrs. Eatonton's honor. "You misunderstand my intentions, sir."

A lanky captain at the other end of the bar bitterly asked, "How so?"

Jason realized he had to plead his case with the entire group. "I am in search of Captain Graham."

The friendly captain asked, "What business do ya have with him?"

Another piped in, "What's Graham got to do with Max's lady?"

Jason focused on the friendly captain. "He can confirm Mrs. Eatonton's safety."

The middle man leaned forward. A pair of faded blue eyes seem to search Jason's soul as he asked, "And what business is that of yourn's?"

Jason realized these men would need most of the story if he was to gain their trust. "I am a family friend. I have known Mrs. Eatonton since childhood. She and Miss Lambert got themselves mixed up in some foolishness with a Captain Talmage and felt the need to have Captain Graham sneak Mrs. Eatonton out to her husband's ship. If she is with Captain Max, then all is well, and I will be on my way home. But, think sir, what if she was waylaid from reaching her husband? He would be unaware of her plight. I doubt that is the case, but it seems only prudent to confirm it with Captain Graham."

The friendly captain's eyes lightened. He nodded in agreement. "Aye."

Jason saw a wealth of understanding in his gaze and heard it in the single word. Though he hadn't said much, he felt the man had grasped the whole situation.

"I'm Captain Simms, and you be?"

"Jason Malwbry."

He turned to his comrades. "Has anyone seen Captain Graham of late?"

They all looked blankly at each other.

Captain Simms stepped down from his bar stool after draining off the last of his ale. "Follow me. I'll take you to Graham's boat."

After the ordeal of finding the elusive Captain Graham, the result was a bit anti-climactic. The sun was nearly set when Captain Simms had one of his men row them out to Captain Graham's sloop. Every stroke of the oars accentuated Jason's worry of what to do if Abigail hadn't reached Max. Finally, they were alongside the ship where the smell of old wood, tar, and wet hemp blended with the salty air. It took several calls before the disheveled man appeared on deck. They had apparently awoken him. Jason promptly stated his quest to which Captain Graham replied, "Aye, she is aboard the *Mystic*." He then turned away, effectively dismissing them. Jason breathed a sigh of relief. His quest was complete.

They returned to shore and Jason thanked Captain Simms for his assistance. He thought he should let Victoria know Abigail was safe, but it was too late to call on her. It would wait until tomorrow. Tired, he returned to the boardinghouse.

* * *

Late Saturday morning, Jason left the boardinghouse under an overcast sky with patches of blue and filtered sunlight. He walked to the Lambert's with mixed feelings. He was looking forward to seeing Victoria even knowing he would have to keep a tight rein on his emotions.

Abigail's maid, Maria, opened the door and showed him to the parlour. Mrs. Lambert laid down her embroidery and rose to greet him. Victoria entered the room in a stunning Prussian blue dress with a wide neckline. Although her chest was decently covered, it left most of her exquisite neck and shoulders bare. The color nicely contrasted with her flushed skin, dark honeyed eyes, and kissable apricot lips. Jason was enthralled. He had to mentally shake himself to pull his eyes away from her as he recalled her mother's presence beside him. His emotional distress made his greeting stiff. He knew she noticed by the confusion he saw in her eyes. He stepped to the side so she could enter the room, but she hesitated.

"You still owe me a chess match to break our tie. The sun is chasing away the clouds. Shall we play out on the piazza?"

Jason glanced at Mrs. Lambert and seeing no objection from her turned back to Victoria. "As you wish." He could survive one last friendly game of chess.

The board was set up in their usual place on the right side of the front piazza. Maria and Lydia occupied the rush woven rocking chairs on the left side; one shelling peas and the other darning socks, to act as chaperones.

Jason tried to focus on the game, but his gaze kept wandering to her animated face. He was fascinated by her deep concentration, her smirk when she discovered a clever move, and the victory when she claimed one of his pieces. More than once, upon his turn, he would have no idea what move she had made. In the end, of course, she won. Her smile of satisfaction imprinted on his soul. He must have hid his inattention well enough, since she didn't accuse him of throwing the game.

He rose to his feet and reached to pick up a few pieces. She followed suit. Keeping in mind their agreement to be friends, they were careful not to touch, but that only seemed to emphasize the need to do so. When they were done with the task, he lifted his eyes to hers. He was caught as effectively as a fish in a net. She viscerally pulled him to her. Everything else faded away. It was only him and her, and his overwhelming need to know if her lips felt as soft as they looked. He leaned toward her. She leaned toward him. Her lids lowered and her lips softly parted.

The creak of a rocking chair behind him broke the spell. He promptly stepped away. Jason was determined to put the moment from his mind. He hoped she was thinking the same. He desperately wanted to kiss Victoria, but only an engaged couple was allowed to kiss, and they were far from engaged. He shook his head. They would never be engaged. He couldn't subject her free spirit to the rigors of the duchy, therefore, he could never ask for her hand in marriage. No engagement. No kisses. He would have to guard against any further moments of weakness. The only way to do that was to remain distant. These last two hours proved simple friendship with Victoria was not possible.

He mumbled an excuse to leave and made a hasty retreat. Walking home his head finally cleared. He realized he never told her of Abigail's safety which was his sole purpose for the visit. Perhaps he should send her a note. He certainly had no intention of repeating this afternoon's torture. His will was not strong enough to break from her again. Even as he walked away, he still felt pulled to return.

Victoria watched Jason walk away. Thrice now he had almost kissed her, and thrice they had been interrupted. Would she never know the feel of his lips pressed to hers?

* * *

Sunday morning Jason waited until the last minute to join the worship service at the custom house. He took up a place behind several other men standing in the back, so they would block his view of the other worshippers. He turned to leave almost before the final 'amen' was said, thereby avoiding even a glimpse of the lady haunting his dreams. If only he could bar her from his mind as easily, he could be more at peace. His fervent prayer was tomorrow he would find a ship to bring an end to his torture.

Victoria felt like stomping her foot in frustration. Jason was nowhere to be seen at church this morning. Now, she was committed to visiting a neighbor with her mother, and tonight they were entertaining her father's clients for dinner. She would have to wait until tomorrow for any hope of seeing Jason again.

* * *

Morning sun touched Jason's face chasing away the slumber that finally overtook him in the wee hours of the morning. He awoke ill-tempered and hungry. The second was easily resolved, but his mood was not likely to improve. A tour of the ship offices only increased his ire. No ships today. Plenty were arriving from across the Atlantic, but none were returning. He needed to get off this island and away from temptation before he lost the will to stay away from *her*.

Passing one of the bars he had visited in his search for Captain Graham, he was lured in by the thought of an afternoon drink to take the edge off his frustration. The room was long and narrow with the bar taking up most of the right side. It was simply made and sanded, but time and use had given it a polished smoothness. The building walls were unadorned bare wood, weathered grey on the outside, and a faded butter on the inside. A few tables and chairs were scattered about the room, but none lined the bar. Jason ordered a whiskey from the barkeep. He turned to survey the other patrons. Two tables were occupied with serious drinkers. In the far corner, a game of faro was taking place with three players crowding the banker and one hovering spectator. Jason thought about joining. He liked the fast paced game. When honestly played, the odds were better than most for players. Unfortunately, banker cheating was rampant to increase the house take. He decided to observe from afar rather than risk any of his remaining travel funds.

All of the men, including the banker, had the look of seasoned sailors. The players wore the authoritative manner of sea captains. The two on the right were well past their prime with thinning hair, more grey than blond, and weathered faces. The one on the left appeared to be a score younger with only a little grey fanning the temples of his dark hair. He was a large man, not in height but in breadth, and sturdily built.

At the end of the latest deal, the two older men groaned while the younger eagerly collected his winnings. The one in the middle said, "Talmage, you have the darndest luck."

Jason's gaze sharpened at the name. This was the man behind Abigail's quest to reach Max. As the next round started, Jason studied Captain Talmage. His beady dark eyes and Castilian nose would have made Jason distrust him even without the knowledge of his threat to Abigail's safety. Feeling the weight of Jason's stare, the man turned to look directly at him. Jason held his gaze. Talmage's eyes narrowed as if recalling an elusive memory. He turned his attention back to the game leaving Jason to wonder if Talmage knew him.

The rounds continued and Jason was only idly watching when he happened to notice a movement of Talmage's left arm and a flash of copper while the other players' attention was held by the observer. It didn't take much for Jason to figure out Talmage had pulled his copper token from the table that would have reversed his bet on the deuce turning what would have been a loss into a win. Unfortunately for Talmage, Jason wasn't the only one who noticed. The man on the far left took one look at the board and bound to his feet pointing his bony finger at the burly man. "You cheat!"

Talmage backed out of his chair in one swift motion to face his accuser with a six inch knife in his hand. For a heavy man, he could move fast. "What did you say?"

The observer sidled his way away from the other two captains. Jason would bet his bottom dollar the man was working with

Talmage. The banker also rose and stepped away from the table to press his back against the wall behind him. Only the middle player remained calmly seated, as if he was a curious observer, seemingly unconcerned with the knife or with being centered between escalating tempers.

The grey captain said, "You heard me. You palmed your copper. It was on the table before the draw and it's not there now."

The seated captain looked to his friend, "Careful Smyth."

Smyth threw an angry look at his friend. "You taking his side, Brantley?"

"Of course not."

Talmage fiercely stared at Smyth. "There was no copper. Call me a cheat again you old fool."

Brantley opened his mouth to intervene but it was too late.

Smyth glared at Talmage. "You're a liar and a cheat."

In a blink, the knife arced across the table and into Smyth's chest. Jaws dropped, including Smyth's. Brantley rose to catch his friend as his knees buckled. Talmage scooped up his chips and presented them to the banker who refused to budge from the wall. Talmage threw the chips at him and reached into the banker's box grabbing all the cash he could in one fistful, and then strode to the door, all before the barkeep came up from behind the counter with a shotgun. He fired a wild shot that went high into the doorframe. The observer, too, ran out before he could reload.

Brantley looked around the room. "Someone get Doc Waterhouse and the sheriff."

The barkeep motioned to a kid, Jason hadn't notice earlier, and sent him running out the door.

Jason walked to the captains. He was relieved to see the knife was in Smyth's shoulder and not his heart. "You know that has to come out." Smyth gave a bare nod in response. Brantley reached for it but Jason waived him off. "I have the better angle." He pulled his handkerchief from his pocket and knelt down beside the injured man. He neatly pulled the knife straight out with his left hand and quickly covered the wound with the folded linen in his right, applying pressure. He let the blade fall to the floor.

The three of them held their pose until the aging Dr. Waterhouse arrived some ten minutes later. Jason moved away to allow the doctor to examine the wound, removing the blood soaked handkerchief. When Jason looked down at his hand to see a blood covered palm, his stomach rolled, not because of the blood, but belatedly realizing, he had just witnessed an attempted murder. He turned to the barkeep who without a word gestured to a bucket of water at the end of the bar used for dish washing. He poured another shot of whiskey in Jason's glass and slide it down the bar for Jason to down when he was finished washing.

The sheriff and Mr. Lambert arrived a few moments later to investigate. Captain Smyth was lifted onto two a table for the doctor to suture his wound while the rest of them were held for questioning. The sheriff took statements from all the witnesses, and then left to hunt down Talmage. Mr. Lambert ordered a drink and turned to Jason, eyeing him critically.

"I gather it's not the first time you've seen violence."

Jason's brow furrowed. "Why do you say that?"

"You're pretty calm for someone who got blood on his hands."

"I've seen my share of bar fights and boxing matches, but I have to admit, it was the first time I've seen someone attempt to kill another."

"Ugly business, isn't it? I hope we can make this charge stick on Talmage. It's not the first time he's committed violence, but his witnesses tend to later forget what they saw. Will you testify against him? If we can catch him. Marshal put a guard on his ship, but he has friends who will help get him off the island."

"If I'm still here when he stands trial I will certainly testify."

Mr. Lambert nodded. "When are you leaving?"

"As soon as I can find passage on a ship headed north. There doesn't seem to be many of them headed that way, at least not any which stop here on their way."

Mr. Lambert looked as if he wanted to say more, but instead set his empty shot glass on the counter and bid them good-day. Jason watched him leave. He wondered if Victoria's father knew how badly he had wanted to ask after his daughter. Jason came in here trying to get her off his mind, and now after speaking with her father, thoughts of her were too strong for the whiskey. He spun around and pounded a frustrated fist against the solid wood counter making the barkeep jump. Jason threw the man an apologetic look and then strode from the bar wondering what he was going to do with himself. The island suddenly felt like a prison.

Weary of everything, it was dusk when Jason trudged back to the boardinghouse and up to his room. As he reached to turn the brass knob, a shadow at the end of the hall moved, taking on the shape of a man, a large husky man. Jason's heart began to race. Sweat broke out across the back of his neck as the threatening voice he heard in the bar was directed at him.

"I've seen you before. You were in that same bar on Friday looking for Captain Graham. I asked myself what's a dandy like you doing looking for some old fisherman? It was bothering me but I finally let it go. You see it was none of my business. But today you became my business. Why don't you and I step into your room for a little talk?"

Jason tried to think of an excuse to thwart Talmage until he saw the flintlock pointed at his chest. The two men entered the sparsely furnished room with a colorful quilt on the single bed and a small dresser. Talmage shut the door behind them. He motioned for Jason to sit on the bed while he went to check the window. Jason guessed he was likely looking to see if the marshal or sheriff's men were waiting outside. Satisfied he was in the clear, Talmage turned to face Jason.

"I need a place to hole-up till dark and I figured you and I could settle a matter between us while I wait. You see that sheriff and that fancy lawyer are looking to do me in. Don't know why they've got it in for me, but they do. They'd like nothing better than to put me behind bars and today's accident is just the kind of thing they're looking for. The other men in the bar, they know me. They know I didn't mean no harm. They'll say it was an accident which leaves only you to say different. Is that how you see it? An accident?"

Jason kept his tone neutral, but he wasn't about to give in to Talmage. "How is trying to kill someone an accident?"

Talmage shook his head. "I wasn't trying to kill anyone. I was aiming for the wall. I only meant to scare Smyth, so he would quit calling me a cheat."

Jason purposefully made his tone sound agreeable even though his words were far from it. "The truth is hard to accept."

Talmage's beady eyes were mere slits. "Are you calling me a cheat?"

The gun was pointed at him once more, but Jason refused to back down. "I saw you cheat. I heard you lie about it, and I saw you throw a knife at your accuser with murderous intent. If you missed your mark, it was because you were aiming at his heart, not the wall."

Talmage, his jaw clenched tight, stepped forward until the muzzle of the gun touched Jason's chest.

Jason tilted his head back in defiance. "If you shoot me, you'll never get out of here undetected."

Talmage tilted his head to stare down his nose. "I've seen you spending time with the lawyer's lovely daughter. Would be a shame to see her come to harm over your stubbornness."

Jason swallowed hard, fully understanding the threat, and fully believing the sincerity behind it. It gave him little choice in the moment but to cajole his enemy. "What are you worried about? Nothing I say matters as long as you don't get caught, and you're too smart to let anyone catch you."

The flattery worked. Talmage took a step back and lowered the gun with a satisfied smile. "You're right. I still control my destiny." He turned to the window to check the street once again. Fitzpatrick was such a small street the window provided a clear view from one end to the other.

Dusk had turned to night while they talked, and the room was in heavy shadows. Jason wasn't going to suggest lighting anything. The darkness was his best defense at this point.

A few minutes later, Talmage turned from the window. "Time to go, I think." He looked around the room and then purposefully stepped to the dresser to rummage through the drawers. He pulled out three cravats and turned to Jason. "Can't have you raising the alarm too quickly."

Talmage stepped closer and Jason jumped to his feet and backed away.

"Now sir," Talmage frowned, "What is your name?"

Jason stared mutely at him, and once again, Talmage raised his gun.

"Malwbry."

"Well Malwbry, if you don't want me to send my men to accost your girl tomorrow, you'll cooperate nicely, and let me tie you up without a fuss."

Jason couldn't see a way out of it, so he offered up his hands to be bound. Talmage quickly tied his wrists together behind him, gagged him with the second cravat, sat him on the bed, and bound his ankles with the third. With one final check at the window, he walked out the door.

Jason immediately started to work on his bonds, but it was of no use. He would need help to get out of them. The only way he could summon help was to make a ruckus, but first he had to be sure Talmage was out of the building. He couldn't risk him making good on his threat to Victoria. Jason stood up and took short bunny hops over to the window to watch for Talmage's departure. After what seemed like twenty minutes with no sight of him, he decided Talmage must have left out the back. He hopped to the hall door and proceeded to bang his head against it until someone finally came to check on him.

Through the door he heard a maid timidly ask, "Sir, are you okay? Do you need assistance?"

Not being able to speak, Jason continued banging his head on the wall until she finally opened the door. He thrust his tied wrists out to the surprised maid. It took her precious moments to get the knots undone. He yanked off the gag as he hopped back to the bed to undo his feet. He flew past the astonished maid still standing in the hall observing his every move.

Jason flew down the stairs and out the door without pause. He continued running in the dark guided by the faint light of the moon and his memory to the end of Fitzpatrick and right onto Front Street. He didn't stop until he reached the sheriff's office. Finding it empty, he paused to catch his breath while he decided what to do next. The streets were deserted. He had no idea where the sheriff or the marshal lived. He could go back to the boardinghouse and ask someone. It occurred to him, Talmage was probably safely on his way out of the harbour by now. He supposed as long as he was out he could verify the latter.

He cautiously made his way down the side of Mr. Greene's warehouse wishing he had thought to grab his pistol. He peered around the corner of the building. There was no activity between the warehouses and the water. His gaze moved to the closest wharf, and again, he saw no movement. As he stepped around the building to make his way to the second wharf, he looked out into the harbour and stopped. There was a single ship under sail passing slowly by the other ships at anchor. He knew without a doubt it was Talmage.

Jason made his way back to the boardinghouse suddenly feeling drained after the day's drama. He would sleep now and advise the sheriff tomorrow, not that he expected it to do any good.

Chapter 10

Monday, Victoria held her parasol against the sun as she strolled the length of Front Street. Her eyes darted everywhere on constant vigil for a certain someone. Lydia and Maria trailed behind her holding their own conversation. Visiting Betsy was just an excuse to walk the length of town. Victoria was really trying to run into Jason having not seen him for nearly two days. The longing for him was her constant companion. She missed his flirtatious banter that made her spirit come alive, his deep smoldering looks that made her stomach flutter, and his keen mind that challenged her chess skills. She yearned for just the sight of his proud aristocratic visage, his dark tousled hair her hands ached to touch, and a whiff of his *Eau de Cologne* that drew her to him like a bee to nectar.

Yesterday, she endured with all the patience she could muster, but today she was without. Her need for action gave rise to the only thing she could do—take a walk and hope to run across him. Fortunately, Betsy's house on Whitehead Street was perfectly situated to take her past the boardinghouse, thereby increasing the odds of catching sight of him.

Despite her leisurely pace through town and lingering near Clinton Place—a triangle patch of ground where Front, Whitehead and Green streets converged—under the pretense of watching the harbour, she did not see Jason. Disappointed but holding onto hope for the return walk, she continued on to Betsy's door. She stepped onto the porch and inhaled the spicy sweet fragrance of Betsy's prized frangipani profusely covered in bright yellow flowers. The lovely scent never failed to make Victoria smile. Betsy's shingle was turned to open and her door stood open allowing the breeze to freshen her shop. Victoria was warmly greeted by Betsy from behind the counter.

"Good morning ladies what a nice surprise and perfect timing. I have cinnamon bread in the oven. It should be done soon."

Victoria's mouth began to water. Betsy's bread was famous on the island. She was kept well supplied in the coveted spice by adoring bread connoisseurs. In exchange, they received a whole loaf of bread and considered it a worthy trade. "Good morning to you too and how fortuitous for me."

Lydia and Maria echoed her greeting.

Betsy lifted the divider in the counter that allowed access to her personal space in the house. She asked as Victoria as she passed through, "Is today's visit for business or pleasure?"

Victoria had decided early this morning that a new dress was the perfect excuse for making several trips to Betsy's shop. "Visiting you is always a pleasure, but today I also bring you an order. I would like a new dress."

Betsy's smile deepened. "A day dress or special occasion?"

Victoria lips quirked. "A special dress." She needed something complicated that would require several fittings.

"Have you thought of a color? I would want to get the fabric ordered right away."

Oh dear! She hadn't considered that delay. "You don't have any fabric on hand?"

"Not much in the way of fancy dress fabric."

"Can we see what you do have? I'm in a bit of a hurry for it."

Bewildered, but more than willing to accommodate, Betsy said, "Certainly. Follow me." She led Victoria into a small room with a large work table. The far wall was lined with wooden shelves filled with neatly stored bolts of fabric and notions. After quickly scanning the contents, Betsy pointed out the choices to Victoria. "I have a pale pink which would not suit you at all nor would this bright yellow." She sighed, "Nothing else I have is suitable for a formal dress."

Victoria's face fell. No fabric would mean no fittings, and she would have to find another excuse.

Betsy scanned the contents once more and then bent down to inspect the bottom shelf closer. She reached in and tugged until she pulled free a bolt wrapped in paper. She turned to Victoria with the sparkle of triumph in her big blue eyes. Victoria anxiously watched as Betsy blew off the dust and carefully unwrapped a bolt of high-quality satin in the deepest plum Victoria had ever seen.

Betsy beamed. "And I believe I have ribbon to match." She turned to rummage some more until she found the box she was looking for. She placed it on the table, opened it up, and pulled out a roll of four inch wide solid plum brocade ribbon followed by several yards of plain one inch ribbon. Both matched the dress perfectly.

"How lovely!" Victoria couldn't have ordered anything as beautiful as the rich fabric shimmering before her.

Betsy ran her hand over the glossy silk. "This was in with the lot of fabrics I bought at a salvage auction. Fortunately, it was untouched by the salt water." She looked up at Victoria with bright eyes. "I can't wait to get started on this. Shall we discuss the design over tea and bread?"

Victoria followed Betsy to the back door where fragrant warm cinnamon drifted in the air.

Betsy asked as she opened the back door, "What is the occasion?"

Victoria frowned. "The occasion?"

"For the dress."

"Oh, yes. Well, there is none yet, but I hope for there to be one soon."

They entered the kitchen and Betsy opened the little cast iron door of the brick oven flooding the room with aroma. She pulled out the bread pans and placed them on her wooden work table to cool. Next, she filled the tea kettle, placed it on the stove, and stoked the fire. She then retrieved two tea cups, the tea canister, and two spoons, and placed them on a tray to wait for the water to heat. She looked to Victoria, "Do you have any ideas for the design of your dress?"

"Nothing in particular."

"Let's start simple then. Do you want long sleeves or short?"

"Short, I think."

"Neckline, high or low?"

Victoria smiled, "Low."

"Square or rounded?"

"What do you recommend?"

"Hum, let me think on it. Should it be solid plum or shall we break it up with perhaps an ecru under skirt or maybe a lace bodice?"

Victoria shrugged. She really wanted something unique. "What about a new style?"

Betsy took a long knife from the drawer and began working a loaf of bread loose from the pan. "I just received a new fashion magazine in this month's mail. We could look at it while we enjoy our refreshment."

"Yes, what a grand idea." Victoria's excitement grew not only to see the new magazine, but her mouth watered as Betsy began placing slices of the fragrant bread on a plate. The tea kettle finally began to whistle. Victoria removed it from the stove to fill the tea cups on the tray. Betsy added the plate of bread and then carried it all to her small dining table rather than the parlour where they normally took tea. She placed the tray on the table and then went to retrieve the magazine and ask Lydia and Maria to join them.

A half hour later, Betsy made a rough sketch of the dress taking ideas from two different designs in the magazines. The trend remained of shorter ankle length hem lines but they both preferred full length. The neckline would be scooped with short capped sleeves starting at the edge of her shoulders. The thin ribbon would adorn the gathering below the puffed sleeves. The waist would fall mid-torso accentuated by the wide brocade ribbon. From the waist, the shimmering satin skirt would fall, unadorned, to the floor with added fullness to catch the light from all angles and loosely swirl about Victoria's legs as she danced. The rest of the wide ribbon would be used to trim a lavender lace shawl.

Victoria was well pleased with Betsy's design. They left shortly after tea. She walked home as slowly as she could manage, still she failed to see Jason.

The sun rose Tuesday morning in a cloudless sky typical for the island during the dry season of the fall and winter solstice. Victoria went through her usual morning routine biding her time until the hour was late enough for social calls. At the strike of ten on the grandfather clock, she gathered her gloves and parasol.

Her mother appeared in the foyer. "Where are heading in such a tizzy?"

"To see what progress Betsy has made on my new gown."

"Give her my warm regards."

"I shall." Victoria sailed out the door, trailed by Maria. Lydia was staying behind to help her mother with a project.

The walk to Betsy's shop proved as disappointing as yesterday's but she put on a bright face to greet her friend.

Betsy was surprised by her guests but welcomed them into her parlour. "Good morning, Victoria, Maria. If you've come to see your dress, I'm afraid I've only had enough time to cut some of the pieces."

Victoria waved off her concern. "I'm not here for the dress, merely a social visit. Yesterday, I seem to have been remiss in asking after your family. How are they?"

Betsy's eyebrows lifted as she gave her a skeptic smile. "They are doing quite well, thank you. Come summer, I shall have another niece or nephew."

"Congratulations!"

"Thank you." Betsy scrutinized her friend's placid demeanor. "Now tell me, what mischief are you making that I am to provide your excuse for gallivanting about town?"

Victoria colored slightly and stumbled to think of a believable pretense.

Betsy answered her own question. "It must be a man. A certain dashingly handsome Englishman, if I'm not mistaken."

Victoria gave Betsy a sheepish smile before admitting the truth. "Yes." She sighed, "We were getting along so very well and I know the attraction was mutual." Victoria leaned in to whisper although Maria could still hear her, "We almost kissed."

Betsy's eyebrows rose turning her bright blue eyes into saucers. "Victoria! How scandalous."

She smiled, unrepentant. "We were standing close after putting away the chess pieces. He leaned in like he was going to kiss me, that is, until Lydia made a noise to remind him we were not alone."

Out of the corner of her eye, Betsy saw Maria's lip twitch. To Victoria, she said, "Has he stated his intentions?"

Victoria's face fell into a frown. "No." She perked up. "But I know we are both attracted to each other. I can feel his interest in me, except for some reason, he hasn't come to visit since Saturday."

"Perhaps he needs an invitation."

"Wouldn't that be improper?"

"For you to do so, yes, but your parents could issue an invite."

"What if he refuses?"

"Why would he?"

Victoria grimaced. "Because my mother put the idea in his head that I would make a lousy duchess."

Betsy's eyes flew wide again. "Your mother said that? In front of you?"

Victoria tilted her head. "Well not in those exact words but that was her meaning. I think Jason took it to heart."

Betsy's eyes narrowed. "What are you trying to accomplish by visiting me?"

"I slowly walk from my house to yours in the hopes of seeing him."

"And what do you plan to do if you succeed?"

Victoria shrugged. "I'm not sure. I can't just plead my case even though that's what I want to do."

"True."

"But so far we haven't crossed paths. Today, I nearly turned on Fitzpatrick to cross in front of the boardinghouse."

Betsy gave a horrified gasp. "No! Victoria, you mustn't. You cannot appear to be chasing him. Trust me, it would go against you if he caught you. Men don't like to be chased."

A self-deprecating smile bloomed on Victoria's face as she recalled saying similar words to Abby. Somehow she must find the patience to wait him out.

Betsy watched the play of emotions on her friend's face. She had never known Victoria to be this serious about a gentleman. Her mother was probably right to be concerned. "Tria, what if this all turns out as you would hope? Have you given any serious consideration of what it would mean to be a duchess? In England? They are not known for tolerating free spirits, and you have a predilection for not conforming to formality."

Victoria's eyes grew solemn. "For him, I would. Betsy, you don't understand how he makes me feel."

Betsy gave her an indulgent smile. "Being near him makes your palms moisten, your blood race, and your insides go all flighty. The way he looks at you draws you in and drowns out everyone and everything around you. He makes you feel like the most precious person on earth." To Victoria's incredulous look she said, "Did you forget I was once happily married?"

"Not at all. It's just that you perfectly described exactly what I'm feeling."

"Do you think your mother would issue an invitation despite her discouragement? It's really your best option."

"I suppose she would if I swallowed my pride and begged her."

Betsy gave her a consoling smile. "We do what we must for love."

Victoria and Maria left a short while later.

Upon returning to her house, once again thwarted in her mission, Victoria sought out her mother in her morning room. She was writing letters and Victoria took that as an omen. She sat down on a nearby chaise and patiently waited for her mother to acknowledge her presence.

After dusting the ink on her finished letter to her sister in Charleston, Mrs. Lambert turned to her forlorn daughter. "What is it dear?"

"I need your assistance."

Her mother waited while Victoria tried to find the right words.

"I would like to send Lord Malwbry an invitation to dine with us this evening."

"Is that really a wise idea, daughter? It would serve you ill to appear aggressive."

"But mother...."

"Victoria, you are trying too hard. You must have patience. If it is meant to be, it will work out in the end."

Victoria fought to hold back her tears of frustration. She could see by the set of her jaw, her mother was firmly against the idea. "I suppose you're right. It's just so hard to wait. To have no say in the matter."

Her mother gave her a bitter smile. "It is always that way for women, especially when dealing with men."

Having nothing more to say, Victoria rose and kissed her mother's cheek. She wandered outside into the garden to sit on the wooden bench under the shade of a stately mahogany. She needed another plan.

Wednesday morning Victoria, trailed by Maria, arrived at Betsy's shop barely containing her frustration. Again there was no sign of Jason, and she had failed to come up with any ideas to change the situation, at least not any suitable ideas. She had several unsuitable ideas no proper lady would ever consider.

Betsy saw her distress. "Your mother refused your request."

Victoria sadly nodded.

"Then you must try to be patient. If he truly feels the way you think, he will find a way to see you."

"That's what mother said too but after visiting three days in a row, the last being Saturday, I can't help feeling like he's avoiding me."

"Nonsense. Chin up and stay the course. Odds are you will eventually run into him."

"Not if he leaves soon."

"Yes, there is that possibility." Betsy laid a comforting hand on Victoria's. "Have faith that what will be, will be." After a moment of silence, Betsy decided it was best to change the subject. "On a brighter note, I have your bodice cut and pinned together. Shall we see how it fits?"

The remainder of her visit was spent talking of her dress and little bits of island news. Again, the walk home was fruitless. She hadn't seen Jason for four days and the longing was plaguing her even in slumber. She often dreamt of him. They were usually flirting, but sometimes he would tell her he loved her and wanted her for his wife. His blue-grey eyes would hold hers with a loving gaze before drifting shut as his head dropped down. She always woke up frustrated because their lips never quite met. She supposed having never been kissed her mind could not conjure what happens next.

Thursday morning was overcast and threatening. Victoria gave a wary eye to the unusual leaden sky but refused to let it keep her from her vigilance but she saw no need for Maria to risk getting caught in the rain. She stepped out alone hoping to at least make it to Betsy's before the clouds let loose. It was not to be. Halfway past the business district, the rain suddenly started with a pelting ferocity. With nothing but saloons in the immediate area, Victoria lifted her skirts and ducked her head, making a run for the shelter of the covered storefront two buildings away.

After leaving the wharf, Jason was feeling frustrated by another unsuccessful day of searching for passage home and bedeviled by recollections of Victoria. No matter how he tried to distract himself, she was never far from his thoughts. Lack of a ship not only meant further delay in returning home, but it also brought no end to the daily tug-o-war of his emotions. Each day it was becoming harder to keep his distance from her. He was physically aching to see her lovely smile and limpid eyes, to hear her lively voice and rich laughter. Her scent still lingered in his mind. It often beguiled him at odd moments. Loneliness was his constant companion. He knew how easily she could dispel it, but he was determined to hold his course, sure that if he could just leave this island, the distance between them would lessen the ache. It was the temptation making it worse.

He was trudging between two warehouses, a few steps from Front Street, when the heavens opened up and sent down a torrential rain. He went running across the street headed for the mercantile to escape the deluge. Head down against the onslaught, Jason didn't notice the figure dashing before him. They collided at the bottom of the stairs. The glimpse of swirling skirts had his hand going out to steady the poor woman he had inadvertently run into. "Pardon me..." The contact with her arm sent a lightning bolt of sensation through his system as he raised his head and his eyes met her honeyed-brown ones; their living version more powerful than the ones haunting his dreams. Incapable of coherent thought, he reflexively finished his sentence, "... miss." His nose flared as it was flooded with a fresh dose of her teasing scent. The combination overwhelmed him with awareness. The only word his muddled brain could manage was a whispered, "Victoria."

For a moment they stood motionless as the rain soaked them through.

Victoria hardly felt the pelting water, but she was intensely aware of the warmth of Jason's hand holding her arm. She was still recovering her wits from the unexpectedness of him standing before her. After days of searching with the intention of speaking her mind, she now had not a lucid thought in her head.

Jason finally came to his senses. He moved his hand from her arm to the small of her back encouraging her up the steps and into the store. A quick glance around the interior revealed one elderly gentleman being helped at the counter by the clerk. The rest of the store was empty. Jason guided her to the notions section by the front window.

"Miss Victoria, are you unharmed?"

She gave him a searching look, but his face was blank. "Yes, I am fine other than a bit wet."

"You should wait here till the storm passes, and then go home for dry clothes." He blushed a little at mentioning something so intimate. Her clothes, wet or otherwise, were none of his concern. "Good day, Miss Lambert." He turned, intending to leave before he found himself entangled in her essence again.

Astounded by his intention to walk away, her sole thought escaped on a breath, "Why?"

The soft pleading of her voice, more than the whispered question, stopped him, but he didn't turn. He leaving suspended, waiting for her to say more.

Victoria took a step closer to his rigid back and said it again, "Why?"

His brow furrowed as his head told him to move to the door, and his heart begged him to stay and answer her. He knew what she wanted to know, and if he turned around to answer, he would be lost. He was about to step to the door when he caught a fresh whiff of gardenia. The scent, his mind could not erase from his memory, curled around him like a living thing and pulled him to her. He fought the urge to turn. His fists clenched as he struggled against his desire.

Victoria sensed his weakening. She took another step closer to whisper, as tears gathered in her eyes, "Why have you stayed away? What have I done to cause..?"

The tremble in her voice was his undoing. He turned and reached out his hand intending to caress her cheek, to soothe her hurt feelings, but at the last moment he caught himself and let his hand fall away. "It is nothing you have done."

Jason and Victoria were unaware of the rain pelting the window, or the mellow voices of the clerk and the shopper drifting across the expanse of the store. The intensity of their emotions, after their long separation, made everything else fade away. Nothing else existed in this moment except each other.

"Then why?"

"You know why."

She shook her head. "I know what I believe to be the cause. I know what others think to be the reason. But, I don't know what you are thinking. I know how I feel. I think I know how you feel, but I don't know why you're fighting your feelings. Please. Tell me."

They were so close the warmth of their mingled breaths lingered in the air between them as intimate as a kiss. Jason moistened his suddenly dry lips and fought the urge to tell her what she wanted to hear, to tell her what he really wanted to say. He took a deep breath, "You heard your mother. It will never work between us."

"Why?"

Anger flared in his breast. "Are you going to make me say it?" Her mutinous look pushed him to say it. "You do not have the qualities of a duchess." At her indrawn breath, he rushed to explain, "Oh, you are certainly smart enough but not refined in nature. The demands of society would destroy you. It would break your spirit." He paused before admitting the true reason, "And that would destroy me."

The building anger and frustration deserted her in a rush. His last words left her feeling empty, hollow, and hopeless, and yet at the same time cherished. She gathered her resolve to make one last plea. "You don't know me well enough to draw such a conclusion, and my mother was being protective. You should have let me decide if I can handle being a duchess." Her tears started to fall. "I might have surprised you." Victoria brushed past a stunned Jason as she rushed to leave the store. Heedless of the rain, she held up her skirts and ran home to the sanctity of her bedroom where she could cry out all her frustrations alone.

Jason eventually turned to leave the mercantile headed for his own room.

Two puddles and some footprints remained on the plank floor to mark the scene of such overwhelming emotions so quietly displayed.

Chapter 11

Friday morning Jason made his way to the docks following his usual routine under a clear blue sky with cheerful, puffy white clouds, not that he noticed. His feet were leaden after tossing and turning all night in a fitful slumber with Victoria's final words replaying over and over in his mind.

You should have let me decide if I can handle being a duchess. I might have surprised you.

The resigned pain in her amber eyes as she left haunted him still. Was she right or was her mother? Victoria was too emotional to be thinking reasonably. Surely her mother understood her daughter well enough to know what was best for her. Or was she being overprotective? Jason's mind circled round and round without any true understanding.

He walked into the first shipping office and was startled when the owner rose from his desk to greet him with a jubilant smile. "Good morning, Lord Malwbry."

"Good morning sir."

"I have excellent news. There is a ship leaving Monday bound for France. I am sure you will have no trouble making your way home from there. Shall I book you passage?"

Jason was too stunned for a moment to speak. Finally he could finish this dismally disappointing trip abroad. He could return home to take charge of his estate. He could finally put in motion his ideas to increase profits and ease his tenants' burdens. He could find a suitable wife and produce an heir or two. Perhaps Lady Jane Torrington was still unattached. And perhaps his tormented heart could find peace. He nodded to the waiting clerk. "Yes, please book it. Thank you, sir."

After paying his fare, Jason left the office. He normally visited two more offices, but now that he had his passage, he turned away from the bight headed back to the boardinghouse. He nodded or lifted his bowler in greeting to the occasional passerby, but he was feeling far from sociable. When he reached the turn for Fitzpatrick Street, he instead kept going to round the bend at Clinton place and slowly walk down Whitehead Street. As he passed Mrs. Wheeler's little house he could faintly hear two voices coming from the outdoor kitchen behind the house. He instantly recognized them. Desperately wanting to avoid another encounter, he did a quick about face and hurried to the safety of the boardinghouse.

Victoria lifted her red-rimmed eyes to the sympathetic blue ones. Her tears were finally spent having cried herself to sleep the night before, and again just now in the retelling of yesterday's encounter with Jason. They were in Betsy's kitchen waiting on the water to heat for a soothing chamomile tea. Thankfully, Betsy didn't try to cheer her. Her mother and Lydia had both tried, and failed. Betsy simply hugged her for a long moment after hearing her tale and allowed the silence to fill the room. It was a companionable silence. It helped to sooth Victoria's wounded spirit. She returned home a short while later and retreated to her bedroom until she was called for supper.

Saturday, Jason didn't set foot outside the boardinghouse. He was moody and morose and unfit company for those around him.

Victoria kept to her room all day. The food trays brought by Lydia were left untouched. All in the household respected her need for solitude but grew more worried as the day progressed.

Sunday morning, Victoria dressed and sat in front of her vanity mirror wondering how to repair her ravaged face. She wished she could stay home and hide from the world another day, but she knew her mother would not allow her to miss Sunday worship. She hoped to see Jason, but knew even if she did, it would be bittersweet.

She had to face facts. He didn't stop her from leaving the store nor did he seek her out yesterday, so she knew he still believed she could not be his duchess. The irony was he thought being a duchess would break her spirit, but here she sat, broken in spirit, because he refused to make her one.

Her mother called from downstairs. It was time to leave. Victoria sighed at the face staring back from her mirror. Only time could erase the ravages of her tears and return color to her washed out complexion. She rose from her chair and drifted down the stairs, to face her father's concern, and her mother's sympathetic hovering. She trailed her parents to the Custom House and to their usual seats in the second row. She tried to quiet her soul and prepare her mind and heart to focus on the Word. She couldn't help casting surreptitious glances behind her, hoping to catch sight of Jason. She wasn't sure why she bothered. Although she was sure he was a God-fearing Christian, she didn't see him last week, so why would she think he would be here today? Still, she kept a hopeful vigilance until the visiting minister took the podium.

Jason waited until the last possible moment to slip through the door of the Custom House just as the minister began his opening prayer. He paused in the entry, head bowed, until the minister said, "Amen." He then made his way behind the standing parishioners to the far corner of the room. He positioned himself to the left of a taller gentlemen, effectively blocking the line of sight between him and Victoria, much as he had the previous week.

At the end of the service, Jason waited to exit last. It was foolish to go to such lengths to avoid her, but he was feeling weak in spirit. He couldn't face her dismay when she learned he was leaving. He knew, where she was concerned, his resolve was tenuous. He was going to have to tell her eventually, but it would be cruel to both of them to do so now in such a public setting.

As he stepped into the doorway, he was caught off guard to see Victoria and her family socializing in the front yard. He quickly stepped back into the shadows of the room but hovered close enough to the opening to observe them. Victoria was partially facing away from him, standing on her father's left, her mother on his right. Both of her parents had their backs to him. He watched her smile and politely greet friends, neighbors, and men who were likely her father's clients. Jason was entranced by the glow of morning sunlight on her skin and the play of copper highlights in her hair. He remembered feeling as if he could conquer the world when she smiled at him. His spirits fell flat to realize this may be the last time he would see her. He was leaving in less than eighteen hours.

A man came to speak to her father and in a few moments it appeared as if their words grew heated. Victoria covertly touched her father's arm and turned a charming smile to the gentleman. Jason wished he could have heard her words, for the tension drained from both men, and a hearty chuckle soon drifted to his ears. Of course, how could a man not soften under her honeyed gaze? When the man left, her father turned to Victoria. Jason guessed he was thanking her before the next couple approached to say hello.

Victoria happened to glance his way. He instinctively stepped back. A moment later he cautiously peeked out, relieved to find her attention drawn to the other side of the yard. He followed her line of sight to a mother and child speaking with the minister. Both seemed to be suffering under a heavy burden of grief. He glanced back to

Victoria to find she was excusing herself from the group and gingerly making her way to the forlorn pair, patiently waiting for the minister to finish speaking with them and move on. She spoke with the woman, coaxing a weak and tentative smile from her. She dropped down to the child's level and spoke to him as well. Jason wished again he could hear what she had to say. The child gave her a nod and she rose to face the mother. She reached into her reticule and pressed something into the other woman's hand. She then abruptly turned to rejoin her parents. The woman, whom Jason decided must be recently widowed, watched Victoria walk away in bewilderment before opening her palm to reveal several coins. The surprise on her face was clear evidence the gift was unexpected. Somehow, Victoria managed to help the poor woman while leaving her dignity intact. It showed compassion and a finesse Jason couldn't help but admire.

His heart ached at the thought of never seeing her again.

He looked back to where Victoria and her family had been standing to find they were now walking home. He waited a few more minutes before stepping from the Custom House. He spoke a few words to the minister and then made his way back to the boardinghouse to pack his belongings. Many thoughts weighed heavy on his mind as he prepared for his departure in the morning, not the least of which was reminding himself, he was doing the right thing. He was also trying to work up the nerve to visit the Lambert's to say goodbye.

It didn't take long to pack his valise, leaving out only what he would need in the morning. It was approaching tea time. If he didn't go now, he wouldn't have another opportunity. Suddenly, he felt the urgent need to see Victoria and to speak with her one last time. He snatched up his bowler and left the room before he lost his nerve again.

Briskly, he walked through town and up to the Lambert's door. Nervously, he raised his hand and rapped on the wooden frame. He took a step back and waited. Lydia soon opened the door. He took his hat off and greeted her formally before asking to see the family. Quietly she led him, not to the parlour, but to Mr. Lambert's study. A quick glance showed the elder gentleman to be the sole occupant of the room. Disappointment was sharp, but Jason consoled himself with the hope he would see her in a few moments.

Mr. Lambert rose to greet him with a firm handshake. "Good afternoon, Lord Malwbry."

"Good afternoon, Mr. Lambert."

"What brings you here on this fine day?"

Nervously, Jason turned his hat brim in his hand. "I have come to say goodbye. I shall be sailing for home on the morning tide."

"I see. I would not have been surprised if you had been delayed a few months longer. It is good you found passage."

"Yes sir, it is."

"It's a shame though, the ladies aren't home at present. I know Victoria would have wanted to say her farewell. She and Mrs. Lambert took food and gifts to a new mother."

Jason's heart dropped. He struggled not to let it show on his face. "You will give them my regards, won't you?"

"Of course."

"Please thank your wife for her hospitality. Your family helped to make my stay here pleasant."

"Glad we could be of service. I wish you a safe journey home."

"Thank you, sir."

Moments later, he was back on the front porch placing his hat on his head. The bright afternoon sun could not cheer his despondency. He had missed his last chance to speak with Victoria. He raised his chin and took a deep breath. It was just as well. Seeing her again would only deepen the agony.

He stepped down from the porch and began walking back to the boardinghouse. He further depressed him to realize it would be the last time he did so. When next he left his temporary home on the island, it would be for good. As he passed Simonton Street, he glanced at Abigail's home. He would have liked to say goodbye to her too. He would have to settle for leaving a letter. If only, he could write one to Victoria. As an old family friend, he could do so with Abigail, but it would be improper to write Victoria. Unless, he turned around and asked her father for permission. His step faltered in hopeful consideration but soon resumed. It would imply a desire for a more meaningful relationship which he could not offer.

He walked slowly, taking in his surroundings, once so foreign, but now, oh so familiar; the white limestone streets, the unique plants and trees, the constant ocean breeze, and the unpainted wooden structures. It was all part of the charm of this tiny island. He only now realized how deeply it etched itself on his soul. He longed for home, but he knew there would be days in his future when he would long to be back here on this tiny, wonderful island. The woman he was leaving behind, he feared, would leave him aching for far longer. The thought of it almost made him change his mind. *How could he leave her?*

Ahead two ladies were walking towards him. He blinked in surprise. It was almost as if he had conjured her. Victoria's smile bloomed when she noticed him, and her pace quickened ahead of her mother. It made his heart beat faster in response. He came to a halt in front of them removing his hat and bowing his head in greeting. He looked up and couldn't help his smile as his eyes met Victoria's warm brown ones. He spoke the expected niceties by rote. His attention was deeply focused on Victoria and hers on him. How he wished he wasn't about to dash her burgeoning hope, again. "Mrs. Lambert, Miss Lambert, I wanted to thank you for your hospitality during my stay in Key West. You have made my time here enjoyable."

Mrs. Lambert smiled politely. "You are most welcome."

Victoria fought not to show a foreboding frown. She didn't want to accept what she knew he was going to say next. She confronted him still hoping against hope he would deny it. "You are leaving us?"

He flinched at the hint of anger in her words. "Yes."

"When?"

"With the morning tide."

He watched her mouth work to form words she dared not utter in front of her mother much less in a public place. He couldn't blame her. There was much he would like to say but couldn't.

Victoria stoically accepted the news. Her mother's presence kept her from speaking what was on her heart.

Instead, they each hoped the other could read the unspoken words in their eyes.

Mrs. Lambert looked from one to the other bringing concern to her eyes. "It is good you have found passage home so soon. I am sure you are anxious to begin work on all your ideas for your tenant farms, not to mention, continue your search for a *proper* duchess."

Jason was aware of the not so subtle reminder; her daughter was not right for him. He gave her a bare nod in acknowledgement.

Victoria was afraid to say anything more for fear her voice would betray her emotion. She thought she had more time to convince him. If she had known their last conversation was going to be the last, she would not have left it as she did. Resigning herself to the inevitable, she tried to absorb every nuance of his features. She couldn't believe this brief meeting was to be the last she would ever see him. How cruel fate was to take away the one man who brought her to life, who made her feel whole, who made her heart sing. She felt tears begin to weld and quickly looked away. Her lips compressed as she breathed deeply in an effort to control her emotions. She could cry in the safety of her room. Here and now, she had to keep her emotions tightly reigned.

Jason understood her struggle, for it mirrored his own. He swallowed hard to hold his emotions at bay. The breeze blew past lifting Victoria's tendrils and carrying to Jason her intoxicating gardenia infused scent. His nostrils flared, and his desire rose. He was fighting a physical ache to be with her. Fighting the need to throw off his responsibilities and declare his feelings for her.

Mrs. Lambert, seeing the wavering emotion on his face, quickly intervened. "You are doing what's best. You will soon be home and your time here will be a pleasant memory as you take up the burdens of your inheritance. May you have a pleasant journey, Lord Malwbry."

Jason heard the veiled message behind her words and had no choice but to respect her wishes.

Victoria swallowed tightly and softly echoed her mother's last sentiment. It was all she could say in this setting. If only she could have spoken to him alone and pleaded one more time.

Jason tried to give a pleasant smile. It felt stiff with all the longing he was holding back as did his words. "Thank you." He stepped aside for them to move past and turned to watch them walk away. Victoria turned her head to give him one final look even though her mother nudged her in disapproval.

Jason had never felt so forlorn in his life. He promptly returned to his room to pace in frustration. It was a long time later before he could bring himself to write his letter to Abigail. He tried to go to bed early but ended up tossing and turning more than sleeping.

He was doing the right thing leaving her behind.

So why did it feel so wrong?

* * *

After parting with Jason, Victoria was silent. She was thankful her mother didn't try to engage her in conversation. She felt as if one word would crumble the shattered wall holding her together. Upon reaching the house, she sought the solace of her room where she curled up on the bed and cried inconsolably. Lydia brought her tea and later a dinner tray. Both went untouched. It wasn't until the wee hours of the morning that she finally fell into a brief and fitful slumber.

* * *

Jason awoke hours sooner than he needed to and recognizing the futility of staying abed any longer, he rose to face the coming day. After two weeks of actively trying to find his way home, he was now reluctant to leave. By the light of a candle, he rose, dressed, and packed his last remaining items. He left the room to make his way down the stairs as quietly as he could so as not to disturb the other sleeping guests. It was not easy to do while holding a chamberstick to light his way and carrying both his travel bags. He had settled his account with Mrs. Mallory the night before, so all he had to do was leave his key on the counter. He blew out the candle and left it there as well before carefully making his way to the front door in the darkest hour before dawn.

He stepped out into the street and drew his coat tighter against the cool morning breeze. He supposed he should get used to the chill. He was returning to England where winter still held firm. He reached the dock under the meager light of the waning moon. The streets were deserted at this hour. The drunks were passed out and even the sailors were not yet stirring. At the appropriate pier, he settled in to wait with his back against a post until he could board the ship.

The solitude and the lack of anything else to occupy his mind left it free to recall every conversation, every smile, every moment of his time spent with Victoria. The recollection of their first meeting and the novelty of her open flirtation made his heart race. He smiled at how he must have looked 'tarred and feathered' on their return walk from the salt ponds. His breath deepened and his body tightened recalling her gentle ministrations and coy stolen glances as she cleaned his arms later. Her captivating gardenia scent lingered so strongly in his mind, it was as if he smelled it still. He smiled, recalling her quick wit and unusual strategies at chess. She kept him guessing at her every move. She would challenge him for years to come, if they had the chance.

But, he was never going to see her again.

His heart gave a wrench. Oh, how he was going to miss her.

He loved her bold bravery as she admitted her feelings the night he dined with her family. He knew then her feelings ran true and would have admitted his own to her shortly afterwards, in private, if not for her mother's cautioning. Mrs. Lambert was right. It would be unfair to ask anyone to be his duchess who wasn't already groomed for the task. It was true Victoria was far from the reserved genteel expectations of a duchess, but she was refreshingly audacious with strength and fortitude. Perhaps she had more strength than her mother believed her capable of. His mind slid to her impromptu visit to the boardinghouse. It was Victoria's cavalier unconcern for propriety that gave credence to her mother's words. Victoria could easily find herself on the wrong side of favor with *The Ton* or worse, the Royals. They, in turn, would ostracize her and that would break his heart.

She had his heart. He knew it was hers when she confessed to helping Abigail board Max's ship while evading Talmage. The concern for the danger she put herself in scared him as nothing else ever had. He had to protect her. He may not have been able to get Talmage arrested but at least he helped get him far enough away to keep Victoria safe. It was her unawareness of her vulnerability and lack of concern for propriety that made him realize no matter what his heart felt, her temerity was unacceptable in a duchess.

But then again, she was young. She would mature and learn the boundaries of society.

He pushed the thought aside. He had made his decision. It was too late to change it now. He tried to turn his thoughts to home and his plans for his estate, but he had lost his zest for the project. He should be planning how best to go about implementing his new ideas. He should consider how he was going to go about finding a bride when he returned, but a certain dark-haired honey-eyed beauty would not leave his thoughts. Her words in the mercantile taunted him: *You should have let me decide if I can handle being a duchess. I might have surprised you.*

Yesterday's scene after church floated before him. He looked past her beauty to her actions, especially when greeting the men who were likely her father's clients. She was polite and demure. She showed the proper amount of interest to flatter without incurring undo attention. In short, she was everything mature and proper for the daughter of a prominent lawyer, and everything desirable in his future wife. *I might have surprised you.* Perhaps he underestimated her. After all, she did skillfully diffuse the situation with the disgruntled man confronting her father. Jason couldn't help his building excitement as he gave her further consideration. She recognized the needs of the mourning mother and child and did what she could to soothe them. Then there was her concern for Abigail's loneliness, and going with her mother to take food to a neighbor in need. These were all the caring concerns of a duchess. Victoria was used to money and social status and managing servants. Again, all things a duchess would have to handle. His heart lightened and his spirits began to soar the more he realized, he and her mother had misjudged her. She had grace and strength. And love. Didn't the Bible say 'love endures all things'?

He was in love with Victoria.

Fully admitting it to himself felt good. Really good. He loved her.

The excitement of it brought him up straight. There was no other woman for him. He was a fool to believe he could leave her behind, much less marry another. He looked at the ship in front of him finally hearing the faint stirrings of the crew. Leaving didn't feel right because he would be leaving his heart behind. He bent down to pick up his bags and turned back to the island. He was going to follow his heart and trust in their love to conquer any obstacles they might face, and he was determined, they would face them together.

She was his destiny. It felt right and good and he quickened his pace now in a hurry to share it with her; at least as soon as it was a decent hour to do so. First, he would leave a message at the shipping office informing them of his change of plans. After that, he had no idea how he would survive the hours until he could call on her.

Chapter 12

Coming to the end of the dock, Jason paused as a figure materialized from the darkness. His heart leapt to see the object of his desire standing before him, effectively ending his wait before it even began.

Victoria took another step forward. "I couldn't let you leave without saying goodbye."

He was thrilled to see her even if she was recklessly out alone before dawn. Lydia came into view. Well at least she brought her maid. It was still unsafe but two was better than one. Foolish girl. He inwardly grinned. She was going to be his foolish girl. He kept his voice neutral as he teased her, "You said goodbye yesterday."

Victoria struggled to keep her emotions in check. "I had to see you. At least one last time."

There was a catch in her voice and her eyes filled with unshed tears. Jason dropped his bags and took another step towards her. "I am glad you did."

They stood there silently reading the depths of emotion in each other's eyes.

Softly, so softly he barely heard her, Victoria whispered on a breath, "Please don't go."

"I have to go." He took a step closer at her indrawn breath. "But not without you."

Her lips parted and a smile wavered as if she was unsure she heard him correctly. He took another step closer, breaking the boundaries of propriety, bringing them close enough to embrace, although he didn't touch her. He inhaled her gardenia scent. It gave him the feeling of coming home. Looking deeply in her troubled eyes, he said the words he knew she needed to hear, "I love you, Victoria."

Her wavering smile took hold as a single tear rolled down her cheek. His name came out on a released sigh, "Oh Jason," and then she drew a charged breath, "I love you too." Her voice tightened at the end as she tried to contain her emotions. In his gaze, she saw his heart now wholly given and knew her reflected gaze told him the same.

Jason longed to pull her into his embrace, but they were not alone. Lydia was standing five feet away and sailors were beginning to move about behind him. The eastern horizon was brightening stealing their intimate cloak of darkness. The love shining in Victoria's eyes made his heart feel light and carefree. He was a man in love and he was ready to take on the world but first it would have to be her father. "Shall we return to your house?"

Understanding dawned in Victoria's eyes as she watched him pick up his bags. Her voice was full of wonder, "You already decided to stay." Shyly she added, as her limpid eyes met his, "For me?"

"Yes, my love, for you."

His words were the sweetest she had ever heard. She was sure as long as she lived she would never tire of hearing the word love from his lips. It would probably always pull at her heart.

They walked side by side back to Victoria's house. Words were not spoken but their shared looks said much in a lover's language all their own.

When they entered the house, Victoria directed him to wait in the parlour. She headed to the dining room where she was not surprised to find her father dressed and reading by candlelight as he savored his first cup of coffee.

Mr. Lambert looked up from his book, surprised to see his daughter. Taking in her dressed state and rosy cheeks, his eyes narrowed as he recalled hearing the front door open and realized it must have been her, and not one of the servants as he assumed. He frowned. "Have you been out this morning?"

Victoria meekly lowered her head. She needed to avoid angering her sire. "Yes, father."

"And what, pray tell, we're you doing out alone at this hour?"

She side-stepped the real question by diversion. "I was not alone. Lydia was with me."

"That does not make it better, young lady. There are all kinds of peril for a maiden walking without a protector at such an unseemly hour. What was your purpose?"

"Father, we have a guest. He is waiting for you in the parlour." Her statement effectively changed his line of questioning as she knew it would.

"He?" Mr. Lambert marked the page in his book and rose from his seat. "It can only mean trouble this early in the morning."

She smiled. "Not this time father."

He gave her a questioning look and then realized it was excitement staining her cheeks and not the cool morning air as he originally assumed. He had a good idea who his guest might be. He gave her a shrewd look. "Daughter, have you done something shameful?"

Her gaze sobered. "No father, at least not anything worse than usual." Knowing he would pull it from her eventually, she admitted, "I did take Lydia down to the wharf so I could say goodbye to Lord Malwbry."

His lips compressed in disapproval but it didn't surprise him. She was too upset yesterday to let their momentary meeting in the street be the end of her desire to become Jason's wife. "Please tell me you didn't drag him off that ship?"

She smiled ruefully knowing she would have tried if it had come to that. "No, father. I didn't have to. He had already decided to stay when I arrived. He is waiting to speak with you in the parlour." Her father moved to leave the room. She didn't think she needed to say so, but she wasn't leaving anything to chance. Before he passed by her she meekly said, "Please, father, be agreeable."

Mr. Lambert's pace faltered. He had a suspicion before, but at his daughter's words, he was certain of the context of the coming conversation. He wasn't ready for this. At the doorway, he turned back almost surprised to see the grown woman who was once his little girl. *Where had the time gone?* With a heavy heart, he made his way to the waiting gentleman who would all too soon whisk his daughter away. His time with her had come to an end, and it saddened him.

Today he felt old.

Jason made a conscious effort to sober his euphoric countenance before turning to greet Mr. Lambert as he entered the parlour. Nervousness fluttered through him as he realized this was perhaps the most important meeting of his life, and here he was, disturbing the gentleman before the sun was even fully risen. "Good morning, sir. I apologize for the earliness of the hour."

Keeping his expression unreadable, Mr. Lambert replied, "Some things just can't wait until a man has finished his coffee."

Jason wasn't exactly sure how he should interpret his statement. Was Mr. Lambert toying with him or seriously vexed by his interruption? He would have to tread carefully. If her father was already irritated with him, it could bode ill for his purpose. "Again, I apologize sir." He wanted to say more but hesitated to do so feeling any excuse he could add would sound feeble.

"Pray sir, tell me what is on your mind that couldn't wait at least until the cock crowed."

Jason grimaced, reminded once again of the early hour and the unseemliness of his visit, but the damage was done, and he could not think of a prevarication more important than the truth to justify the disturbance. He would have to push forward and hope he wasn't turned down out of hand for his impertinence. "Sir, as you were aware from our conversation yesterday, I was set to leave this morning." He took a fortifying breath to calm his nerves and tried to surreptitiously wipe his sweating palms against his legs.

Mr. Lambert uttered a non-committal, "Yes."

"I was waiting to board this morning trying to convince myself it was the right thing to do, but in doing so, I came to realize all of my reasons were wrong. I thought by leaving, I was protecting your daughter and, in time, our feelings would diminish. I was wrong. Separation was only going to cause more pain, and the protection I thought I was giving her was a sham. Your daughter's spirit is strong. She is compassionate, courteous, and even refined, when the occasion calls for it. Yes, she is brash and bold, and at first, it seemed unsuitable, though I was captivated by her charms. But as I have come to know her, I have seen beyond the surface to the depths of the woman she truly is, and in doing so, I lost my heart."

Jason carefully watched Mr. Lambert's expression as he spoke and finding only openness pushed forward with his request. "Sir, I couldn't leave today because, I would be leaving part of me behind. Your daughter holds my heart, and so, I am before you now to humbly ask for her hand in marriage."

Mr. Lambert's breath escaped him. He knew Jason's intent before entering the room, but the words still took the wind from him. He wished he could object, so he could selfishly keep his daughter, but he knew her heart was taken too. Jason was a fine young man. There were plenty of temptations for corruption and deprivation on this island. He knew without a doubt, Jason had steered clear of them. He came from an established family with an English title of all things. *His daughter a future duchess!* Any father would be proud to claim the match for social status alone. But he was fortunate in that his future son-in-law loved and cherished his only child. Though it pained him to say it, there was only one answer to give to the young man's quest. "You have my blessing." Jason's face broke into the happiest grin he had ever seen on a man.

Jason leaned forward to shake Mr. Lambert's hand unable to contain his joy. He started for the door, then realizing he was forgetting his manners, turned back to his host. "May I go to her?"

"No."

Jason's mouth dropped open in surprise.

Mr. Lambert's lips quirked. "Wait here. I will send her to you."

Moments later a radiantly smiling Victoria entered the room alone. The door was left open but her father didn't join them. Victoria gave him a coy smile. "We have a few moments alone. Please make the most of them, milord."

Jason obediently did as she requested. He closed the distance between them, and taking her hands, he dropped to one knee. "Victoria, my love, will you marry me?" It seemed as if he had used up his flowery speech on her father. He was left with only the words of a simple life changing request for her. The deafening squeal of delight that followed caught him by surprise.

"Yes, yes, a thousand times yes." Her joyous laughter brought him to his feet with an answering smile. Their eyes locked and nothing more needed to be said. He looked forward to a lifetime of getting lost in her beautiful honeyed gaze. He would never tire of studying the emotions churning in their depths. His gaze drifted lower. The longing to kiss her took hold.

The sound of feet hurriedly descending the stairs, followed by her mother's voice, drifted in the open door. "What on earth was that noise?" Her father's hushed answer had the new lovers guiltily stepping apart knowing the interruption was timely. But Jason was willing to move only a step away to stand by her side. He held out his hand to her. The jolt of awareness as she slipped her slender hand into his was unexpected drawing their surprised gaze to each other as her parents entered the room.

Her mother's hastily donned dressing gown trailed behind her and then swirled around her legs as she came to a sudden halt just inside the room. The enchanted scene before them brought an indulgent smile to her father's face and a momentary look of horror on her mother's. "Victoria Marie Lambert, what have you done?"

The lover's combined gaze flew to the distraught woman shocked by her dismay.

Mr. Lambert laid a comforting arm across his wife's shoulders urging her to turn toward him. "It is time to let her go. Our daughter is a woman now as you have so often reminded me of late. The decision is hers as well as the consequences." Softly he added, "We must let her go." He drew his wife's gaze to the couple as he said, "And she has chosen a fine young man of noble blood, hasn't she? You will be the envy of all the other mamas in town to have made such a splendid match for your daughter, and now, you have a wedding to plan." Feeling her anger drain away, he kissed her temple before turning back to the couple. "You are engaged, are you not?"

Victoria mutely shook her head still reeling from her mother's anger, and her father's unexpectedly calm acceptance. Jason squeezed her hand, and firmly replied, "Yes, sir."

Mr. Lambert stepped forward to shake Jason's hand forcing him to drop Victoria's. "Congratulations!"

Mrs. Lambert didn't move. Victoria approached her mother and in close proximity she could see the pooled tears in her eyes. "Mother, please be happy for us. I love him so."

"Have you really given this careful consideration? I don't think you have." Her stricken eyes pleaded with Victoria. "Child, you will be moving to England. We will never see you again."

At this, both the men turned towards her. Mr. Lambert laid a comforting hand on his wife's shoulder. "Nonsense, we can visit her in England."

Jason offered, "I promise you we will come to visit as often as we can between babies."

Mrs. Lambert's eyes softened. "Babies."

Victoria's mouth went dry. She factored moving into her decision and welcomed it. She took heed of Jason's warnings of his parents' faults. She knew she may struggle to get along with the Duchess. She accepted those challenges. But having children failed to cross her mind. Victoria eagerly anticipated being Jason's wife, but was she ready to be a mother? Of course children were a natural outcome of marriage. He once mentioned the need of an heir as the reason for seeking Abby's hand in marriage. The full portent of his comment did not register with her at the time. It did now. The idea of being in a family way frightened her, especially as she would be so far away from her mother.

Mrs. Lambert saw the flicker of uncertainty and the settling fear on Victoria's face. She pulled her into a tight embrace. Against her temple she whispered, "Daughter, let us go to the morning room and talk." The two ladies exited the parlour leaving bewildered men in their wake.

Jason had no idea how he so quickly lost his connection with Victoria. One moment they were standing united in love ready to face her parents and eager to take the next step. In the next moment, he felt her emotionally pull away from him just when her mother seemed to find a reason to be excited for them. *Did her doubts infect Victoria after all?* Nervously he glanced at Mr. Lambert who shrugged his shoulders. Even after years of marriage, he had no better understanding of the female mind. It gave Jason pause for concern. *Had he acted too rashly?*

Mrs. Lambert ushered her stunned daughter into the morning room now awash with the golden glow of sunrise. She gently led Victoria to the deep mahogany and cream brocade sofa and then settled in close beside her. She waited for Victoria to gather her thoughts and speak first. She had a good idea what was bothering her daughter but wanted to be sure. It gave her time to gather her own thoughts. For many moments, the only sound to be heard was the soft ticking of the mantel clock.

Victoria finally raised her eyes to the gentle, concerned gaze of her mother. "I love Jason. I want to be his wife with all my heart." She looked down at her lap. The subject of intimacy embarrassed her. "But I am not sure I am ready to have children. I mean to actually have a child. To bear..."

Her mother's lips quirked, unseen. For all she wanted to discourage the sudden marriage, she had to give her daughter full encouragement in this matter. She lifted Victoria's chin forcing their eyes to meet. "Becoming a mother is not a sudden thing. There are nine months in which to prepare, not only physically, but mentally as well. As for the rest of it, well, women have been having babies since the beginning of time. It is God's way, and the Lord will see you through it. And afterwards, you have this new miracle entrusted to your care, and your love for it will have no bounds. It is the most wonderful experience a woman can have, and when the time comes, I know you will be ready. Put your fear aside, dearest. It is borrowed trouble anyway. The more important question is, are you sure you want Lord Malwbry to be the father of your children?"

Victoria gave the question the due consideration her mother expected. In all ways, the answer was yes. Could she submit to Jason in producing a child? Yes. Could she see him as a good father to their children? Yes. She only hoped it would not happen too soon, although she did find comfort in her mother's words. Her thoughts circled back to her mother's earlier reaction to their betrothal. "Do you find fault with Jason?"

Her mother took a heavy breath. "No, dear. My greatest concern is the old adage, 'marry in haste and repent at leisure.'"

"What do you mean?"

"When you let your heart or your," she hesitated in search of the right word, "passion guide your decision to rush into marriage, later you may discover you made a mistake, and end up spending the rest of your life in misery. At least, you will have the engagement period to carefully consider your decision."

"How long is the engagement?"

"It varies with circumstances, but it should be at least a year."

"A year? Jason can't stay here a year. He has to get back to his estate. He was boarding a ship this morning."

"All the better. The separation will give you time to ensure you have made a wise decision."

"But mother..." She hesitated knowing what she was going to say would sound petulant.

Her mother patted her hand. "Absence makes the heart grow fonder."

Victoria remained silent. The thought of letting Jason leave without her was unbearable, but she knew better than to argue with her mother. It would only end in the certainty of Jason leaving without her. She was going to have to bide her time, and let Jason and her father settle the matter.

Her mother stood and held out a hand for Victoria to do so as well. "Let us breakfast with your young man so we may get to know him better."

Their meal of toast, eggs, and fruit was accompanied with pleasant conversation. Her parents mostly asked about his family and descriptions of Southampton, Midanbury, and his estate. It was at the end of the meal when their cups of tea and coffee were refilled that her father again broached the sensitive subject of Jason's departure.

"Lord Malwbry, when do you plan to leave for England?"

"I am not sure, sir. It took two weeks to find this morning's ship bound for France. I don't know how long we will have to wait for the next one. It could take weeks."

Victoria saw her mother's head snap up at his use of 'we' but her father silenced any protest from her with a firm look.

Finally, the meal was concluded. The young couple was allowed to have some time together, albeit, chaperoned by Lydia. Victoria led Jason by the hand to her mother's garden behind the house. They sat together on the same wooden bench she had retreated to in despair earlier in the week. How different she felt now!

Lydia paced nearby until she grew weary of walking. She retrieved a stool from the outdoor kitchen, and placed it so she could sit and lean against the building. The lovers were in sight, but she could not easily overhear them.

Jason picked up Victoria's hand and laced his fingers with hers. Neither of them were wearing gloves. The contact was exhilarating, bringing a becoming flush to Victoria's cheeks. He brushed his thumb lightly across hers. The simple touch had a profound effect on her amplified senses.

Jason leaned his head down to rub his cheek against the downy softness of hers. Her lure was potent. He could not resist tilting his head to place a kiss against the corner of her lips. Emboldened, he lifted his hand to her chin to turn her face to meet his. His eyes drifted closed as he pressed a light kiss against her dewy soft lips. The sensation was akin to a heady wine, and he would have explored more if not for Lydia's intentional cough. Reluctantly, he pulled back to see Victoria slowly open her luminescent eyes. Her lips curved into a pleasurable smile. Oh yes, he was looking forward to wedded bliss.

Her first romantic kiss. Victoria savored the magical wonder of the fleeting sensations wrought by the mere touch of his lips to hers. It was unlike anything she had ever experienced. It also somehow intensified her feelings toward her betrothed. She was eager to discover what other intimate wonders would be revealed in time. She hoped in a very short time. Patience was not one of her strong suits. Apparently, it wasn't one of Jason's either.

He touched his forehead to hers. "When can we be married? Very soon, I hope."

Victoria frowned recalling her mother's words.

Jason pulled back, his brow furrowed in concern. "You want to wait?"

Victoria quickly shook her head. "No I don't, but I'm afraid my mother may insist upon it. She said a year's engagement would be wise, and even suggested it would be good if you went home for a while."

Jason unconsciously shook his head. It was even less likely he could stand to board a ship without her now that they were betrothed. And to wait a year? He didn't want to wait another day.

Victoria squeezed his hand bringing his attention back to her. "You must speak with my father. He may be able to persuade her."

"Shall we speak with him together?"

"We could."

Hopefully, Jason asked, "Now?"

Victoria was surprised, "Now?"

"Yes, why not now? I want this settled. I need to know how long I must wait to make you mine." He raised their clasped hands to place a kiss against the back of hers.

She smiled at his impatience and the thrill of sensation his lips generated. She didn't want to wait either. The last two weeks were the longest of her life. A year would be unendurable. It wouldn't matter if he was here or away. Either would be senseless torture. She knew it wouldn't matter how long they waited; she was not going to change her mind. He was the man for her.

Seeing the acquiescence in her eyes, Jason stood and turned to her, using their still joined hands to pull her to her feet. Silently, they sought out her father. They hardly even noticed Lydia trailing behind them and dropping back to wait as they entered her father's study. He was busy writing out a business contract when they entered. He finished his sentence and returned the quill to its resting place before standing to greet them.

Victoria spoke first, "Mother speaks of a long engagement. A year at least."

Her father nodded. "It is always wise to take one's time in considering such a serious commitment."

Victoria stepped forward pleading with her eyes. "Time will not change my heart. I am sure of my decision."

Jason stepped forward as well. "Sir, my heart will not let me leave this island without her, and yet I must return. There are matters I need to attend to at home." Sheepishly he added, "And my travel funds are not unlimited."

Mr. Lambert's look turned shrewd. It was the first money had been mentioned. He wondered if it was not the young man's true intent in starting this conversation. "Meaning you could not extend your visit without replenishing your funds."

Jason's head came up at the tone of Mr. Lambert's voice. Pride firmed his chin. "I can procure the funds to stay. That is not the issue. It is more that, I have plans to implement to increase our family's income, and the state of things when I left were not in such a way as to allow the luxury of time."

Mr. Lambert leaned back in his chair the better to carefully study his future son-in-law's reactions. "It is customary to settle a dowry on one's daughter and it is commonly done between English aristocrats and wealthy Americans—the exchange of wealth for title."

Jason inhaled sharply. "I assure you sir, I am not seeking your wealth. I do admit it was the original intent in leaving England. At least, it was my parents' intent. I have since discovered, I would rather earn back the wealth of my family's holdings than have it propped up with a bridal dowry."

"A very noble and satisfactory answer. Still, I will see my daughter properly settled. I have my pride too."

"If you insist, then attach it to her alone. It will be her security should I fail."

"Do you have so little confidence in your success?"

Jason's jaw clenched. "For my part, I fully intend to succeed, but if I cannot control my father, my efforts may be for naught, and if something should happen to me before I fully inherit, Victoria would be at the mercy of my mother instead of the other way around. Having funds solely her own would be beneficial in either situation."

Mr. Lambert's respect for the young man rose several notches effectively erasing some of the lingering doubts he had for the young lord his daughter professed to love. He still wasn't ready to see her wed, but it was based on the pain of separation and not fear for her future. It still seemed unreal. His daughter—a duchess. A smile hovered on his lips. He held out his hand to Lord Jason. "I will do as you suggest. You are a sensible young man. I will be proud to have you as a son-in-law."

Victoria's face beamed. It was high praise indeed coming from her father. She was proud of Jason for earning his approval. But then her smile faded. "Father, what of our engagement? Can we not be married right away?"

Mr. Lambert turned his softened gaze on his only child and placed a hand along her cheek. "I will see what I can do, but please tell me you aren't thinking of today."

Jason turned a pleading look to his bride-to-be but left the decision to her.

Victoria saw the opposing requests in the eyes of the men she loved and for some reason it brought her friend to mind. "I couldn't possibly get married without Abby standing beside me." She turned to Jason. "Could we please wait for her to return?"

"Of course." It was still an unknown date, but at least it was less than a year.

Her father, ever the lawyer, made a counter proposal. "Once Mrs. Eatonton returns, you may marry just before the next ship sails for England."

Victoria and Jason's eyes both flew to Mr. Lambert's. He silenced Victoria's protest with a firm look. Jason accepted his decision having momentarily forgotten about needing replacement passage. It could be several weeks before he found another ship. Perhaps he should consider waiting in Charleston where passage might be more readily available. He sighed in frustration. He would wait until Abigail returned to broach the subject with his future father-in-law.

The couple left Mr. Lambert's study hand in hand. Jason turned to his love. "Walk me to the door?"

Victoria was surprised by his request. "You are leaving?"

He lifted their joined hands to his lips to press a tender kiss to the finger that would soon wear his ring—a ring he would first have to find. His grandmother's heirloom ring was in his father's safe in England. He would have to purchase a temporary substitute. And that was just one of many tasks. "I regret we must part for now. I need to see Mrs. Mallory about a room and see to a refund for my passage this morning." He paused for effect with a hovering smile. "And I must let the shipping offices know I am now looking for passage for two."

Victoria's petulance quickly turned to pleasure. "I suppose I could let you out of my sight for a little while."

They walked to the front door where Jason turned and curled a hand around the back of her neck. Victoria sucked in her breath in anticipatory surprise as Jason leaned in. Seeing Lydia's appearance out of the corner of his eye changed his intended kiss on Victoria's sweet lips to a brush across her cheek. "I will return before supper, my love." He opened the door and picked up his bags turning back after stepping out on the piazza. "Promise to think of me until then."

Victoria gave him a glowing smile. "With pleasure, my love."

Jason lingered in her soft gaze for a moment absorbing the radiant beauty of her, framed as she was in the entry. The gentle morning breeze caressed the escaped tendrils of her sable hair against her alabaster cheek. His fingers ached to do the same. Leaving her, even for a few hours was torture. How had he ever thought he could leave the island without her? With slow reluctance, he turned to walk down the steps. He reached the street and had yet to hear the door close behind him. The corner of his mouth lifted knowing she felt the same

159

reluctance.

The shadows were lengthening as Victoria and her mother took their afternoon tea in the parlour. Her father left the house shortly after Jason having several court cases on the docket to present to Judge Webb.

Victoria was lost in thought and growing impatient for Jason's return. Her mother had to ask her question twice to garner her attention. "Have you given any thought to a wedding dress?"

Victoria smiled sheepishly. "Not yet. Do you have a suggestion?"

"Perhaps we should visit Mrs. Wheeler tomorrow for her advice. We will also need to give consideration to what should be included in your trousseau. And you will need more trunks. One will not be enough for packing all your clothes and other belongings." The enormity of her daughter's leaving overcame her. She was unable to say another word for holding back her tears.

Seeing her mother's distress, Victoria rose to comfort her and in so doing felt the enormity of her decision making it difficult to breath. She would be packing all she owned to leave her home for another country, leaving all she knew behind. Under Jason's loving gaze, it was easy to make the decision. Now, when faced with the reality of all that her decision entailed, while still exciting, it was also daunting.

Knocking on the front door dispelled the moment. Victoria's heart leapt in anticipation of welcoming Jason's return. She left her mother to rush to the foyer in time to see the butler step aside to reveal Max and Abby. Victoria squealed in delight for the second time that day. She couldn't help releasing her joy, for Abby's return removed one impediment to her nuptials, plus the look of radiant happiness she and Max both wore must mean their scheme was successful.

The two ladies embraced and as the happy couple was welcomed into the Lambert home, Abby said, "We had to come tell you the news right away before you heard it elsewhere, after we freshened up, of course. I am afraid my dress was ghastly after a week at sea." She cast a loving smile to Max before returning her attention to Victoria. "We have returned from the reef victorious. Talmage is in custody and my father's ship is safely returned to her course." She placed her hand on Max's arm. "And we wanted to thank you."

Victoria put her hand to her chest, glancing from one to the other. "Thank me? Whatever for?"

Abby cast a loving gaze to her husband before answering,

"Because of your encouragement, we have come to understand each other, and now enjoy a happy marriage."

Victoria shook her head. "It was all your doing. I simply gave you a nudge. And, you say Talmage is under arrest? That is good news to be celebrated. Come into the parlour and have some refreshment." Abby started to protest so she added, "I have news to share as well."

Abby cast a look to Max who shrugged. Taking it as acceptance, Victoria turned and led them to the parlour. After greeting Mrs. Lambert and receiving their tea and biscuits, Abby asked, "What is your news Victoria? Please do not keep us in suspense any longer."

Victoria could no longer hide her delight. Her smile encompassed all her features. "As of this morning, Jason and I are engaged to be married." Expecting her friends to share her joy, she was greatly disappointed to see deep concern in Abby's eyes and Max's frown of disapproval. Her smile faded into confusion. Victoria gave Abby a probing look. "You do not approve?"

Mrs. Lambert asked, "Is there a concern with Lord Malwbry?"

Abby quickly shook her head. "No ma'am. Lord Malwbry is of fine character. It is merely the precipitousness of the betrothal which bears concern."

"Yes, I agree." Mrs. Lambert turned her gaze to Victoria. "But my daughter has always been headstrong. She set her cap for Lord Malwbry the moment she laid eyes on him. I fear there is no dissuading her."

Victoria's smile was tight. "No, there is not." She turned beseechingly to her friend for understanding. "Abby, I see you are concerned, but please believe, Jason and I are of one mind. We wish to be wed right away, so he may return to England and begin work managing his inheritance. He'll be here soon and you will see for yourself. I do have a favor to ask of you." Abby's eyes widened but Victoria rushed on before she could say anything. "Will you be my maid of honor?"

After a bare moment's hesitation, Abby smiled. "Of course, I will. You need only tell me when."

Victoria's face bloomed again. "Now that you have returned, we need only wait for a ship. Father stipulated we must wait until Jason finds passage to England again."

Max nodded. "Another two months and there should be plenty of ships sailing in that direction."

Victoria's smile fell. "Oh dear, we were hoping for much sooner."

Chapter 13

Jason's pace was lively as he returned to the Lambert's in the fading January sunlight. All in all, it was quite a remarkable day. From the depths of despair as he boarded a ship this morning, to the joyous high of securing the hand of the woman he loved, all in the space of time it took the sun to rise. He was once again settled in at the boardinghouse. The shipping offices had all been notified he was now looking for passage for two to England. Of course, his request generated curious questions, and his response brought hearty congratulations, well aware as they were of Mr. Lambert and his beautiful daughter.

The door opened as he turned from the street to the Lambert's front steps. The golden glow of the afternoon softened the stark contrast of Victoria's dark hair against her pale face. His heart jumped noting her pleasure in welcoming him enhanced her smile. He took the steps two at a time and came to an abrupt halt in front of his pleasantly startled fiancée. He gave her a quick kiss not caring who might witness it. The hours they were apart had been too long. Victoria's pretty blush in response made him feel like he could conquer the world.

Victoria was caught off guard by Jason's amorous attentions, but she had no objections to his kiss or pushing the boundaries of proper behaviour for a betrothed couple in public. That he was willing to do so was one of the things she loved about him. She stepped aside to let him in, and closed the door, shutting out the world. Knowing Lydia was in the kitchen and her parents were in the parlour, she leaned in to give him a full lingering kiss letting the novel sensations and his musky scent wash over her. It was a heady combination causing her knees to go weak and the world around them to fade from existence. Jason's hands grasped her elbows, steadying her, as he moved his lips against hers creating a delicious friction she had no idea existed.

Neither of them heard the approaching footsteps. The surprised gasp of her mother's maid startled them. Jason guiltily jerked away from Victoria. The maid continued past them and started up the stairs bringing her into Victoria's line of sight. Victoria's color increased at being caught, but then, she burst into relieved laughter that it wasn't one of her parents. Coyly, she met Jason's gaze and found the same mirth in the depths of his irises. The risk of being chastised was well worth the experience of his magical kiss. Her lips still tingled from the sensation. Reaching for his hand, she led him towards the parlour. "I have good news to share. Max and Abby have returned and Captain Talmage is in custody."

He lifted their entwined hands to place a kiss on the back of hers. "The only way this day could have been better is if I had found us passage home."

Jason held her parents enthralled for the entire meal with the story of his journey from England to Key West. His ability to share his faults and weakness with humor, and have his audience think nonetheless of him, was a gift. It also gave Victoria time to lovingly study all the nuances of his features; from his firm jaw line to his supple lips which even now colored her cheeks with remembered pleasure. She liked how he gestured with his hands when he was excited, how merriment turned his eyes bright blue, and embarrassment flushed his neck more than his cheeks. But mostly, she liked how every once in a while his eyes would catch hers with a deep soulful look as if they were sharing a lover's secret.

After supper her father kept Jason busy with talk of politics and the differences between England and America. When tempers heated while disagreeing on the results of the War of 1812 her mother promptly called an end to the evening. The two young lovers were given precisely two minutes alone in the foyer to say good night. Victoria didn't object when Jason used the time to employ his lips in another manner ending with a whispered good-bye when her father loudly cleared his throat before stepping out of the parlour. She watched her beloved leave, reluctantly closing the door when Jason was no longer in sight.

Victoria sat before her vanity mirror absently brushing her hair as she recalled every moment of the most amazing day of her life. Deep in thought, her mother's appearance at her shoulder startled her.

Mrs. Lambert smiled indulgently. "I did knock, dear, but you didn't hear." She gently took the brush from Victoria's still hand and resumed the task of brushing out her long tresses.

Victoria closed her eyes enjoying the soothing sensation.

Her mother made a soft sound and Victoria's questioning eyes met her smiling gaze in the mirror. "I was just recalling how you hated to have your hair brushed as a child."

"I hated having to sit still and endure the tangles."

"You also hated the time it took to braid your hair to prevent the tangles, my impatient little girl."

Their eyes met in the mirror. Victoria whispered, "I'm sorry I wasn't the daughter you wanted me to be."

The brushing stopped. Her mother leaned forward to look directly in her eyes. "I was never disappointed in you, Victoria Marie, don't even for a minute think that I was. I love you for who you are not who I wanted you to be."

Tears pricked Victoria's eyes. Her mother's words touched her heart. "Thank you."

Her mother resumed brushing her hair and several moments passed in comfortable silence before she once again met Victoria's gaze in the mirror. "Are you sure Lord Malwbry is the one?"

Victoria steadily held her gaze as she firmly said, "Yes."

"Darling, don't misunderstand. Your father and I like him but England is so very far away."

"I know. I am going to miss you terribly, but my love for Jason is strong. As much as I hate leaving you and father, now, knowing Jason loves me too, I will go wherever he goes."

Her mother laid the brush on the vanity and smiled benevolently. "My daughter, one day a duchess. I never dreamed of such a thing."

Victoria dropped her head in shame. "I know I'm not worthy..."

Her mother's anger was unexpected. "Hush child." She moved to stand in front of Victoria and lifted her chin with her right hand. When their eyes met she continued speaking with urgent firmness. "You most certainly are worthy. You may not have been raised from birth in nobility, but you have nothing to be ashamed of. I have every faith that you will learn to be a very noble duchess—perhaps not an entirely proper one, but certainly a noble one."

They both smiled as her mother leaned down to press her forehead to Victoria's. "However, I am very concerned about the hastiness of your plans and the certainty of your heart. Take this night to search your soul, question your heart, think it through with your head and not your emotions. If by morning, you are still sure you have found your true love, then I am happy for you. It is a gift. I will miss you dearest." She placed a kiss on her forehead and turned to leave. At the door she paused, her face wistful. "Goodnight Victoria."

Victoria was left in the candlelit quiet to sift through her churning emotions. She thought it strange her mother was more certain she could be a duchess than believe her truly in love. She was certain of her feelings for Jason. She loved him beyond reason from the moment of their meeting. Each day had only strengthened the bond, but thoughts of being a duchess terrified her. Almost enough to call off the wedding. The sharp wrenching pain around her heart every time she considered doing so kept her from it. Instead, she shied away from any thoughts of what awaited her in England, but her mother was right. She needed to carefully consider everything including her ability to be a duchess. In that regard, her mother's confidence did much to bolster her own.

Victoria awoke late and lethargic having spent much of the night tossing and turning in turmoil over her future role, but she also had sweet moments reliving and cherishing the events of the day. Especially the moment Jason first told her he loved her down by the dock and his later proposal in the parlour. Her first kiss; a kiss that awakened physical desire. She felt the excitement of it even now, shimmering below the surface of her being. She wanted to feel even more.

Knowing she would see him soon, and the thrill of maybe finding a private moment in which to kiss again, chased away her lethargy. Excitement had her throwing off the covers and racing to face the new day. Duchess worries could wait. As far as she was concerned, they could wait until the moment the title transfer was imminent. Didn't her mother like to say 'worry was only borrowed trouble'? She smiled at her reflection as she poured fresh water in the basin and dipped a clean cloth to wash her face.

A short while later, she was breakfasting alone in the dining room when the butler ushered in Jason, hat in hand, flushed with exuberance. Victoria rose from her seat as Jason crossed the room in hurried strides to greet her.

Jason could contain his news no longer, it burst from him as soon as their hands touched. "A ship will be leaving this port Monday bound for England. I have booked our passage."

Victoria was speechless. She was prepared to wait weeks, now it would be days. A few days in which to pack all her belongings, prepare for a wedding, and say goodbye to her parents and all her friends.

Her continued silence worried Jason. He tilted his head to meet her wayward gaze. "Are you having doubts, my love?"

She smiled for him. "No, of course not. I was thinking of all I would need to do in less than a week. I became a bit overwhelmed, I suppose."

Fearing her answer, Jason offered, "Would you prefer to wait for the next one?"

Victoria shook her head. "No. Monday is fine." She smiled and her breath contracted as excitement grew in her breast.

Jason breathed a sigh of relief.

Mr. Lambert entered the room, having heard Jason's voice.

Victoria moved from Jason to her father excited to share the good news. "Father, Abby is returned and a ship is imminent. The criteria you set for our wedding has been met. All we need now is your blessing. Could we marry this Saturday?"

"You seem to have overlooked one important thing. There currently is not a clergyman present on the island."

Victoria stomped her foot. "Drat this small island. This would not be an issue if we still lived in Charleston."

Jason frowned. "But my love, we would never have met if you lived in Charleston."

Victoria gave him a rueful smile.

Mr. Lambert muttered, "You still would not be able to marry so soon as your mother would insist on waiting for the banns to be posted. Actually, I am sure your mother would prefer a church wedding. Perhaps the wedding should be held in Charleston."

Victoria shook her head. "Then we would have to wait on another ship." She grabbed Jason's hand and tugged him towards the door. "We should see Captain Max right away."

Jason followed her without question trusting that she had an idea.

Her father called after her, "What can he do?"

She paused to answer. "He can take us to find a minister. Surely there is one to be found in Cuba or the Bahamas and brought here."

Her father strode forward. "Wait just a minute daughter. You may ask Captain Eatonton to search for a minister. Lord Malwbry may join him if he likes, but under no circumstances are you to go with them. Is that understood?"

Victoria ducked her head to hide her smile. "Yes, father."

"Very well then, off with you now."

It only took a few minutes for them to walk from the Lambert's dining room to the Eatonton's front door. Victoria knocked with impertinence despite the earliness of the hour.

Maria answered the door. "Good to see you, Miss Lambert, Lord Malwbry."

"Good morning Maria. Could we speak with Captain Max?"

Max and Abby appeared behind Maria to welcome Jason and Victoria into their home. While the men shook hands, Victoria kissed Abby's cheek in greeting. She whispered, "You two seem to be happily in love with each other."

Abby blushed and whispered back, "As do you," before stepping back to greet Jason.

Victoria reached for Jason's hand as she turned to Max. "We are in need of your assistance."

Max's head tilted as he studied the pair before him. "How so?"

"Jason found passage to England for us on Monday. We need to marry right away except there is no minister present."

Max smiled. "So you would like for me to marry you at sea. I happen to be doing just that for Thomas and Maria on Friday. It could be a double ceremony."

Victoria sputtered in dismay. "Well, I hadn't thought, um..." She turned to Jason for help.

Jason said, "It is a generous offer but..."

Victoria regained her voice. "I'm afraid mother would not approve. We are pushing her limits by not having a proper church wedding. She would never allow us to forego clergy as well."

Jason nodded. "My family would feel the same."

Max's brow furrowed. "Then what is it you are asking?"

Victoria's eyes implored him. "To help us find such a person and bring him here."

"I am afraid I cannot help." Max turned his gaze to his wife. "I promised Abby a week on shore, and I'll not break it."

Jason gave a nod of acceptance, but Victoria turned her pleading eyes to Abby.

Abby lifted her hand to caress the back of Max's bicep. "For this, I will release you from your promise as long as you take me with you."

Max's gaze moved from Abby to Victoria to Jason before he sighed in surrender. "Very well. Where do you suggest we start?"

Victoria breathed a sigh of relief. "Cuba is closest if you think a priest could be found who speaks English. There are British colonies in the Bahama. Loyalists fled there after the war. Surely you could find a priest or minister among them willing to travel."

Jason handed Max a black drawstring bag. "A donation to their church may prove a useful persuasion."

Max nodded. "It may indeed. Does it matter the denomination?"

Jason said, "My mother would prefer Anglican or Protestant, but I will settle for whatever gets us married by Sunday."

Victoria smiled. "My parent's would prefer Episcopalian, but I agree with Jason."

"Very well." Max turned to Abby. "If I can persuade enough of the crew to give up their liberty to sail the ship on this lover's errand, could you be ready to leave in a few hours?"

Abby smiled, "Of course."

"Good. I think the Bahamas is the better choice. I would like to be there and back before Friday." He turned to Jason. "You are welcome to join us if you can handle sleeping in a crewman's hammock."

Jason wanted nothing more than to turn down the offer, but Max's challenging look made him say, "I accept." Besides, this mission was for his cause. The more people looking, the faster it could be a *fait accompli,* and it would give him something to do while Victoria was busy with wedding plans and packing.

"Good. Meet us at Mr. Browne's wharf in an hour."

* * *

Thursday afternoon the sunlight streamed through Victoria's window highlighting the chaotic pile of discarded clothing and trinkets strewn across her bed. Most of the floor space was taken up with three packed trunks and one open chest she was almost finished packing. It was just as well Jason sailed with Max and Abby. It had taken every moment since they left on Tuesday for Victoria to reduce her worldly possessions to fit within the confines of four pieces of luggage. She also managed a few fittings with Betsy. The plum dress was almost finished. It was turning out even more luxurious than she imagined. She couldn't wait to don it for her wedding.

Assuming there would be a wedding come Saturday. The *Mystic* had yet to return with her beloved and a minister. She missed Jason terribly. She felt lonely, despite the constant attention of servants and her mother as they helped her pack. Thankfully, the task of packing occupied her during the day. She wasn't sure how she was going to cope when she was done, for the nights were interminably long as she lay awake thinking of Jason and imagining what her life will be like in

England.

She straightened from the chest pressing her hands against the ache in her lower back. She wandered over to the window facing the north end of the harbour. Idly, she watched the slow progress of a small fishing boat when a commotion downstairs caught her attention. She left her room to investigate. Her pace and her heartbeat quickened as the robust timbre of Jason's voice drifted up the stairs. Her excitement was such that she wanted to fly down the stairs and into his arms. Her parents' presence held her to decorum.

Jason's gaze was drawn to Victoria's as she appeared at the top of the stairs. He wanted nothing more than to race up the stairs, sweep her into his arms, and indulge in her sweet kisses. Propriety held his feet still but his eyes never left hers as she descended the steps. Halfway down a slow sweet smile blossomed on her face and his heart raced. Absence indeed made his heart grow fonder. Two days ago, he would not have thought it possible to love her more, but now, he could not deny the strength of his affection for her expanded deep in his soul. How much more would he love her tomorrow? After their vows? In twenty years? It was a wonderful, yet overwhelming, consideration.

As she reached the bottom step, he held his hand out for her. She placed her slender fingers on his open palm. He curled his hand around them bringing the back of her hand to his lips. His eyes never left hers. It was a far cry from what he wanted, but he would take what he could for now. He need only wait two more days before they would be pronounced man and wife. On that night, he would claim her lips with all the passion and desire he now must withhold.

Mr. Lambert cleared his throat.

Jason reluctantly lifted his lips from her skin, but he refused to release her hand.

Victoria finally found her voice to ask the only question that mattered, "Did you find a minster?"

Jason smiled. "We did indeed. He is a Protestant, Reverend John Forsyth. Captain Max and Abigail are currently seeing him settled in at Mrs. Mallory's."

Mrs. Lambert frowned. "An Episcopalian would have been better. I suppose a Protestant will do."

Mr. Lambert laid an arm across his wife's shoulders. "I am sure Reverend Forsyth will do just fine."

Jason turned back to Victoria. "Would you care for a stroll? The weather this afternoon is quite pleasant."

Victoria smiled. "I would love to."

As they reached the street, Jason held his arm out for Victoria. She curled her arm around his bicep getting as close to him as she could. Close enough to pick up the musky smell of sailing under his recent application of *Eau de Cologne*. Lydia trailed behind as chaperone.

Victoria looked up at the smooth jawline of her beloved. "I apologize for my mother's disparage of the reverend. I, for one, am grateful you met with success, for I would hate to miss this sailing."

Jason smiled down at his love. "I took no offense. I suppose I am so used to listening to my mother's complaints that hearing your mother's was almost expected."

Victoria frowned. "How sad. Is your mother never pleased?"

"I have rarely seen it. Besides, I am sure her disapproval is governed as much by their struggle to accept your coming departure as it is the denomination of the reverend."

She sighed. "I daresay you are correct."

Enjoying the late afternoon sun, they walked all the way out to the lighthouse and were now following the shoreline back to town, hand in hand, sharing whispered sweet sentiments. Occasionally, Jason would stop to pick up a seashell that garnered his attention and sometimes add them to the growing collection in his pocket.

After a dozen or so, Victoria asked, "What do you plan to do with those?"

Sheepishly he said. "I have no idea."

Victoria couldn't help but join in the hunt adding her finds to his other coat pocket.

Coming in line with Clinton Place, they made their way back to Front Street. Slowly they walked the length of it to return to her house in time for supper.

Time flew from then until the day of her wedding. The lovers reluctantly parted company after supper on Thursday. Friday, she and Jason boarded the Mystic along with all the other invited guests to sail out into the Atlantic where Captain Max performed the marriage of his deck hand, Thomas, to Abby's maid, Maria.

The bride and groom chose Max as officiator over Reverend Forsyth since they were not familiar with his religion and Max was their friend. A meal of fish, rice, and beans was served aboard ship. It was followed with Maria's mother's recipe for Jamaican rock buns which Abby likened to fruit and spice scones.

It was a simple affair, but touching. It made Victoria all the more impatient for her day. Her stomach was knotted with nervous excitement and a bit of trepidation. Jason seemed to be very calm and assured. She wished she felt the same. Upon their return, Mrs. Lambert insisted they part company until the ceremony. Victoria reluctantly wished her bridegroom a good evening. Jason lightly kissed her cheek. "Until tomorrow, my love."

Saturday morning Victoria sat before her vanity in her underclothes as Lydia put the finishing touches to her upswept hair. She pressed both hands to her middle hoping to calm the nervous fluttering. The silky plum gown waited on her bed. Soon she would don it and make her way downstairs and out to the garden to take her vows. Two days after she would leave her home for England. Panic bloomed. She took a deep breath to quell it. She wanted this. All her life she dreamed of marrying someone who would take her to the unknown. Now that her dreams were coming true, and on a grander scale than she imagined, she should be ecstatic, not panicked.

Jason impatiently paced the length of the study with a barely touched drink in his hand. Mr. Lambert ushered him into the room upon his arrival to await the ceremony. He was early, over an hour early, but he would rather wait here than in his cramped boardinghouse room all alone. After a few stilted attempts at conversation, Mr. Lambert picked up his paper and left Jason to his thoughts.

Jason was anxious to get the wedding done. He was fearful that at any moment, his bride would get cold feet and call off their nuptials. She was giving up her family, her home, and her country, for him. He couldn't believe he was fortunate enough to have found a woman who loved him enough to make such a sacrifice.

A short while later, Captain Max and Abby were ushered into the room. Jason rushed forward to greet them.

Abby said, "Excuse me gentlemen, I am going to check on the bride."

Jason bowed to her and then turned to Max. "Thank you again for agreeing to stand up with me."

Max clapped him on the back. "Glad to do it."

Lydia answered the knock on Victoria's bedroom door and opened it wide to allow Abby to enter.

Abby's smile widened as she approached her friend. "You look beautiful."

Victoria ran her fingers over the full skirt. "Betsy worked late into the night finishing it. You don't think it's too dark for a wedding dress?"

Abby shook her head. "No. It gives your skin an alabaster glow."

Victoria pinched her cheeks again. "My reflection looks pale."

Abby grinned. "You look like a blushing bride." At Victoria's skeptical look she added, "Are you going to trust me or your mirror?"

"You're biased."

"Your mirror is faulty."

Victoria gave her friend a false horrified look before both ladies broke down in laughter. Lydia smiled indulgently at their silliness.

Abby sobered first. "I brought you something borrowed, Tria."

Victoria shook her head. "You didn't need to."

"No. But I wanted to." She laid a velvet bag of royal blue on Victoria's bed and proceeded to pull out its content.

Victoria gasped, recognizing it instantly. "Oh, Abby, I couldn't! It's your family heirloom."

Abby smiled benevolently. "Hence the reason it is borrowed. You will wear it. I insist." She carefully held the gold and jeweled tiara out for Victoria.

Victoria accepted it with trembling fingers, afraid that she would drop it. She passed it to Lydia to place in her hair. Sunlight sparkled off the facets of exquisitely cut sapphires, diamonds, and emeralds. It brought to mind for Victoria, the way the bright sun would play off the rippled water surrounding the island.

Mrs. Lambert walked in and gazed at her daughter in wonder. Tears sprang to her eyes. "Oh my, you are a stunning bride." She recognized the tiara from Abby's wedding and turned to her. "Something borrowed, I hope?"

Abby nodded.

"What a beautiful gesture of friendship." She turned to Victoria. "I brought you this handkerchief to borrow, but I see you have no need of it."

Victoria rose to hug her mother, accepting the handkerchief. She lifted it to dab at her tear filled eyes. "I beg to differ."

Mrs. Lambert cleared her throat and reached into her pocket.

"You have your borrowed handkerchief and crown with blue sapphires and your new dress." She took Victoria's hand and turned it over to place a pair of diamond earbobs on her palm. "And here is something old. They belonged to your grandmother. They are yours now." Mrs. Lambert held up a coin. "And from your father, a penny for your shoe."

Victoria's eyes watered anew as she hugged her mother. She looked around the room from her mother, to her best friend, to the woman who cared for her daily needs in so many ways, and whispered, "I am blessed."

A disquiet downstairs announced the arrival of the reverend and soon after guests began to arrive. Victoria's father knocked on her door ready to usher her to her wedding. A few deep breaths were required to calm her nerves and square her shoulders.

On the final day of January, 1829, Victoria Marie Lambert married Lord Jason Albert Duncan Malwbry in the dappled sunlight beneath the mahogany tree in her mother's garden. All who attended declared her a beautiful blushing bride and Jason to be a dashing bridegroom. Together they made a stunning pair. The ceremony was followed with a decadent luncheon of roasted meats and vegetables, served from silver platters on white damask covered tables adorned with flowering tree limbs, accompanied with plenty of wine. Afterwards, the guests were treated to a delicate, iced, almond flavored cake.

Jason's gaze sought out his bride across the parlour. The guests had dwindled down to a half dozen of the Lambert's closest friends. She looked as fresh and lovely now as when she first appeared in the doorway leading to the garden. And now, as it did then, his heart nearly stopped as he took in her delicate creamy skin against the dark purple silk, and her dark tresses framing her face, smiling just for him. The sunlight catching on the jeweled tiara completed the picture of his perfect duchess-to-be. Pride surged in him that he would call this beauty his wife. He wished an artist had been available to capture the moment to grace the hall of Rothebury forever. He promised himself, one of the first things he would do upon returning home, was commission an artist to paint her.

The ceremony was hours ago. The servants were clearing the last vestiges of the reception from the yard. The sun was dropping low on the horizon. Soon they would have a late supper and then the wedding night could begin. Soon he would be able to claim his beautiful bride.

Victoria felt the weight of Jason's gaze from across the room much as she was acutely aware of the unaccustomed weight of the gold band on her left hand. She looked to find his hooded gaze focused on her. Her middle tightened. Tonight she was a bride. The full meaning of it came rushing to her in a fluttering, flushing panic.

Abby leaned in, startling her, as she whisper, "Relax. You will eventually enjoy what is to come. Just follow his lead." She offered Victoria a fortifying smile.

In a private moment only a little while ago, Abby had given Victoria a cursory, albeit more than her mother had told her, description of what to expect. It had only served to increase Victoria's tension.

It was time for bed. Victoria watched with trepidation as her father handed Jason a lit candelabra and wished him good night. Their simple supper of soup and bread churned in her belly. Her parents came to wish her a good night before passing by and leaving her alone in the parlour with Jason. He approached her with an enigmatic smile.

Jason lifted her hand to his lips and pressed a gentle kiss against her knuckles. "Shall we retire, my love?"

The warmth of the candles heated her right cheek. His hand released hers to brush across her left cheekbone and curl around her neck.

Her voice was surprisingly weak when she answered him, "Yes."

His lips descended to hers in a feather light kiss that eased some of her tension and left her wanting more. He took her hand again and led her from the room, up the stairs, to the door of her bedroom.

"Wait here."

Victoria thought the request odd but did as he asked. Jason entered the room and placed the candelabra on her dresser. He then returned to her with a confident air. In the next heartbeat, he scooped her up into his arms cradling her against his chest. After another quick kiss, he carried her across the threshold. "Wouldn't want to risk any evil spirits."

"Don't tell me you believe in that nonsense."

He kicked the door shut with his foot and walked over to the bed before letting her slip to her feet. "No, but I do believe in traditions and that was one, in particular, I looked forward to carrying out."

He kissed her deeply arousing all the awareness and excitement he had once before, and then he showed her what it meant to be truly man and wife.

Chapter 14

The salty wind blew loose tendrils about her face as Victoria stood at the rail of the brig having crossed the English Channel. She pulled her cape tighter to ward off the chilly March air. She grew anxious as she watched the Southampton shore grow closer. So too, did she notice the tension increase in her husband's shoulders. Over the course of their voyage across the Atlantic sharing a compact cabin, she learned to read his moods and had grown used to thinking of him as her husband. The last seven weeks had passed pleasurably.

She smiled to herself remembering the Sunday service following their wedding day; the strangeness of being called Lady Malwbry and answering questions regarding her husband and their plans. While strange, it made her joyful and happy.

Her smile turned wistful as she relived the tearful goodbyes of the Monday. As they boarded the ship bound for France, she clung to Jason for the strength to walk away from all that was safe and familiar. She still felt all the mixed emotions of standing at the railing waving goodbye to loved ones and marveling at all that had occurred in a week's time. It was just the previous early Monday morning, she had walked to the dock expecting to say a final farewell to Jason.

Victoria turned to look up at her husband. Seeing his tightened jaw, she squeezed his hand. He looked down at her and smiled reassuringly but she wasn't fooled. He was worried how his parents would receive her. She knew his concern was for her feelings and not for theirs, but she also knew, even if he didn't admit it to himself, he longed for their approval. And so did she.

Upon their arrival in France, Jason announced they would spend a week or two in Paris. Now she wondered if it wasn't an excuse to further delay their arrival at Rothebury.

Whatever the reason, she thoroughly enjoyed the afternoons they spent wandering the streets surrounding the Seine River, and visiting palaces, museums, and churches. Her favorites were the intricate details of the Pantheon's interior and the grandeur of the *Cathédrale Notre-Dame,* especially the gorgeous colours of its intricate stained glass. One day was spent strolling hand in hand along the footpaths and gardens of the *Champs-Élysées* finally reaching its end at Napoleon's partially built *Arc de Triomphe de l'Étoile.* It wasn't much more than the beginnings of the four base footings and had stood as such for over a decade as the current regime would not spend any money to complete it. She couldn't discern what it was supposed to end up looking like until they discovered the completed *Arc de Triomphe du Carrousel* at the east end of the city. The oddest thing they saw was Napoleon's large plaster version of what was to be a bronze statue of an imperial elephant. It was to be built on the remains of the *Bastille,* destroyed in July, 1789, at the start of the French Revolution.

On their last night in the city, he took her to the *Comédie-Française* housed in the *Salle Richelieu.* Her less than adequate French made the play hard to understand, but she enjoyed it nonetheless. The architecture of the building, the music, elaborate costumes, and set designs enchanted and delighted her like nothing she had ever seen before.

Their time in Paris were cherished memories to last forever; not only for the sights they had seen, but also for the time spent alone. Their only concerns of the moment were in pleasing each other. But all good things come to an end. This morning, they sailed from Le Havre, France to Southampton.

The brig was docked, and they were preparing to debark. Jason turned to Victoria at the top of the gangway. "It's going to be late by the time we reach Midanbury. Perhaps we should stay the night in the city and get a fresh start in the morning."

Victoria gave him a sympathetic smile as she laid a hand on his forearm. "I am weary of travelling. For better or worse, I am ready to meet your parents and get settled in your home."

Jason gave her a searching look. "Very well. Wait for me here on the ship. I will see to our transportation."

Victoria pulled her cloak tighter as she watched him leave and then cast a weary eye to the grey overcast sky. Cold had been her constant companion since leaving the Caribbean. She missed the warmth of the tropical sun. She wondered how long it would take for her to acclimate to the English climate. She was thankful Betsy had been thoughtful enough to make her the warm cloak she now wore, recommending she have it lined with fur once she was settled in England. Jason also had insisted they make a few purchases in Paris to supplement her wardrobe with woolen undergarments.

Jason soon returned with a hired carriage. It wasn't long before their luggage was loaded and they started off on the final leg of their journey.

Jason nudged Victoria awake as the carriage passed through the gates of Rothebury. Victoria did her best to freshen her appearance while stealing quick glances out the window, anxious to see her new home. The trees lining either side of the drive opened up as they circled in front of the house, and her view was filled by the impressive three story, seven bay, Georgian manor. The pale stone was bathed in the golden glow of twilight lending the home an ethereal beauty. Victoria fell in love with it on sight. She sighed, "It's lovely."

Jason smiled. He had to agree. In this light, the house was exquisite. He exited the carriage and held out his hand to assist her. The central door beneath the carved stone, arched hood opened to reveal an elderly gentleman dressed in a black suit with white gloves that she correctly assumed to be the butler.

"Welcome home, Lord Malwbry."

"Thank you, Mr. Flynn." Jason turned to Victoria. "And this is my wife, Lady Victoria Malwbry."

"Pleased to meet you, milady. Welcome to Rothebury Hall."

Victoria marveled at the total lack of surprise the butler displayed, for there was no time for Jason to send word to his family of their nuptials or their pending arrival. She frowned, unless unbeknownst to her, he posted them at their arrival in France. As she followed Jason into the house, the butler directed servants that seemed to appear as needed to tend to the horses and their luggage before following them into the narrow foyer with a surprisingly high ceiling to take their coats and gloves. To Jason he said, "Shall I have a chamber made up for Lady Malwbry?"

"Yes, the one to the right of mine. Her trunks can be deposited there. Will you also see that a bath is drawn for her in my room?"

"Of course, milord. Shall I announce your arrival?"

Jason grimaced. "Yes, I suppose so. Tell my parents to expect us down for dinner."

"Very good, milord. Will there be anything else?"

Jason waived him away and then turned to Victoria. "Let us adjourn to my chamber until yours is ready." He picked up the candelabra from the entry table as dusk made the interior light dim.

Mutely, she followed him from the foyer into an open area with white marble flooring and a large curved staircase with red carpeted steps which they ascended to the second floor. In the deepening shadows of the interior, she was only able to take in hints of the grandeur of her new home. She was excited to do some exploring tomorrow. They walked to the end of the upper hall which she guessed to be twice the length of her entire former home. At the end of the hall, she glanced into the room on the right, done in cream and gold, to see sheets being changed and furniture polished. Jason opened the door in front of them and walked inside a chamber twice the size of the one they just passed. Large double windows covered with heavy drapes filled two walls. Against the third wall was a grand four poster bed with a navy duvet. A bench stood at the foot of it beckoning her forward to rest. A marble fireplace filled the fourth wall next to the entry door with a cheery blaze to warm the room. In the corner next to it was a claw foot tub.

It wasn't long before a parade of servants piled her trunks in the cream and gold room and returned a short while later with buckets of steaming water for her bath. She would have liked to enjoy a long soak, but she needed to hurry if they were not going to be late for the evening meal. Lacking a maid, Jason helped her dress. She choose the plum gown as it was her best garment.

When they were ready, Jason paused at the door. "Don't expect my mother's approval. She will find fault in something, to be sure. Please don't let her make you feel inferior. Just remember, I love you and I have faith in you. Nothing else matters, certainly not her opinion."

"You really expect her to disapprove of me?"

"I hope she will approve, but you are not of her choosing so I wanted to prepare you for the worst."

"Thank you." She was already nervous to meet his parents. His words were meant to bolster her confidence, but they had the opposite effect. Her stomach tightened in response to her trepidation.

Jason saw her worry increase and knew not how to help. He kissed her hoping to convey his faith in her. He gave her his arm and led her downstairs through another lengthy hall to the dining room. He paused before entering to offer a smile of reassurance.

Victoria took a deep breath and donned a smile for her new in-laws, bracing for the worst. At their appearance, both his parents rose from their seats at either end of the long table and came forward to greet them under the glow of a multi-candle wall sconce. Victoria noted they both appeared to be a bit older than her parents. The Duchess was an inch taller than her and of slender build. She held herself tautly erect. She did approach them smiling in welcome, but it was stiff as if the expression were seldom worn. The Duke had a bit of a paunch and thinning hair, though his sideburns were bushy, giving him a squat appearance even though he was really a little taller than his wife. His welcome smile seemed jovial and sincere. Jason stood stiffly at her side as if bracing for a storm.

The Duke was first to speak. "Jason, welcome home. I see your journey was a fruitful endeavour."

Jason smiled tightly. "Mother, father, this is my wife, Lady Victoria."

Victoria curtsied, tilting her head low. When she looked up, she kept her features neutral. "Your Graces, it is a pleasure to meet you." Nervously, Victoria worried if she should have said Grace instead of Graces even though she meant both of them. *Was Graces even a word?*

The Duke genuinely smiled at her. "Welcome to Rothebury Hall, Lady Victoria. May I say you are quite beautiful? My son has chosen well for his bride."

Victoria returned the smile. "Thank you, Your Grace." *Oh no, wasn't it milord or sir after the initial greeting?* She wished now she had paid more attention to Abby when she was explaining these things, but she found it so boring at the time.

"So you have returned with a wife and thwarted the whole of Midanbury from an expected wedding. I suppose we will just have to tell everyone her family would not allow her to travel unmarried."

Jason was surprised his mother cared about the ceremony. "I honestly didn't think anyone would mind."

"Why ever would you assume that? We are an example to this community and events such as weddings are to be grand affairs. I suppose a reception will have to suffice."

"My apologies, mother."

The Duchess looked Victoria over thoroughly. "I trust your journey was uneventful?"

"Yes ma'am."

"You are American by birth?"

The disdain in which the Duchess said *American* made her face pucker as if she sucked on a sour plum. Victoria had to swallow hard to hide her amusement. "Yes ma'am. I was born in Charleston, South Carolina."

"And do you have siblings?"

"No ma'am. I am an only child."

The Duchess frowned. "Was your mother not capable of having more children?"

Victoria knew her face betrayed her shock at such a rudely personal question. In the next heartbeat, she bit her tongue to keep from asking the Duchess the same question.

Jason's anger was instantaneous. "Mother!"

To Jason, the Duchess said, "I was merely trying to learn something of this woman you have foisted on the family." She turned back to Victoria. "And what is your father's occupation?"

"He is a lawyer, ma'am."

Jason knew very well where his mother's line of questioning was leading. He sought to momentarily satisfy her curiosity without revealing confrontational information just yet. "He is a highly successful lawyer representing very lucrative cases of maritime salvage."

His mother's eyebrows rose and her head tilted slightly in silent acknowledgement to Jason for doing his duty. For now he was happy to let her believe there was a sizeable dowry to fill their estate. It would make this first night easier for Victoria.

"Shall we dine?" The Duchess abruptly returned to her chair to be seated by a waiting servant.

The Duke returned to his end of the long table. Jason led Victoria into the large room and held a chair for her at the center of the table that could easily seat twenty. Two large candelabras were the only adornment on the highly polished walnut surface. A few other candelabras on the side pieces provided additional lighting. Still much of the room was in shadows. As far as Victoria could tell the walls were painted maroon with gold stenciling above darkly stained wainscoting. Jason circled the table and upon sitting across from Victoria, the Duchess signaled for the pheasant *consommé* to be served.

Since one had to raise their voice to be heard across the room, very little was said as they made their way through the courses of the meal. Afterwards, they adjourned to the library across the hall from the dining room. Jason seated Victoria in a wing-back chair by the fire realizing she was unused to the cool English weather. His mother took up position in the opposite chair. Jason brought them each a glass of sherry. He meant to stay close to Victoria for support, but his father summoned him to the other end of the room for "a drink and a chat". As Jason walked away, he heard his mother ask Victoria for a list of her accomplishments.

His father lifted his brandy snifter in salute. "My congratulations son, she is a beauty and of a sweet disposition as well. And her father is a wealthy lawyer? How much of a dowry did she bring?"

Jason grimaced. He knew he wouldn't be able to put it off for long, but he had hoped to escape this night without having to face this confrontation. Perhaps a half-truth could delay the inevitable. "A rather sizeable one." His father's face lit with what could only be described as glee. Jason could well imagine he was thinking of the excitement of betting on races. Fear of what his father might do on the morrow, without the full truth, forced Jason's hand. With a deep sigh he added, "However, he is a very good lawyer. The dowry is in Victoria's name." He waited for this news to sink in. It didn't take long.

"Can it be transferred?"

"Not without her consent."

"Then, by God, you will get her to consent."

"No father."

The Duke frowned, "She is defying you already?"

"No." Jason inhaled deeply preparing for his father's wrath. "I requested it to be so."

His father's apoplectic response carried across the room. "You requested it!"

Jason grimaced as Victoria's gaze swung to meet his. "Yes."

"You have doomed us to debtor's prison."

"Don't be melodramatic. I have a plan to rebuild our estates."

"Rebuild? Even if you could, it will take too long."

Jason's brow furrowed. His father's dejected tone gave rise to suspicion. "Have you been gambling while I was away?" The slight rise of his shoulders was all the answer Jason needed. "Bloody hell." The curse slid out quietly so as not to alarm the ladies but no less vehemently. He turned away from his father to face the darkness outside the diamond pattern leaded glass. He wasn't going to be able to save both estates if his father didn't cease his gaming. Depending on how bad the losses were this time, he may very well have to ask Victoria for the money. It took a moment for him to calm down enough to turn around and ask, "How much did you lose?"

His father sheepishly shrugged again. "I don't know, a few guineas I suppose."

Skeptically, Jason said, "A few?" He suspected it was significantly more than a few.

His father's eyes narrowed as he let righteous anger flare. "You are my child. I do not answer to you."

Jason was unprepared to take on this battle with his father. It needed to happen but nothing would be accomplished tonight while they were both angry. Jason set his unfinished drink on the sideboard. "I find I am still weary from my travels. I will bid you good night." He didn't wait for a response but proceeded across the room to Victoria and offered her his hand. "My dear, are you ready to retire?"

With a silent nod in answer to his question, Victoria accepted his hand and rose to her feet. She noted the increased tension in Jason's face and shoulders. She herself was more than ready to abandon the Duchess' inquisition. She had asked for a detailed account of Victoria's education and accomplishments and was quite free in dispensing her opinion of perceived inadequacies. The Duchess was subtle in her attack for the conversation started comfortably open and Victoria willing was forthcoming with the details of her upbringing under the matriarch's encouragement. It was only after she had finished that the Duchess under the guise of a compliment declared her unsuitable to succeed her title. Victoria was trying to come up with a defense for an opinion she basically agreed with when Jason approached.

As Jason turned from closing the door of his bedroom, Victoria said, "You warned me but I didn't believe your mother could be such a nosey shrew."

At the same time, Jason declared, "My father is going to be the ruination of this family."

They both stopped and looked at each other in dismay, and then Jason laughed. The sound was infectious and Victoria couldn't help giggling too. He wrapped his arms around her and leaned his forehead to hers. "I am sorry."

"Why? You cannot control your parents."

"I know. I am sorry I took you away from your sunny island and lovely parents to this cold, damp, inhospitable house."

Victoria smiled, tilted her chin up to kiss him, and then pulled away to look in Jason's eyes. "I'm not sorry. This house, at least what I have been able to see so far, is magnificently splendid. I love it already, damp and all." She raised her hand to caress his cheek, "And because of you, we shared two wonderful weeks in Paris where I fell even deeper in love with you." She shook her head. "We will find a way to deal with your parents, together."

The sincerity shining in her eyes renewed his hope. He kissed her deeply and from there all thoughts of his parents or further discussion disappeared.

Morning sun streamed in through the drapes they had neglected to close the previous evening to fall across Jason's face, pulling him from slumber. He placed a kiss atop Victoria's head nestled into his shoulder before carefully extricating himself from her and the covers. He pulled fresh clothes from his wardrobe, absently thinking he would need to get around to hiring a new valet. Maybe he should start with inquiring after his former valet, Reginald, on the off chance he was not gainfully employed elsewhere. Victoria was in need of a new maid as well.

Jason was fully dressed and prepared to leave the room when Victoria began to stir. She sat up in bed and stretched her arms upward immediately pulling Jason's thoughts away from his plans for the day. She coyly smiled at him, and he moved her way to claim a kiss. Waking up to her smile was one of his favorite things about being married. Victoria rose to her knees the better to cling to him and deepen the kiss. Jason pulled away with a smile. "You keep that up, my lady, and we will never leave this chamber today."

"And where is the harm in that?"

"I have things that need tending today."

Victoria smiled. "Yes you do. I am looking forward to you showing me around my new home."

Jason frowned. He had planned to drag his father to their solicitors to learn how great his recent gambling losses were and how the affairs stood with both the Rothebury and Malwbry estates. Then, he wanted to visit his steward and tenants and see first-hand how his land was being managed. Victoria's smile wilted tugging on his resolve. It would be cruel to leave her alone on her first day. Surely, one more day would not change anything. "Right you are, my lady. We shall spend the day exploring the grounds together." Her smile was restored making Jason happy, and then she frowned again.

"You know, it is deucedly inconvenient for my clothes to be in the other room if I am sleeping in here."

Jason gave her a secretive smile as he held out his hand. He led her off the bed and over to an open area of wall in the corner beside his dresser. "There was a particular reason I chose your room to be to the right of mine." He pushed his hand against a specific piece of wood trim and a hidden door swung open into her adjoining room.

Victoria was beguiled. "How clandestine!" She moved through the open doorway, and then turned as a disturbing thought occurred. "How many times have you used this passage?"

"Only once."

Victoria couldn't help the jealousy filling her. "Did you care for her?"

Jason's lip quirked in amusement at her misconception but seeing the storm of emotion in her eyes he quelled it. "I used it once, alone, when I was much younger to avoid a confrontation with my mother."

"Oh." Victoria's relieved smile could not be held in check.

"I believe some long distant great uncle had it installed when he married for the same reason you are using it now. He could have commissioned an ordinary door, but he chose a hidden one to please his wife's whimsy."

"Are there any other secret passages in the house?"

"None that I know of, unless, you want to count the servants hall between the north and west wing."

She held her hand to him. "Come help me dress. I am anxious to explore."

Jason followed her into the room. "After the house, it would be best to see the rest of the estate on horseback."

Victoria turned to him with a bright smile. It had been ever so long since she had rode a horse.

Jason tucked a strand of hair behind her ear. "Do you have riding habit?"

Her face fell. "No. But I can make do with my oldest dress."

"I see that besides a maid more additions to your wardrobe are in order."

Victoria turned her back to Jason so he could tighten the stays of her corset. "Are you weary of dressing me already?"

He placed a kiss on her nape as he pulled the strings of her stay. "I do find it difficult to cover your tempting flesh when I much prefer ravishing it."

A short while later, they began their tour from the upper story of the south wing where Jason's room was located to the dining room. In the light of day, Victoria could see the many paintings and tapestries hung along the hall, and the richness of the burgundy carpet with floral outlines running the length of the hall. The walls were white plaster and the brass sconces placed at regular intervals gleamed. The housekeeper and maids kept the house well cleaned.

The walls in the dining room were indeed maroon with ornate gold stenciling. Two large oil paintings of the house facade in spring and fall dominated the walls of the room while the huge walnut table filled the breadth of it. They filled their plates from the covered platters on the sideboard of scrambled eggs, bacon, sausage, fried tomatoes and mushrooms, and baked beans, along with toast and wild honey served at the table.

Jason conspiratorially whispered to her, "In my boyhood, I considered this room a torture chamber. I was forever being admonished to mind my manners, and do you know what Nanny's method was for instilling proper posture?"

Victoria smirked in amusement. "No. What did she do?"

"She would tie a knife to the back of my chair, so that if I dared to lean back, I would get the sharp end between my shoulders."

Victoria was horrified. "You can't be serious."

"Oh, but I am."

She noticed, even though it was just the two of them eating at the large table, Jason sat erect, his back several inches from the back of the chair. It made her smile and then frown thinking of Jason's sad childhood.

The tour continued after their breakfast with the morning room, library, drawing room, and parlour of the downstairs. All were tastefully decorated in rich colors except for the morning room which was done in pale rose. Next he took her upstairs into the north wing, where his parents resided. He showed her the currently unused nursery where he spent his tender years before proudly leading her down the east gallery hall. He pointed out portraits of his various ancestors ending with one of his mother as a young girl of perhaps sixteen. Victoria was mesmerized by the young woman with soft brown hair, warm brown eyes, and a smile hovering on her lips; so completely opposite of the woman she was now. "She was beautiful. I see you get your nose and chin from her."

"Hmm, I hadn't really given it any thought."

Victoria looked back down the row of paintings. "These are all of your mother's family. What of your father or his family?"

"There are none."

Her chin dropped as she puzzled out this information. "So your father became a duke by marriage. The title is from your mother's family?"

"Yes."

"And what of the Malwbry estate?"

"I inherited it from a cousin on my mother's side. My father is the second son of a baron."

"Oh." She gave a last glance to the portrait of the young Duchess as she followed Jason from the hall. What she learned helped explain some of the tension between Jason's parents.

Next, he pointed out the stairs to the third floor servants quarters as he led her to the back stairs and down to the kitchen at the back of the house. He introduced her to the plump French cook and the other staff lingering nearby. She was surprised he knew them all by name. So far she had met well over a dozen footmen and maids in addition to the butler and the housekeeper. She supposed it took many to keep a house of this size in proper order.

Rather than leave the house from the kitchen door, Jason led them back into the interior, so they could exit from the Gothic door in the south facade leading directly into the gardens. This section was different in style from the front of the house. One or the other must have been an addition, but Victoria couldn't say for certain which part came first. They both appeared to have been constructed more than a century ago.

Jason paused at the door to assist Victoria into her warm cape. The moderately cool temperature felt good to him, but he was sure his wife would find it quite chilly. They did not linger overlong in the gardens for it was too early in the season for much to be seen; only a few early spring bulbs, the winter camellias in bloom, and a budding maple tree. He assured Victoria in a few weeks the garden would burst into an abundance of colour for her to enjoy.

From the garden, they made their way to the stables. The groom, having seen Jason outside, had Shelton waiting for him. Jason sent him off to retrieve a well-behaved bay to saddle for Victoria. When all was ready, he assisted Victoria to mount side-saddle before settling on Shelton. Jason led them first across the informal lawns to the south so Victoria could see more of the house. He then led them down a close trail into a shallow valley with a series of pools surrounded by well-placed trees. Victoria could easily imagine how pleasing the spot would be come summer when leaves would provide dappled sunlight and ample shade.

They climbed out of the valley on the western side to pass the kitchen gardens and follow the grounds to the north side of the house edging the woods. The impressive large double bow windows spanning the full height of the house drew Victoria's gaze upward to discover the Duchess watching them from her bedroom window. Disconcerted, Victoria dropped her gaze. She swore she could feel the Duchess' disapproval even out here.

Jason led her to the front of the house to see what she had missed upon her arrival. Standing opposite the house, on the other side of the carriage drive, was a small stone church. A domed cupola rose high above the roof line with arched openings on all four sides surrounding the bell. Its base formed the church entry with a matching arched opening. The lawn was neatly trimmed all around the church. The only part of nature allowed to grow wild was some ivy left alone to climb the height of the weathered stone on the left side of the entry; at once out of place and yet part of the church. Victoria empathized with the ivy and hoped to do as well claiming her niche within the structures of her new home and family.

Jason helped her to dismount and led her inside to inspect the nave and apse. Devoid of parishioners and clergy, the carved stone walls and high ceiling echoed with solemn emptiness. The design was Baroque in style giving the parochial church an impressive and yet quaint appeal.

At her nod to continue on, they remounted and headed away from the house. Jason challenged her to a race across the meadow to the forest. He beat her, of course, but only by a few strides. The exhilaration felt wonderful. He led her into the trees following a narrow path. She had been quietly following him for some time up a gentle incline when she began to wonder at their destination. Suddenly the trees opened up along a ridge where Jason came to a halt. Victoria carefully led the bay to stand beside his stallion. A peaceful river valley opened up below them.

"This is one of my favorite places." He turned to her, his face placid. "You are the first person I've ever brought here."

Victoria smiled. "It's charming."

Jason couldn't help kissing her. The exhilaration of the ride still shone in her eyes and her cheeks were pink from the cold making her irresistible. She belonged here with him. How did he ever think he could leave her in Key West? His gaze returned to the valley. "That is River Itchen. One day when the weather is nicer, we'll ride the path along the water's edge. It's too far to go today." He turned his horse and paused. "Are you hungry? We could ride a bit further to a local tavern or return now to the house."

Recalling the Duchess in the window, it was an easy decision to delay their return for as long as possible, despite being chilled. "I would not be averse to riding a little further."

Victoria scanned the dark interior of the simple tavern as Jason led her to a table in the corner. She listened to him direct the proprietor to have mead and stew served immediately. Suddenly, she realized the difference in him, she had been vaguely aware of since their arrival in England. He was stiffly formal—with everyone. He only seemed to relax when they were alone. In Key West, he may have been standoffish at times but never lordly. She smiled to herself, yes, that was exactly how she would describe his attitude—lordly. She also noticed as they were touring the house and the grounds that many of his stories echoed of a lonely childhood. His circumstance likely created his demeanor. As an only child in a remote area, most of his contact would have been with his parents and servants, especially as a small boy. It was easy to see how he would have acquired his lordly manner growing up in Rothebury Hall with his parents as role models. She too, being an only child, had experienced isolation but fortunately friends lived nearby to keep her grounded. It was sad that Jason had not made friends until he was older. It also explained the paradox of his friendliness with the house servants when his parents weren't around. For many years, they likely were his only friends.

The newlyweds spoke of the countryside and things they had seen on their ride until the steaming bowls of mutton stew were placed before them along with thick slices of fresh baked bread. It may have been because she was cold and hungry, but Victoria thought it was the best stew she had ever tasted. It was thick and savory with tender meat and plenty of vegetables.

They were nearly done eating when a handsome man approached the table, hat in hand, and close in age to Jason. Victoria's gaze drew Jason's attention to the newcomer and he eagerly rose to greet him. "It's good to see you, old friend."

"So you have finally returned, Malwbry. How were your travels?"

"Enlightening. Let me introduce you to my wife, Lady Victoria." Jason turned to her. "My dear, this is Sir Marcus Danvers, a longtime friend."

Marc's smile showed his bewilderment. "Pleased to meet you Lady

Malwbry."

Victoria rose to greet the newcomer with little interest until she heard his name. "Victoria is fine. I am pleased to meet you as well. May I call you Marc?"

"I would be pleased if you did."

"Abby mentioned you to me."

"Abby? Do you mean Abigail Bennington? You know her?"

Jason's jaw quirked as Victoria replied, "She is Abigail Eatonton now."

Marc cast Jason a quizzical glance.

Victoria said, "We became instant friends. She said you encouraged her to leave England." Jason's astonished anger toward Marc caught her off guard.

"You encouraged her to leave? Why?"

"It was good for her."

"And what of me? I thought you were my friend."

Victoria's concern that Jason still held tender feelings for Abby returned. Despite all the intimacy between them, was she just a convenient replacement?

Marc laid a hand on his shoulder. "I am your friend and it appears as if I did you a favor." He smiled for Victoria and watched her struggle to return it.

Jason suddenly was aware of how his words must have sounded to Victoria. He turned to her with an affectionate smile, eager to soothe her hurt feelings. "Yes, a favor indeed. Victoria is all I could want in a wife and more."

Victoria tried to let the hurt slip away, but the damage was done. Her confidence was shaken. Her mother's words echoed in her mind. *Marry in haste, repent in leisure.* Had her headlong desires blinded her to the truth of his regard?

She missed some of the exchange between the two men. Marc bowing to her brought her attention back to him.

"Good day, Victoria. I look forward to seeing you this evening."

"Good day, Marc."

When Marc left, Jason turned to her. "I hope you don't mind having dinner with Marc and Mary."

"No, of course not." It was better than the alternative; another strained meal at the oversized dining table with his parents.

The ride back was silent. Victoria didn't feel like contributing to the conversation and Jason respected her silence while puzzling out how best to undo the inadvertent rift he created between them.

Returning home from their evening with the Danvers, Victoria stepped from the carriage much improved in spirits from when they left a few hours ago. Mary Danvers was a very petite and very proper English lady but she also possessed a charming wit and sweet, caring demeanor. Victoria couldn't help but appreciate and admire her and even wished to emulate her, though she knew she hadn't the patience for it. They were bosom friends before dinner was served.

Through the courses of the meal, Jason regaled his host and hostess with the tale of his journey alone on horseback from Montgomery to the Bennington plantation and back again. His description of the pony's antics and his sad attempts at making fire had them all laughing. Even for her, hearing it a second time, it was still amusing.

The four of them were having so much fun, they hated for the night to end. But end it must, and here they were, not three steps into Rothebury Hall, when they were summoned into the library. Victoria's good humor evaporated as did Jason's from the concerned look he cast her way. He reached for her hand in support. The Duke rose from his chair as they entered the library. Jason said, "Father, mother, I hope you can understand it has been a tiring day and we wish to retire early."

His mother rose from her chair, "You have been avoiding us all day. I suppose it's understandable since your father tells me you have returned with a wife but no dowry—the sole purpose of your journey, was it not? You told us you were leaving to marry Abigail Bennington, barely a tolerable candidate, but at least she had the money and the upbringing. Instead, you have foisted us with this American chit and no money to pay the debts of this household." Temper raised her voice to a fevered pitch by the end of her tirade.

Jason dropped Victoria's hand to step towards his mother. He spoke through clenched teeth, "I beg you to have a care how you speak of my wife, for she has done nothing to bear your disrespect. Don't forget one day she will take your place and have every reason to banish you to the cottage for your contempt."

Victoria appreciated Jason's defense of her, especially after her earlier misgivings, but she didn't wish to further any bad feelings between them. Besides, his efforts were futile. His mother was determined not to accept her.

Jason continued, "I have not changed my mind. I want to rebuild our estates rather than waste money propping them up. As for the debts, I suggest father and I visit the solicitor tomorrow to determine exactly what needs to be done to satisfy any immediate concerns. Meanwhile, Mother, I expect you to help Victoria with hiring a new lady's maid and valet to suit our needs. Good night." He turned Victoria from the room while his mother was still sputtering in indignation.

He knew he was being disrespectful, but he didn't know how else to get them to listen to reason, and fleeing seemed more prudent than continuing the argument tonight. Certainly, his mother had tried for years to curtail his father's gambling. Now it was up to Jason to make the Duke see reason or all of his other plans would be for naught.

Once they were far enough away not to be overheard, Victoria softly said to Jason, "Do you think you were a bit harsh?"

"I learned long ago my parents only take notice when the message is forcefully spoken."

Victoria bowed her head to keep Jason from noticing her anxiety. She knew there were families who treated one another callously, but she never expected to become part of one. To be fair, Jason gave her fair warning before their marriage, but from the idyllic glow of new love the prospect was of little consequence. Unfortunately, the reality of living in such an environment was going to be rather difficult to bear, but bear it she must, for there was no other alternative.

She lifted her head as she recalled something Abby once told her. "I thought the British were known for their stiff upper lip and their reticence in addressing anything uncomfortable or acting in any way outside expected behaviour?"

"You will encounter much of that outside this house or on the occasion we have visitors, but otherwise, within this family we express ourselves quite freely. It is one aspect in which your forthright nature will serve you well." Jason took her hand as they ascended the stairs. "We will find a way to make this work."

* * *

Jason ran a hand over his face while the bald-headed solicitor his father employed was tallying the numbers written in a ledger. His father was fidgeting in the chair beside him. They both knew the outstanding debt was going to be a large sum. The list of accounts due was larger than Jason anticipated.

In an effort to distract his nervous apprehension while they waited, his thoughts turned to Victoria. He wondered how she was fairing today in his mother's company. They planned to visit the modiste to commission a riding habit and would make social calls on her mother's friends in search of a lady's maid and valet. He could well imagine, it would be a trying day. He wished now he had thought yesterday to suggest Mary accompany her on these tasks instead. He supposed he could hope the day would allow his wife and mother to become more comfortable with each other. His mouth quirked knowing it wasn't likely.

The solicitor cleared his throat pulling Jason from his musings.

"Three thousand, four hundred and twenty seven pounds not including any recent expenditures."

Jason was aghast. He couldn't look at either man. "Could you give us a moment?" He was grateful the solicitor left the room without question, closing the door behind him.

Eyes still cast to the far wall, he said, "Father, that is over a thousand pounds greater than before I left. What have you to say for yourself?"

"Your mother..."

"Come now, we both know this is not her doing."

"It is my affair, not yours. I will not answer to you."

Jason swung his gaze to meet his father's so that he could see the fury behind his words. "I beg to differ. It is our home you risk and my inheritance you squander to compensate for your unhappiness."

His father abruptly stood sending his chair sliding backwards. "Now see here..."

Jason rose in kind, towering a few inches over his father's rotund frame. "No father, you see here. This stops. Now! It must end or I will leave for good."

"And go where?"

"America."

"With what funds?"

"I will sell off Malwbry and leave. I refuse to put time and effort into saving Rothebury just so you can piss it all away."

"Mind your tongue, boy."

"I am a boy no longer. And from this day forward the only way you will have my respect is by refraining from gaming. Of any kind. Do you understand me? Nothing. For if you do, I will sever all ties and renounce my titles. The estate will have no heir from you. It will be the last you will see of me."

"Have you not a care for your mother?"

"Haven't you?" He shook his head. "What am I saying? Obviously you don't for I have never seen one ounce of concern from you for her well-being and you certainly have never listened to her pleas."

"That is none of your concern."

"Of course it isn't. I am only a son forced to watch his parents emotionally batter each other on a daily basis. If not for how you treat the staff, I would believe there was not a caring bone in your body."

"I am the Duke of Rothebury and I will do as I please."

Jason's shoulders slumped. "Then Victoria and I shall leave."

Quietly the Duke added, "And, I find I am weary of the tracks."

Jason's head came up. He studied his father face and realized he was agreeing to his demands while trying to maintain honor. "And what of the card tables and side bets?"

"Yes, those too."

Jason silently nodded accepting his agreement.

His father resumed his seat.

Jason took a few steps toward the door but paused at his father's shoulder. "Don't think in a few weeks I will change my mind. It is set." His father said not a word. Jason opened the door signaling for Mr. Rawlings to return. The two of them spent the next hour with only minimal input from the Duke working on a plan to pull some money from the Malwbry estate to relieve the most impendent debts and a reasonable payment plan to satisfy their other creditors.

They returned to Rothebury in time for lunch but the ladies were still away. Afterwards, Jason left to pay a visit to Malwbry's steward. He wore the poor man out with his multitude of questions. He returned in time to dress for dinner feeling quite pleased with all he had learned. There was much in the way of improvements to be made, and he was determined to start on the morrow.

Rustling sounds from the adjoining room caught his attention. He straighten the cuffs of his jacket and cast a final glance in the mirror to assure his appearance was correct before moving through the secret passage.

Victoria smiled at his entrance. "Just in time, my love. I wasn't sure how I was going to finish my buttons without you."

Jason kissed her cheek and then moved behind her to finish her task. "Did you have any success in the search for servants?"

"There were none available to be recommended by your mother's friends, so we have placed advertisements." She turned to Jason with a sigh. "Your mother insists I must have a French maid and nothing less will be good enough."

"And what is wrong with a French maid?"

"Nothing, I suppose, so long as she can speak English. I am afraid my French is dismal at best."

Jason smiled and lifted her hand to kiss the back of it. "I believe most of them speak English."

"I wish we could dine in our room."

"Has my mother been too much for you today?"

"No. Well, yes. I cannot do anything well enough to please her. Her complaints..."

"Yes, I know. Just do your best and know that I love you. In my eyes you can do no wrong."

She laughed as she caressed his lapel. "Will you tell her that when next she disparages me?"

"Of course, if it please you."

"It would." She playfully swatted him. "But you will do no such thing. Now we best be going before we are chastised for being late."

They arrived in the parlour to be cheerfully greeted by the Duke and Duchess. Neither of them were quite sure what to make of their change in attitude. Jason didn't trust it, but he wasn't going to say anything to dispel it either.

The Duchess reached out her gloved hand to her son. "I was thinking we should have a reception to celebrate your marriage and so everyone can meet Victoria."

Jason's first thought was the cost of such an event. "Mother, it is not necessary. We don't need a reception. She will meet them all in good time."

"Nonsense and it's not for you, it's for everyone else. A wedding was expected. A reception is the only respectable thing to do. Surely we are not that destitute yet."

Jason grimaced. He knew his mother would wear him down eventually. Perhaps he should give in now and keep her in good spirits. "Very well, but keep it reasonable. Nothing lavish. Neither Victoria nor I wish it."

The Duchess smiled. "Of course." She turned to Victoria. "You and I can get to know each other better in the planning."

Victoria inwardly grimaced while outwardly she smiled in

agreement.

Chapter 15

For two days, the Duke kept to the estate according to the report Jason received from the stable master. Jason, on the other hand, spent the better part of those two days interviewing his tenants and inspecting the farms that made up Malwbry. He was ready to earn his income. He had been handed too much already. Using what he learned from James Bennington's plantation, he decided what improvements to make and how best to implement them. His father's cooperation was a relief and he began to relax in the confidence his plans would be successful. Spring was nearly upon them which worked well in his favor. It was an excellent time to experiment with crop rotation and new fertilizers.

At the end of the first week, he presented his ideas to his steward who received them with little descent if not enthusiasm. The following week, Jason gathered the tenants to present his plans to them. The meeting did not go well. Only a few were open to change, they being the younger men. Most of the others were belligerent if not outright hostile against him. One man even dared to tell him what they all were thinking.

"I've been tillin' this land longer than you've been drawing breath lad. I believe I know what I'm a doin' and don't need a frivolous young lord with fancy notions tellin' me otherwise."

Jason looked from one face to the other as he debated the wisdom of outright demanding they implement his ideas or keeping peace and working only with those open to making changes. It would slow the progress down by years but a higher crop yield would do more to convince these men than his words, especially if they ever learned where the ideas came from. He could hear them now saying no respectable Englishman would listen to a traitorous American.

Maybe a bribe would work.

Loudly so as to be heard over the crowd, Jason said, "I have an offer for you." He waited until the men settled down to listen. "For those who are willing to try my ideas, I will not only provide the fertilizer, I will also cut their rent by ten percent." The ensuing shocked silence was at least some gratification out of the disappointing meeting. "I will give you the night to think about it. Any willing to take up my offer should meet me here tomorrow."

Jason walked Shelton into the stable feeling cast down by the lackluster response of his tenants. He was nervous that tomorrow would only see a few willing to try his experiments. It was in this sad state of mind that his groomsman, Graham, approached to take his horse.

"My lord, I have kept watch on the Duke's comings and goings as you asked. A short while ago, he called for the carriage to be brought around. I overheard him instruct the driver to take him to his club."

Jason turned his head from the groom as he sighed deeply in dismay. He had been looking forward to pouring out his troubles to Victoria and relaxing before dinner. Now he must swiftly ride to ensure his father was not breaking his word. "Thank you, Graham."

Reluctantly he turned Shelton and rode for Midanbury. A quarter hour later, he dismounted in front of the gentlemen's club. Friends greeted him as he entered the richly paneled foyer. He paused to remove his riding gloves, and spotted his father across the drawing room in conversation with a longtime friend and neighboring lord. Perhaps he had worried for naught. As he stood there debating whether to stay or leave, the two men were approached by another and then moved off toward the card room.

"The devil take him," slipped out from under his breath.

Jason strode forward determined to remove his father, forcibly if necessary. He entered the game room as the Duke and his companions were being seated. His father's back was to him, so he was at his shoulder before his presence was known. Jason glanced around the table and nodded a greeting to each of the men.

One of the lords said, "Welcome home, Lord Jason. Did you enjoy your travels?"

"Yes, Lord Markum. It was a valuable experience but I am glad to be home again."

"I heard you have returned with a beautiful American heiress. Congratulations."

"Thank you, Sir Beechen."

"When will we meet her?"

"Soon. My bride and my mother are planning a reception." Jason squeezed his father's shoulder. "Father, I am afraid you are needed at home." Feeling his shoulder tense, Jason firmly added, "At once."

The Duke stood and gave his son an arched look before bidding farewell to his friends. Together they purposefully strode from the room. Out front, after the footman was dispatched to call for his carriage, the Duke turned to Jason seething with anger. "Are you having me watched in my own home?"

"Apparently that is what it takes to impress upon you the seriousness of our situation."

"You'll not embarrass me like that again. Send a servant next time."

Jason turned to fully face his father still speaking in undertones so as not to attract attention. "Have you so quickly forgotten our understanding? You gamble, and I leave. There will not be a next time. A servant will not be sent to call you home, but to retrieve the trunks for packing."

His father chose to remain silent as the carriage approached followed by a groomsman leading Shelton. Another son may have tied his horse behind the carriage to ride with his father, but Jason had nothing further to say to his father, and apparently, the Duke felt the same. Rather than gallop ahead as he would prefer, Jason kept behind the carriage ensuring his father did not turn back. He wouldn't put it past him to consider it.

They arrived home in time to dress for dinner.

Victoria waited for Jason in his dressing room. "I have good news to share." She helped him off with his coat and laid it on the back of a chair as she spoke. "We have found a valet I think you will get on with very nicely. A Mr. Scott from Winchester. He will arrive tomorrow."

Jason kissed her cheek. "Thank you, my love. Well done."

"I am afraid the search for a maid continues. There have been no less than three I would have gladly hired but your mother is insistent none of them will do since they are not French. I should think my lady's maid would be my decision. Can you not say something to her?"

Jason sighed. "Have you not tried telling her this yourself?' Stepping into battle between his wife and mother would not solve the problem, and he had enough of his own battles to fight. Festering anger and frustration made him pull at his cravat harder than necessary.

Victoria stared at her husband's back feeling let down. "Of course I have and her response was 'what would the daughter of a common colonist know of noble expectations.'"

Jason heard the despondency in her voice and it tugged at his heart. It wasn't fair to take his anger out on her. He turned and placed his hands gently on her upper arms. "I'm afraid you must learn to deal with my mother on your own. If I involve myself in every disagreement, she will never learn to respect you."

Victoria gave him a weak smile. "I suppose you know best. I will find a way. She's just worn me down this week especially since you and I have hardly spent any time together."

"I warned you, I have a lot to do to get ready for spring planting."

""I know. I don't mean to complain. I just miss you."

"We are together every night."

"I..." She swallowed hard to hold back the building hurt and anger. She had always thought of herself as a strong, independent woman. It distressed her to realize how much she was depending on Jason for her happiness. Besides, she didn't mean to add to his burdens. She donned a bright smile. "Of course and it is enough... for now."

Jason moved his hands to her cheeks and bent to kiss her fully. "I promise, after spring planting, we can spend more time together. The summer is yours, my love." Her watery smile enticed him to kiss her again. "Now I must finish dressing, or we will be late for dinner." He glanced at her dress, realizing she had changed already. "Who helped you dress?"

"I asked one of the downstairs maids after I saw you ride off again, in case you weren't back in time. The overheard the housekeeper gave her a hard time about leaving her other duties so I suppose I should speak to her tomorrow."

"I shouldn't worry about it. You are my wife, the Lady Malwbry, and as such you are entitled to make special requests of the servants."

"I don't want to be a burden."

Jason kissed her cheek. "My dear, you could never be a burden."

"It is sweet of you to say, but I am not sure the maid would agree with you." Victoria handed him her necklace to fasten and presented him her back. "Did you know your mother is planning a service with vows spoken in the chapel to sanctify our marriage as if we aren't truly married?"

"I am not surprised." When he finished with the clasp, Jason ran his hands down her arms. "In her mind it has not been properly done if she didn't witness it."

Victoria turned around to lift her eyes to her beloved. "There is to be a dinner the night before with titled guests, and after the service a gathering in the banquet hall for all. I am to have a different dress for each occasion. I thought the point was to curtail expenses. This flamboyance is a bit ridiculous."

Jason shook his head, feeling defeated. "Please, go along with it." He forestalled her protest. "I agree with you but these are expected traditions, and it is much better than the alternative."

"Which is?"

"She could have refused to accept you or acknowledge the marriage which would make our lives very difficult."

"You think she would dare cause such a scandal?"

"I choose to be thankful not to find out if she would or not. Come darling, let us not keep dinner waiting. An angry cook is even worse than my mother."

Victoria chuckled. "I didn't think that was possible."

* * *

The following morning, Jason arrived a few minutes late to meet the interested tenants. Nervously, he approached the crude building afraid he would find the meeting room empty. Fear of such an outcome kept him awake much of the previous night. Taking a deep breath he opened the door. At first, he could see nothing in the dark interior but as he stepped across the threshold faces began to appear. Once his eyes fully adjusted, he counted eleven men. Not as many as he had hoped for but certainly more than none. As he pulled off his gloves and considered what to say three more slipped in behind him. When a dozen more showed up in the next few minutes, he was pleased but he began to fear his offer was too generous. The ten percent loss on so many farms was going to be a burden if his ideas didn't increase production.

He placed his gloves on the center table and looked around the room. "Gentlemen, shall we get started."

There was still resistance to his ideas but the gathered men agreed to try and so the next few weeks were busy overseeing the planting of crops and application of fertilizers, first with the early crops, and later implemented with the summer crops.

* * *

Victoria awoke to April sunlight streaming across her pillow. She stretched and turned to find she was alone. After more than a month of Jason leaving their bed before dawn, it didn't surprise her but still disappointed her. Rising she donned her silk dressing gown and walked to the window to enjoy the sight of budding trees and the blooms of spring bulbs strategically placed around the yard.

Having heard her stir, Sophia, her new lady's maid, cheerfully entered the room. "And what are madam's plans today?"

Her new maid arrived a week ago. She missed Lydia now serving as Abby's maid since Maria was married, but she and Sophia were getting along well. "I believe the Duchess mentioned we would visit the village this morning."

"Very well, would the green striped lawn be suitable?"

"Perhaps something heavier. The weather is still a bit cool for me."

"Of course."

When the reception was first suggested, Victoria offered suggestions of what she would like, but she was overruled on all counts. She ended up docilely accepting all of the Duchess's plans having quickly learned disagreement only earned her insults. Besides, giving the Duchess free rein kept her occupied and less inclined to spend her day finding fault with everything Victoria said or did. Today, with the reception a week away, the Duchess insisted Victoria accompany her in visiting all the merchants providing for the affair to be sure all was going according to plan. Accepting the housekeeper's word that all was well was not sufficient enough for Her Grace.

Victoria trailed her gloved hand along the smooth oak banister as she descended the main staircase. She loved everything about her new home; the grandeur of the estate, the respect of the community, the dignity of the titles, the expansive gardens to wander, and servants to see to her every need. It was all more than she ever imagined, and it was wonderful, except for her mother-in-law. She had learned the Duchess' given name was Henrietta. She didn't dare address her as such, not even in private, but out of spite she thought of her as plain old Henrietta.

Henrietta constantly criticized her every move, complaining her posture wasn't straight enough, her head not held high enough, she used the wrong silverware, spoke at inappropriate times about inappropriate subjects, and on and on it went. If Victoria called her 'Your Grace' she was told to use 'Duchess' and if she used 'Duchess' she was told 'Your Grace' was more appropriate. Victoria did her best not to let the hen-pecking get to her. If it was only Henrietta's opinion she would not care, but she was quite concerned about the upcoming reception. She did not want any of the guests to find fault with Jason for choosing her as his bride or worse to make a fool of herself. The only way she could see to avoid such a catastrophe was to swallow her pride and ask Henrietta for guidance.

On the way to the village in the close confines of Henrietta's barouche, Victoria drew her breath and turned to her mother-in-law. "Your Grace, I know I am not well versed in English customs, and I don't wish to disappoint Jason. I was hoping you could give me some guidance for the upcoming events, especially the dinner, and all the titles, so I may address our guests properly."

Henrietta was silent until she felt Victoria's discomfort. She conceded, "I suppose you may as well learn to be a duchess, since this weekend will declare to all you will one day become one."

Victoria suffered her sarcasm and icily replied, "Thank you." She intentionally left off any form of address as a silent protest.

"Upon our return, we will start your education with how to properly serve and take tea, then we will move on to the dining room. There is much for you to learn of posture, deportment, manners, etiquette, formalities, and address. I am not sure we can do enough in a week to get you ready, but it will not be because I failed to try."

Victoria sighed. It was going to be a long and trying day.

Dinner that night was a silent affair. The Duchess had talked herself out instructing Victoria having spoken non-stop for the better part of the day. For Victoria, her head was reeling with all the information received. She was too mentally drained to converse. One look at Jason, and it was easy to see he was too fatigued from his day's labors to care much for conversation, and the Duke, as usual, was more interested in his meal than discourse.

Afterwards, Jason begged his parents leave to turn in early. Victoria was more than happy to join him. Upon reaching the sanctity of their room, she intended to unburden her frustration of the day on Jason. She ended up holding her peace when he released the torrent of his frustrations. It seemed the farmers were not following his instructions, and he discovered the land agent was undermining him behind his back forcing him to terminate his employ. Jason would now have to take on the extra work until a replacement could be found. He was tired, frustrated, and disheartened. Victoria could well sympathize, feeling the same herself.

She did her best to assure her husband all would turn out well in the end. "You know what you need to regain your prospective?" She didn't wait for him to answer. "You need to take some time for yourself."

"Have you not been listening? I have too much to do. Come summer I can rest but now I must persevere."

"Surely you can spare a few hours to refresh yourself. I was thinking of a morning ride, just the two of us. We have hardly spent any time together since we got here."

"Have I not spent nearly every night pleasing you?"

She smiled, recalling the pleasure he often gave her. "Of course, but a little time spent having fun in the daylight would do us both some good. Surely you cannot deny me that?"

"Have I denied you so much?"

"Of you? Yes, you have. I know we agreed you would make up for it in summer, still you cannot find fault with me for wanting a little bit of your time to see me through till then, especially if now you will be working even harder than before."

Jason's mouth quirked. "How can I deny you what I really want as well? So be it. Will tomorrow morning satisfy you, my love?"

"Exquisitely, my dear."

Jason and Victoria cantered across the freshly cut grass of the south lawn having spent an enjoyable hour riding through the woodlands and round the ponds. The gardener's assistant could be seen in the distance working with a scythe on the eastern slope in preparation of the weekend's festivities.

Victoria breathed deeply of the sweetly scented air.

Jason caught her rapturous expression as he brought his mount beside hers, "Penny for your thoughts."

She turned to him. "Mmm, I've missed the smell of freshly cut grass. There's precious little of it on the island. It reminds me of summers growing up in Charleston."

"Did you enjoy your childhood?"

"Yes, I did." She frowned, "I suppose you didn't."

"Oh, it wasn't all bad, especially once I was able to make friends outside the estate."

"Yes, I got the impression Marc Danvers saved you from loneliness and isolation."

He smiled. "And led a susceptible and I imagine gullible lad on a great many risky adventures."

"I shall have to thank him."

Jason laughed. "For what?"

"For keeping you from being stodgy and boring, for I am sure, I would not have fallen in love with you otherwise."

"My dear, if not for him, it is likely we would have never met."

"See there, I have much to thank him for."

"Are you implying that without Marc's influence, I would be unsuitable to you?"

"Well, you have as much as admitted that is likely."

"Now that I think on it, perhaps I was the one encouraging Marc, and it is Mary who should be thanking me for making him a better man."

Victoria laughed, amused by his affronted pride. "No doubt, you are both the better for having known each other."

Jason pulled her to him for a quick kiss before slapping her horse on the rump and kneeing his. "Race you to the stable."

They came to a halt together in the stable yard only because Jason held Shelton in check. Otherwise, the stallion would have easily overtaken her mare, not to mention Victoria was not about to ride sidesaddle at a full gallop. He jumped down from his mount and came to her, placing his hands around her waist to help her dismount. With her hands on his shoulders, her feet gently touched the ground. She looked up to thank him with a smile and received an unexpected kiss in exchange. The nearness of the stable boy made her blush. Jason couldn't resist kissing her again. She ducked her head and he smiled. This morning's ride was exactly what they both needed; a chance to rekindle the excitement of their young love.

* * *

Saturday afternoon, Victoria was supervising the arrangement of flowers and greenery for tonight's table and the hall for tomorrow's reception. She had never seen so many flowers gathered all together and thoroughly enjoyed arranging them in the large silver urns. The flowers alone would outdo the grandest ball in Charleston. Then there were all the silver service pieces, hundreds of candles, and yards and yards of ribbon to adorn everything. It was all very lush and elaborate. Part of her reveled in the extravagance and desperately wished her mother could see it. The other part of her despised it for the detriment to Jason's goals. However, when she mentioned her misgivings to Jason, he merely shrugged his shoulders and told her to enjoy it as it would be some time before they would entertain in such a fashion again.

At five, Sophia came to her under strict orders from the Duchess that she was to go upstairs and rest before dressing for dinner. Victoria sighed in frustration but conceded giving final instructions to the housekeeper as she was ushered toward the stairs.

Two hours later, excited and enchanted, she descended from the upper story on Jason's arm wearing a dark blue gown with a low cut square neckline decorated with white embroidery and puffy short sleeves. It draped from the high waist gathering in silky folds to the floor. The collective sound of appreciation from early guests gathered in the foyer did much to bolster her confidence. She was also still glowing from Jason's appreciative looks when he came to collect her dressed in his finest dark waistcoat and breeches, navy vest richly embroidered with gold thread, and snow white dress shirt and cravat. He cut a fine figure and she was proud to call him her husband.

Facing the gathered crowd with nervous trepidation she listened carefully to the names as Jason began introducing her to their guests. It was all Lord and Lady this or that followed by titles and names she would never have been able to recall if not for having spent hours studying the guest list. She smiled and nodded appropriately and hoped she carried on reasonably well. By the time they moved into the parlour to await more guests, she was feeling overwhelmed. By the time dinner was announced, she was feeling inferior to the task despite her determination otherwise.

Lady Elizabeth Kendall paused beside her on the way into the dining room to whisper, "Relax, you're doing fine."

Victoria released the breath she hadn't realized she had been holding and genuinely smiled for her new found friend. "Thank you." She could easily see why Abby was so fond of the sweet natured, beautiful blond. She was thankful the Duchess placed her nearby in the seating. With Elizabeth's help, the conversation around them flowed smoothly.

Afterwards, the ladies adjourned to the parlour. Victoria left the room to freshen up. Upon her return and before entering the room, she inadvertently overheard two ladies speaking ill of her. She pasted a smile on her face and walked past without acknowledging them. She didn't stop until she reached Elizabeth who quickly offered her comfort.

"Pay them no mind. They are gossips of the worst sort and we have all at one time or another suffered from their wagging tongues."

It was such an uncharitable speech from someone she had already come to understand saw only the good in everyone that Victoria unexpectedly laughed in response. Perhaps it was the built up tension or nerves that caused it, but the relief it brought was immediate and immense. Elizabeth smiled broadly in understanding and they both ignored the questioning looks from the other matrons about the room, especially the Duchess' disparaging regard.

* * *

Early Sunday, Sophia helped Victoria dress for church. Since it was not going to be a full wedding but a simple vow renewal, the minister convinced Her Grace that including it as part of the Sunday services would be sufficient, forcing her to abandon the idea of the traditional Wednesday nuptials. Jason's mother also tried to route him from their bedroom the previous night, but he refused the idea firmly reminding her, they were already married. Once they got past their irritation, her effort amused them. Their laughter lasted long after her troubled departure.

In one thing, the Duchess refused to be swayed. An elaborate wedding dress was ordered for the day. It was made in the same empire style of Princess Charlotte's 1816 wedding gown, although done all in white, without the costly silver embroidery. Victoria failed to talk her out of the expensive Brussels lace around the neckline and sleeves. The train was edged in scalloped lace and the dress hem was embroidered with shells and flowers. It was the most beautiful dress Victoria had ever worn.

Upon Sophia's arrival, Victoria slipped from their bed to pad barefoot into her room to begin dressing. An hour later, Jason entered the room wearing a white morning coat with tails looking every bit as debonair as she imagined Beau Brummell.

He approached Victoria with a large, red, velvet lined box. He opened it to reveal an intricately woven diamond necklace and earbobs.

"Oh my!" Victoria reached out to delicately trace the dainty settings.

"These belonged to my grandmother. Shall I help you?" He transferred the box to her hands and withdrew the necklace as Sophia stepped aside.

Victoria turned and watched in the mirror as he placed the chain around her neck. Its length settled very pleasingly in line with her collarbones. Jason then held the box so that she could fasten the earbobs. They were heavier than expected. She turned to fully face Jason waiting for his approval.

"You are beautiful, my love."

"No regrets?"

"No. And you?"

She smiled. "No."

"Not even my parents?"

"As long as we have each other, nothing else matters."

She made him smile. Sophia chased him from the room, so she could put the finishing touches on Victoria's coiffure. He returned a half hour later and offered Victoria his arm. "Shall we go?"

Jason and Victoria walked across the gravel drive to enter the quaint chapel filled beyond capacity. They were nearly last to arrive, sedately slipping into their place in the first pew beside the Duke and Duchess. The service was led by the local bishop in ceremonial dress. Though the service was more elaborate than she was used to in recent years, Victoria found comfort in the similarities to her Episcopalian upbringing.

After communion, the Bishop called Jason and Victoria to stand before the altar. Once again, they took their vows of matrimony. This time, Jason slipped a diamond encrusted heavy gold band, once belonging to his grandmother, in place of the first band which she had moved to her right hand. The Bishop then blessed them and pronounced them husband and wife. As they came together to kiss, their eyes caught and held sharing a secret mirth at the irony of the pronouncement.

Hand in hand, they left the church followed by the Bishop, the Duke, and Duchess. Outside in the yard, they lined up to greet the rest of the congregation. For the next ten minutes, they received the well wishes from the departing worshippers.

Last to leave the church, Jason and Victoria walked back to Rothebury Hall to join his parents and their overnight guests for a lavish breakfast. Afterwards, they leisurely strolled the lawn and gardens admiring the early roses. After an hour of fresh air and sunshine, Jason and Victoria returned to their rooms where Sophia helped Victoria remove the wedding gown to change into the wine colored silk Betsy made for her. She was still pleased to have won that particular battle with Henrietta and saved the cost of an unnecessary third gown. She swapped the heavy diamond earbobs for her grandmother's lighter diamond settings as her lobes were feeling much abused. She pinched her cheeks and then joined Jason to descend the stairs to await the start of the afternoon banquet.

The servants scurried about tending last minute details, as they made their way to the library. The Duke and his friends were already in the room visiting. The Duchess and the other lady guests were napping. Victoria assured Jason she would be fine entertaining herself and settled in with a book while he joined the other men in conversation.

At the appointed time, Jason and Victoria stood with the Duke and Duchess to receive their guests. This party consisted of many in attendance of the previous dinner plus most of the villagers. Victoria was disappointed to receive Lady Kendall's regrets. She was feeling unwell due to her delicate condition. Victoria would have enjoyed it more with her presence as a buffer. At least she found this party easier to mingle since there were less titles to worry over.

The guests attended the buffet tables with the aid of servants to fill their plates and carry them to the tables set up in the yard. Jason and Victoria were allowed to sit together to eat, but duties kept them separated for the rest of the afternoon until the last guest departed. They climbed the stairs together very tired. Although pleased with the day, they were glad it was over.

Jason undid the buttons of Victoria's dress and loosened her stays. He helped her slip off the garments and laid them over the back of the velvet dressing chair. Victoria faced him in her silk chemise and stockings illuminated by the glow of soft candlelight. Even after two months of marriage, she could still take his breath away. Jason stepped closer to softly caress her cheek. Victoria tilted her head, savoring his touch. They shared a slow, gentle kiss, savoring the night and the pleasures to come.

Jason wrapped his arm around her waist, bringing them close. "Congratulations, my love. You were well received. I could not have been more proud to introduce my wife. You handled the past two days splendidly."

His approval released the last of her tension. Victoria let out a sigh of relief. "I can do this."

Jason's grin turned mischievous. "You certainly can do this."

Victoria easily read his thoughts. Playfully, she slapped his shoulder. "No. I meant be a duchess. Eventually."

Jason's expression sobered. He ran his fingers down her temple, lovingly gazing in her eyes. "Yes, you will. I am sorry I ever doubted you. I never will again." He sealed his promise with a solemn kiss.

Chapter 16

The following day, Jason resumed his work. When Victoria came down later that morning, the Duchess declared they would continue her training. Victoria assumed the lessons would end with the reception, but once started, the Duchess felt it her duty to instruct Victoria in all that her future title would require of her.

When her mother-in-law wasn't commanding, she was criticizing Victoria didn't have a single moment of peace outside her bedroom. What seemed like a humongous castle upon her arrival now felt as claustrophobic as a one room cabin. By the following week, Victoria had had enough. She exploded as soon as she could get Jason alone.

Victoria couldn't help the anger seething in her words. "There is not enough space in this house for the both of us."

Jason, caught unawares, was shocked. "I thought we were doing fine?"

Frustrated and gritting her teeth, she said, "You and I are fine. It's your mother I can no longer tolerate. We have to move."

"Move? What do you mean?"

"I cannot abide living under the same roof as her any longer. She is impossible."

"Where do you propose we move to?"

"Your estate! Is there not a house on the Malwbry estate?"

Jason reluctantly said, "Yes. A small one, but it hasn't been occupied in a very long time."

"Surely with a little cleaning it could be habitable. Promise you will take me tomorrow to see it."

Knowing it useless to argue when her mind was set, Jason reluctantly agreed. "Very well. We will ride over in the morning."

Victoria calmed down now that she had hopes of escape. The rest of the evening was spent pleasantly. In the morning, she followed Jason on horseback to his estate as curious about the property as she was the house.

Jason brought them to a halt on a crest of road overlooking his estate. Newly planted fields stretched out to the east broken only by the occasional tenant keep. The earthy smell of freshly turned soil mixed with manure permeated the moist air. Jason's gaze proudly wandered over the furrows covered in sprouted growth. Victoria showed polite interest in the fields but her eyes glazed over as he tried to share with her the details of the planting. Resigned, he turned them toward the trees.

Victoria was forced to maneuver her mare close to Jason at the entrance of a wooded path. It was once a wide enough for a carriage but now was overgrown with barely enough clearing for them to ride together. Victoria grew pensive as she worried over the state of the dwelling if the way was this neglected.

The road wound around a knoll covered in wild greenery and on the other side stood a small, sad, two-story, brick cottage with five single windows and a sagging door. Sunlight filtered through the trees to play along the moss covered roof shingles. The chimney at one end was missing a section of bricks that had fallen to the ground below. Victoria dismounted with the intent of going inside, hoping, against hope, the interior was still in good shape. Jason followed without saying a word.

He pushed against the lodged door with his shoulder. The pressure snapped the worn out upper hinge. Now the door hung at an odd angle allowing just enough room for Victoria to step past the threshold and walk right through a tangle of dusty old cobwebs. She checked her frightened squeal and brushed the gossamer threads aside to assess the dim room. If it were only a matter of cleaning, the project would be intimidating enough, but she knew without Jason's confirmation any hope of them living here was futile. There was a bow in the ceiling suggesting it would be unsafe to walk on the upper floor, if one could even get past the rotted stair treads due to water damage from the broken window above it. They could not spend the money it would take to make the house livable again.

She turned to leave, lifting her troubled eyes to Jason's. "I know you told me, but I had to see it in order to resign myself to remaining in Rothebury Hall."

Jason helped her past the leaning door and then attempted to pull it back to some semblance of being closed. Before helping Victoria into the saddle, he solemnly said, "I am sorry it was not what you had hoped for. Perhaps in a few years we can manage something with it."

Victoria bit back the retort on the tip of her tongue born from her frustration. She didn't want to quarrel with Jason. He was trying to help. "Perhaps. Until then I shall just have to manage as best I can with your mother."

He kissed her cheek. "I have faith in you."

* * *

And so the weeks continued as before with Victoria daily testing her forbearance with the Duchess and Jason pushing onward despite the obstinacy of his tenants. He usually returned late with mere moments to change before dinner was served. Afterwards, he would go straight to their room and fall asleep exhausted. They rarely spoke in private having soon discovered airing their daily grievances was not as cathartic as they needed. Victoria's problems increased Jason's feelings of inadequacy. His reticence to share his problems increased her frustrations. They were miserable and didn't know how to fix the problem.

* * *

The 'Duchess Lessons' finally dwindled, and now Victoria's days were spent almost pleasantly when Henrietta wasn't needling her about producing an heir. Victoria usually held her tongue, but on one occasion she felt the need to lash back, and so she opened a subject she thought sure to annoy Henrietta.

"Your Grace, I have long been puzzled by something. Why is Jason's father a duke when it is your family's portraits that hang in the hall? If I recall correctly, you once told me you were the duchess *suo jure* before you married. Wouldn't that make him a 'Sir' and not a 'Duke'?"

Henrietta gave her daughter-in-law an inscrutable look, surprised she knew so much already. The girl was far too keen. It was an annoyance in this moment, but Henrietta was not above acknowledging the trait would serve Victoria well in future. "How quite observant of you."

When she said no more, Victoria prodded. "I suppose if you won't tell me, I could ask His Grace, or maybe my friend, Lady Kendall, could explain it. I could try writing to Abigail. She has known the family a long time, hasn't she?"

Henrietta blanched. The idea of Victoria dredging up the past with all her friends was abhorrent. Getting past the scandal in her youth was bad enough. Henrietta certainly didn't want to relieve it again. "Very well. If you must know. My father and brother were both killed in battle when I was very young. I was determined to hold onto the estate and was doing quite well until King George III decided I must marry so there would be a man to protect the lands from enemy invasion. I delayed doing so in the hopes the idea would fade." She pursed her lips in remembered frustration. "It did not."

Victoria worked to hide her grin. "What did the King do?"

"He gave me a few months to pick someone or he would choose for me. When he lost patience with my reticence, he sent his favored officer. I found the man insufferable and the whole situation intolerable, but I knew better than to outright refuse the King, so I agreed to take him for a husband but I did everything I could to delay the marriage."

"I suppose that didn't go over well with King George."

"No, it did not. He removed the title from my family and gave it to his officer making George, the Duke of Rothebury."

"Thereby forcing you to marry him in order to regain your title."

Bitterly she replied, "Yes."

"And you hate him still for it."

Henrietta frowned. "I wouldn't say hate."

"Despise, then."

"Yes, I suppose I do still despise him for forcing my hand."

"Despise the King or your husband? Or both?"

Henrietta spoke absently as if considering the idea for the first time. "Honor would not allow me to despise the King, so I suppose I have held it against the Duke all these years."

"Do you not think you could let it go? He was only doing as his King commanded, same as you."

The Duchess returned to the present and snapped at Victoria, "Do you not think I know that? I am not so foolish as to believe he actually cared for me."

Victoria chose to disregard her rudeness. "Why couldn't he?"

"I have had enough of this conversation."

Curiosity made Victoria ask, "Have you never been in love?"

"I have said all I am going to say today. Be off with you."

Victoria rose with a smile. She found out something interesting and she accomplished her goal of being dismissed. It was not a bad result from needling the Duchess, but she couldn't help feeling sorry for Henrietta. To have never loved, and to be forced to marry a man she could never respect, was a sad lot in life. Victoria quit the house to wander the grounds and soon found herself down by the ponds. It was a breezy day causing the water to ripple and catch the sunlight. It reminded her of the waters surrounding Key West. She was suddenly awash in homesickness. She missed her parents, the easy flow of island life, her friends, and especially Abby.

She played with the diamond wedding band. Nothing was as it should be. She and Jason loved each other which made their situation infinitely better than his parents, but they barely spoke to each other these days. She was feeling isolated and lonely. Briefly she thought of visiting her new friends but dismissed it. Seeing Elizabeth so advanced in her condition would only reminded her she wasn't likewise, and Mary Danvers had confessed the other day to also being with child. A baby would end the Duchess' complaints and give Victoria something to focus on other than her misery, but getting with child was difficult when she and Jason weren't doing less of their part to make it happen. She wistfully smiled recalling how she had dreaded the idea of motherhood the day Jason proposed. Now she was anxious for it to happen.

She wandered a little further reluctant to return to the house. The warmth of the sun reminded her she neglected to wear a hat, or bring a parasol, and that summer was approaching. Jason promised to spend more time with her come summer. She dearly hoped it would be the case. She missed him terribly.

* * *

The following week brought a surprise visitor. It was almost time for afternoon tea. Victoria and Henrietta were in the parlour doing needlepoint when the butler stepped into the room to announce Captain Bennington's arrival. Eager for news from home, Victoria rose from her seat excited to greet Abby's father. She curtsied and then stepped forward to kiss his cheek in her exuberance to see him.

The captain chuckled with delight. "Lady Malwbry, I must say, marriage rather becomes you." He turned to bow over Henrietta's hand. "Your Grace, you are looking as well as ever."

"Thank you, Captain Bennington. You are a long way from your merchant ship."

"Yes, I am, but I promised Abigail I would look in on her friend, and when Mr. Lambert heard I was headed this way he insisted I bear a gift for his daughter." He turned back to Victoria and pulled a wooden box from his coat pocket.

Victoria accepted it, noting the familiar box. Eagerly, she opened it to find the expected perfume bottle nestled in layers of cotton to protect it during its journey. It was the gardenia scent her father always gave her. She held the bottle tightly to her chest savoring the sweet memories it engendered, just as her father likely intended. Captain Bennington pulled letters from his other pocket to hand to her.

"Thank you sir. It was so kind of you to bring these to me. Would you care to stay for dinner?" Henrietta gave her a sharp look, but she didn't care. It was her home too, and if she wanted company for dinner, she would invite them.

"I must admit, a good meal is tempting, but it would be rather late afterwards to travel back to Southampton. I am afraid I must leave now if I am to return to my ship before dark."

Henrietta was not about to let her daughter-in-law outdo her in hospitality. "Nonsense, Captain Bennington. I insist you spend the night here so that you may enjoy a fine meal and a comfortable slumber before once again taking to the trials of sea."

The captain bowed to his hostess. "Very well. I can spare one night away from the crew, but more than that and they will scatter like the wind on me."

"Victoria, dear, please show our guest to the blue room."

Victoria rose from her chair with a smile. "This way, Captain Bennington."

"Do you find England to your liking, Lady Victoria?"

She paused and half turned to look at him. "Just Victoria, please."

"You don't like your title?"

"No. I mean, I do like it from everyone else, but you have always known me as plain old Victoria. Seeing you is a reminder of home, so when you call me Lady Victoria it..." She faltered looking for the right words, "ruins the feeling I suppose."

"I think I understand."

"As for your question, my new home has taken some getting used to, but on the whole, I find it agreeable."

"And married life?" He saw the flash of sadness cross her face before she hid it behind a smile.

"Jason is wonderful. I have no regrets marrying him." She resumed leading him up the stairs to his bedroom for the evening in the same wing she and Jason occupied.

"Abigail will be glad to hear it. I must admit she asked me to visit, so that, I might ascertain your true happiness since she found your letters, insufficient, shall we say."

Victoria laughed lightly in self-deprecation. "I did warn her I was a poor correspondent. I seem to lack the patience for putting pen to paper for any sufficient amount of time conducive to conveying one's feelings." Reaching the corridor of bedrooms, she paused at the second door on the left, so he could proceed her into the room. Captain Bennington paused. His intent look gave her the impression he was studying her true feelings. A little flustered, she added, "Dinner is served at seven. We usually gather in the parlour a half hour beforehand. She gave him a brief curtsey and abruptly took her leave lest he discover the sadness she wished to keep hidden.

* * *

Jason pulled the door closed to the land agent's office. He had spent the last several weeks going over all the books kept by the former Malwbry stewards. Today he was finally done. He had to make corrections to the last steward's poor work, but the ledgers were now in good order. After months of hard won battles with his tenants and the long hours of spring planting, he was finally seeing hope for the future. His belief that the estates could once again be profitable was another step closer to fruition. He felt like celebrating. He mounted Shelton and rode for home anticipating Victoria's delight to have his company hours before dinner.

As he passed between the fields it gave him great pleasure to see those under his guidance were doing better than the others. It was justifiable proof his ideas were working. Next year, he would have an easier time getting all of the farmers to participate. He had expectations of a high yield. Perhaps even high enough to put a dent in the Rothebury debts. He couldn't help the satisfied grin he knew he was wearing.

He made his way down the road and turned into the tree covered lane leading to Rothebury Hall. The great oak sentinels gave way to the welcoming sight of his ancestral home on the hilltop. He loved the house, but his parents never made it feel like home the way it did now knowing Victoria was waiting for him. He nudged Shelton into a gallop toward the stables, anxious to kiss his wife.

Leaving Shelton in the hands of the stable boy, Jason dismounted absently seeing, but failing to register, the empty space where his father's carriage belonged. He entered the house and went straight to the parlour expecting to find Victoria and his parents in the room. He was, therefore, surprised when only his mother was there to greet him

After kissing her cheek, he moved to the sideboard for a glass of water. "Where is Victoria?"

"I couldn't say. She left a while ago to show Captain Bennington to his room."

"Captain Bennington, did you say?"

"Yes. He surprised us with a visit and will be staying for dinner. After, it would be too late to return to his ship, so he will remain overnight."

"I look forward to seeing him. Is he with father now?"

"No. I don't believe so."

Something in her tone made Jason's hackles rise. Awareness surfaced. "Father's carriage is gone."

Henrietta affected unconcern. "Is it?"

"Where did he go?"

"I wouldn't know. He didn't say anything to me."

Jason gave up his questioning. He had a feeling his mother had a good idea where his father had gone and was keeping it from him. What he couldn't understand was why she would do so. For certain, she had always been against his father's gaming.

He made his way to his room intending to change out of his work clothes before searching for Victoria. He was surprised to hear her call out to him as he passed the open door to her room. He turned back to find her excitedly making her way to him.

She greeted him with a charmingly coy smile. "Hello husband. I am happy to see you."

He welcomed her into his arms. "I am happy to see you too." They shared a kiss mindful of the open doorway. He then took her hand and led her into his room. He closed the door behind them, so he could kiss her as thoroughly as he pleased.

When they parted, Victoria asked, "What brings you home so early?"

Jason smiled. "You."

Her smile brightened. "I would love to keep you in this room all to myself until dinner, but we have a guest."

"Yes, mother mentioned Captain Bennington is here." He realized, he had passed a closed door on his way down the hall and now assumed it was because it was occupied. "When did he arrive?"

"About a half hour ago."

"And how long has my father been gone?"

"He left sometime after breakfast as he usually does. Likely he will be home soon. He usually returns shortly after tea."

"Are you saying he leaves the house almost daily?"

"Yes, at least for the last few weeks after the weather turned warm."

Jason stepped from her and turned away as he contemplated the meaning of his father's absence. He felt betrayed. Knowing his father would likely deny it if confronted, he determined he must find out first-hand. He turned, taking angry strides from the room while throwing his words to Victoria. "I am sorry to leave you. I shall return in time for dinner."

In no time at all, Jason was astride Shelton and galloping down the drive. He headed straight for his father's club intending to catch him before he left. He would have proof his father was gaming while he toiled in the fields and ledgers. Jason's anger mounted with every body-jolting, distance-eating stride. Reaching the front of the club, he slid from the horse, tossing the reins to the stable hand. "Just hold him. I shan't be long." He tossed back over his shoulder. "Some water wouldn't be amiss." He didn't even wait to see if the stable hand complied.

Taking the steps two at a time, he burst through the door feeling a bit of *deja vu*. His father was not in the main room. He continued walking towards the game rooms, desperately hoping he was wrong, uncaring of the stares following him, knowing he must look a sight in work clothes and in a temper. He heard his father's voice before he saw him sitting at the second table waiting on the latest hand to be dealt. Jason stopped in his tracks. His father's eyes met his. Moments passed as they stared at each other before Jason turned and walked away, defeated. He told his father what would happen. Now, he would have to see it through. He was angry and hurt, but later, it was going to devastate him.

He heard his father excusing himself from the table and hurried his strides toward the door. He refused to have a confrontation here for all the neighbors to witness. Jason made it out the door and into the saddle before his father appeared on the threshold. Aware of him but refusing to look in his direction, Jason turned Shelton and galloped away.

When he reached Rothebury Hall, he was on a mission to speak with Captain Bennington. He found him with his mother and Victoria in the parlour. The ride made him sweaty and disheveled, but he cared not about his appearance nor the sensibilities of etiquette. Without benefit of greetings, he said, "Captain Bennington, might I have a word with you in private?" He held his arm out, indicating for his guest to follow him elsewhere. He shook his head at Victoria when she rose as if to speak to him.

Jason led Captain Bennington to his father's library and closed the door behind him. He took up a position from the side of the room where he had a good view of the window overlooking the drive, so he would have advanced warning of his father's approach in the carriage.

Captain Bennington asked, "What is this about?"

"We have business to discuss."

"If you don't mind my saying so, you seem agitated."

"It is urgent business, I'm afraid. What is the itinerary of the *Abigail Rose*?"

Captain Bennington's curiosity was no greater than his concern for Jason's request. "She sails tomorrow on the afternoon tide for Boston."

Jason's face fell, but then he asked, "And after?"

"Charleston and Mobile."

"Would you be willing to add Key West to your ports of call?"

Captain Bennington smiled. "That is a given whenever I am passing by."

"Then would you have room for two passengers?"

He frowned for a moment, considering whether he should offer passage more than if he could. "We have a full load, but I suppose I could make free one cabin with two berths. It would be tight accommodations, not at all what you are used to, I'm afraid."

Jason smiled tightly. "It will do. And what would you charge?"

The captain swallowed hard not at all sure he was doing the right thing. He named a price half his normal fee being a lesser cabin.

Jason shook his hand. "I'll take it. What time should we be ready to leave in the morning?"

"Would eight o'clock be sufficient?"

"I will see that we are ready." No sooner had the words been spoken, the carriage was seen emerging from the shadow of the great oaks. "Do not speak of this. I will tell my parents in good time."

"Very well."

"As you can imagine, I must make haste if we are to be ready to leave with you."

They returned to the parlour where Jason strode to Victoria and abruptly took her hand. "Come with me." He rushed her from the room. They turned out of sight at the top of the stairs, just as the front door flew open. His father's hurried steps faded towards the parlour.

Victoria turned to Jason in a flurry as they entered his room, and he let go of her hand. "What is the meaning of this? Jason, what is going on?"

Jason was wildly pacing the room, before turning his anger on his wife. "Why did you not tell me father has been leaving the house every day?"

Victoria gasped. "I didn't know it was important. Why shouldn't he leave the house?"

"Because he was breaking our agreement."

"You mean he was still gambling? Are you sure?"

"Yes. I found him at the club sitting at a gaming table."

"Perhaps there was no money involved."

Jason gave her a disparaging look. "The opening bids were on the table. There was money involved, and the stakes were quite high."

Victoria's face fell. She laid a hand on Jason's arm. "I'm sorry."

Her touch softened his temper. He placed his hand over hers. "So am I, for he has left us no choice. For the sake of our future, we must leave. Captain Bennington's presence makes it very expedient."

"Surely you don't mean to leave tomorrow?"

"Yes, that is exactly what I mean."

"But we could never pack in time."

"We can if you only pack what is necessary. The rest can be sent later."

"Sent where? Where are we going?"

"Back to Key West for now."

"Are you sure this is necessary? While I certainly don't mind returning to the island, this is your home. What about all your plans?"

"They mean nothing if it can't save Rothebury."

"There is my money..."

"No."

He was so emphatic, she didn't even try to argue it further. While she feared he would later regret today's decision, she could do nothing more than go along with it. "Very well. Are we sharing a trunk or should I have one brought for each of us?"

"I suppose we each may have one."

Victoria rang for the servant and shortly Jason's valet appeared.

Jason stepped to his man. "Discretely as you can, please have two trunks brought down. One for each of our rooms." The well trained servant kept his surprise hidden.

"Yes, my lord." Smartly he left the room.

Jason turned to Victoria. "Can you help me dress for dinner?"

"Certainly. When will you tell to your parents?"

"If it can be helped, I hope to say nothing until after the staff has all gone down to their dinner."

Dinner was a stilted, silent affair. Jason refused to speak to either one of his parents leaving Victoria and Captain Bennington to carry on much of the conversation. They did their best to avoid answering any of the more pointed questions concerning their earlier conversations with Jason. Most of these inquires came from the Duchess. The Duke said very little after ascertaining Jason's state of mind.

Jason did not say anything of his plans to his parents until after Captain Bennington left the room to retire for the evening. His mother rose to bid them goodnight and Jason halted her with, "I have an announcement." Both his parents turned to him expectantly; his mother with a puzzled look and his father with dread. "Victoria and I will be leaving in the morning with Captain Bennington. It is unknown when we will return, or indeed, if we will ever return." Before his mother could ask, Jason added, "Father knows why. You may direct your inquiries to him. As you can imagine, Victoria and I have much to do before retiring, so we will bid you goodnight."

Victoria spent much of the evening in thought of what should be packed. Upon reaching her room, she quickly gathered the clothes she would take. While Sophia was packing those, she pulled together the rest of her needs. In a half hours' time, she was looking around the room in contemplation of anything she might have missed. Another quarter of an hour later, her trunk stood ready at the door of her room. Sophia soon left after helping her change for bed.

Victoria paused at the secret passage to look around again, only this time, it was at all she would be leaving behind—the seldom used bed, the vanity, the intricately carved wardrobe, and the comfortable arm chair in front of the large window overlooking the gardens. She had come to love the room and its secret door. She turned to enter Jason's room and paused again. They had made some happy memories in this room as well.

Jason approached. He kissed her on the forehead as he pulled her into his arms. They stood there silent for a moment each lost in their thoughts. At length, Jason pulled away. "We will be fine. They will be fine. I hate knowing this house will eventually be sold to pay my father's debts, but I refuse to sacrifice our future to save it."

Victoria heard the heartbreak in his words. "You are brave." She reached up to stroke his cheek. "And you are strong." She placed both hands on his shoulders. "And you are courageous in doing something that must be so difficult for you to do. I love you and it hurts me too to leave this home we love so well. But I know my true home is wherever you are, and so it matters not where we live, as long as we are together."

Emotions nearly smothered him. He was reminded in that moment of what was most important in his life. He gently placed his hands on either side of her face. "I love you, Victoria. You are my heart and my home, and I have neglected you so." He kissed her deeply trying to convey all his feelings to her. When at last their lips parted, he said, "Perhaps this change really is for the best."

Victoria grasped his hand as her other untied the ribbon closure of her robe. "Come husband, we must take our rest if we are to leave so early in the morning."

* * *

On the other side of the house a much different conversation was taking place. Angry words and accusations flew across the Duke's bedchamber fueled by years of built up resentment.

"George, you did this by breaking your word to Jason, and by God, you will fix it. Rothebury must have an heir."

He scoffed at his wife's dramatics. "There will be regardless of Jason's whereabouts. Any child of his will be heir."

"In case you don't recall, he threatened to disown us. We will never know our grandchildren. That is unacceptable, not to mention your continued actions will cause us to lose Rothebury." She walked around the four poster bed to corner him in the far side of the room. "I have put up with an awful lot from you, but this, I will not stand for. You will go speak to Jason and promise him whatever you must to get him to stay. What's more, you will keep your promise this time if I have to have you watched every minute of the day."

"I will speak with him—in the morning. He is too angry now to listen to reason. Morning will be better. Perhaps he will have changed his own mind by then. He loves this house more than you do. Mark my words, he'll come to his senses. All of this flustering is hardly needed. Now, madam, if you would kindly return to your chamber, I would like to get some sleep. It will be an early morning for me if I am to do your bidding."

Reluctantly, Henrietta retreated. His reasoning made sense. Morning would be better for persuading Jason to stay. There was nothing more to be done until then.

* * *

Jason awoke several hours earlier than needed. He slipped from the bed to dress simply in trousers, drawstring shirt, and a sweater to ward off the early morning chill. He left the room and his sleeping wife with the intention of wandering the estate until daybreak. He was well aware it would be his last hours spent in his childhood home, his family's estate, his heritage, and with his beloved horse. He was surprised to find Captain Bennington leaving his room as well.

"Good morning, Captain."

"Good morning, Lord Jason."

"I trust you slept well."

"Yes, as well as can be expected when I don't have the sea to rock me to sleep."

Jason smiled.

"Young man, are you awake so early because you are having doubts or because you are anxious to be gone?"

"The latter, sir."

"I am at your disposal. We can leave earlier if you like."

Jason considered the scene his mother was likely to cause and decided an early start might be for the best of all concerned. "Thank you. I'll go rouse Victoria. Mayhap we can depart in less than an hour's time. Our trunks should already be loaded and we can have the cook pack us some food."

By quarter to six, Captain Bennington was driving the hired buggy he had arrived in away from Rothebury Hall. Jason and Victoria were beside him and their luggage strapped behind. They made good time reaching the wharf. While the couple settled into their tiny cabin,

Captain Bennington checked the crew's preparations for departure.

* * *

Meanwhile, at Rothebury Hall, Henrietta arrived in the dining room to find George unconcernedly partaking of breakfast. When she asked if he had spoken to Jason, he simply replied that he was already gone. In a rage, she stood over him, "What do you mean he is already gone? They hadn't planned to leave for another hour." She turned to Mr. Flynn for confirmation. The butler silently nodded.

After fuming in silence for a few minutes, she leaned over her husband's shoulder and removed his plate from in front of him. "I would dearly love to dump this on your head, but as it would only further delay your departure, I will refrain. I insist you go after our son and bring him back. You make whatever promises you must make—and you *will* keep them because I promise I will see that you do. And George," she waited until he fully looked at her, "if you thought your life with me was miserable before, you have no idea how bad it will get if you fail." When the Duke remained unmoving she railed, pointing towards the door. "GO! Stop them from boarding that ship."

* * *

A commotion on the dock brought Jason topside to investigate. It was with great surprise, he saw his father arguing with one of the sailors in an attempt to board the ship. Captain Bennington approached him. "Shall I allow him to board?"

Jason watched his father in silent contemplation, unable to come to a decision. Finally, he looked to Abigail's father, a man he respected. "Sir, what would you advise me to do?"

"Hard to say since I don't have full understanding of the situation, but I believe you have a father desperately trying to make amends. If you turn your back now, it will likely lead to lifelong regret by one if not both of you."

"And if I give him another chance, and he fails me again?"

"Then you can leave with a clear conscience knowing you did all you could."

Jason considered his words. During the night he made peace with leaving his home so changing course now felt like being pulled backwards. On the other hand, starting over somewhere else, leaving his heritage behind, felt wrong. He came home prepared to fight for his birthright. His father was one of those battles and just because he lost the first engagement didn't mean he had to abandon the goal. For everyone's sake, he would give his father another chance. "I suppose you are right, but he need not come aboard. I will go down to meet him and at least listen to what he has to say."

"Be quick about it. Time and tide wait for no man."

Jason stepped down on the wharf as Victoria appeared at the railing. She anxiously watched the confrontation between father and son.

Jason came to a stop in front of his father without speaking, but with a hard glint in his eye, he waited to hear what he would say.

Faced with his angry son, George was at a loss for words. He knew not how to make him stay. At length he came to realize, he had to let go of his pride. "I am sorry."

When it seemed he would say no more, Jason prompted, "For?"

"For breaking my promise not to gamble."

"I told you, if you did, I would leave. Did you not believe me?"

"I am a weak man. The cards called to me. It wasn't a matter of believing you," his voice trailed off in shame, "because I was thinking of naught but the game."

"Do you not understand, father? Rothebury Hall will be lost if you don't stop."

"The chit's money..."

Jason pulled up straight. "Victoria! My wife's name is Victoria and you will show her respect."

George sighed, "Victoria's money can save Rothebury. The solicitor told me how much her dowry is worth. It is plenty to resolve all our debts."

"I have already told you we will not be using her money."

"Son, it's your turn to put aside your pride for the good of the family."

"No. It is not my pride that keeps me from doing so. It's my future, our future, hers and mine, and we won't have one if I give in to you."

"Nonsense."

Jason sighed in frustration. "It's no use. You will never change." He turned to leave.

George began to grasp his son's determination to leave and panicked. He could not return to Henrietta without bringing his son home. "I will change." Jason stopped walking but didn't turn. "You can take away my carriage, have me watched, whatever you must, just please don't go. Your mother needs you. Rothebury needs you."

Jason turned around. He studied his father trying to determine the sincerity of his words. "You promised me once before. What will make this time different?"

"I fully believe you will take your leave and never look back."

As Jason watched, the hard mantle of pride slipped from his father's face revealing the wretchedness of a man who realized he was broken. And despite everything, Jason cared. "Very well. We will try this one more time..." His father looked up with hope. "If you agree to be watched... and... all your friends must know you cannot gamble."

Anger stiffened George's back. "This is a private matter."

Jason was firm. "Not anymore. You can choose to tell them and give them a story of saving money to reinvest in the estate, or I can tell them it is because you gambled all the money away."

Defeated again, his father muttered, "I will tell them."

"Good. Maybe with them to hold you accountable, it will be easier not to give way to temptation on the occasion you find yourself tempted. Since I don't mean to make you give up your friends all together, at least for the foreseeable future, we will visit the club together. Can you accept these terms?"

George swallowed hard. Pride was a difficult thing to let go of. "I accept."

Jason breathed a sigh of relief. They would try one more time. "Did you bring the carriage?"

"No."

"Then will you go hire a conveyance to get us home while I go tell my wife we are staying." He turned from his father without waiting for an answer. He looked up to the ship's rail not surprised to see Victoria leaning over it, anxiously waiting.

He boarded the ship and approached a wide-eyed Victoria with a half-smile. "I hope you don't mind if we stay."

Her face bloomed into a broad grin. "Not at all. I am quite relieved actually."

He gave her a questioning look. Something about her tone...

"I am sure it would have been a troublesome voyage in my

delicate condition." She watched as her words registered. He struggled to speak, his mouth forming many words but no sound emerged.

She grinned and nodded. "It is too soon to tell anyone, and I didn't want to burden you yesterday with one more factor to consider in your decision."

In his joy, Jason lifted her to him and swung her around. "I love you."

Victoria smiled brightly. "Let's go home, my love."

The End

Become a Key Friend

You can sign up to receive email updates on upcoming books, contests, sneak peaks, promotions, and more.

Visit www.susanblackmonauthor.com for more details

Check out the 'Behind the Scenes' page for more details, photos, history, resource lists, character lists of who is real and who's not, and many other behind the scenes extras.

See my Pinterest boards for images of people, places, and things that have inspired the writing of each book.
www.pinterest.com/susanblackmonauthor

If you enjoyed reading *Love in Key West*
please consider posting an honest review on
Amazon and/or Goodreads

Your recommendation is the best gift an author can receive

Read on to catch a sneak peek of

Love Again

The next installment of the Love in Key West series.

Published December 2016

LOVE AGAIN

New York City, February, 1831

It wasn't supposed to be like this....

Theodore Whitmore was exasperated. He ran a hand through his russet hair as he reminded his young son for the third time, as gently as his frustration would allow, to stop playing with the spindle top and find his missing shoes.

They were late leaving the house again. A noon deadline at the newspaper weighed heavy on his mind. It was mornings like this Theodore missed his wife the most. He was having a hard time finding the patience to deal with his five year old son. Granted Henry turned five just this week. Still, Theodore hoped five would bring more independence. He watched as the child half-heartedly searched for his shoes in the parlor only to be distracted by a wooden boat he found in the corner. Interesting how he could find these things now but couldn't see them last night when he was supposed to put away his toys.

Theodore straightened the stack of work papers he gathered from the table and dropped them into his satchel. He then closed his eyes and breathed deeply to control the building frustration. Feeling a little calmer, he walked over to his son and crouched down to his level. Removing the boat from Henry's grasp and tilting his chin up, Theodore waited until his son's light blue eyes met his hazel. "Henry, where did you take off your shoes last night?"

Henry scrunched up his face as if thinking real hard.

Theodore's eyes narrowed. "Hmm." He realized the rational approach was not going to work. Taking Henry by the hand, Theodore walked him room to room visually searching the floor of each and asking, "Did you leave them in here?"

Each time Henry shook his head.

Where in heaven's name could he have hidden them?

Margaret would have known where to find them. Of course, if Margaret were still alive Theodore would have been at work by now, and she would be taking care of their son. A sudden unbidden memory arose of his wife standing on the doorstep holding their baby boy on her hip, teaching him to wave goodbye as Theodore left for the office. His throat tightened and his step faltered.

He missed her so.

It had only been a few months, but it felt like years since he last saw her face or held her to him. They both missed her, father and son. Henry still cried for her at bedtime although it was occurring with less frequency.

Theodore brushed his hand over Henry's blond head, and noticed he was in need of a haircut. It was hard raising his son by himself, but he refused to take the easy way out and turn him over to his cantankerous old aunt or worse yet, strangers, to see to his rearing. And as he so often did since Margaret got sick, he wished his parents were here to help. Ten years ago they decided to relocate to his mother's birth country of Austria leaving their home to Theodore. No other relatives existed from either side of Henry's bloodline. His peers ridiculed him—rearing children was woman's work—still he refused to have it any other way.

Reaching the nursery upstairs, Theodore realized this should have been the first place he looked. The shoes were lying haphazardly on the floor at the end of the bed, as if having been kicked off in a hurry. He would have thought five years old mature enough to manage a pair of shoes, but apparently he was wrong. Sitting his son on the bed, he straightened his socks, slipped his feet into the leather shoes, and buckled them rather than wait the countless minutes it would have taken Henry to do it. Then, taking the trusting little hand in his big one, Theodore waited for Henry to hop off the bed, and together they returned downstairs.

They donned their winter coats to walk the three blocks to his Aunt Agatha's house where he would leave Henry in her care while he worked. The arrangement was made out of desperation in those awful days before Margaret's passing, and now, although he would prefer to leave his son with someone younger and more congenial, his aunt would take it as a betrayal, and so the situation remained status quo.

The morning air filled with the whinny of horses pulling their burdens. The steady sound of carriage wheels against cobblestones underlined with the harsh staccato of hooves emphasized his need to hurry. He desperately wanted to take longer distance-eating strides but necessarily restrained his gait to match the smaller steps of his son. Henry, oblivious to his father's angst, cheerfully waved to the grocer sweeping the walkway.

The aroma of fresh baked bread as they passed the bakery had Theodore wishing, just once, they might have the time to stop. Another block and they turned the corner to pass a cluster of houses before coming to the iron fenced yard of his aunt's abode. He opened the gate and ushered his son through and up the steps to the front door of her brick three story, two chimney house. Theodore impatiently knocked and waited for the aging butler to open it and usher them into the pristine morning room. He unconsciously paused to smooth his russet hair back from his forehead and run his hands down the front of his clothing, making sure all was in place before entering the room. It was a leftover habit from his childhood when Aunt Agatha would chastise him anytime his appearance was less than pleasing.

As usual, his aunt was dressed in black, still mourning the loss of her love over three decades ago; although if asked, she would say it was in deference to her parents whose deaths were more recent. At her throat rested a cameo pendant she had worn for as long as Theodore could remember. A white lace cap covered her gray hair, loosely knotted on her crown. It was an oddity, her loose hair, when everything else about her was straight laced and starched.

She pierced him with a glare. "You're late."

Preferring not to cross words with her, he agreed without speaking. "Hmm."

Her frown deepened with the hated non-response.

Henry cheerfully said, "Good morning, Aunt Aggie," before climbing onto the sofa with a primer in his hands.

Theodore ruffled his son's head and gave his aunt a perfunctory kiss on the cheek before hurrying to the door.

She called after him. "At least your son has respectable manners."

"Maybe from local thievery?"

Theodore tilted his head. "Probable. There is a lot of money flowing through the salvage courts."

"There must be a lot of money if they are taking Simonton's request serious enough to send the army. Then again, maybe there is some kind of conflict building we are as yet unaware of." Bob gave him a cocky grin. "Theodore, I want you to follow the army down there and find out what is going on. If there is something brewing in the Caribbean, Key West would be right in the thick of it. It's a good place to test this new idea of ours."

For half a second, Theodore's heart raced at the idea of tracking down the details and writing a full unbiased news story to impress the entire city of New York, maybe even the country, until reality returned pressing down on his shoulders.

Henry.

"Bob, you know I can't do it. I have my son to consider. I can't leave him for that long."

Bob expected his objection. "Take him with you. The paper will pay the hotel room and someone to stay with him while you're working."

"Have you gone daft?"

Bob pretended not to hear him. "A brother of a friend lives down there, William Whitehead. He can assist with all the arrangements."

"It is a generous offer, but you will have to give it to someone else. My son suffers enough without his mother. I'll not take him from the only home he has ever known to live in a hotel on some island while I'm chasing a story."

Bob countered with a ready argument. "A home as full of memories for him as it is for you. A change of scenery will do you both good, and Key West is a booming place. Maybe you'll find a secondary story there too."

Theodore inwardly flinched. His friend struck a nerve. Margaret's presence seemed to linger in every room. But he said no, and he meant it. Theodore stood up, placed his hands on the edge of the desk, and leaned towards Bob to make his point. "I will not take Henry to Key West. I can't and won't leave my son to the care of strangers at the drop of a hat, and I won't leave him here with my aunt. The answer is no."

"I knew you would feel that way so I arranged for my niece to accompany you as his caregiver. You have no objections to her, I assume." Bob had the confident smile of someone about to win his argument. "You could really make a name for yourself as a top reporter in this town." Seeing no change in Theodore's face, Bob played his trump card. "If this endeavor is successful, I'll make you a partner."

The offer surprised him. Bob really knew how to play on his deepest desire for his career, and he knew Theodore wouldn't object to his niece, Annalise. She took care of Henry during those dark days when Margaret first became ill while he kept vigil at her bedside. His mind immediately shied away from the memories. They were still too raw.

Bob added, "It will be good for both you and Henry to put some distance to this city and that house. Some new experiences are just what you need." He opened his desk drawer and took out an envelope dropping it on the desk in front of Theodore. "Here is an advance on the travel expenses. How soon can you be ready to leave?"

Theodore stood up straight and firmly said, "The answer is still no." He held Bob's stare for a moment longer, then turned on his heel and left the office.

* * *

Normally when Theodore made a decision it was cut and dried, firmly made, not to be questioned, not even by him. He certainly never had a decision give him second thoughts like he was currently experiencing. Theodore was in turmoil.

Why was this one so different?

He knew why. It had everything to do with what was best for Henry.

Decisions used to be easy. College, career, and wife were straightforward choices. There was never a doubt when he decided not to follow his father in business. He attended Union College because it was prestigious and close to home. He didn't give marriage a second thought. He knew within three days of meeting Margaret he would marry her and did so six months later. Even after marriage, the decisions he had to make were clear. It was only now that he alone was responsible for Henry's well-being, something he was ill-equipped to handle, was he unsure of his decisions.

As if the opportunity of field reporting and a possible partnership were not enticing enough, the story was of interest to him as well. His wants were juxtaposed against Henry's needs. He would lay aside his wants in a heartbeat to do what was right by Henry. The real reason for the confliction was not knowing what was best for his son. Bob made a good point about getting away from the memories. Maybe it would be good for Henry to experience something new. He wanted to do what was best for his son. If only he knew what that was.

Love in Key West series

Salvaged Love

Love in Key West – a novella

Love Again

Enduring Love

Once Upon an Island Christmas – a novella
Fall 2020

Divided Love
2021

ABOUT THE AUTHOR

Susan Blackmon has enjoyed reading historical novels all her life. With a talent for writing, it was only natural for her to try her hand at creating one of her own. All that was missing was inspiration. An unexpected cruise ship detour to Key West and a few history tours later, Max and Abby's story began.

When Susan isn't writing, she enjoys being with her family, hiking waterfalls, reading, and scrapbooking.

Visit www.susanblackmonauthor.com to learn more about her books or to find your favorite way to connect via social media.

Made in the USA
Monee, IL
06 December 2020

51135084R00146